THE
MIGRANTS

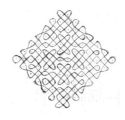

This is not an autobiography. Those are written by the rich and famous; I am neither. This is the story of a migrant family who left their motherland, sacrificing all that was dear to them, in search of a better future. It is based on stories I have heard, mostly from my mother and the treasure trove of my own memories, which have deliquesced into my being from an early age. Those stories and memories are part of my heritage, intrinsic to who I am today. I share them here with you before they too, disappear, like the people who inhabit these pages...

THE
MIGRANTS

SALMA A SIDDIQUI

ISBN: 978-93-52010-38-7
© Salma A. Siddiqui, 2018
Cover Design: Paramita Bhattacharjee
Layouts: Chandravardan Shiroorkar, Leadstart Design
Printing: Printed In India by Nutech Print Services - India

First published in 2018 by

PLATINUM PRESS

An imprint of LEADSTART PUBLISHING PVT LTD
Unit 25, Building A/1, Near Wadala RTO,
Wadala (E), Mumbai 400 037, INDIA
T + 91 96 9993 3000 **E** info@leadstartcorp.com
W www.leadstartcorp.com

Disclaimer This is a work of fiction. The opinions expressed
in this book are exclusively those of the Author and do not
pertain to be the views of the Publisher.

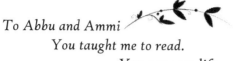

To Abbu and Ammi
You taught me to read.
You gave me life.

Islamabad
Rawalpindi
Lahore
Muslims
Hindus, Sikhs
PAKISTAN
Delhi
Karachi
Bhagalpur
Calcutta
Dhaka (Dacca)
Mumbai (Bombay)
INDIA
Chennai (Madras)
The Partition of British India, 1947

In tribute to all those who sacrificed their lives
for the betterment of others.
They live on within us.

About the Author

SALMA SIDDIQUI was born in Rawalpindi. She migrated to the United Kingdom with her family when she was nine years old. Her formative years have left a lasting impact on her life. Following graduation, Salma pursued a career as a research biochemist, at St Georges Hospital Medical School. Some years later, she began teaching 'A' Level Biology. She has published several science textbooks which are now part of school syllabi in both Britain and Pakistan. She spends her time teaching, writing and travelling. This is her first novel.

Salma lives in London with her husband, Asif, and their children – Kashif, Nimra, Samirah and Saif.

CONTENTS

PART I

RAWALPINDI (PINDI)

PAKISTAN 1960s

PRAYER BEFORE BIRTH

~ Louis MacNeice

I am not yet born; O hear me.
Let not the bloodsucking bat or the rat or the stoat
or the club-footed ghoul come near me.

I am not yet born, console me.
I fear that the human race may with tall walls wall me,
with strong drugs dope me, with wise lies lure me,
on black racks rack me, in blood-baths roll me.

I am not yet born; provide me
With water to dandle me, grass to grow for me, trees to talk
to me, sky to sing to me, birds and a white light
in the back of my mind to guide me.

I am not yet born; forgive me
For the sins that in me the world shall commit, my words
when they speak me, my thoughts when they think me,
my treason engendered by traitors beyond me,
my life when they murder by means of my
hands, my death when they live me.

I am not yet born; O hear me,
Let not the man who is beast or who thinks he is God
come near me.

Let them not make me a stone and let them not spill me.
Otherwise kill me.

1
PINDI

Returning from one of our expeditions, we took a shortcut through the forbidden territory, *Shah di Tallian* – a dark eerie graveyard overshadowed by huge trees and dense thorny overgrowth. Lying atop a fresh grave, I found a tiny dead baby. It was like a miniature doll – its skin moist, shiny and translucent. I could see the organs within. I bent forward and stared closely before calling to my cousin, 'Farooq!'

Farooq looked back and almost lost his balance as he gasped and recoiled. For a few minutes we both stared at it, transfixed and wide-eyed. I would have picked up the lifeless infant had he not pulled me away. Grabbing my arm, his fingers wrapped themselves around my wrist like the tendrils of a creeper, his face white as a sheet. 'Let's go, Salmi! Let's go!' he whispered, breathing deeply.

'You're hurting me,' I protested. He relaxed his grip a little.

I secretly recited the *Ayatul-Kursi,* the prayer of protection, in my head, with some trepidation, not wanting to let Farooq know I was scared.

Noting my twitching lips he enquired, 'What are you muttering?'

'*Ayatul-Kursi.*'

'Say it out loud.'

'Why, don't you know it?' I snapped and then began reciting loudly.

Realizing the significance of our find, he tightened his grip on my arm and hissed, 'Don't say a word to anyone, Salmi! Promise me...promise.'

'I promise,' I said, irritated, jerking my arm free.

'Word of honour? We'll be in dead trouble if...'

'Why? It's only a baby. We didn't put it there!'

'We're not supposed to be here at all. We're sure to get a good beating if Abba Jaan finds out.'

Carefully sidestepping graves, avoiding stinging nettles and anthills, crushing fallen leaves underfoot, we rushed out of the graveyard at a run. Neither of us said another word as we dashed across busy Murree Road and turned into the *gali* between Qamar Bakery and the free government clinic where we had our BCG jabs; past the large yellow colonial houses; beneath overhanging balconies dripping water from hanging bougainvillea, fragrant *Raat ki Rani* and *Chambaili*; past the butcher's shop exhibiting a gruesome selection of blood-drenched black goat heads, eyes wide open, staring straight at us. A live goat, its hind leg tethered to a lamp post, was munching on fodder standing in its own urine, oblivious of its impending fate. Overstepping the urine trailing across the *gali*, I moved furtively to get on the other side of Farooq, in case the goat butted us.

As we neared home I dreaded going past hawkish Mirza Sahib's grocery shop. He had shouted so fiercely at my cousin Rosy the other day – for picking at the fresh tamarind – that she had wet herself. I breathed a sigh of relief on seeing him busy weighing rice on his pan balance. As always, he was dressed in a crisp white *kurta shalwar*, far too well dressed for a grocer, his thick mop of silver hair kept under control by his maroon *fez*. The usual group of cronies who gradually gathered in his shop during the day, like vultures around a corpse, sat puffing the tall *hookah* while putting the world to rights.

Farooq and I tried to slip past without being noticed. But Mirza Sahib looked up from over the Gandhi glasses perched on his nose. Knotting his thick white brows he said curtly, '*Salaam Alaykum*,' to remind us of our manners.

'*Salaam Alaykum*,' I blurted quickly.

Unperturbed by Mirza Sahib's terse greeting, Farooq gave him a sideways glance and continued walking. I admired his sangfroid. Thankfully, Mirza Sahib became distracted just then by a boy demanding his change or we would certainly have had to listen to a sermon on the blessings of saying *salaam*, and a lot more no doubt.

Having forgotten the reason for our haste, I lingered at fat Bashir's sweet shop, breathing in the intoxicating aromas while Farooq walked ahead. Bashir sat like a Buddha, seated behind a huge cauldron in which he was frying *jalebi*. Perspiration made his bald patch shine and the pockmarks on his Mongolian features more prominent. His grubby vest and black and white chequered *dhoti* were wet with sweat despite the revolving fan that kept the flies away from the tall pyramids of sweetmeats – *ladoo, burfi, gulab-jaman* – on stainless steel platters.

As Bashir squeezed the grubby piping bag, streaks of batter oozed out like earthworms emerging from the ground after rain. With surprising dexterity he twisted the worms into figures of eight as they fell into the boiling oil, whereupon they immediately turned dark orange. Bashir then transferred his perfect creations into a cauldron of hot sugar syrup. Wiping the sweat from his brow with the greasy towel flung over his shoulder, he carefully scooped out the *jalebis* and placed them in a wire basket to drain before arranging them on a steel platter.

Mesmerised, I watched, licking my lips, a safe distance from the huge cauldron of milk that had been simmering since dawn and which by now had turned almost pink, with a thick layer of cream on top. Intermittently, Bashir served the men sitting on colourful jute *mooras*, skilfully pouring the milk back and forth from one steel glass to another, raising them higher and higher until the milk turned frothy. Noticing me from the corner of his eye, he nodded his head to indicate I could take a *jalebi*.

Farooq was waiting impatiently for me at our front door. I offered him a piece of *jalebi* with a forced smile. He shook his head in refusal. Before entering, he looked straight at me to remind me of my promise. I nodded as I licked my fingers.

Rosy was waiting for us in the courtyard. She seemed to sense my unease and asked, 'Where were you? I was looking for you. You always sneak off without me.'

'Your pretty dress would have got dirty and you'd have whined like a baby,' I taunted. The word 'baby' suddenly reminded me of why we had raced home and I shuddered.

'*He* didn't want you to come with us either,' I said, glancing up at Farooq. 'You can never keep up and you are such a...' I stopped as Rosy's mother, my aunt Wazir Khala, walked past, carrying a vegetable laden tray.

Rosy and I were the same age but being the long anticipated daughter after three sons, she was indulged by her parents. She resented the fact that her brother Farooq and I preferred each other's company to hers. But now, unable to keep my secret to myself a moment longer, I told her everything. 'There was a dead baby lying on top of a grave in the graveyard!' I whispered.

'You went to the graveyard?' Rosy's dark eyes widened. She seized my shoulder and moved closer to hear the details. 'Ammi will kill you if she finds out.'

'She won't 'cause she *isn't* going to find out, *is she?*'

'What did you do?'

'Nothing! Farooq wouldn't let me pick it up. He made me rush home. Don't...*don't* tell anyone!' I said, making unwavering eye contact. 'Farooq will kill me if you do.'

But Rosy was never good at keeping secrets. She blabbed it all to her mother, who immediately summoned the two of us.

Wazir Khala, my mother's eldest sister, sat cross-legged on the prayer *chowki*. She was preparing vegetables for the evening meal. With thin lips pursed and thick eyebrows knotted, she squinted in deep concentration as she continued chopping okra with pernickety attention, ensuring she cut out the wormy bits. Ammi sat beside her, her feet dangling above her discarded slippers. Ammi's complexion was flushed, her nose red and her tiny eyes swollen, clouded by recent tears. In her hand she clutched the blue aerogram that had arrived from India a couple of days ago, causing such turmoil in our household.

They were talking in hushed tones but stopped as we approached. I heard Wazir Khala whisper *harami!* I knew this to be a bad word though I did not know precisely what it meant. From the stern look on their faces I sensed serious trouble. Ammi opened her mouth to say something but before she could utter a word, Wazir Khala raised her hand with a move of distaste, signalling Ammi to stop and said firmly, 'Jugnu, let me handle this.'

Ammi drew in a sharp breath between gritted teeth, pinching her thin lips and frowning as she reached for the fan lying on the *chowki* and began fanning herself with unnecessary vigour.

'Did you see anyone at the graveyard; anyone at all?' Wazir Khala demanded, looking first at Farooq and then at me. I shook my head from side to side, silent, unable to speak.

'Farooq you know this is serious. Tell me the truth.'

'No, we were only there a few minutes,' he said, turning to face her.

'How many times have I told you not to roam in unearthly places? And with your hair open like this, some *Djinn* will possess you.' Ammi couldn't restrain herself from clouting me.

Wazir Khala pulled me away. Although she was fierce, she seldom hit us. Ammi frequently lashed out at us. 'Jugnu, I said let *me* handle it,' Wazir Khala said irritably.

I stood immobile, staring at my trembling hands. She looked at us intently, silently, for what seemed like an eternity. A tall cone of mosquitoes spiralled above her head in the dusk, dispersing and regrouping with each turn of the lazily revolving fan. Sweat trickled from the folds of waxy skin on her neck and meandered down between her ample breasts, causing her diaphanous pink cotton shirt to turn almost purple and cling to her breasts, making them uncomfortably prominent. She seldom wore a bra at home.

She picked up her *dupatta* and wiped the sweat with the sluggishness that seems to infect everyone in that sweltering heat, and flung it across her chest, suddenly aware of my gaze. Her eyes magnified behind her thick glasses, her bony hand holding the knife had prominent blue veins visible under the pale insipid skin. The evening shadows across her face made her even more intimidating.

Massi the maid, who had been cleaning the floor with an old towel, moving from side to side on her haunches, added phenyl to the water in the bucket, scattering droplets as she dipped the towel in and out. Teeth clenched, her knuckles turned pale and her glass bangles jangled as she wrung it tight. She looked up, her *kajal* smudged around her big eyes and deep arched furrows on her forehead in the shape of her eyebrows. Pushing back wisps of hair with a crooked finger, she said, 'Ah, let them be. No harm will come to them in the graveyard. My husband, Allahrakha, is always there... Besides, these two are as sharp as razors. Who would mess with them?'

'Massi, she is only seven and her guru here...' Ammi paused and glared at Farooq. 'How old are you, Farooq?' Without waiting for a reply, she snapped, 'Nine!' Turning her attention to Massi again she said, 'And besides, your old man is always fast asleep. What would *he* know?'

'Now, how would *you* know that?' responded Massi in her tangy native dialect, widening her big eyes and flashing her *paan* stained teeth in a cynical smile. Turning back to her task she said, 'Clip her wings whilst you can. No one wants a girl they cannot control!'

Wazir Khala put down the knife and slowly took off her glasses. Her eyes now appeared sunken and smaller. She wiped her hands with her *dupatta*. Gently massaging the puffy dark half-moons under her eyes with the back of her clenched fist, she suddenly grabbed me by the arm and pulled me close. Without shifting her gaze and clenching her stained uneven teeth, the right canine of which was missing, she warned us in a low husky voice, as if telling us a deep dark secret, 'You know the tall, dark gypsy women on Murree Road with the long flared skirts, thick bangles and bead necklaces? The ones pretending to sell fruit...' She paused. 'They will snatch you both, hide you under their skirts and sell you to *horrible, horrible* men, who will maim you and force you to beg.' She spoke slowly, emphasizing each word, staring at us from between her almost shut eyelids.

The exaggerated tone did not rob her words of authority. Transfixed by her intense gaze, I averted my own. Terror caused my heart to beat so loudly I thought it would jump right out of my chest. It set up a throbbing in my temples and found reflection deep down in my stomach. Twisting my fingers I chewed my lips, tasting the salty blood in my mouth. I squirmed in anticipation of what was to come. I berated myself for telling Rosy.

'Stop fidgeting!' shouted Ammi, eyes flashing.

'You are not to go there again, understand?' Wazir Khala commanded as she tugged at my arm sharply.

'Yes, yes,' I warbled, nodding my head like a rag doll. One more tug and I would have collapsed.

Shifting her ferocious gaze she looked at her son questioningly. 'Farooq!' she boomed.

'Yeees?' he replied in an insolent, belligerent tone.

She half raised her hand to strike him but changed her mind in mid-action. Her wrinkled upper lip twitched as she tried to suppress her anger. He flinched and ducked in anticipation. 'There will be consequences if I *ever* hear you've been there again,' she said, waving a stained, bony finger.

Realising the seriousness of the situation, even Farooq was silent. We waited patiently for a sign of dismissal. Resting her hand on her knee, Wazir Khala rose laboriously, stretching to ease her aching back, and then hobbled towards the kitchen with unhurried steps, complaining about her aching knees. Handing the tray to Massi she said, '*You* must know whose it could be.'

'*Naa*, no one I know,' Massi replied.

Wazir Khala shouted instructions over her shoulder to wash properly around the bin and to clean the chicken coop. 'And Massi, remember to tell the *dhobi* my bedcover – the yellow and black floral one – is missing from my laundry,' she said before finally disappearing behind a door.

'I will deal with you later,' Ammi warned me as she searched for her slippers with her feet and then rushed downstairs.

As soon as they were out of sight I took a deep

breath, for my aunt epitomised the pernicious stepmother of my storybooks and I was terrified of her. My relief was short lived however, for I knew I was in for it in other quarters.

Farooq stared at me judicially and pulled my ear, twisting it mercilessly. 'I told you not to tell!' he whispered through clenched teeth.

Flinching in pain, I hissed in indignation. My ear tingling, I looked at him with unconcealed anger. 'What's the big deal? Why couldn't I take it? I don't have a doll. No one else wanted it.'

'It wasn't a doll. It was a dead baby, you idiot!' he yelled.

'Yes, but it was just lying there. No one wanted it.'

Farooq shook his head in despair, hissing through his teeth. I lowered my eyes sulkily so he would not see the tears welling in them, and ran out of the room, my mouth trembling uncontrollably. I made a mental note never to trust Rosy with a secret again, ever.

I could hear Wazir Khala talking to Salahuddin Khalo in hushed tones in the kitchen. Soon Salahuddin Khalo appeared, grabbed Farooq by the arm, almost dragging him along and slammed the door behind them. From the balcony I watched Salahuddin Khalo, Farooq and Abbu hurrying down the *gali* towards the main road which led to the graveyard. Farooq turned and looked up. I quickly hid behind a pillar.

Rosy was watching from behind the door, guilt written all over her face. Annoyed at her treachery, I poked out my tongue at her and crooked my little finger, indicating the end of our friendship. '*Kutti!*' I muttered under my breath as I pushed past. 'That's why we don't take you with us, tattle-tale!'

Her eyes followed me to the door. I knew she hadn't meant to be malicious; she had just been feeling dejected at being left behind as usual and blurted it out to Wazir Khala, just as I had blurted it out to her. In my heart, I forgave her.

2
SALMI

My father, Abbu, always said he had named me Salma because I had bright twinkling eyes – a sign of intelligence he maintained, and to rhyme with Najma, my sister, eighteen months my senior. Affectionately, everyone called us Salmi and Najmi. Out of respect I called my elder sister Baji. Being a poet, Abbu habitually rhymed words. He then named my younger sisters Rukhsana and Farhana, and my brothers Ather and Muzher. Poor Farhana was nicknamed *Nunni* (Tiny), for being so small at birth, but no one can quite remember why Rukhsana came to be nicknamed Shano.

Abbu chanted 'Salma *sitara, chunda tarra mujhe jaan se pyara*' (Salma the star, moon and stars; dearer to me than life itself). Full of fiery vitality, I seldom walked, preferring to hop and skip, so he also called me *Para* (mercury), never still.

My early memories are fragmented but my mother, Ammi, tells me I was an impetuous and mischievous little girl. One of the earliest recollections I have is of losing my way home. Ammi is still surprised I remember it since I was not more than four years old. It happened in the Shah Chan Chiragh house in Pindi, where Abbu rented an apartment in a large pre-Partition era house. Some occupants like Abbu's friend Ajaz Uncle, rented a single room. *Dadi*, an old lady, and her family, occupied the entire upper floor. *Dadi* was not related to any of us but everyone called her that and like a typical *Dadi*, she scolded and offered advice whether one needed it, wanted it, liked it, or not.

***

I must have been about six when my friend Noor and I ventured out to buy the orange segment-shaped sweets I so loved. After several wrong turns we eventually found the sweet shop. Delighted, Noor fished out the coins from her frock pocket, purchased the sweets and handed me one before putting another into her own mouth. Going back home, we lost our way.

Holding clammy hands we walked and walked, unable to recognize the *galis*. Panicked, we both began to cry. Scared and teary eyed, I looked up to find three bearded, very tall men in long black *sherwanis* coming out of a mosque.

'What's the matter *baita*? Why are you crying?' one of them bent down and asked sympathetically.

'We're lost!' we sobbed in unison, crying harder.

When we told them where we lived, they escorted us back to our neighbourhood. As soon as we turned the corner of our street, a group of boys ran up to us. 'Where were you? Everyone is looking for you,' they babbled.

Azra, a neighbour, who was filling her bucket from the tap at the corner of the street, left the tap running and rushed up to us. 'Where did you go?' she yelled.

By the time we reached our door, the group following us had turned into a procession. Uncle Ajaz appeared from somewhere, grabbed Noor's arm and began questioning her. Unaware of the commotion we had caused, I ran in, followed by the neighbours who had been out searching for us. As I entered the house, two huge hands scooped me up me into the air like a rag doll and perched me on the mantelpiece next to the radio covered in its crochet lace cover. A dark angry face with knotted eyebrows loomed before me. I could see the hair in his nose. The big mouth opened and closed, exposing large teeth; spit flew into my face and onto the mirror and my frock as he shouted.

'Where were you?' Without waiting for a reply, Abbu waved a fat finger in front of my petrified face. 'Don't ever do that again!' he warned, his voice booming across the room. Startled, I fell back, convulsed in fear. Tears rolled down my cheeks. A yellow dribble trickled down from the mantelpiece onto his shiny black boots. Ignoring the wetness he picked me up and hugged me. I sobbed into his neck.

'Don't ever do that again! Your Ammi and I were frantic with worry,' he whispered urgently as he cuddled me lovingly, wiping my wet cheeks.

***

The next time I was in trouble I wasn't so lucky. I was smacked all the way down the spiral staircase, watched by all the children in the building. The older girls in the building had pooled money for a tea party. They asked me to bring some from Ammi, and I did. Then they asked me to bring more. I knew Ammi would not give me anymore since she was busy chatting with her friends on the roof, so I stole a coin from her *paandan*. I was sneaking up the stairs with the coin safely tucked in my cheek when Ammi happened to come down the stairs. Sensing my fear, she looked at me suspiciously.

'And where are you going?' she asked in a sing-song voice.

'Mmmm...' I replied, coin firmly in cheek.

She asked again. When she got the same reply, she said, 'Have you been eating sugar again? I told you not to...' She whacked me across the face. The coin flew out of my mouth and rolled down the stairs, never to be seen again. Rubbing my stinging cheek I yelled in pain. 'You little *chorni!* Who taught you to steal?' Ammi screeched as she continued to smack my bottom and legs.

Humiliated and angry at being beaten in front of all my friends, I screamed all the way down to our room. I called her *kutti*, which resulted in my being locked in the store room. I sat inside, rocking to and fro, chanting 'Ammi *kutti*, Ammi *kutti*...' When Abbu tried to persuade me to apologize, I defiantly amended my chant to 'Ammi *kutti*, Abbu *kutai*...'

Hearing the hullabaloo, the other occupants of the building, including *Dadi*, emerged from their rooms.

'What's the commotion about?' demanded *Dadi*.

'She *stole* money from my *paandan*,' *Ammi* told her.

'She is only a child, Jugnu. What does she know about stealing? She wanted money. She took it. Why are you making such a fuss about it?'

Through the store room door I could hear Ammi sobbing. Abbu was consoling her, which infuriated me even more. Instead of telling her off and comforting *me*, he was comforting *her*.

Dadi unlocked the door and said to me, 'Come *baita*, come. You must not swear at your *Ammi* and *Abbu*.' Holding me by the arm she lead me to the roof, where several women sat chatting in a congenial group, enjoying the late winter afternoon sun. They chewed sugarcane, ate oranges, knitted, and oiled each other's hair. Picking up a large loop of wool from the *pulang*, *Dadi* held it up between outstretched hands. Shaida Auntie began to unwind and then wrap the wool into a ball while continuing her previous narrative. She threw the occasional sympathetic glance towards me.

Crying and sobbing I sat alone and morose, watching , through the holes in the brick wall the fat old lady down below, roasting popcorn and corn-on-the-cob in hot sand on a *tandoor*, while eager buyers waited. When I remembered my beating I began to cry again.

Dadi came over and hugged me. 'Look at you, still sobbing,' she said, patting my cheek affectionately and kissing me. 'You must never swear child, especially at your Ammi and Abbu.' She combed my hair with her fingers and then led me downstairs to make peace with my parents.

3
LETTER FROM INDIA

Amongst the adults there was a great deal of talk about India, passports and our paternal grandmother, Dadi Jaan. At last we were going to India by train to see her. It was a big deal for all of us, especially Abbu. We had never met our paternal family and Abbu would see his mother after seventeen years of painful separation. We were all very excited about our first ever trip outside Pindi.

Having waited all this time for the border between India and Pakistan to open, Abbu sighed with relief, holding our green and gold passports in his hands. He took us shopping to buy new shoes, suitcases, presents for his family, and yards and yards of colourful floral fabric to make new outfits for us all. Ammi, with Wazir Khala's assistance, sat sewing every free minute she had.

One afternoon, Abbu returned from work as usual, his bicycle overladen with mangoes and other groceries. Ammi quickly put aside her sewing machine and rushed to help him. She placed the mangoes in a bucket of water to cool and began heating the meal she had prepared, instructing us to go wash our hands and lay the *dastarkhan*. When Abbu went to shower and change and while Ammi was busy in the kitchen, we sneaked a mango each, softened the pulp in its skin, pierced a hole and sucked the delicious juice. Eventually we ripped off the skin to suck the stone.

Ammi returned just then, pinched her lips in disapproval but didn't say anything. She indicated with her eyes that we should sit. Abbu came in, fresh from his shower. And we began squabbling about who would sit next to him. Ignoring us, Ammi began to tell him bits of news and gossip. Just then there was a knock on the door.

My brother Ather, returned from opening the door, a blue aerogramme in his hand. As soon as Abbu saw the blackened corner, indicative of bad news, he dropped the *chapatti* in his hand and shot up like a spring uncoiled, snatching the letter from

Ather's hand. As he read, he put a hand to his head. Resting his forehead on his arm, he leaned against the wall and wept.

Ammi went to stand nervously beside him. 'What has happened? Is it Ammi Jaan? What's wrong?' When he did not reply, she grabbed the letter from him, her brow furrowed in concern.

We knew better than to ask questions and merely watched in silence as she read the letter. Then she too, began to cry. She ushered us out of the house, telling us to go out and play. Baji and I looked at each other in bewilderment. We were usually severely ticked off for staying out in the scorching sun. Holding hands, we peeped in through the window.

Ammi was trying in vain to comfort Abbu. He was inconsolable. That was the only time in my life I saw my father sob like a baby.

'Lines scratched on a map have cost me my family!' was all he said.

Later, Abbu having refused to eat, Ammi took off our frocks (to reduce her wash load later), and left us gathered around the bucket, sucking mangoes, dressed only in our knickers. She picked up baby Muzher saying, 'Najmi, Salmi, clear up when you finish. Wash up and *all* of you lie down.' Accompanied by Abbu she headed upstairs to Wazir Khala's. 'Salmi, switch off the fan!' she shouted over her shoulder.

We knew the routine of bathing after eating mangoes before lying down for the afternoon siesta.

'Why was Abbu crying?' I asked Baji.

'I think Dadi Jaan is dead.'

'So we are not going to India then!' I said petulantly.

'I don't know,' she responded, shrugging her shoulders.

We placed the mango skins and seeds in the empty bucket. Then we hosed each other down, got dressed again and then lay down to rest. By the time Ammi and Abbu returned, my siblings were asleep, but I lay awake, tossing and turning, seething about our jeopardized trip.

Ammi rushed about sullen faced, in glum silence, frantically packing.

That night I scrambled into Abbu's bed, as I often did but awoke when Abbu's snoring changed to mumbling. He suddenly sat up, arms flaying, and began shouting for his sister. 'Sultanat, Sultanat!'

By now Ammi too, had awoken in alarm. She

switched on the light and stroked his arm saying, 'What's the matter? Wake up! Wake up!'

Abbu's face gleamed with perspiration. Tiny bubbles appeared on his brow and trickled down into his eyebrows. He was breathing heavily, a perplexed expression on his face. For a while his eyes continued to stare ahead without blinking. Finally he looked at Ammi, and then at me, with a confused look, as if trying to recognize us. Ammi was used to Abbu mumbling in his sleep, but never like this. She poured him a glass of water, which he drank in one go. 'I had a bad dream,' he said, patting me soothingly. 'Go to sleep, *baita*.'

He lay there breathing deeply for a long while. I knew he was murmuring verses from the *Quran*. I pretended to be asleep.

When Ammi thought I was really asleep, she asked him, 'What happened?'

'I saw Sultanat on fire! A mob had caught her and set her alight. She was burning from the legs upwards. I was running and calling out to her but the faster I ran the further she got from me. No sound came out of my mouth. I can still see her horrified face, disappearing in the flames...'

I couldn't sleep for a long time. I always went to Abbu when I was scared. To see him terrified was disconcerting. Somewhere in the distance I heard the night watchman tapping the metal end of his stick. The only sound in the room was the *tick-tock* of the clock.

Within days, and without any explanation to us children, Abbu departed for India – alone.

4
BAJI AND FAROOQ

*B*aji and Farooq were born on the same day. Farooq was Wazir Khala's third son while Baji was Ammi's firstborn. Farooq, like all his siblings, had a buttermilk complexion but was a tiny, premature baby – a fragile doll with elfin features. In fact, he was so petite that everyone feared he would not survive the night. He reminded Amma Ji, my maternal grandmother, of baby Tauseef, the baby she had lost on the ominous and nightmarish journey to Pakistan from India. She nursed Farooq devotedly, taking charge of feeding him at two-hour intervals, twenty-four-seven.

In contrast, Baji was a massive nine pounder. She had a dark complexion, large dark eyes and a flat stubby nose. It was bad enough that Ammi's firstborn was a girl and thus a burden, but worse still, she was dark and ugly. All the members of our maternal family had fair 'English rose' complexions. A dark skin was an unforgivable sin, especially in Amma Ji's eyes. She tut-tutted over the baby, fearing for her future. Notorious for her tactlessness, she sighed, 'May *Allah* bestow her with a good fate. What *bud-naseebi* to have a girl like this as your firstborn, with such dark skin!'

'Amma Ji, I thank the Lord that she is healthy and has ten fingers and toes,' Ammi responded in irritation.

'It is well to keep quiet sometimes,' Massi said, being among the minority who could snap at Amma Ji with impunity.

'You agreed to *Bhai* Azhar as your son-in-law. How come you didn't object to his dark complexion?' enquired Tauqeer Khala, my aunt.

'Perhaps having four daughters to marry off, his striking features, impeccable *Lucknawi* manners, *and* the fact that he was from a Syed family [direct descendants of Prophet Mohammed PBUH], may have had something to do with it,' remarked Wazir Khala, raising an eyebrow.

'It seems I raised my daughters to talk back to me!' snapped Amma Ji. 'It's hard enough marrying off pretty daughters, let alone ugly ones, especially when you have nothing to give as dowry.' She stood up and stormed out.

Ammi began to cry. Massi hugged Ammi, shaking her head in disbelief at Amma Ji's words.

Baji would not take Ammi's milk, so she tried goat's milk, cow's milk, and even camel's milk, as well as various formulae. But Baji could not digest any of them. She was taken from one doctor to the next, but she continued to throw up and scream day and night.

'I have seen many babies but none as fussy as this little one,' confessed Massi.

Has she fed? Did she throw up? The baby's digestion became a topic of general conversation. The relatives and friends who came round to congratulate Ammi and Abbu on the birth of their baby, showed initial concern but ended up commiserating instead. Soon, only Ammi and Abbu were left to fret and cope with the baby that was becoming thinner before their eyes. While Farooq gained weight, Baji became a bag of skin and bones, and even darker and uglier. They spent their ever-depleting resources on medical expenses and new formulae. Doctors, homeopaths and herbalists were all consulted.

Much to Ammi's dismay, the neighbours and so-called friends, and even some of the family, began to suspect she might be possessed. 'Often the case for the firstborn,' they whispered behind her back amongst themselves.

As soon as Massi thought Ammi was out of earshot, she whispered to Amma Ji, 'It's the evil eye. She has had it too easy. She had her firstborn even before her first wedding anniversary. Look at poor Irshad, Jamal's daughter, she's been married seven years and not produced as much as a mouse! Her husband's family have sent her back to her parents.'

Massi couldn't keep her voice down even if she tried and Ammi heard. 'I gave generous *sadka* and have never wished ill on anyone. Why would I be cursed?' she snapped, suppressing her tears.

'No *baiti*, I know you are a sweet soul but sometimes it's others' envy that gets you. That's why they say, hide your pregnancy from strangers,' Massi said a little sheepishly. 'Take her to the *pir* by the big *peepal* tree. He'll take care of the evil eye.'

'You know today's kids; they don't listen to their elders. How often I have told her not to gallivant shamelessly in front of strangers, especially in early pregnancy. But would she listen?' Amma Ji added, shaking her head as she popped a *paan* into her toothless mouth, oblivious to her daughter's distress.

'I don't believe in *Taveez ganday*. Abba Ji says it's a sin to go to shrines. We should pray directly to *Allah*,' Ammi said.

'Yes, yes, but the *pir* is a *holy* man and he *too* prays to *Allah*. He knows the appropriate verses to ward off evil,' Massi told her with the air of the most faithful.

Ammi gritted her teeth and walked away to tend to her screaming baby with a heavy heart.

When all else failed, in desperation Ammi and Tauqeer Khala decided there was no harm in taking Massi's advice and they secretly took Baji to the *pir*. They huddled together, squatting on their haunches under the huge *peepal* tree. Clutching the skinny infant, they eyed each other amongst the mass of sweaty, smelly women who had come from far and wide, all hoping for divine intervention and fast forwarding of their prayers to a higher being. Not knowing what to expect or do, Ammi anxiously observed the others going in one by one into the shrine through a tiny wooden door, worn and shiny from the hands of countless devotees and desperate souls pushing past to enter. She thanked the Lord in her heart that the baby was asleep. Clearing her throat, she held back the urge to cough, brought on by the rancid smell of mustard oil lamps and incense and whispered in her sister's ear, 'How much should I give?' indicating with her eyes the tall menacing man whose head seemed far too small for his body, who guarded the entrance. 'Loose change,' came the brief reply.

Finally it was their turn to go in. Avoiding eye contact, Ammi dropped some coins into the bowl, hoping it was enough. She hugged her bundle closer and edged past the guard. As the ladies ducked inside, they found themselves in a dark courtyard overshadowed by a tree with a ghostly aura. Under it was a *kuchi* grave draped with a green satin sheet scattered with rose petals. There were more smoky clay oil lamps and the place reeked of incense. Several women, dressed in white, sat on jute mats some way off, rocking to and fro, reading from the *Quran*.

A sullen old man, his face almost invisible behind his long white hair and beard, sat crossed-legged beside the shrine. Gesturing with a nod of his head, he told the ladies to sit down. Ammi and Tauqeer Khala squatted awkwardly in front of him.

'What do you want?' he barked without looking up, continuing to turn the beads of his *tusbi*. His beard twitched as he chewed tobacco.

Haltingly Ammi told him about her child's ill health. Before she could launch into the details of the doctors she had seen and the remedies they had tried, he raised his skeletal hand, commanding silence. He gestured with his bony finger to bring the baby closer. He removed the shawl from the baby's head, dipped his index finger in the oil of the lamp on the grave and smeared a black mark on the baby's forehead. The baby squirmed but did not awaken.

His eyes closed, the old man mumbled verses from the *Quran*. Looking up, he said in a firm tone, 'You are struck by the evil eye. You girls don't take care when you are with child.' Pointing to a pile on the floor beside the women reading the *Quran*, he instructed, 'Buy a green *chaader* to drape on the shrine.'

Ammi and Tauqeer Khala returned home several hundred rupees poorer, reeking of incense. They had pounding headaches. In a minuscule black pouch tied around Baji's neck was a *taveez*, along with several others to burn at sunset every Thursday for the next seven weeks.

Meanwhile, Abbu continued to scout for formula until Baji finally took to Cow and Gate and soon gained weight. As she recovered her complexion became lighter and she morphed into a beautiful, chubby little girl. Ammi was left wondering whether it was the miracle of the *taveez* or Cow and Gate milk.

***

Farooq remained petite and fragile despite the fact that he was breastfed till three and hand fed by Wazir Khala till he was over twelve years old. He resented the fact that I, eighteen months his junior, was taller than him, that I came first in my class and earned a double promotion. He snubbed me by pointing out that I only did well because I went to an Urdu medium school whereas he went to an English medium one, which was much harder. He was a brilliant student and wanted to be a doctor.

Our grandfather, Abba Ji, sometimes teased him as he ruffled his hair, saying, 'Farooq, how will you ever become a doctor with those tiny feet?'

As it happened, Farooq did become a doctor, despite his small stature and tiny feet – a cardiologist, in fact. But he sacrificed much to do so.

5
MURREE ROAD

W e moved to a ground floor place on Murree Road from Shah Chan Chiragh, soon after Shano's birth. Wazir Khala, Salahuddin Khalo, and our six cousins, lived upstairs. Our house was the tallest in the neighbourhood. It towered over all the other buildings – an adult amongst toddlers. It was the only house in our neighbourhood with a large mosaic tiled *thara* over the open drain that ran on either side of the *gali*.

Baji and I often sat on our haunches, knees tucked under our chins, playing jacks using carefully picked stones and a ball. We chanted nonsense rhymes that we made up or had learnt from our friends, to the tunes of the latest pop songs, while our friends and siblings watched mesmerized by the dancing ball and stones.

Sometimes we opened our shop, selling *kugoo gorai*, the clay animals and pots we had purchased from street vendors. The main entrance to the house had grand wooden double doors with metal stars at the centre of carved flowers that were part of in an intricate wooden floral design. The left side of the double doors remained permanently locked, with a thick iron chain and bulky rusty padlock. A brass plaque boldly inscribed with my father's name: Dr. Syed Azhar-uddin Ahmed 127C, Murree Road, Rawalpindi, adorned the outside wall. There was no mention of Salahuddin Khalo, who lived upstairs.

The majestic entrance to the house gave onto a dark hallway with stairs to the right and a mosaic tiled courtyard to the left. The colourful design spilled outwards, making the area seem larger than it was. Ornate wrought iron balconies overhung the courtyard, around which whitewashed rooms extended. The courtyard was the soul of our house. It served as our living area and playground during the day and, in the summer, to escape the heat of the tiny kitchen, Ammi constructed a temporary brick stove under the shade of the balconies. On hot sweltering nights, we pulled the *palungs* out and slept under the stars. We escaped to the roof when it became still hotter.

Occasionally, Massi came to the house, a beaming smile on her face and a huge bundle tied in a discoloured bed sheet precariously balanced on her head. She unloaded her bundle in the middle of the courtyard and untied the knots. A whole array of hand embroidered fabrics, *dupattas* and shawls tumbled out from within. She knew her place and squatted on her haunches while Ammi and Wazir Khala pulled up jute stools to inspect the mound. They picked up this piece and that, scrutinized it and asked its price. Before Massi could reply, they had moved on to another piece that had caught their eye.

'Call Naz's mother,' Ammi shouted over her shoulder to whoever was within hearing range, without turning her attention from the treasure.

In no time Naz's mum and a few other women from across the *gali*, would join the preoccupied ladies. We knew Ammi and Wazir Khala would be lost to the world for the next few hours. Taking full advantage of their distraction, we went into the kitchen and helped ourselves to the homemade sweets – *soji ki barfi*, *daal halva* and other goodies – that Ammi had prepared and hoarded for unexpected guests. We were prepared to face the consequences later.

***

In winter, Ammi and Abbu slept in the small back room while we slept cocooned in thick *lehafs* on *palungs* in the larger multipurpose room. It was bright and airy, with the *palungs* pushed against the walls. Ammi was forever fixing the floral bedcovers since we used the *palungs* to sleep on, to sit on, to play on, and eat on. The *palungs* themselves were simple wooden frames strung with thick rope. Abbu tightened them regularly by pulling the ropes at the foot end. The *palungs* were not as comfortable as Ammi and Abbu's webbed *masiari* and we could feel the ropes through the thin cotton-filled homemade bedding.

When the worn rope gave way, Ammi and Massi would unwind the entire network from the wooden frame and rework it, nimbly weaving the rope in and out in intricate patterns. It blistered their hands but Ammi never stopped the street hawkers who went by chanting their trades, to do such arduous tasks, as Wazir Khala and most of the other neighbourhood women did.

Occasionally, we dragged the *masiari* and the *palungs* out into the courtyard, sprayed them with stinking insecticide oil, using a leaking hand pump and beat the beds with sticks to dislodge the bugs that bothered us at night. We squashed the little beasts under our feet leaving bloodstains on the floor tiles.

One afternoon, I stood on a *palung* by the window, holding a glass jar to catch the wasps that entered through the hole in the wire mesh, escaping from the scorching afternoon sun,

'Stop it Salmi, you'll get stung,' Ammi implored as she oiled Shano's hair. 'Stop it! You hear me?'

Ignoring her pleas I carefully held a wasp with a *dupatta*, pulled out the sting with tweezers, tied a thread to its leg and chased my terrified siblings around the room.

'Ammi, Ammi tell her to stop!' screamed Ather, hiding behind her.

Gritting her teeth, Ammi rose to hit me. She knocked over the bottle of oil, which further infuriated her. I ran round and round the prayer *chowki* to save myself, tripped, and broke my jar. The wasps escaped into the room, causing chaos, and the jagged glass made a big gash in my palm. Everyone, Ammi included, took refuge in the adjacent room.

'Serves you right! Just you wait, I'll sort you

out, good and proper!' Ammi shouted from behind the screen door.

Blood gushed from the deep cut in my hand. I knew I would get no sympathy from Ammi, so I ran to Khala Ji, my *Quran* teacher, down the *gali*. Seeing my bloody hand, she rushed to me, arms outstretched. 'Oh *Sadqay*, what happened? Come, let me see. Kubra, quickly get some *lassi!*' she called to her daughter. Reassuring me as she cleaned my hand affectionately, she asked, 'How did you do this?'

'I fell with a glass jar,' I sobbed, sensing sympathy.

'Ooh, I hope there is no glass in your hand,' she said concerned, bandaging my hand. Then she fed me buttered corn *roti* and spinach, stroking my hair between mouthfuls, as I sipped my cold yogurt drink.

On returning home, I found Ammi in the kitchen, preparing tea on the new clay stove she had so lovingly constructed. It was a U-shaped brick and clay structure which burnt firewood. To the left of it she had made an interconnected circular hole, which she used for simmering. The bricks were moulded over with red clay so that the pans and the *tava,* the hot plate for cooking *chapattis*, sat snuggly. In the winter, it was tough to keep the damp firewood burning. Tears ran down Ammi's flushed face as she blew into the dying embers with a *phookni*, dislodging ash and creating acrid smoke that twisted and curled in all directions. But the quivering flames sprang back into new life, dancing to an invisible tune as the boiling pot of water on the stove hissed and gurgled accompaniment. Ammi added several teaspoons of tea leaves, sugar and milk into the pan and covered it to let it brew.

Glancing at my bandaged hand, she gestured for me to sit beside her. She brushed away the hair from my face and, with a sympathetic smile said, 'Who bandaged it? Khala Ji?' I nodded. 'When your Abbu comes home he will take you to the clinic on Murree Road.'

Knees pressed against her chest, Ammi kneaded dough and prepared square, round and even triangular *parathas* for us and our cousins on demand. She poked the logs with a *chimta*; sparks flying in all directions like fireflies. 'Shano move!' Ammi ordered without averting her gaze from the fire as we squabbled over the next *paratha* that ballooned and puffed up on the *tava*. Sprinkling sugar on them, we would roll them up and wolf them down with hot milky tea in ceramic cups.

When she finished cooking, Ammi brushed away the coal and ash, saving the charcoal to scrub her pans. She wiped the stove with a cloth dipped in a watered down clay solution, making it appear as good as new and leaving a permanent, fresh earthy smell in the kitchen.

One day, on discovering squirming, tiny pink baby mice in the kitchen cupboard, Ammi closed the cabinet in disgust and said, 'Perhaps you should get that cat after all. It would get rid of these wretched vermin.' She made room for the crockery in the *namutkhana*, the wooden cabinet with wire mesh panels, stacked with milk, fruit, vegetables and sugar.

'May I? Can I please get the kittens?' I beamed gleefully.

'*Kitten*,' Ammi emphasized. As I turned to rush off, she held my arm and said, 'It's a lot of responsibility, keeping a pet. If you don't look after it, *you* will have to answer to *Allah*.'

'I will...promise!' I shouted as I ran to the park to find the kittens behind the bushes.

I was relieved to find the mother absent, so I had time to select one from the litter of four. Eventually, I settled on the black and white one.

There after, every day, before going to school, I salvaged scraps from the butcher for my cat, *Billi*. On meat-free Tuesdays, she survived on leftover tid-bits and milk. After Ammi hit her for sneaking a piece of meat from the *qorma* she had just prepared, *Billi* took to indignantly retreating into the kitchen chimney as soon as I left for school. She only came out when I returned home, tail held high, purring and nuzzling my legs and finally rolling into a ball on the soft cushion on her favourite wicker chair.

***

A welcome addition to the kitchen was our paraffin cooker. It was portable, more efficient and less hassle than the clay stove. But Ammi continued to cook *chapattis* on her clay stove since the *chapattis* smelt of paraffin when made on the new cooker. Baji's arm was severely burnt one day, when her red dress caught fire from the paraffin stove as it flared up.

'It's Shamshad's *nazar,*' Ammi shrieked, mouthing soundless prayers as we all rushed about screaming.

Only that morning Shamshad Auntie had admired without adding *Mashallah* (May *Allah* protect you), the pretty red frocks Ammi had so painstakingly made from the parachute fabric Abbu had brought from the army depot. The material charred and stuck to Baji's sizzled skin. Abbu rushed her to Holy Family Hospital in a *tonga*, where the nuns gave her old Christmas cards to distract her while they treated her burn.

I was envious of Baji's lovely cards, and whenever anyone went to the hospital, I made it a point to accompany them. There, I pestered the nuns for cards, unaware that they did not have them all year round.

***

Ammi believed fervently in the curse of the evil eye. Whenever we were ill, she blamed one Auntie or the other, saying they had looked at us with envy or not uttered *Mashallah;* hence, we had been struck by the evil eye and jinxed. She immediately circled a few coins around our heads and set them aside to give to beggars. Then she read ritualistic verses from the *Quran* and blew on us to ward off evil, and make us better. Abbu, in turn, administered appropriate medicines from his dispensary.

At our slightest achievements Ammi set aside a few coins to give to the poor in a gesture of thanksgiving – a lifelong habit we all acquired.

***

Next to the kitchen was a small tiled room that served as our bathroom. It was no bigger than a closet with a metal bucket under a tap tied with a long piece of fabric to prevent the water from splashing. On hot summer afternoons, while the adults napped, we played in the bathroom. One day, I locked the bathroom from the outside and climbed in through the window. I then blocked the drain and the gap under the door with my clothes and towels and filled the room with water.

Ammi was awakened by the din I made. When she opened the bathroom door, she was thrown back by the flood of water. Knowing my fate, I ran out of the house, knocking over the huge ceramic jar of mango pickle Ammi had left to mature in the sun. She had spent several afternoons slicing and pitting the rock-hard, green mangoes and rubbing them with a unique blend of salt and spices – a recipe she had acquired from Khala Ji. She then dried the mangoes in the sun and soaked them in hot mustard oil. Now, yellow spicy oil and slices of green mango lay strewn across the yard amongst the shards from the broken jar.

I ran out into the *gali*, knowing Ammi could not chase after me there as she observed *purdah*. Furious, Ammi stood at the window shouting, 'Come in *now!*'

'No, you'll hit me!' I yelled back.

'I said, *come this instant!*'

This went on for some time, and many of the neighbourhood children gathered outside, awaiting the inevitable. When I eventually ventured into the house again, Ammi had not forgotten or forgiven. She hit me with her slipper.

It was in this bathroom that the girls running away from home hid. Baji and I were playing jacks on the *thara* and enjoying fresh, tangy pineapple Abbu's brother, Nadir Chacha, had brought from Dhaka.

'Why has Nadir Chacha come?' I asked. 'He's never come before.'

'To say goodbye to Abbu before he goes to London,' Baji told me, apparently in the know.

Suddenly two girls ran past us into our house. 'Don't tell anyone!' shouted the taller one as they hid in the bathroom adjacent to the entrance.

Four burly men charged into the house behind them. 'Where are the girls?' barked one. Baji and I sat in silence, blinking at them.

'Did two girls run in here?' shouted the fat one. We sat tight-lipped. I shook my head from side to side.

The men ran up the stairs. On hearing their footsteps recede, the girls dashed out of the house.

'Where are they?' shouted the fat one again as they rushed back down.

Scared, we fled to the back room. Soon police officers invaded our house. The intruders insisted the girls had entered our house, and our family must have had a hand in assisting their escape. The police questioned Abbu, Nadir **Chacha** and us.

'Don't be scared *baita*, tell them the truth,' coaxed Abbu, gently pulling me closer.

We told Abbu exactly what happened. He assured the police our family had nothing to do with the incident. Nadir **Chacha** fretted that if the police detained him, he would miss his flight back home.

Finally, it took Abbu's Army connections to get us out of the mess. The girls had run away from home to escape forced marriages. Despite their spunky revolt, they were located several days later and married off immediately.

***

Our drawing room doubled as Abbu's dispensary. It had a separate side entrance for the men so they did not have to enter the main house, as Ammi observed *purdah*. Behind Abbu's rickety swivel chair, on the whitewashed wall, was a map of the world, London encircled in red. The medical charts Abbu had procured from visiting medical reps adorned the walls.

The room was furnished with a large examination table, covered in black leatherette, a large sofa, a few chairs, and a massive desk. The green embossed leather-covered desk was protected by a sheet of glass, under which Abbu kept many visiting cards, prescriptions and small handwritten notes. A carved wooden box containing an array of treasures, sharpened pencils, labels, pens and string, were placed to the right, and a metal kidney dish containing syringes, thermometers, scalpels, pointers, scissors and a blood pressure monitoring set, was placed to the left of the marble fountain pen and ink holder. These we were not allowed to touch.

In the evening, chairs were put outside the dispensary door for patients. Women, children and old men began arriving well before opening time, and we could hear the buzz of their chatter from our courtyard. Sometimes, even people not waiting to see Abbu, sat chatting with their friends on the chairs we had put out. But no one objected.

We were strictly forbidden to play in the dispensary. But we sneaked in when the adults were napping. There, Rosy and I played doctors and nurses. 'Open wide, say *ahh*,' I copied Abbu, bending forward to shine a torch into Rosy's open mouth. '*Ummh*,' I nodded knowingly. 'Don't drink iced drinks and no tangy sweets,' I would instruct, waving my finger at her. Then, using a *jharoo* stick as an injection, we giggled as I injected her in the bottom and administered sweet homeopathic pills. One day Farooq caught me with my *shalwar* down, receiving my injection.

'Where do you pee from?' he enquired.

'Piss off!' I said irritably, quickly pulling up my *shalwar*.

'Right! I am going to tell Ammi what you two are up to,' he said, smiling maliciously. We thought he was bluffing but sneaked out of the room, just to be sure.

Abbu occasionally allowed me into the dispensary to help fetch and carry bottles of white homeopathic tablets from the shelves, because I was going to be a doctor when I grew up. I felt very proud and privileged. He examined the patients, transferred a small batch of tablets onto a tiny square of white paper, then he added a few drops of liquid from the vast array of brown bottles he kept locked in his black leather case. Twisting the paper into a small cone, he transferred the tiny tablets into a little bottle, firmly sealing it with a cork. He scribbled on the bottle while instructing the patient to take them at least half an hour before each meal.

Most women came accompanied by a man, or at least a child. If Abbu needed to examine an unaccompanied female, he called Ammi to sit in. After surgery hours Abbu's friends gathered in the dispensary to recite poetry, play chess and drink endless cups of tea till the early hours of the morning.

Late one evening, having served several pots of tea, Ammi lost her patience and, forgetting *purdah,* stormed into the dispensary. 'Right...that's it! I'm fed up with this crazy game that never ends!' she said decisively and flung the chessboard across the room. She stormed out, putting a sudden end to the game and the late-night gatherings for a while.

Abbu's friends, who had never before seen Ammi, watched the tiny lady in stunned silence, then sheepishly rose and departed in haste, apologizing profusely.

'Is that why she is named Jugnu?' asked Ajaz Uncle.

Abbu looked at him quizzically. 'Firefly,' he said, smiling. He didn't talk to Ammi for a couple of days but, realizing he was the one at fault, finally apologised. 'I didn't realize I was keeping you up.'

'It was past two o'clock!' Ammi replied, suppressing a smile.

'My friends think you are named Jugnu because of your fiery temper!'

They both chuckled.

***

My cousin Bader claimed the small room on the first floor landing as his library. Unlike other households nearby, the *Jang* newspaper and monthly *Taleem-o-Tarbiat* and *Bachon ki Dunya* children's magazines, were delivered to our house. Bader cut out the daily cartoon strips of the adventures of *Kirby* and had them bound. These, along with our collection of magazines, he rented out to children in the neighbourhood. With the five rupees he saved, he bought a Monopoly set. During the siesta hours we played Monopoly, hiding our currency and property cards under pillows. Misbah once sneaked a 1,000 rupee note from Farooq and put it under Bader's pillow. Salahuddin Khalo and Wazir Khala were rudely awakened from their nap by the resulting argument that escalated into a punch-up. Without asking any questions, Salahuddin Khalo ripped the Monopoly board in two. All we could do was watch in horror and cry. Wazir Khala smacked Misbah and helped us stick the board together again.

I spent hours making a Ludo board, using coloured buttons as counters and the dice from the Monopoly set, we played all afternoon. We collected and cut out cigarette packs and wrote letters of the alphabet on them to make our own *Talimi Tash*, with which we played a game similar to Scrabble. We glued together matchboxes to make doll furniture, and made clay animals and fruit, which Salahuddin Khalo then helped us paint. Abbu cut out the sailor from a Woodbine cigarette packet and attached a weighted string to it. We hung the sailor outside the library door. When the door opened, the sailor saluted.

Rosy and I often retreated to the library to play with her doll and draw on our slates. My drawings always had a cottage with a sloping roof, mountains in the background, a winding path leading to the house, bordered with flowerbeds, a river and pine trees. God knows where I dreamt up such a scene from. Perhaps it was a premonition of the future. When we asked Wazir Khala whose drawing was better, she always said Rosy's, even though we all knew mine was the best. When we asked Ammi, she pointed out the good parts in each, saying both were lovely. Why couldn't she just have been honest and say mine was better, I will never know.

6
WAZIR KHALA AND SALAHUDDIN KHALO

Making the most of the natural light in the balcony, Salahuddin Khalo was engrossed in the intricate details of the flowers he was painting. The sensuous, heavy fragrance of seasonal flowers and turpentine was overpowering. Rosy and I sat playing with our dolls.

'Why are you wasting your time painting *that?* Why don't you paint Brigadier Adnan's portrait? He's been asking you for months!' snapped Wazir Khala as she walked past.

'*Because I don't paint portraits,*' Salahuddin Khalo replied, enunciating every word.

'If you can paint that, you can paint portraits. At least he'll pay you generously,' she goaded.

'I *do not paint for the money. I paint for myself!'* Salahuddin Khalo snapped. The lady in the painting looked on languorously with slanting eyes, as if bemused by the sudden drama.

As I ran past, I nearly knocked over the easel. He threw his pallet and paint brush on the floor and gave me a stern look. With eyes flashing and forehead creased, he yelled angrily, 'Salmi *aur nacho!* That's it, keep dancing!'

I froze. He marched off to the library with a sullen face and banging the door shut, locked it behind him. We knew he would sulk there for the rest of the day in seclusion and solitude, and a frosty atmosphere would persist in the whole household for days, with neither husband nor wife talking directly to each other.

Ammi was engrossed in her sewing on the *chowki*. She stopped the sewing machine. Shaking her head she addressed her sister. 'Baji, why do you pester him when you know…'

'*Because* it would pay the school fees for a whole year,' Wazir Khala retorted but she knew she had gone too far. Picking up a frock, she began hemming the garment.

Ammi opened her mouth to say something but thought better of it. Sighing deeply, she resumed her sewing.

Wazir Khala was the eldest of nine siblings and by far the prettiest. Since her mother, Amma Ji, was often ill, she became matriarchal at an early age. Not only did she bully her siblings, but even her poor husband Salahuddin Khalo lived under her thumb. Wazir Khala had a caustic tongue and a curious aristocratic manner about her – something she hadn't lost from pre-Partition days, when she was queen bee, with a privileged life. Having tasted the sweet joy of plenty, she found it hard to swallow the bitter pill of frugal living. She seemed to think she was better than the rest. Perhaps she was. After all, she was the firstborn of Shehzadi, the Princess, and had witnessed her grandfather's lordly existence in pre-Partition India, where everyone called him *Badshah* because of his magnanimous nature, and treated her like fragile porcelain. Now all she had left were her precious memories.

Long after everyone else had accepted their compromised circumstances as a reality, she retained her lofty airs and continued to muse over her past high connections and lost affluence, yearning for the comfortable existence she had taken for granted as her birth-right. Perhaps her loss was greater, for she had been engaged to a most eligible bachelor, a wealthy landlord, who thereafter jilted her and moved to England after Partition, and married an English girl. Wazir Khala was left bitter and dejected.

Her splendour spent and having lost the freshness of youth, she became bitter and acid-tongued. A lifetime of resentment pickled her heart. Perhaps she felt fate had short-changed her and she deserved better.

Wazir Khala still stood uncompromisingly erect, in an aristocratic, haughty manner – a relic of great beauty. But the bitterness of a hard life was evident on her face. When she looked at you, she narrowed her sunken sorrowful eyes, underlined by dark puffy half-moons, as if pondering something in the distance she had seen for the first time, lost in an inward maze of contemplation. Deep lines etched on her forehead gave her a continually troubled look. She had beautiful, sharp cheekbones, a characteristic of all her siblings as well. Her flaccid and waxy cheeks were pulled down on either side of her pursed pink lips, though she had a tinkling childlike laugh. With time she had grown a little stout, giving her a matronly figure. But it didn't detract an iota from her grace and poise.

After Partition, Wazir Khala married Salahuddin Khalo, a distant relative. Physically they made a handsome couple but were poles apart in nature. They were both tall, with the sharp features and fair complexions so crucial to being considered beautiful in Asian society. Wazir Khala was very proud of the fact that she had produced two beautiful daughters – Rosy and Ruby – and four sons – Misbah, Bader, Farooq and Mustafa. The children had inherited their parents' fair complexion and good looks, and Wazir Khala idolized them. We, on the other hand, had inherited olive skins from Abbu and were considered *nasal biggaar*, the black sheep of the family, especially by our grandmother, Amma Ji.

Wazir Khala had a voracious desire to snatch from life more than it could give – not for herself but for her children, whom she indulged recklessly, depriving herself not only of the luxuries of life but at times its bare essentials. She sent her children to English medium schools despite the fact that the fees were well beyond her means. She considered education as the only way out of the financial drudgery she experienced. Since her children mingled with the children of the high gentry, she pedantically ensured they were dressed appropriately, leaving her chronically short of cash and dependent on her family.

Salahuddin Khalo, an obdurate capricious man, was economical with his words. His expressive face and soft eyes communicated more than his speech. Once he said something it became etched in stone. He must have been a dashing young man in his youth for even in later life his clean-shaven face remained handsome. He had chiselled features with an Aryan nose and sharp jawline, as if carved with a sharp knife; dark wavy hair, and large fleshy ears – features he passed on to all his children. His high arched eyebrows above clear, soulful eyes, gave him an almost surprised look, belying his quick temper. The crow's feet at the corners of his eyes, the receding hairline, sharp jaw and full lips, though austere, gave him the appearance of a man who had lived.

Salahuddin Khalo dressed impeccably. In fact, Abbu said that when he first saw him, wearing dark glasses, a cotton chequered shirt with the top button undone, loose fitting fawn trousers, stylish tan moccasins, and his hair brushed back under his trilby, he had thought he looked like an Italian gangster. But I was reminded of Clark Gable in *Gone with the Wind*. He remained graceful, appearing younger than his years, to the end. He put his youthful appearance down to the clove of fresh garlic and sliver of fresh ginger he consumed with a large glass of water first thing in the morning.

He was a gifted artist and painted huge canvases of mounted soldiers in British colonial uniform, historical war scenes, and portraits in the style of Vermeer and Chughtai. He handled his brushes with a certain ease and freedom that came from close acquaintance and natural aptitude. His paintings are displayed in the Army Museum in Rawalpindi and have been published in PIA calendars as well. Much to Wazir Khala's annoyance, he did not utilize his talent for financial gain. She failed to appreciate his finer, artistic qualities and found him both tiresome and perplexing. She considered him a failure for not being able to meet her material demands; not necessarily for herself but for her children. She resented his thwarted ambition and selfish nature for he did not share her aspirations. She mistook his artistic nature for indolence and blamed it on his upbringing in the small city of Gujranwala.

'None of them are willing to venture out of Gujranwala and explore the world – *kowain kai mainduck* (toads in a well),' she scoffed of his family.

Wazir Khala had a keen interest in medicine. She knew the names and cures to all the common ailments and confidently prescribed for the neighbours who came round to seek free medical advice. She resented the fact that her parents had not permitted her to continue her education.

'On the day of Judgment, I will challenge Abba Ji and ask him why he deprived me of education,' she said, turning her mouth down in contempt and setting aside the garment she was hemming. 'If I were educated I wouldn't have to skimp and save, and be dependent on *him*. I would be able to provide for my children.'

'*Baaaji*, how could you?' Ammi snapped back as if stung. Her sister's words pierced her heart and she turned crimson with anger. Rage choked her throat and the veins stood out on her forehead and neck. She couldn't stomach the bile in her sister's vitriolic remarks about her beloved father. 'You have such a barbed tongue. That is such a harsh thing to say. It was hard enough for Abba Ji to send the boys to college. Besides, there *were* no colleges for girls in Pindi then!'

Wazir Khala straightened her already stiff posture and grimaced, pursing her lips. Unperturbed by Ammi's impertinence, she added acerbically, 'Amma Ji never gave any importance to our schooling. Whenever she was ill, *which was all the time*, or if anyone of *you* was sick, she kept *me* back from school.'

'It wasn't her fault that she was ill. You weren't

the only one who suffered. You escaped by getting married. It was Tauqeer and me who made mounds of *chapattis* and food for the family and all those who just dropped in unannounced. Besides, no one could afford to send girls to school then!'

'Those who cared did. Look at Iqbal.' Wazir Khala paused. 'And Amma Ji was forever pregnant. That took a toll on her health. She could have done something about that.'

Ammi placed her hand on the wheel of the sewing machine and looked up in genuine consternation, unable to listen to the venomous remarks any longer.

'You know Abba Ji believed in providence – He who giveth life will provide. Besides, Iqbal was an exception. Her father was a wealthy *nawab*, with drivers and cars!'

'Amma Ji always considered us girls as burdens. She treated us like servants and thrust us at the first man that darkened our door,' Wazir Khala said dismissively.

'*She did not!* You are such a spiteful soul. *You* were hurt because your fiancé broke off the engagement and went to England. You can't blame Amma Ji for that. That wasn't her fault,' Ammi said, throwing back her head and narrowing her eyes that shone like two steely dagger points.

Wazir Khala glared at Ammi. Every feature in her stern face became statuesque. She set aside her work, letting her hands lie listlessly in her lap while gazing into the distance. Softly, she said, 'Some things wound you to the core, leaving a permanent scar on your heart. The deeper the wound, the longer it takes to heal. Unfortunately, you can't tell the severity of the injury by looking at the scar.'

Ammi looked up, startled. She weighed the words, a shadow crossing her face. 'Baji, I never realized how deeply it had hurt you...you never said...'

Before Ammi could finish, Naz ran in breathlessly. Pulling Wazir Khala by the hand, she shouted, 'Please come! Come quickly! Javaid can't breathe; he's having an asthma attack!'

Wazir Khala threw Ammi an alarmed look and rushed off with Naz, leaving Ammi to ponder the gravity of the situation. Wazir Khala accompanied Javaid's distraught family to the hospital.

A few days later, when Javaid's mother came over to see Ammi, she excitedly narrated her first ever encounter with the nuns at the Holy Family Hospital in her high-pitched voice, the Pashto peppered with Urdu and Punjabi: 'Jugnu, you won't believe what those white women with black clothes did at the hospital!'

'You mean the nuns?'

'Yes, yes...they put Javaid on a bed and, as if by magic, the bed went up a tunnel. I would have screamed had it not been for Baji Wazir holding my hand.'

'They took him up in the lift?' Ammi chuckled.

'Baji Wazir is a saint. She saved Javaid's life.'

'Yes, she is brilliant in a crisis, but it's *Allah* who grants life, not Baji Wazir.'

I regularly mimicked this incident to our amused Urdu-speaking family, who loved to hear me speak Punjabi. Rolling with laughter, they would ask me to repeat the story again and again. Exaggerating her actions and her Punjabi-Urdu-Pushto speech, I happily obliged, relishing the attention I received.

7
ROSY AND ME

Ye dolut bhi ley lo, ye shuhrat bhi ley lo
(Take my wealth, take my fame),

Bhale cheehn lo mujh say meri javani
(Snatch from me my youth if you will),

Magar mujh ko lauta do bachpan purana
(But return to me the spring of childhood),

Vo kaghaz ki hashti, vo barish ka pani
(The paper boat that sails in the rain water).

Jagjit Singh's melancholy voice poured from the radio. I sang the next couplet in my head before I heard them...

Bhulaye nahin bhool sakta hai koi
(Unable to forget even when one wants to)

Vo chhoti si raaten vo lumbii kahaani
(Those long stories in the short nights).

Wazir Khala's raspy voice boomed above the song: 'Salmi, keep an eye on Ruby! See she doesn't roll off the bed.'

Wazir Khala had left the baby on the bed, with the radio switched on. Ruby happily played with her uplifted feet. I rushed to the room but seeing my cousins Bader and Farooq where Ruby should have been, unnerved me. They lay on the beds, separated by the writing desk, knees bent, a thin sheet covering their mutilated delicate parts. Ruby gurgled beside Farooq. It was strange that Farooq, nearly twelve, and fourteen-year-old Bader, had only just been circumcised. Most boys underwent this in the first few days of their lives. Wazir Khala said Farooq was too small and weak when he was born, but God knows why Bader was still a Hindu. I thought it was quite brave and daring of them to go through the humiliation and embarrassment at this age. But no doubt a lifetime of teasing and being called Hindu at every opportune moment by their siblings, cousins and friends, had taken its toll. Besides, ever the maverick, Farooq liked to shock. It was he who had called the barber to ` do the dread deed.

In the living room, sunlight poured in from the balcony and windows. The bright clean room smelt of fresh flowers and phenyl. As always, a vase of awkwardly arranged maroon *Kalgha* (Celosia), drooping in the heat, stood on the writing desk next to the radio. Salahuddin Khalo brought the flowers from the gardens of the Army General Headquarters where he worked. I loved stroking the velvety *Kalgha*, which caused a cascade of tiny black seeds to fall. I quickly blew them off the table before Wazir Khala saw.

The ephemeral late afternoon light streamed in, casting a long rhomboid of light on Salahuddin Khalo's prayer *chowki*. The once navy blue velvet prayer mat, now faded to grey, with only a few matted tassels remaining at the ends, was spread out as always, ready for the next prayer. A stack of crisply ironed laundry, just brought by the *dhobi*, lay next to the tattered red notebook and stub of a pencil Wazir Khala used to itemize it.

On the mantelpiece, a copy of the *Holy Quran*, carefully wrapped in a faded pink brocade cover, sat on a carved wooden bookstand. To the right of it stood Salahuddin Khalo's exquisite, unframed painting, inspired by Omar Khayyam, of an ethereal lady with angular features and slanting eyes; a long pale robe cascading behind her, a delicate pink orchid arranged in her flowing hair. The lady held the edge of her *duppatta* as it slid off her head.

In the centre of the mantelpiece stood a clock, once gold, now a dull yellow, frozen in time at 6.30 many decades ago. The lazily rotating ceiling fan churning hot air was reflected in the glass of the framed photograph of Wazir Khala standing proudly beside her children – Misbah, Badar, Farooq, Mustafa and cherub-like Rosy, with her curly hair and cheeky smile. A gecko hid patiently behind the picture, waiting to catch flies and mosquitoes. Abbu must have taken that photograph since he was the only one with a camera, brought back from England in the year of the Queen's coronation.

Chiaroscuros of light and shade danced intricate patterns on the crumbling whitewashed wall as the lace curtain fluttered and flapped in the fickle breeze of the ceiling fan. A dark streak ran around the room at the base of the wall and the furniture, caused by the daily mopping. The song continued on the radio:

Vo budhiya jise bache kehte the naanii
(The old woman the kids called granny)

Vo naanii kii baaton mein pariyon kaa deraa
(The fairy stories told to me by the granny)

I sang along, teasing Farooq and dancing between the beds. I was always dancing and singing the latest songs, nonsense rhymes, times tables or even verses from the *Quran*, while playing Jacks or hopscotch. Sometimes I tried to read *Ayatul Kursi* and other verses from the *Quran* to erase the songs from my head, but they soon crept back, wriggling into my brain quietly, uninvited, as if they possessed me.

Just as in the *ghazal*, there was an old lady in our *gali* – crazy Mai Phuttan – with her shaven head, dressed in long frocks people forced her to wear, for left alone she would strip and run naked down the street. Children teased her mercilessly and chased her chanting, '*Pugli, pugli*-crazy, crazy.' She would run down the *gali* crying and screaming abuse, spit drooling down her prickly chin, making incoherent sounds.

Although we lived downstairs, flowers were always absent from our house. But that was not all we didn't have – Rosy used a toothbrush with toothpaste; we used a homemade *munjun* powder that Ammi prepared by grinding charcoal, salt and herbs. This we rubbed onto our teeth with our fingers or *miswak* sticks. While we did not have toothbrushes or toothpaste, we always had Imperial Leather soap, Ammi's favourite, while everyone else used the horrible, smelly, pink Lifebuoy.

I envied Rosy. She had better clothes than I did. She was pretty, with dark, curly hair and chubby pink cheeks. Everyone commented on her fair complexion and lovely dresses. Abbu sometimes called her Shirley Temple. Neither she nor I knew who that was, but we knew it was a compliment. Rosy went to St Mary's, and her brothers went to St Andrew's, the posh English medium schools on the main road, while we went to the Urdu medium school in our *gali*. Wazir Khala made it a point to mention their schools whenever she introduced her children to anyone so as to make it quite clear they went to English medium schools.

***

Appi and Baji from across the *gali* were talking about going to their village. When I said I had never seen a village, they offered to take both Rosy and me. We rushed home to ask our Ammis. Wazir Khala gave her consent immediately, but Ammi refused. When I protested, she said, 'What clothes will you take?'

'I can take my red and pink frock, and Baji's yellow one. That'll fit me.'

'No, you'll need new shoes and more clothes, and I can't buy new shoes just yet.'

Wazir Khala said I could take Rosy's shoes; we were the same size. But Ammi said no. Despite all my cries and pleas, I wasn't allowed to go. When Rosy returned after a whole week, I did not ask her about her trip. I did not even ask if she had travelled by train. And she, feeling guilty at having gone without me, did not tell me either.

*****

Rosy went to Gujranwala by train to see her grandparents every holiday. I had never even seen a train, let alone travelled in one. Nor had I seen my grandparents since they lived in India. The only form of transport I had sat on was Mamo Zahid's motorbike or the *tonga*, the horse-drawn carriage, to go to the Holy Family Hospital in Satellite Town with Ammi.

Rosy always returned from Gujranwala with beautiful clothes, presents from her aunts and uncles, and anecdotes of the trip. Her grandmother made gorgeous dolls with fingers, pointed chin and nose, dressed in gorgeous red wedding outfits trimmed with lace and gold braid that matched those she made for Rosy. The only doll I had was the one I made myself, using fabrics I had scrounged from the fat seamstress Phama, in return for massaging her forever aching back. I rolled up two pieces of white fabric, bent one in half to serve as the face and trunk and tied the other to the trunk in a cross, to serve as arms. Then I drew eyes, mouth and a nose on the face and stitched pieces of long, thick, black thread for hair. I plaited and tied the hair with red ribbon. When dressed in long, flared printed frocks, it looked quite decent.

Not totally satisfied with my creation, I went over to Humaira Baji, who was brilliant with her hands and could work magic with fabrics. I was forbidden to go to her house because she was possessed. Though she was perfectly normal most of the time, occasionally she fell without warning and went funny. Unfortunately, when I arrived, it was one of 'those' times. Humaira Baji was lying on the floor, twisted and jerking and thrashing about in a most peculiar manner. Her eyes rolled back to show just the whites and she was frothing at the mouth. Her arms and legs lashed out uncontrollably before her body convulsed into a rigid abnormal position. Her mother rushed about in terrified panic, shouting, 'Oh dear Lord have mercy on my child! Please help her, help me. Have mercy on my child!' Reading *Ayatul Kursi* and other verses from the *Quran* out loud, she tried to force a teaspoon between Humaira Baji's clenched teeth.

'Shall I call Ammi or Wazir Khala?' I hollered in fright.

Without replying, she rushed about, moving furniture out of the way. I dashed home. Ammi was sitting enjoying the winter afternoon sun, unpicking her knitting. Naz's mother from across the *gali* was with her, and Massi was oiling her hair.

'*Ammi*, come quick! Humaira Baji is dying!' I screamed.

Alarmed, Ammi dropped her knitting and they all rushed over to Humaira Baji's house. Naz's mother tried to calm Humaira Baji's mother, forcing her to sit down. Ammi placed a pillow under Humaira Baji's head, and Massi rubbed the soles of her feet, instructing me to get some warm milk.

'Just hang in there, it'll pass. Just hang in there,' Ammi continued to whisper as she stroked Humaira Baji's hair. After what seemed an eternity, Humaira Baji went limp and wet herself. She remained unconscious for some time. When she finally came round, she remained disorientated and listless for a long time.

'You must take her to the hospital. They have medicines that can help her,' Ammi told Humaira Baji's mother when everyone had calmed down.

'Yes, take her to the hospital. The women in those black clothes – what d'you call 'em?' asked Naz's mother.

'Nuns,' Ammi whispered, fixing Humaira Baji's clothes.

'Yes, those nuns are wonderful. Angels... they are angels. They saved Javaid's life when he stopped breathing.' She was about to narrate the whole incident when Ammi gently shook her head.

'If it gets about that she is possessed, who will marry her?' sobbed Humaira Baji's mother. 'Promise me you will keep this to yourself.'

'She is *not* possessed, she is ill. She will be fine once she gets proper medication. And don't worry; we have daughters of our own. We won't mention it to anyone. Just take her to the hospital. I'll come with you,' Ammi said in a soft, soothing tone, patting her hand.

'Change her name. Some names are unlucky', suggested Massi. 'I don't know anyone called Humaira who is happy and healthy.' She went on to name several Humairas who were ill-fated, culminating with the story of the beautiful baby she had helped a *Pathani* woman deliver, who named the baby Humaira. 'That baby was *munhoos* (cursed),' Massi stated with conviction.

'Massi, how can a baby be *munhoos*? All babies are innocent angels,' Ammi chided.

'She had an extra finger, nail and all, hanging off a thread on her little finger. Everyone knows that's unlucky. When I pointed it out to the

Pathani, she made me cut it off. If that weren't bad enough, the afterbirth wouldn't come. She bled so much I ran out of cotton wool and had to cut up her *lehaf.* I was pulling out wad after wad but the bleeding wouldn't stop. There were two men in the house, her brothers. I told them to take her to the hospital. It was a treacherous night; rain, thunder, lightning….' Massi shook her head. 'They couldn't find a *tonga* and she died. If that's not *munhoos,* what is? One of the men placed a thousand rupees in my hand and told me to leave the ill-fated infant at Pir Haroon Rasheed's shrine.'

'No, you didn't!' Ammi exclaimed, wide-eyed.

'We'll soon be burying both of them since there is no one to look after the child here. She has a better chance of surviving there than with us,' he told me. What could I do? With them carrying those big rifles and all...'

Naz's mother nudged Ammi and looked towards me to indicate I was listening.

'What happened to the baby?' Ammi asked, unperturbed.

'I don't know. I asked the *malung* at the shrine the following day and he denied all knowledge of it; said he didn't know what I was talking about.' Massi shrugged her shoulders. 'He began questioning *me,* so I let it go.'

'How long ago *was* this?' Ammi asked thoughtfully.

'Oh, don't know exactly; long before Partition.'

'*How long?*' Ammi asked.

'*I don't know*...long time. My Rani was about three.. so thirty, forty years... Why are *you* so interested'

'Oh no...just wondered,' Ammi replied dismissively.

'I better get back before Jamal gets home or I'll get a beating,' sighed Naz's mother. She hovered about, torn between staying to help and facing the wrath of her violent husband.

'I don't know how you can live with a man who treats you so badly. You should stand up to him,' Ammi said, shaking her head.

'A man's not a man unless he beats his woman. Besides what *can* I do?' Naz's mother gave a nervous laugh but her face immediately tightened when she saw the look in Ammi's eyes.

Annoyed at her tame acquiescence, Ammi snapped, 'I know what I'd do. In my view a man is not a man *if* he beats his woman.'

Naz's mother giggled and left. Ammi helped Humaira Baji's mother tidy up before she too left with the promise to take her to the hospital as soon as Humaira Baji was up to it.

For days, Ammi wondered about Massi's story about Humaira. I felt sorry for Humaira Baji and didn't care what anyone said because it wasn't her fault that she was named Humaira, or possessed. When Humaira Baji felt better, I went to see her. She was very upset that I had witnessed her having a fit.

'That's why I don't go anywhere. I'd hate to make a spectacle of myself in public,' she said, trying to hold back the tears welling up in her eyes. She asked me to describe what had happened.

Realizing she was upset, I said, 'Oh nothing much; you just fainted,' and quickly changed the subject by telling her about my fight with Rosy.

Humaira Baji then had a brilliant idea. She sent me to Phama, the seamstress to collect remnants. Phama was a huge woman. Her chocolate coloured skin stretched taut and smooth like satin over her oval face. Her obese body shone like polished mahogany. Beads of perspiration gleamed on her fuzzy upper lip and forehead. She sat on the floor under the huge *Sukh Chain* tree in her courtyard, with one knee drawn up to her chin and the other leg folded beneath her body, surrounded by garments, fabrics and laces. She worked her hand-powered sewing machine, propped up on a low wooden platform, with a preoccupied, intent look.

'*Salaam-Alaykum*, Phama.'

'*Walaikum Assalam*,' she replied above the clatter of the sewing machine. Her warm fleeting glance welcomed me without words in a benevolent embrace. She continued to work the machine with one hand manoeuvring the fabric this way and that with the other. Her ample bosoms bounced up and down rhythmically with each turn of the wheel. Her coconut oiled, dark hair, pulled tight in a thick plait, danced like a python about to strike over her right shoulder as she swayed to and fro. A rebel strand had managed to escape and hung defiantly by her temple, teasing her mischievously. She grabbed it between her index finger and thumb and absentmindedly swept it behind her ear.

She paused. In the lull she held up the stitched garment and, narrowing her large, deer-like eyes, scrutinized it for defects. Finding none, she shook it out and flattened it on the wooden platform. Then, she carefully snipped the loose threads, trimming and nipping the finished garment here and there, her teeth biting on her protruding tongue with each cut. She finally looked up with a long sigh. 'What are you after? Remnants for your dolls?' she asked.

I smiled a begging smile.

Irritated by the fluff, she sniffed and twitched her petite nose, rubbing it with the back of her plump hand and bending forward, revealing the black *taveez* hanging between her ample breasts. She turned the garment the right way round, held it up and examined her handiwork, and then pursed her full lips in self-satisfaction on a job well done. She sat up on her haunches, surprisingly nimble for her size, yawned inwardly without opening her mouth and flexed her shoulders. Taking a deep breath, she said, 'How's your mother?'

'She is fine.'

'Tell your aunt her clothes are ready,' she said, changing the thread on her machine.

'I'll tell her… Shall I take them for her?'

'Yes…no… Let her send for them so she can pay me at the same time.'

'You'll be lucky! But I'll tell her.'

She gestured with her eyes to the pile of remnants in the corner, while she ironed the garment. 'Take the lot, I need the space,' she said dismissively.

I ran up, gave her a hug and kissed her on her soft coconut smelling cheek. She smiled and hugged me back with her free hand. I made a bundle of the multitude of coloured fabrics and then ran home, delighted with my loot.

'You have to rub my aching shoulders this evening!' Phama shouted after me.

'Okay!' I yelled back. I knew that if I went home, Wazir Khala and Ammi would take many of the larger pieces to make their brassieres and frocks for baby Ruby, so I ran straight to Humaira Baji.

She made me lots of clothes for my dolls and a handsome male doll dressed in a green *kurta* and white pyjama. Showing it off to Rosy, I suggested we marry him with her doll with the red outfit trimmed with gold braid. She agreed. We held our dolls' wedding in the library. When all the girls I had invited to the party turned up for the wedding, Ammi had no choice but to make *biryani* for us all. She was *not* pleased. We sang wedding songs and danced the *bhangra* to the beat of Ammi's wooden sewing machine cover improvised as a drum. We even had the ceremony of showing the bride and the groom's faces for the first time to the guests, and they gave money as gifts to the couple.

I had conspired with Humaira Baji to acquire Rosy's doll after the wedding, as was the custom that the bride comes away with the groom, but Rosy refused to hand over the doll after the wedding and we quarrelled. We didn't speak to each other for several days. Rosy complained to Wazir Khala. Without asking any questions, Wazir Khala shouted at me, reminding me of how sensitive Rosy was.

When I told my tale of woe to Khala Ji, my *Quran* teacher, she consoled me by showing me a plant she had purchased from a street hawker. Its leaves folded as soon as I touched it. I was fascinated.

'*Chohi-moie* (touch-me-not),' Khala Ji said, nodding with a broad smile.

I nicknamed Rosy *Chohi-moie*, and much to Wazir Khala and Rosy's annoyance, almost everyone adopted it too.

***

Much later, Abbu finally sent us *real* dolls from London – our reward for good exam results. Mine was a beautiful Barbie dressed in a white bridal outfit, complete with a silver tiara. Baji's was quite a lot larger than mine and dressed in school uniform, with a white blouse, blue skirt and a red cardigan. I really should have had the bigger doll since I came first in my class, but I suppose Baji was older and besides, my doll was much prettier.

Our treasured dolls were carefully stashed away in the large trunk under Ammi's bed, where she kept her special outfits and valuables. When she occasionally opened the trunk, we gathered around her. I loved the musky smell of stale perfume and mothballs and held up her outfits against my body to see if they would fit me. Admiring the gold and silver embroidery on silks and velvets, I said, 'Ammi, can I have these when I get married?'

'*Besharam!* Girls don't talk about getting married,' she chided. But from her smile I knew she wasn't angry. '*Inshallah,* I'll make you better ones when you get married; lots of them,' she said, hugging me.

'No, I want *these*,' I insisted.

'Alright, alright, you can have them,' she agreed, smiling and folding them to put back in the trunk.

We were briefly allowed to play with our dolls before she put them back in their plastic covers and locked them in the trunk too, along with the thick beaded necklaces and fountain pens Abbu had also sent us.

I never forgave Ammi for burning many of her outfits to extract the silver from the embroidery, which she sold for pittance before our departure to London. I also never forgave her for giving away our dolls as gifts to our cousins Fareeda and Saadia, when we went to stay with them in Karachi on our way to London, for they were the first *proper* dolls we had ever had.

8
STORIES FROM THE ROOFTOP

We had a bird's eye view of the entire neighbourhood from our roof. Below us, Rawalpindi sprawled in all directions. While eunuchs danced the *bhangra* in the streets below, up above, colourful paper kites danced in the sky, competing with crows and kites of the avian variety. The pungent smell of smoke and curry mingled with the refreshing aroma of fresh *roti* from Aslam's *tandoor*, whetting our insatiable appetites.

The flat roof of our house was our playground by day and as it got hotter, our bedroom by night. The brickwork on the roof and its walls were painstakingly elaborate, with geometric designs. The lattice work made mysterious patterns on the ground in the sun. In the absence of television, video games, mobile phones and even toys, we had to seek our own entertainment, and the vantage point of our towering rooftop provided plenty. It also gave us an added advantage for kite flying. In the relentless, sweltering heat of Punjab, we spent our afternoons and weekends skipping rope, playing jacks, and hopscotch barefoot, jumping from foot to foot, to prevent our feet from blistering on the scorching roof.

Across the *gali*, opposite our house, was a row of ten single storied brick houses, abutting each other; a single step leading to the doorway above the drain. These houses had been originally built for the labourers who had served the landlord who owned our house and all the land around it. All the houses were identical – two rooms with windows opening onto the courtyard. Next to the main entrance to the courtyard were stairs leading to the roof, under which was the kitchen, where a cowpat fire polluted the atmosphere, morning and evening. Women sat on low wooden stools, fanning the smoky fire to keep the smelly cowpats alight, cooking *chapattis* and curry, their shiny pots and pans stacked in alcoves behind them. The other corner, with a corrugated roof, served as the bathroom.

In the first of these houses, right opposite our house, lived my friend Naz and her family. Her father, Jamal, owned the dairy at the end of the *gali*. Khala Ji lived in the very last house.

In the sun-drenched winter afternoons, after completing their chores, women sat on *palungs*, chewing sugarcane, eating oranges, sewing, knitting, picking nits from each other's hair or oiling and combing it, or simply gossiping until the men returned home from work. College girls reclined on *palungs* reading *Urdu Digest*, *Shama* magazine, *Zaibun Nissa* and *Khwateen ki Dunya*. Little girls played with their dolls, skipped, played hopscotch, jacks, and cat's cradle, either in their homes or out in the *gali*.

I knew everyone in the neighbourhood. I would cross the *gali* to Jamal's house to play with Naz. Like most *Pathans*, Jamal carried a rifle and was famed for his fiery temper. He was feared by most people in the neighbourhood, especially after he hung a local bully, Zulfi, upside down by his ankles in the dairy amongst the water buffalos, for stealing Naz's ring. He also beat his wife and children at the slightest provocation.

Naz's mum was an obsessive cleaner. Each morning after serving breakfast to her family, she dragged the *palungs* out into the courtyard to air the bedding and proceeded to wash the rooms, the courtyard, and the stairs. The bricks in her house were bright red with the constant onslaught. She then attacked her laundry under the tap, pounding the clothes with a thick, wooden stick. The parapet of her roof was always adorned with laundry. Exhausted after finishing her chores, she spent the late afternoon resting in a shaded part of the courtyard.

Naz and I climbed onto her roof and then over the walls, drifting from house to house, exchanging greetings and news, like bees collecting nectar, finally ending up at Khala Ji's, where I, along with all the girls in the neighbourhood, congregated to read the *Quran*. Khala Ji's was the only house with bougainvillea covering the entire front wall. She also had roses, snapdragons and marigolds in pots around the courtyard. These she lovingly watered and tended.

I spent a lot of my free time at Khala Ji's, for she was a kind, loving *Pathani*, who spent most of the day teaching *Quran* to the neighbourhood girls. She always listened to my loquacious chatter with great attention, and I adored her. Like Abbu, she called me Salma *Sitara* (Salma, the Star).

Khala Ji had a smooth buttermilk complexion and snow-white hair. A delicate rose fragrance hung about her from her homemade soap. Her pink cheeks had seldom been kissed by the sun, for whenever she went out she wore a white shuttlecock *burqa* that covered her from head to toe, and she never ventured onto the roof because, she protested, 'Those men in the *aeroplanes* peer down through binoculars!'

Her husband was a small stout man with a pugnacious face, a large closely cropped head, and skin as dark and wrinkled as tanned old leather. None of her gentle nature had rubbed off on him. Dark bushy eyebrows knotted over his bloodshot eyes. Twisting his moustache, he roared at us in his raucous voice, 'Get off those *palungs!* You break one daily. Haven't you got homes to go to? Go, all of you, go home!'

'May *Allah* have mercy on you! Leave the children alone; they are reading the *Quran,*' Khala Ji said, shooing him away. He would leave, slamming the door behind him, cursing and swearing in Pashto and wiping the spittle from his mouth with the back of his clenched fist. Khala Ji shook her head in despair. Sighing sorrowfully, she continued to mutter prayers for her husband's salvation under her breath.

She indulged me and allowed me to comb her long, white hair. I sometimes plaited it in one plait and at other times in two, like a little girl. She wore numerous silver earrings along the entire edge of her ear lobes, the weight of which permanently disfigured her ears. She looked pious and elegant in her lace trimmed, white muslin *dupatta* and white shirts with tiny floral prints.

'Khala Ji, you look so pretty, you will go straight to heaven,' I said one day, showing her the mirror after tying her plaits with my red ribbon and nuzzling into her soft body.

'*Sadqay!* May *Allah* give you a long happy life!' Beaming, she blessed me, and holding my head in her plump hands planted soft moist kisses on both cheeks.

Khala Ji was an incredible teacher. Twenty-five girls would sit rocking back and forth, all reading out aloud different passages from the *Quran*, while Khala Ji sat on her low wooden stool, feeding cowpats into her stove, fanning away the resulting smoke and stirring her pot. She called out above the cacophony in her golden syrupy voice, 'Ayy Salma *Sitara,* read it again,' and corrected a mistake. 'Saeda, read it again.'

The rules of the class were clear to all and revolved around 'three'. Find your *separa* from the pile in the alcove by the fragrant *Gollai Dawoodi* bush on arrival; read your lesson aloud three times; await your turn and recite it to Khala Ji. If you made more than three mistakes, you automatically went back and read it again three times. If you had fewer than three mistakes, you moved on and read the next passage to Khala Ji. She helped with difficult words and you returned to your place, read it again three times and put away the *separa*. We recited the verse from the *Quran* we had memorized parrot fashion, to Khala Ji's daughter, Kubra Baji, and that was that – c*huhtti* and home time!

***

Bashir's house was across the *gali* to the right. Despite the fact that he had grown-up daughters, it was very messy. The entire roof was piled high with empty hessian sacks and *ghee* tins, amongst broken and discarded furniture. The rancid smell of stale *ghee* polluted the neighbourhood. Bashir was eventually forced to sell the tins and sacks to street vendors when the neighbours complained about the smell, the rats that scurried amongst them and the cats that chased the rats. The beds in his house remained unmade. The quilts remained on the bed, even in summer, for there was nowhere to store them. Bashir's teenage daughter, Azra, and her friend often giggled under the bedding until Wazir Khala yelled from our roof. 'What are you two up to?' The girls then scampered off, ashen-faced.

Our house backed onto a vacant plot where there was a huge berry tree, under which Aslam had made a *tandoor*, where he made *naan* for the entire neighbourhood. I leaned over the parapet from Wazir Khala's courtyard and watched Aslam expertly flatten the ball of dough onto a moist circular pad and stick it firmly on the inner wall of the *tandoor* with clockwork monotony. His lean dark body glistened like polished mahogany with perspiration and his drenched vest and *dhoti* stuck to his body. Occasionally he stopped for a second and blew away the sweat that dripped from his brow and nose or wiped his forehead and chin with the back of his arm. Children and old women sat huddled on their haunches, cowering under the tree or the inadequate and discoloured hessian shelter in the intolerable sun, with their platters of dough beside them, all patiently awaiting their turns to have their *naans* made.

Hanging over the wall in Wazir Khala's courtyard, I teased Aslam, chanting the poem in my schoolbook:

Aslam ki Khala ki shadi thee

(It was Aslam's aunt's wedding)

Guddi Lahore se Karachi janai wali thee.

(The train was about to depart from Lahore to Karachi.)

Aslam looked up and smiled his crooked smile and winked, as if to say 'Hmmm, I'll sort you out later.' He scooped out the hot crispy *naans* with a long metal hook and piled them in a wooden crate. His little helper gathered and wrapped them in old newspaper and handed them over to the waiting customers.

***

A barrage of stones, old shoes and sticks landed in our courtyard as passing children threw them up at the berry tree to knock down the ripe berries. Poor Shano bore the brunt of someone's hunger for berries when a large piece of wood struck her on the head, splitting it open. Surprisingly, though there was a big white gash, there was no blood. Had Ammi taken her to the doctor, she would have needed several stitches.

***

Bader found a gorgeous cream coloured puppy in Liaqat Park, which he smuggled to our rooftop.

'Don't tell anyone. *Abba Jaan* (his father, Salahuddin Khalo), won't let us keep him.'

'Why not?' I asked incredulously. 'How could anyone not love such a beautiful creature?'

'He just won't. He hates dogs,' Bader said as he tickled the pup's belly.

For several days we managed to keep the secret, but eventually I confided in Ammi when she caught me sneaking food to the roof.

'I was wondering what you were up to! Get rid of it!' she said at once. 'Your Khalo won't like it, and the roof is no place for a dog.'

Ignoring her instructions and convinced the rooftop was the ideal home for our puppy, we built a shelter with upturned *palangs* and old bedding. But we were unable to confine the playful puppy or prevent him from gnawing. He scratched and gouged the *palangs,* ravaged the bedding, and bounded around the rooftop. We argued over names. Bader insisted on Tiger and instructed him in the few words of English he knew.

'Why should we call a dog Tiger? Besides, he is a Pakistani dog, so why do you speak to him in English?' I demanded.

Thereafter we called the dog 'Doggy', and he soon began responding to it. We all played with the overfed Doggy, sneaking tid-bits to him, but no one was willing to clean up after him. The roof was littered with dog poo, unfit to play hopscotch or anything else.

One day, Salahuddin Khalo was engrossed in a book and Wazir Khala was sorting the laundry when Hamida, the *jamadarni* (sweeper) came charging into the room.

'I am not going to clean the dog shit on the roof! My job is hard enough with your chickens and that monstrous cockerel. I am not cleaning dog shit!' she announced.

With her back to Salahuddin Khalo, Wazir Khala indicated with her eyes to keep quiet and accompanied Hamida to the roof. Salahuddin

Khalo continued to read in sublime indifference. We children looked at each other, knowing we were in trouble.

The same evening when we were in our courtyard, with the adults drinking tea and chatting, our playtime came to an abrupt end when Bader gasped and pointed up at the roof, his eyes wide with shock. We all looked up to see Doggy scampering along the narrow ledge, trying to find a way down to us. Time froze as sixteen eyes stared in horror, mouths wide open in silent screams. Petrified, we watched the puppy tumble from the fourth floor, hurtling down towards us, his limbs flailing in all directions, for what seemed an eternity. I covered my eyes.

With a a high-pitched piercing yelp of pain, he landed on the first-floor balcony railing and then on the ground in front of us. Reluctantly, I parted my fingers and peeked to see Bader walk up to where the puppy lay twitching and making muffled guttural sounds. Blood trickled out of his eyes and nose. Bader gazed at it, lips quivering. With a long deep sob he fell on his knees beside it. Trying not to cry, he gently ran his trembling hand over its limp body. The puppy lay there whimpering in a puddle of blood and urine. Then with one last groan, it became still. Bader gulped. Tears ran down his cheeks.

He slowly and carefully scooped up the lifeless body and, still sobbing, hugged it tenderly to his neck. He walked away with the puppy as we all stood watching.

I was sobbing uncontrollably. Ammi held out her arms and hugged me close. Nearly gagging with nausea, I buried my head in her chest. Silently, she stroked my hair. Salahuddin Khalo opened his mouth to say something but before any sound emerged from his mouth, Wazir Khala gestured with a raised hand for him to keep quiet. He stomped off after Bader, mumbling under his breath.

We never spoke about Doggy again.

***

When Bader acquired his first novel, *Ali Par Kya Guzri* (What Ali Endured), I begged him to let me read it. I eventually persuaded him to loan it to me in exchange for grinding glass in preparation for *Basant*, the kite flying festival, to celebrate the arrival of Spring. All the boys were involved in the long arduous process of crushing and grinding glass bottles they had been collecting on the roof. There was a delicious pleasure and excitement at being at one with the big boys. The glass powder was sieved and mixed with bright dyes and *saresh* – stinky glue slabs that we heated in empty *ghee* tins over twig fires. The smoke and the foul acrid stench of *saresh* and *ghee* made us retreat for short intervals, wiping our runny bloodshot eyes and noses with our sleeves. The gooey mixture was applied with wads of old rags to string wound around the legs of upturned *palungs*. When it dried, the razor-sharp string was carefully wound on spools and stored for the big day. The torturous exercise left our hands raw for days, but we knew it would all be worth it when the sharp string cut other kites during the dogfights in the sky.

The boys made their own kites using tissue paper and thin strips of bamboo sticks. Abbu joined us on Basant, armed with huge shop bought kites in bright colours, eight-shaped *Tukkals, Shahenshah* the Emperor and *Pari*, fairy, with long multi-coloured tails that swished and hissed in the wind. Ammi and Wazir Khala joined us on the roof too. They prepared all kinds of treats - *gulgolay, pakoray, lassi*, and tea in huge pots, sending intoxicating aromas that enticed even the most solemn Salahuddin Khalo to join the roof party.

'*Bhai Azhar, bachoon main bacha ban gai* (Brother Azhar, you have become a child amongst the children)?' he smirked.

Abbu laughed his hearty, guttural laugh, ignoring the sarcasm in Salahuddin Khalo's tone. 'You should try it.'

'No thank you, I'll leave that to you,' Salahuddin Khalo replied with a hint of a smile.

There were dozens of kites of every colour in the rainbow, hissing in the cloudless azure sky, glistening like jewels. The wind was perfect to lift them higher and higher. Oblivious to his bloodied fingers, Abbu had already cut several kites with his red *Pari*. He darted across the roof to cheers, whistles and shouts of glee from us as his kite swished from side to side.

'Abbu, Abbu watch out for that black *Tukkal!*' I shouted, honoured to be his assistant.

'Salmi, give me slack on the string... quick, quick! Hurry up!' I spun the spool as fast as my bandaged fingers could manage.

'More...more...more, Salmi...more!'

I chased after the spool rolling on the roof. Everyone jumped out of the way, careful not to trip and get tangled with the razor-sharp string. All eyes were now on the kites just above our heads. As the wind picked up, Abbu lunged forward and entangled the black *Tukkal*. It tried to escape the manoeuvre but Abbu had him. The black *Tukkal* knew it was in trouble. Both kites dipped and dived in the sky, lurching this way and that. Neighbours ran on nearby rooftops from one end of the roof to the other for a better view, cheering and betting on which one would be cut. Children and cyclists in the *gali* stopped and gazed up at the sky, mesmerized, afraid to blink as the dogfight reached a crescendo. A chorus of *Bo kaata, bo kaata!* (Cut it, cut it) echoed all around. Ammi, Wazir Khala and Salahuddin Khalo joined in the chanting. Abbu ran across the roof, ducking and diving, dancing with the kites. Another gust of wind and he gave out slack and then pulled back hard. It was all over for the *Tukkal...Bo kaata, bo kaata!* The roar rose above the applause as Abbu's *Pari* cut the *Tukkal.* It went gliding off into the distance. We watched the boys running in the *gali*, chasing after the cut kite as it floated aimlessly in the distance.

We all cheered and clapped, dancing with joy as we hugged and congratulated Abbu. 'Shabash Bhai Azhar, *Shabash*, well done!' shouted Wazir Khala and Salahuddin Khalo. Exhausted, Abbu pulled his kite in. Ammi rushed forward and handed him some bandages for his cut fingers, and a glass of *sherbet*. I hugged Abbu's long legs as he patted my head, congratulating me for my part in the victory.

Slumber once again overtook the city and a cloak of darkness shielded its sins. With all our kites torn or lost, the adults applied ointment and bandaged our cuts. Exhausted by the festivities, we sat on *palungs* reliving the events of the day, lauding and exaggerating our triumphs and successes while picking at the remains of the food.

Suddenly we heard the cockerel crowing and several dogs barking.

'What time is this for the cockerel to crow? That's one confused cockerel!' remarked Bader with a laugh.

That was when we felt the first jerk. All chatter ceased. Startled, we looked up at our elders. I ran to Abbu.

'Sit down, sit down, don't run. Stay put everyone; stay put!' shrieked Wazir Khala, pointing to the ground. *'Zalzala* (earthquake)!'

A chorus of *Kalima*, the Muslim declaration of Faith, began to rise from the neighbouring rooftops, *Lā ilāha ill lul-lā ho, Muhammadun rasūl Allāh* (There is one God, and Mohammed is His prophet.)' Holding hands, we huddled closer and joined in. *Lā ilāha ill lul-lā ho, Muhammadun rasūl Allāh.*

Then came another tremor – this one seemed to go on forever. The whole building swayed from side to side, and a crack appeared on the wall facing Bashir's house. We could hear people running out of their homes into the street below. *Allah O Akbar, Allah O Akbar! (Allah* is great!), the *muezzin* called over the loudspeaker from the local mosque. The call to prayer echoed through the city, spreading like Chinese whispers from mosque to mosque; only the message remained the same: *Allah O Akbar, Allah O Akbar!* We snuggled closer together, gazing at each other in fear, anticipating more quakes.

'Ammi, *please* read *Ayatul Kursi,*' pleaded Baji, a tremble in her voice.

'No *baita,* recite the *Kalima: Lā ilāha ill lul-lā ho, Muhammadun rasūl Allāh,*' interjected Abbu, reciting it aloud.

Shano sobbed in Ammi's lap. Ammi stroked her head tenderly while uttering the *Kalima,* gently rocking back and forth. The tremors slowly came to an end.

Abbu turned to us to explain, 'You should recite the *Kalima* during a *zalzala,* just in case...'

'In case of what?'

'In case it is the end, you idiot!' responded Farooq.

Abbu freed his hand from my grip and, narrowing his eyes, peered at the crack in the wall. He walked over to examine the damage. Salahuddin Khalo joined him.

'Don't any of you come near this wall. In fact, *no one* is allowed on the roof till we've seen to it!' said Abbu firmly over his shoulder, as he scrutinised the damage.

Ammi lit a lantern. The sudden brief flaring of the match emphasized the deep darkness. We all sat in petrified silence, gradually gaining the courage to speak.

'Must have been at least six on the Richter scale,' whispered Wazir Khala.

'At least,' agreed Ammi, letting go of the match that threatened to burn her fingers.

Wazir Khala made herself comfortable. Winding into the storytelling pitch she began telling past anecdotes of earthquakes as we all sat around her listening intently, leading up to the Big One in 1935, in Quetta. 'It was nearly eight on the Richter scale. Wiped out all of Quetta and killed 600,000 people – the whole town was flattened...'

'You are frightening the children! I think we should stay up here tonight in case there are any aftershocks,' Ammi said, changing the subject.

We had not yet begun sleeping on the roof as it was still cool enough in our bedrooms.

Reluctantly, we dragged the *palungs* to their places for the night and began squabbling over pillows and bedding. Farooq couldn't help teasing me about the incident last summer when one sweltering evening, I was given the task of sprinkling water on the scorching roof to cool it down before arranging the *palungs*. While spreading the bedding, I decided to make it extra cool for everyone and sprinkled water on the bedding too. I waited eagerly for praise when everyone came upstairs to find their pillows and sheets wet. All I got was a clip on the ear for my trouble. Everyone laughed at the memory while I blushed with embarrassment. The tension caused by the earthquake eased, even thought it was at my expense.

In the stillness of the night, unable to sleep under the starlit sky, I snuggled up to Abbu, wondering which wall would have collapsed first if our house had come down. I watched the scintillating stars glimmer like diamonds in the night sky, and the shooting stars dart across from one end of the heavens to the other.

'It's the angels chasing Satan. He is trying to enter heaven after being expelled for tempting Adam and Eve,' Ammi explained.

With the mosquitoes making every effort to keep me awake, it was a long time before my consciousness clouded and the mournful cricket chorus finally lulled me to sleep.

The following morning it wasn't the sunlight sending rose-tinted hues through my eyelids or the dawn chorus, nor the *muezzin's* calls to prayer from the local mosques that roused me, it was the heat of the sun and the flies buzzing around my face, trying to enter my eyes and nose. They forced me to flee downstairs. Everyone was glued to their radios, listening for updates on the impact of the *zalzala*. Basant left on the back burner, the topic of *zalzala* was on every lip.

At school, everyone had a tale to tell about what they had heard in the news and about homes that had come down. Zarina was absent as were many other girls. Her house had been reduced to rubble, but fortunately they had all evacuated it just before it came down. Shahan's cousins and aunt perished when their roof collapsed. Miss Zohra was absent with a broken leg. We realized how lucky we had been that our house had escaped with just a crack, considering its height.

The kite flying continued for several months until the sun got too hot for us to tolerate the heat. Some diehards continued flying until the *Lu* came – the hot westerly wind forcing them to pack away their kites and spools of string till the next season. The paper kites were replaced by vultures, eagles and kites of a different kind, all of whom soared high in the blue sky over the arid plains of Punjab.

***

Abbu had a khaki mosquito net fixed on a bamboo frame over his *palung*. I think it was an army issue. We all scrambled under it to listen to him narrate the 'never ending story' in his deep melodious voice. He had a sweet tongue and was a great orator. Our cousins came over to our side of the roof to join in. I sat stroking my cat, nestled in my lap, playing with her soft squidgy paws, gently squeezing each toe to watch the claw pop out. The cat initially allowed me this indulgence and then retrieved her paw to continue the leisurely cleaning and licking of her paw and face, swishing her tail from side to side before settling into a soft, ball deep amongst us.

Every evening Abbu asked us to suggest a new topic for the story, and we tried to come up with the most ridiculous or difficult title we could think off. He had no problem conjuring up a tale around it on the spot. He started from where he had left off the previous night and continued until we began to drop off like gorged mosquitoes. Abbu had an incredible ability to paint pictures with words. He transported us across the world, from China to Arabia, from India through Europe to a land of Satan and *Djinn*, fairies and angels, demons and stealthy, grotesque monsters, evoking pictures in our minds tangible enough to touch.

We travelled with Gulliver and Ulysses, shook with fear pretending not to be scared of the one-eyed Cyclops, and listened with awe to tales about the witches of Macbeth. Imagining ourselves to be the beautiful Sheba, we flew into Solomon's glass palace, and counted the animals as they went into Noah's ark. Fists clenched, oohing and aahing; we willed the soldiers to hang on as they huddled in the wooden horse to enter Troy, begging Abbu to continue when he tried to end the story.

One of his most memorable stories was of Rama and Sita. Prince Rama, heir apparent of Ayodhya, was banished to the forest due to the machinations of his stepmother, who wished her own son to become king. Rama begged his beautiful wife Sita, to stay behind at the palace to await his return. But she insisted on going with him. The Asura, Ravana, with ten heads and eyes as red as coal fires, spotted Sita and fell madly in love with her. Since she refused to go with him, he abducted her. Rama followed the trail of golden jewellery Sita cleverly left. Helped by the monkey Hanuman, Rama fought a terrible battle in Lanka, killing Ravana and rescuing Sita. When Rama and Sita finally returned home triumphant, oil lamps were lit in every home to welcome them. To this day lamps are lit during Diwali, to symbolize good triumphing over evil, just as a tiny lamp conquers darkness.

Another interesting story I loved was about the humble onion. The onion pleaded with *Allah* saying, '*Allah mian*, everyone uses me in every curry, *biryani, daal* and chicken dish. It's not fair.' *Allah* said to the onion, 'You should be grateful you are so popular, but if it distresses you, whenever anyone uses you they will cry.' Hence, to this day, whenever anyone cuts an onion, tears come to their eyes.

9
GALLIVANTING

It was a carefree time. We played outdoors and no one cared where we were as long as we returned home before sunset. While the other children played hopscotch, cricket, marbles or *gulli danda* in the street, Farooq and I went exploring, leaving Baji and Rosy behind, which irked them both.

Farooq and I were two of a kind – adventurous and daring. We got up to a lot of mischief together. His desire for congenial company somehow singled me out. We flitted from place to place like Peter Pan and Tinker bell. We didn't need to communicate with words. Like little conspirators, we could almost read each other's minds. While the elders slept during the afternoon siesta, we sneaked off, leaving separately to be less conspicuous. Farooq was my protector and I depended on him for he was older and a boy – the leader of our expeditions. He took me through the back streets to secret hideouts he had unearthed, catching wasps and frogs and chasing butterflies.We roamed behind President Ayub Khan and Fatima Jinnah supporters holding large paper roses or swinging hurricane lamps (their political party symbols), and chanting slogans as they canvassed for the upcoming elections.

Sadar Ayub, paniki tube
(President Ayub, water tube)

Madurai millut, pani ki quilat
(Mother of the nation, water shortage)

We were in the front row, waving green and white Pakistani flags in exuberance, under streams of red Chinese flags across Murree Road, when Zhou Enlai, the Chinese leader, visited Rawalpindi.

Another time, Farooq knocked down the high pyramid the orange seller had carefully constructed, with a single shot from his perfectly aimed slingshot. As anticipated, the orange seller chased after him, and I made off with the oranges in my frock front improvised as a basket and climbed the high wall opposite the bakery. Farooq soon joined me. To add insult to injury, we sat smugly eating them out of the orange seller's reach. As he seethed with rage, we rocked with laughter, overcome by the hilarity of it all. When I got the giggles, it was almost impossible to stop.

From our vantage point we watched the baker knead the dough for bread with his bare feet, sweat pouring down his chest into the dough. I made a mental note never to eat bread, especially from that bakery.

We often waited by the bend near College Road for the over-laden sugarcane trucks. As the trucks slowed down at the sharp bend, we each grabbed a sugarcane stick, pulling it as the truck went past, and rejoiced at our loot. We spent the rest of the afternoon sitting on the bridge watching the traffic below, ripping off the tough skin of the sugarcane with our teeth and chewing the fibre and swallowing the sweet juice. We would spit out the white husk at unsuspecting passersby. Or we went to Liaqat Park, sharing it proudly with the rest of our gang, lounging under the date trees by the stream.

One day, the sky was hazy and orangey-yellow from morning. It hadn't rained for months and you could smell the dust in the air. The sun had been breathing fire on the earth and the scorching ground seemed to vibrate with heat. The hot air shimmered like quicksilver. Ammi caught us sneaking out as she went to lie down for her afternoon siesta. Looking up at the overcast sky, she warned us not to get caught in the sandstorm. Having lived in Multan, where sandstorms were a daily occurrence, Ammi could unerringly predict an upcoming sandstorm.

In Liaqat Park, the trees had lost their leaves, and the grass was scorched brown. The only place where there was any respite from the heat was in the dwindling stream. In the dappled stillness, Farooq walked in the shallows of the serpentine stream, gushing in places, trickling over moss covered rocks in others. I chased waddling geese, trying to catch the chicks trailing behind them. The geese lunged forward, hissing at me with their necks outstretched.

'Come into the stream – it's lovely and cool. Careful Salmi, there might be black scorpions or centipedes hiding behind those rocks,' warned Farooq, wallowing at the deeper end.

'Ugh...have you seen the scar on Amma Ji's calf? It's nearly six inches long,' I said

'Yes, wonder how she got it?'

'She said she was bathing by the well and a centipede dug all its legs into her leg. Her mother had to apply a hot rod on it.'

'Why didn't she just pull it off?'

'She said that if she'd pulled it off, the legs would have remained in her flesh and she would've had to go to the hospital to have them removed,' I said with an exaggerated shiver.

'Ew...' Farooq replied, screwing up his face.

Unperturbed by the mosquitoes and the bluebottles, we avoided the black ants that bit so viciously that their heads came away from their bodies when we tried to pull them off. Shano and Rosy walked along the edge of the stream. Farooq caught a frog and threw it at Rosy, imitating its croaks. Rosy screamed and tried to jump away. Grabbing Shano, she knocked her into the stream. Shano lost one of her new shoes. We could see the sky changing colour but were desperate to catch Shano's shoe. We tried in vain to fish it out with palm leaves and sticks. Suddenly, the dust rose up around us, blowing our hair, lifting our frocks and filling our *shalwars* and shirt sleeves like bellows. We abandoned our quest to rescue the shoe and hurried home through the deserted streets.

'Run children run...*aandhi*...sand storm!' shouted a man speeding past on his bike with his shawl wrapped round his head, desperately trying to keep his balance. The trees swayed violently and the dust rose up around us, getting into our eyes, noses and mouths. Paper bags, leaves, torn branches, bits of cardboard, rubbish, even billboards, chased us as the storm howled like a demented demon. Baji tried to wrap her *dupatta* around her face but it flew off and lodged in a distant tree.

'*Hava mein urta jai mera lal dupatta malmal ka* (My red muslin *dupatta* flies in the wind),' I sang, teasing her.

'Shut up, Salmi! Just shut up!' Baji, who was ahead of me, turned and screamed in irritation.

Squinting through eyes shielded behind our hands, we blindly ran home. Ammi and Massi were anxiously waiting for us. We looked like ghouls, our hair in disarray, panda-faced, our clothes and faces covered with white dust. Initially, Ammi didn't say anything, merely throwing us the 'I told you so' look, her lips twitching in a voiceless prayer of thanks as she ushered us to the bathroom. But when she set eyes on Shano's bare feet, she couldn't resist clouting her.

'Go straight up *now*,' Ammi told Farooq and Rosy, pointing to the stairs.

'Leave him be. Even his mother couldn't keep him inside,' chuckled Massi, referring to Farooq's premature birth.

'This one was just the same; she didn't remain inside full term either,' Ammi said, looking at me.

***

Shah Chan Chiragh was a predominantly Shia neighbourhood. Farooq and I enjoyed going to the religious gatherings at the *Imambara* in anticipation of the sweets distributed there. Despite Ammi's protestations, I joined in the *matum,* the ritualistic self-flagellation, beating my little chest pink, and the singing of the *mersias* – the songs of praise at the gatherings, which I continued to sing as I played and skipped rope.

Saath laitai chalo mujh ko baba,

Karbala tak main paidal chuloon gi

Woo Madinay ki sunsan gulyan...

I watched in wonder as the men built *Tazias* – elaborate, monumental technicolor constructions decorated with silver, gold and multi-coloured tinsel, depicting the tombs of the martyred family of Prophet Mohammad. It was led by an elaborately adorned and henna-decorated white horse, draped in a colourful shawl and garlanded with marigolds, representing the horse of Hazrat Hassan, the martyred grandson of the Prophet[PBUH]. On the 10th of *Muharram* (the first month in the Islamic calendar), we watched from Mumtaz Auntie's balcony, the bare-chested young men carry the ornate *Tazias* chanting, *Ya Ali, Ya Ali,* ahead of the burial procession. As the procession reached the crossroads, the men grouped themselves into a circle and beat their chests harder, reaching a feverish frenzy, as if possessed. The chanting got louder and louder. Old men with sticks darted around the edge of the crowd beating the ground or hitting the legs of the surging crowd to keep control. Some distributed ice-cold sherbet to the participating young men with bleeding bodies.

The young men at the centre of the crowd flagellated themselves with more vigour than the rest, with shimmering knives attached to shining chains, chanting, *Ya ALI, Ya ALI* – their *shalwars* soaked in blood. Thick blue veins appeared like cords in their necks as they stressed 'Ali' over *'Ya'*. A more sombre older group followed, smacking their already crimson chests in unison, creating a loud shuddering thud with each strike, like a drumbeat. A crowd of solemn women and children watched the procession from the roadside, gently tapping their own chests and murmuring, *Ya Ali, Ya Ali*. Many people watched from their balconies, windows and rooftops. Young boys climbed onto walls and into trees for a better view. Where the road narrowed at the bend, idlers and pedestrians, in no hurry to move on, caused a bottleneck.

'Why do they do this to themselves?' I asked Ammi, screwing up my face and awed by the sight.

'To feel the pain and suffering of the martyrs of Karbala.' She was eager to explain in detail but as I leaned forward to get a better view, she moved quickly to hold me back. 'Careful, don't lean so far out, you'll fall. Najmi, keep an eye on Shano and Ather.'

'The procession is getting bigger each year,' shouted a woman above the din.

'And bloodier! I can hardly watch.'

'How do they bear it?'

'They probably apply something to numb the pain.'

'But the blood and cuts are real enough. I wouldn't let my sons do it.'

'Oh their mothers are proud of them.'

'Hajra's son always participates, and you should hear her boasting about it.'

'How old is he now? Wasn't she looking for a bride for him?'

'I don't know, but did you see her husband running around with his stick? At home he's always complaining about his aches and pains.'

'It's Hajra's fault; she fusses over him like a skivvy.'

'Jugnu, when is Bhai Azhar going to England?'

'Next week,' Ammi said gloomily.

'You shouldn't let him go! You know what men

are like. Out of sight, out of mind, and you know what these foreign women are like.'

'Bhai Azhar isn't like that,' Mumtaz Auntie said rather loudly with a stern look at her neighbour. 'Besides, he adores Jugnu.'

'Ammi, I need to pee,' shouted Nunni.

When Ammi took her to the bathroom, Mumtaz Auntie scolded her neighbour, 'Why are you stressing her? It can't be easy for her as it is.'

'Sorry, I wasn't thinking. I …'

When Ammi returned, she quickly changed the subject, tugging at Nunni's dress, 'Where did you buy this pretty frock, Jugnu?'

'I made it myself,' replied Ammi.

After another ten minutes of frenzied flagellation, the *matum* subsided to a gentler pace and the white horse, smothered with garlands, led the procession onwards. The air that seemed to have stretched taut like a tightened bow, relaxed again. We breathed a sigh of relief as the gathering dispersed.

***

Mumtaz Auntie, a distant relative of Abbu's extended family, was a jolly lady from Bihar, with a shiny dark face. She wasn't much older than Ammi, and unlike anyone else I knew, dressed in bright saris, with ornately embroidered borders and matching blouses. Her sour faced acerbic husband was tall and lanky, his skin wrinkled like a hide that had been under water for a long time. The impeccably dressed, stooped old man in a white *kurta pyjama* was so much older than Mumtaz Auntie, that for a long time I thought he was her father. He spent most of his time in his study, from where he occasionally barked at his wife and children. Everyone, including Auntie, addressed him as Hakeem *Sahib*. Auntie chatted joyfully with Ammi as they cooked together amongst squeals of laughter. She spoke very fast, like a record played at the wrong speed.

'Jugnu, when I came home from your house the other day there was a *janaza* (burial casket) being carried out from my front door.'

'No!' Ammi gasped, widening her tiny eyes.

'I panicked for a second. Dear God! I thought. I left my old man in fine form this morning, whose *janaza* is this?' She paused, taking the pan off the cooker, her glass bangles tinkling. 'The old man next door had died, and they couldn't take the *janaza* down their narrow stairs, so they had to bring it over the wall to our roof and carry it down my stairs. Imagine...' she giggled as her plump little body wobbled and quivered. Ammi too, doubled up with laughter, shaking her head in disbelief.

Mumtaz Auntie made a real occasion of our visit, preparing her special steamed *biryani* and Ammi's favourite dish – *taka-tak*. We all ate it happily at the time, loving it, and only squirmed years later when we realized it was offal and tripe.

'I wish Bhai Azhar was here,' Auntie said.

'I know, he loves your *biryani,* but he's got a hundred and one things to do before he goes.'

'Jugnu, are you alright about him going?' Mumtaz Auntie gently held Ammi by the shoulders, looking into her eyes.

'What can I do, even if I wasn't? He's made up his mind and he is sure it's the best thing for the family. It's a blessing that Baji Wazir lives upstairs, otherwise you know it would be impossible for me to live without a man in the house. But you know *Bhai Sahib* is an angel when he wants to be, but when he is in a mood…'

Auntie held Ammi's hands in empathy. 'I know. Don't worry. I will send the boys round often to see if you need anything. And you send word if there is anything – anything at all, you hear.' She didn't let go of Ammi's hands till Ammi nodded with a forced smile.

Later, one of her many sons walked us home,

carrying the big pot of food that Mumtaz Auntie insisted on sending for Abbu.

***

Ammi had a special, almost telepathic bond with her twin sister, Tauqeer Khala, and it was to her Ammi confided. She wasn't just her sister but her best friend. Some days she would ask Abbu to bring extra provisions.

'Why? Is someone coming?' he would ask.

'Yes, Tauqeer.'

'Did she send word?'

'No, my heart is telling me.' Ammi would reply, and she was never wrong.

On Fridays, we dressed in our best and marched to Tauqeer Khala's. It wasn't hard choosing what to wear; every *Eid-ul-Fitar* we had two new outfits each – one silk suit to wear on *Eid* day and a cotton one for the following day, complete with matching ribbons, bangles, socks, shoes and vests. On special occasions we wore the *Eid* suit – with all the accessories. When visiting or expecting guests, we wore the cotton suit. Ammi altered these outfits as we grew out of them and they were passed down from one sibling to the next. Baji, being the eldest, had hand-me-downs from our aunt

Shama Khala, which were more fashionable than the simple outfits Ammi made for us. She even had a *dupatta* of which I was very jealous at the time, but when I *had* to wear one, I realized what a nuisance it was for it was always getting in the way and getting caught in everything. It was like a noose around my neck. I inevitably lost it. So I compromised by tying it around my waist while playing and only wore it around my neck at home.

Tauqeer Khala too, had cooked extra food without being told we were arriving. She greeted us at the door with a broad welcoming smile, as if she hadn't seen us in years. 'Come, come, come,' she chanted excitedly, standing behind the loud printed curtain over the door and beaming from ear to ear.

Despite the fact that she had a scar right across her left cheek, from having been at the wrong place at the wrong time as a child during a fight in the neighbourhood, when a flying brick struck her, she had a beautiful absent face with a drowsy manner. We all adored Tauqeer Khala, for unlike Wazir Khala, who could only see good in her own children, Tauqeer Khala had a way of complimenting us by pointing out a talent we had failed to notice in ourselves, and soon that talent shone so brightly that we were amazed by it. She happily admitted to her failings and at times boasted about her stupidity. We laughed, rolling on the floor until we could laugh no more, when she mispronounced words.

After several promptings by Abbu, Ammi finally found her *burqa*. Replete on good food and exhausted, we prepared to return home. But Ammi's natter didn't end until Abbu had gone a hundred yards down the street, and we tugged at her *burqa,* urging her to leave. We walked home behind Abbu carrying Nunni through the dark *galis*, Ammi following several yards behind, and the rest of us trailing behind in a diminishing line.

Once when we were returning from such an outing and some of Wazir Khala's children had tagged along, a passerby remarked, 'Look at that tiny little woman with so many children.'

'They are not all mine!' retorted Ammi angrily.

10
SIBLINGS

———————— ⌇ ————————

Ather was born earlier than expected, at home. Abbu was at work when Ammi went into labour and, much to Wazir Khala's horror, she had to play midwife. We were all swiftly shooed out of the house with firm instructions to stay out. Baji was told to summon Massi, our maid and local midwife. Farooq was dispatched to fetch our grandmother, Amma Ji and my aunt, Tauqeer Khala. We stood outside on our *thara,* baffled by the frantic activity and the noise from within the house. Finally, soon after Amma Ji and Tauqeer Khala arrived, Wazir Khala popped her head out, her face flushed and sweaty, she breathlessly shouted, 'Come in, come in! You have a baby brother!'

We stormed into Ammi's bedroom to find her clutching a tiny baby wrapped in a white shawl. Massi was on her haunches, absent-mindedly washing the floor and Tauqeer Khala was fussing around rearranging Ammi's bedding. I couldn't understand where this baby had appeared from but knew better than to ask. We took turns to peep at the new-born.

'That's enough; that's enough...go out, all of you!' Amma Ji shooed us out of the room.

Abbu came home from work to find the whole house abuzz with activity.

'Bhai Azhar! Come and recite *Azan* in your *son's* ear,' Wazir Khala announced triumphantly as soon as Abbu entered the house. He looked at her startled but his eyes lit up.

'Abbu, Abbu we have a baby brother!' I shouted.

Abbu darted into the bedroom. '*Alhamdulillah!*' he cried. 'Jugnu, Jugnu...are you alright? Is he healthy?'

Beaming from ear to ear, Ammi handed him the tiny bundle. He buried his face in it and deeply inhaled the sweet fragrance of the newborn. Repeatedly thanking the Lord, he unravelled the bundle and kissed each of the tiny fingers and toes.

I tried to attract his attention but Amma Ji grabbed me and made me sit down beside her. 'Why does *he* have to do it?' I asked her, irritated at being overlooked.

'Do what?'

'A*zan*.'

'The first word a baby should hear when he comes into the world is the name of *Allah*,' she explained.

'But why can't Wazir Khala do it?'

'There are duties for men, and there are duties for women. Abbu goes to work; Ammi cooks the dinner. Abbu has to recite the *Azan*; Ammi feeds the baby. So let him be.'

'But why?' I questioned again, trying to free myself.

She clutched me tighter. 'Stay put. You and your never ending questions, Salmi!' she said, shaking her head with affectionate asperity. 'It is how *Allah* made us, so that's how *it is*.'

Amongst demands for a grand celebratory dinner, Wazir Khala insisted on a special present for being the first to bestow the good news and for delivering Abbu's first son. 'At last a boy, after three girls,' she cried elatedly, not missing the opportunity to remind

Ammi that she had produced three girls on the trot.

Her words pierced Ammi's heart but she remained silent, only exchanging a look with Tauqeer Khala. Aware of Ammi's irritation, Tauqeer Khala, who had five sons and no daughters, sighed. 'Oh, what I wouldn't do to have just *one* girl!' she said.

Ignoring Wazir Khala's gibe, Abbu happily agreed to give her a present as well as throw a party. He dashed out to buy sweetmeats to celebrate.

'Thank the Lord he's fair, not dark like your girls. I pray He grants them good *kismet* for it is hard enough marrying off one daughter, let alone three...I should know!' Looking up at the heavens, Amma Ji rolled her eyes.

Ammi sighed, looking at Tauqeer Khala again.

'Amma Ji, they are gorgeous, all three of them. Look at their features – stunning. Who cares about *white skin?* They have gorgeous complexions,' rebuked Tauqeer Khala.

Exhausted, Ammi shook her head to let it go.

'No, Jugnu, Amma Ji shouldn't say things like that about her granddaughters, especially after you've just given birth,' Tauqeer Khala snapped.

'So it's for my children to tell *me* what I should and shouldn't say?' Amma Ji responded, annoyed.

Fortunately, before the argument could escalate, a group of *hijras* appeared at the front door, dressed in bright clothes and heavy make-up, singing and clapping with exaggerated gestures, demanding alms. Abandoning Ammi, the women rushed into the courtyard.

'I don't know how you people get the news before anyone else!' Wazir Khala squawked in irritation. She tried to shoo them away as if they were polluting the atmosphere, but they refused to budge.

'Let them be, Baji,' shouted Tauqeer Khala. 'It's a happy occasion. How are they supposed to live if everyone turns them away? Besides, you don't want them cursing you. They say *Allah* grants their prayers!'

Wazir Khala sucked her teeth. On seeing Abbu approach, she left him to deal with them. They encircled Abbu, who was carrying boxes of sweetmeats. They shook their tambourines in his face and clapped even louder and began dancing. We stood in a line, along with the other children from our street, to watch the impromptu performance. They remained long after Abbu gave them a generous donation and *metahi*, continuing to sing and dance in our courtyard to several exuberant songs.

Sweetmeats were distributed in the neighbourhood and amongst friends and family, and alms among the poor. Telegrams were sent to India to inform our paternal family of the birth of Abbu's first son and heir.

Ather was a lovely baby and grew into a gorgeous toddler. He had a thick mop of curly brown hair and an endearing, shy way of looking down when anyone addressed him. Abbu adored him – his long awaited son after three daughters – and took him everywhere, even to his office. He bought lovely clothes for him and delighted in personally feeding and bathing him. Dressed in light chequered cotton shirts with matching shorts, he perched Ather on the table for all to see, prompting him to sing songs and recite poems he had taught him, all the while taking photographs. Eyes lowered, Ather obliged and performed obediently like a trained monkey.

***

Ammi tells us that Nunni was almost born in the *tonga* as it clip-clopped along Murree Road, past Gawal Mundi, on its way to the Holy Family Hospital. Thankfully, she managed to hold little Nunni within her bulging belly till they reached the sanctuary of the hospital.

I remember going to the hospital with Wazir Khala, to see the baby, but the gatekeeper refused to allow children under twelve into the hospital. When he allowed Baji to go in but stopped Farooq, he protested that he was the same age. But the attendant didn't believe him. Bader and Baji went in with Wazir Khala, while Misbah, who was carrying baby Ruby, Farooq and I, stood helplessly outside the gate.

Ammi waved from the third floor window and attempted to show us the baby, but we couldn't see much more than a rolled up blanket. Farooq bent to whisper a plan in my ear. Just then, an eagle swooped down and snatched Ruby's rusk from her hand. In the chaos that ensued, as Ruby screamed in terror, Farooq and I made a dash past the attendant. He ran in one direction, I in another. The mortified caretaker chased after Farooq like a cat after a mouse but was unable to catch him. We soon made our way to Ammi's room.

Wazir Khala was commiserating with her on the birth of her fourth daughter. 'What a shame! What a burden! Another girl!' she said, sighing deeply.

'I am not ashamed I have given birth to another daughter,' Ammi snapped.

'Shame has been handed down to us from birth, and we are brought up to be ashamed,' Wazir

Khala remarked with that far-away look in her eyes. Her face wore the same haughty expression she acquired when she suddenly fell to musing, retreating into herself.

Ammi knew that look! She gazed at her sister in indignation and contempt. 'Baji I don't know what...' Leaving her sentence unfinished she sighed, shaking her head. Raising herself on her elbow, she began feeding the crying baby.

We stood at the foot of the bed, too embarrassed to look. When she finished feeding, she bent forward to let us have a peep. 'Look, this is your baby sister!' Ammi beamed.

'Where did you get her from? Why didn't you get a boy?' I asked, screwing up my nose as I peered inquisitively at the little red creature with huge eyes in a moon-shaped face.

'Oh *Allah* sends the babies by helicopter to the hospital roof, and I was a little late!' Ammi explained, with an exaggerated smile. 'All the boys had already gone,' she said, making a sad face.

We nicknamed the baby *Nunni* (tiny). She is called so to this day, even though she has adult children of her own.

***

I was nine when Muzher was born. I adored my baby brother and was very possessive of him, treating him as my personal charge. I carried him in my arms even after he could walk because he liked it and I liked it. If he wanted something, and he often did, for he was stubborn from an early age, I did my best to acquire it for him. I would have stolen for him; I never did, but I probably would have.

Abbu was struggling financially and the arrival of yet another mouth to feed made him even more resolute about fulfilling his lifelong dream to revisit England. Everyone, including Ammi, hoped he would change his mind and postpone his costly adventure. But for him it wasn't a question of if but when.

11
AGONY OF SEPARATION

W e knew something was afoot as Abbu and Ammi stopped talking when we were within earshot. We heard them speaking in hushed tones late into the night. In between shopping trips and long discussions with Salahuddin Khalo and Wazir Khala behind closed doors, one day Abbu sat us all down and said, 'I have something important to tell you: I am going to London.'

'Where is London? I thought we were going to India?' I interrupted.

'Look it up on the map in the dispensary. Now listen, you all have to be very good and help Ammi. It's going to be very hard. Salahuddin Khalo will look after you while I am away.'

'When will you be back?' I questioned.

'I am coming with you,' cried Ather.

'No, you can't come with me. I have to go and find us a nice place to live, and then I will call you,' Abbu said with a forced smile, pulling Ather close.

'I don't want to go to London. I want to go to India by train, to see Dadi Jaan,' I said.

'No, we are not going to India. You will come to London by aeroplane. You have to be very good and…'

'But why can't we go with you?' asked Baji.

'I have to find somewhere for us to live first. Then I'll send for you.'

'Where will you live?'

'With your Zia Mamo, till I find a place of my own.'

'Why can't *we* stay with Zia Mamo?'

'No. Just listen to your Ammi and be good and I will send for you all very soon.'

'I want pretty dolls with *ghararas*, like Rosy's. I don't want to go to London. I want to go to India to see Dadi Jaan!' I protested.

Abbu looked at Ammi for support and found her sobbing. He rose abruptly, touched her shoulder and left the room. Mournfully, we crowded around Ammi. All my dreams were crushed and crumpled up like yesterday's newspaper. A multitude of questions fluttered in my mind but I didn't voice them.

***

One day I overheard Ammi whispering to Wazir Khala that Dadi Jaan had kept such a dark secret from Abbu and Nadir Chacha, that it had broken Abbu.

'What secret?' I butted in.

'Nothing that concerns you! You should *not* be eavesdropping on adult conversations,' Ammi chided curtly. 'Run along and play.'

The next few days were hectic as friends and family came to say good-bye. Within days, amongst a tearful farewell, Abbu departed for London.

Salahuddin Khalo was cornered into agreeing to take care of us in Abbu's absence. Both Ammi and Abbu knew from the outset that he was very moody and most reluctantly fulfilled the demands of his own large family, after much nagging from Wazir Khala. They knew it would be difficult, but just how difficult they had yet to find out!

Soon after Abbu left, Ather fell ill. Ammi too,

felt very lethargic and unwell. Initially she put it down to overwork and depression but eventually visited Holy Family Hospital, where after extensive tests, she was diagnosed with hypothyroidism. Her problems became further compounded when Muz broke his leg and was hospitalized and Ammi had to stay with him for two weeks. The rest of us stayed with Tauqeer Khala.

At night, when the watchman tapped his metal-tipped stick to warn trouble makers of his presence and the crickets sang in chorus, it sounded ever more menacing. When I woke up scared in the middle of the night, there was no one to snuggle up to. I could hear Ammi sobbing in bed with seven-month-old Muz on one side and three-year-old Nunni on the other.

Till then Ammi had never even ventured to the shops by herself, let alone tackle the demands of her large brood. She had never had to manage the household accounts, shop for groceries, visit schools, doctors or do any of the daily chores. Abbu had performed all the outdoor activities, as was the norm in Asian families. Ammi was oblivious about financial matters. Each month Abbu purchased the monthly groceries and bought any essentials needed for the day before he left for work. Any other provisions Ammi needed, she bought from passing street hawkers, from behind the fading curtain that hung just inside our front door. If she needed anything else, one of us happily obliged.

Those early days after Abbu's departure were the most testing for us all, especially Ammi. For the first time she had to manage the limited cash. After paying the rent and school fees, there wasn't much left for food, clothes and unexpected expenses such as doctors and hospital bills. Initially, Salahuddin Khalo purchased our groceries along with his monthly shopping, which wasn't that difficult since Ammi wrote out a shopping list which he handed to the grocer in the *mundi*. He hired two porters, one to carry our groceries and another to carry his. We tagged along for an outing and jostled with the shoppers in the dusty bazaar, scurrying from shop to shop while Salahuddin Khalo aggressively haggled with the vendors sitting on the floor behind pyramids of polished fruit and vegetables and mounds of spices, eggplants, tomatoes, onions, potatoes and okra. The grocer piled the groceries into the basket, emphasizing that the sprig of coriander and a fistful of green chillies were free. The porters trailed us home with fictitious animation and alacrity, carrying the basket of provisions on their heads.

'*Sahab Ji*, take care of your wallet. They'll steal your belt off of your trousers and you wouldn't know,' one porter said, trying to carry favour.

'I wasn't born yesterday,' Khalo replied, glaring.

With time, Ammi had to plead with Salahuddin Khalo to do each little task, almost begging, as politely as she could, before he finally obliged. She gradually began to venture out though it was difficult for a woman to visit offices. It just wasn't the norm. Besides, she didn't know where to go and how to get there, since public transport was so inadequate. She was mortified at her helplessness but resolved to cope as best as she could on her own. When really hard pressed, she asked her younger brother, Fida Mamo or her father, Abba Ji. Never before had she realized that in a patriarchal society such as ours, a woman was so venerable without a man, her protector. With Abbu gone, even her nephews thought they could disrespect her. Occasionally Abbu's friends came to check on us at his postal behest. Ammi had never before spoken to any of them face to face since she observed *purdah*, but now she had no choice but to stand behind the curtain inside the front door and narrate her predicament to them.

The only means of communication with Abbu was the post, and a letter took a minimum of seven days, often longer, to reach its destination. The postman, whom we had hardly noticed before, became the most important man in our lives as we waited for him daily, longing for a letter, or more importantly, a money order, from London. Abbu moved from one job to another. Each aerogramme had a new return address, and many of Ammi's letters were lost or collected late as he had changed his address yet again, to be near his new job. Abbu's spasmodic letters and money orders left Ammi frustrated and financially compromised.

Travelling to foreign lands was a privilege only the rich could afford. Abbu had exhausted his financial means in getting to London. He had sold Ammi's jewellery to finance his trip. The weeks of unemployment between jobs and the extra medical expenses he had neither anticipated nor budgeted for, and if that was not enough, the political instability that led to war between Pakistan and India, sent inflation rocketing sky high, and Abbu's meticulously worked out budget out the window. Ammi began to wonder if Abbu would ever accumulate enough funds to summon us all to London. During this trying time, Ammi and Abbu exchanged heart rending letters.

2nd April 1965

Assalam Alaykum,

This is my third letter since your last aerogramme, each of which I sent to a new address. I don't know if you received them or you are too busy enjoying the gaieties of London and have forgotten us. I have not yet received last month's money order and already the due date for school fees and the rent for this month are upon me. With your last money order, I barely managed to pay the medical bills and settle Mirza Sahib's account since he refused to give any more groceries on chit. I know Mirza Sahib is very expensive but what am I to do when Salahuddin Bhai goes off to the mundi without telling me. I owe him Rs 160 from last month so I can't blame him!

I hope you have found a better job, but why did you leave the last one? Please send me money as soon as possible. If there is a problem, maybe my brother Zia Bhai can help?

The teachers are threatening to strike the girls off the register. You promised me in your last letter that you would send money regularly just as you promised to call us to London within the year. I begged you not to go.

In response to your lecture about praying and being frugal I have written the following couplet:

اوروں کو جو تلقین کیا کرتے ہو اظہر

خود اپنے گریباں میں منہ ڈال کہ دیکھو

Auroon ko jo tulqeen kia kartai ho Azhar
(Before preaching to others, dear Azhar),

Khud apnai geraiban main moon daal kai dekho
(Look within yourself).

I am no poet so correct me if it's not right.

Ather is now a little better, but he is still on medication. He has lost a lot of weight. Muzher is very clingy and cries all the time. I don't know if his leg hasn't healed properly or if he is missing you. I went to Holy Family Hospital. They have given me iodine. It's some problem in my neck. I have started to take it but have not noticed any improvement in my health yet.

The girls have passed their exams. Salmi came first in her class and has written a letter to ask you to send her a prize. Najmi too wrote a letter, but I didn't post them. I didn't have any money. Abba Ji bought me this aerogramme.

When will you be able to send our tickets? If you can't call us, please come back. We will manage somehow. At least, I won't have to beg everyone to lend me money and to do my chores.

Awaiting your prompt reply,

Jugnu

In response, littered amongst the cool stream of Abbu's lyrical words of love were guilt, painful internal struggle, and heartrending pleas to be patient, spend the meagre funds with care, keep faith and look after the children, as well as mundane exchanges regarding daily activities. He sent Ammi a camera and a transistor radio/ tape recorder so that she could listen to him recite his poetry on the BBC World Service, and knowing she could not read the English instructions, he diagrammatically illustrated how to operate them.

Daunted by the vast funds required to summon his large family to England, Abbu remained hesitant and dithered time and again about whether to call us over or return without having achieved his goals. He implored Ammi not to think that his heart had turned to stone and, to him, she was more beautiful than any pretty English girl in London. Ammi's letters were full of more practical and mundane woes and worries, whereas Abbu's letters were tender expressions of love and devotion. They began with *Meri achchhi Jugnu* (My lovely Jugnu) and were signed as Azhar *khasta jigar* (Azhar the tender heart).

20 April 1965

Meri achchhi Jugnu (My lovely Jugnu)

Assalam Alaykum,

I hope this letter finds you and the children well. I am very sorry I received your letters late because I moved, and I was unable to send the money order on time. Your letter was so harsh it seems you are angry with me. *Jugnu, you have a right to be angry especially since you have had to cope with your and the children's illnesses on your own, but you can't imagine what life is like here, unlike in Pakistan, where you come home at 1-2 pm and have the rest of the day to yourself. Here the normal working hours are from 9 am to 5 pm. It takes nearly an hour on the train to get to work and an hour to get back home. It was impossible to go to my old address to collect the post.*

I am working during the day in a factory after which I go to evening classes. On Saturday and Sunday, I have been helping Zia Mian in his travel agency to earn extra cash. I had to take time off on Saturday morning to collect your letters. I am saving every penny so that I can call you and the children soon.

You cannot imagine how difficult it is to find a room to rent and a job that pays enough to cover my expenses and allow me to save some money for your tickets. Angraiz (British people) don't like us Asians and blacks. They write notices on their windows that they don't want to rent their rooms to us. I had to ask Zia Mian to find a room for me. Because of his fair complexion, the landlord thought he was Italian, so he managed to get the room for me. I don't know what will happen when the landlord sees me. Allah Malik (Allah is the master).

Life is very hard here. I am now renting a very small room in Kingston. The only good thing is that it overlooks a beautiful garden full of lilies and azaleas. I have a hand basin, and an electric ring in the room that serves as my kitchen and I share the bathroom with six other people. There is nobody to do the laundry or cleaners to clean. I have to do all my chores myself whenever I can.

English food is totally inedible. They don't use any spices, only salt, and pepper. It is hard to find all our spices here. I had to go a long way by train to a place called Brixton to get halal meat, chillies, and coriander. I cook at weekends and eat the same food all week. My lonely life is totally rice-focused but yesterday I made minced meat and six parathas. (You can't imagine how hard it is to cook on an electric cooker.) Two, I ate last night, two I took for lunch, the other two I will eat this evening. I am counting the days when you will cook wonderful food for me again. I long for you and your chapattis.

I again apologise for the delay in the money order. All the paperwork at my new job delayed my pay, and I had to pay a month's deposit for the room I am renting. I know how hard it must have been for you, but please try and curb the expenses. I know you can't do anything about the medication and the school fees but wait till next month for new shoes for the children. Buy one pair at a time. Ask the landlord to be patient. I will send you a lump sum soon to settle his account.

I have asked Ajaz to lend you Rs 500 till my next money order. When he comes, ask him to go to the hospital and get the medication. Make sure to take your iodine. It is very important. Also, make sure you give Ather his medicine and plenty of milk and perhaps take Muzher to the hospital and have his leg x-rayed to find out why he is crying. I hope his leg has healed properly. Does he limp when he walks? I am so worried about you all. Does Ather still remember me or has he forgotten me? You have done so well to get through the last few months by yourself, nursing the boys, especially since you are not well. My brave Jugnu, well done! I am so proud of you.

I asked you to send me photographs of you and the children and instead you have sent me photographs of a beautiful young girl. You have tricked me. This girl with the chubby cheeks and dark eyes torments me. Now I will have to call her!

You should have posted the letters from the girls. It would have cheered me up. Send them with your reply. I have posted sweaters, fountain pens, and dolls for Najmi and Salmi. There are three necklaces too. The pink and the blue ones are for Najmi, Salmi. The crystal one is for you. I hope you will like them. I have bought a train set for Ather. I will send it with Zia Mian and Nafeesa in June.

I will send your plane tickets soon. I promise. I cannot return now, my dear Jugnu. You have to be strong. I long to return to the sunny frivolities of Pindi and loathe the cold, wet climate in London. I long to be in the sunshine with you and the children but if I return now, it will negate all our struggles. I would never be able to stand on my feet or be able to repay the loans I took to get here. I would fall flat on my face, never again able to stand up. I have to make something of myself for you and our children. We have to make this work for our children.

As for your couplet, I can't believe you wrote that! It is perfect. I have written a whole ghazel in response. I will recite it on BBC Radio Foreign Service on Sunday at 8.00 pm which will be one o'clock at night in Pakistan. If you switch on the radio I sent and set the dial at the mark, I have made, you will be able to hear it.

Tell me what you think.

I yearn for you as a desert yearns for water. The charm and gayeties of London are spurious without you and the children. Piccadilly seems worse than Bhabra Bazar. Not a single day passes when I don't make plans to unite our family somehow.

Main Pareshan Hoon (I am Forlorn)

Punish me no longer for I am forlorn	اب نہ تڑپاؤ میں پریشاں ہوں
Show me your face for I am forlorn	شکل دکھلاؤ میں پریشاں ہوں!
Someone lingered in my thoughts again	پھر مجھے یاد آگیا کوئی
Bring me the wine for I am forlorn	لاؤ مے لاؤ میں پریشاں ہوں!
The world has forsaken me	مجھ کو ٹھکرا دیا ہے دنیا نے
Desert me not for I am forlorn	تم نہ ٹھکراؤ میں پریشاں ہو!
Don't turn away oh friend without reason	بے سبب روٹھے نہیں اے دوست
Come, come back to me for I am forlorn	آؤ لوٹ آؤ میں پریشاں ہوں!
I keep seeing glimpses of again and again	بارہا میں نے تم کو دیکھا ہے
Show yourself for I am forlorn	سامنے آؤ میں پریشاں ہوں!
Oh my friend, my life partner	اے مرے میر کاروان حیات
Show me the way for I am forlorn	راہ دکھلاؤ میں پریشاں ہوں!
The last breath is about to escape my lips	جان ہونٹوں پہ آن پہونچی ہے
Please come no for I am forlorn	اب تو آجاؤ میں پریشاں ہوں!

Issi say jaan loo tum mughko kitnai pyarai ho
(Know by this how much you mean to me)

bana leya hai tumhai apni zindagi main nai
 (I have made you the essence of my life)

Meri nazar main to juchti nahi khudaie bhi,
(In my view even the majesty of God rankles me)

Ye aur baat hai, ki teri bandagi main nai
(It's another issue that I worship you)

اسی سے جان لو تم مجھ کو کتنے پیارے ہو
بنا لیا ہے تمھے اپنی زندگی میں نے

میری نظر میں تو جچتی نہیں خدائی بھی
یہ اور بات ہے کہ تیری بندگی میں نے

Take heart and have faith my darling as do I.

Your, khasta jigar Azhar

Abbu watched the news of the 1965 war
between India and Pakistan on television. As
India advanced into Lahore, he feared for our
safety. He revised his plans yet again to call
for his family sooner. He wrote more frequently
and ended his letters by saying, '*I left you in the care
of Allah, and to Him I pray for your safe keeping.*'

Occasionally he phoned at a pre-planned date and time. We all marched off to Dr. Ghazi's house – the only person with a phone among our neighbours – and waited patiently. When Abbu finally called, a three-minute call, or if we were lucky, five minutes, only Ammi got to talk to him. Sometimes, however, despite the long wait, the much awaited call never came, and we returned home disappointed. After the phone calls Ammi remained depressed for days. She would tearfully repeat his brief conversation to anyone who cared to listen.

The first question from those we met was, 'When are you going to London?' Unable to give a definite reply Ammi became even more despondent and feared Abbu might find someone else and never call for us. Unable to speak her mind, she read and re-read his letters, dissecting them in her head to see if she could read between the lines, till she knew them by heart. Her frustrations were compounded by Misbah and Bader's behaviour towards her, and by Wazir Khala's indifference to her complaints. Misbah and Bader teased and taunted Ammi like monkeys. Just as she cleaned the courtyard, they tore up bits of paper and rained it down from the balcony above.

One day, Ammi asked Salahuddin Khalo to buy a rubber mat to safeguard against Nunni's bedwetting. She washed the mat and hung it to dry. When she went to pick it up later that afternoon, there was a big L-shaped cut into it. Ammi was furious. She had warned Bader to be careful with the blade he had been playing with earlier that day. Knowing she wouldn't get any sympathy from Wazir Khala, she complained to Salahuddin Khalo. But he remained silent. All Ammi could do was to cry in despair.

To vent her pent-up anger and only sanctuary was Tauqeer Khala or Amma Ji's, where she had a sympathetic ear, but no one dared to intervene as they were all aware of Salahuddin Khalo's moods and knew Wazir Khala never found fault with her children.

The final straw was the day Rosy and I sneaked out mid-afternoon to buy the orange sweets that I loved. On our return, Salahuddin Khalo was anxiously waiting by the front door, his hand shielding his eyes as he squinted into the bright midday sun. 'Where have you two been?' he barked as we approached the front door.

'Salmi took me,' Rosy blurted meekly.

Salahuddin Khalo slapped me across the face and shouted, pointing at Rosy, 'Look at her! She is as red as a pomegranate. She'll get sunstroke!' He hugged Rosy.

Wazir Khala was standing by the stairs. 'Get upstairs,' she hissed at Rosy through gritted teeth. 'You shouldn't roam the streets...you are not destined to be a street hawker.'

Ammi had witnessed the incident. Being so vulnerable, she was quick to reprimand us and even quicker to take offence on our behalf. She glared at Wazir Khala and sobbed tearfully, '*Bhai Sahib*, if you had hit them both I wouldn't have minded, but you hugged your daughter and slapped mine. My children are not orphans; they are just as precious as yours.' She grabbed me by the arm and pulled me into our courtyard.

That was a rare occasion when Ammi hugged me and sobbed into my hair, for Ammi was not demonstrative of affection. Wazir Khala's words had wounded her ears and heart and continued to wound her soul for days. She gathered us all and marched to Amma Ji's house in the scorching sun. A few days later, we packed our belongings, loaded them into two *tongas*, and moved to Amma Ji's house in Bhabra Bazaar.

Ammi did not speak to Salahuddin Khalo, not even to say goodbye, when we finally departed for London.

12
BHABRA BAZAR

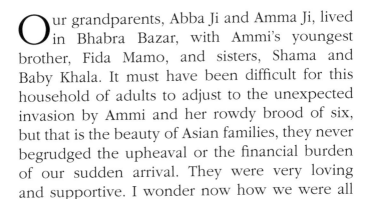

Our grandparents, Abba Ji and Amma Ji, lived in Bhabra Bazar, with Ammi's youngest brother, Fida Mamo, and sisters, Shama and Baby Khala. It must have been difficult for this household of adults to adjust to the unexpected invasion by Ammi and her rowdy brood of six, but that is the beauty of Asian families, they never begrudged the upheaval or the financial burden of our sudden arrival. They were very loving and supportive. I wonder now how we were all accommodated.

The house was of the usual pre-Partition style, with a central courtyard with rooms extending in all directions under overhanging balconies. Before Zia Mamo's family departed to London, the drawing room had been their bedroom and out of bounds to us children. But now, Baji and I were allowed to sleep on the light green divans with the large bolster pillows. Shama Khala and Baby Khala had the small bedroom next door, where a *palung* was dragged in at night to accommodate Ammi and Muz as well. The larger room that spanned the width of the house and faced the entrance, was Abba Ji and Amma Ji's bedroom. Another *palung* was installed there for Ather and Shano. Besides the beds, it had a spotless, white sheet-covered floor seating arrangement, with bolster pillows, where everyone gathered to relax and to eat.

Ammi was mortified at having to move back into her parental home, especially since Abba Ji had once made it clear, when she had returned home after an argument with Abbu, that her home was with her husband. '*Baita* you are welcome if you come for a visit, but now you're married your home is with your husband,' he had said. Ammi had returned home humiliated and had vowed never to do so again. However, having discussed her present circumstances with her parents, it was he who had advised her to move. So Ammi swallowed her pride and prayed it was a short term arrangement.

Abba Ji and Amma Ji spent most of their time sitting propped up by white bolsters on their beds. Abba Ji sat cross-legged, swaying to and fro while reciting the *Quran* in the morning. Even when he traced the lines with his index finger, he kept his thumb closed within his hand. We all knew we were not allowed to ask what had happened to his thumb. With his glasses perched low on his pink bulbous nose, he listened to the news on the radio in the alcove beside him; eyes closed, his hands constantly turning the beads of his amber *tasbih*.

Amma Ji sat in front of her *nuqsheen paandan,* a beautifully engraved silver box, knitting or cutting areca nuts with the *sarotta.* Her *paandan* was a magical box that housed a whole array of tiny containers with various concoctions of pastes that she applied to betel leaves and chewed most of the time, like chewing gum. Fresh betel leaves, wrapped in moist cloth, *kutha* extract from a tree bark, *choona,* (slaked lime), chopped areca nuts, green cardamoms, cloves, aniseed and *misri* (crystallized sugar), were all neatly stored n tiny containers in her *paandan.* It also contained money, keys, and even scissors – serving her as her handbag. No one, not even Abba Ji, was allowed to touch it. Anyone who wanted any of its magical ingredients had to ask Amma Ji and she happily obliged. A spittoon was tucked under her *palung*, into which she spat blood red *paan* extract at regular intervals.

The constant onslaught on her mouth with this concoction stained her teeth and the inside of her mouth pomegranate red. Years later, when she was in London, and I had to take her to the Royal Dental Hospital to have dentures made, the dentist was shocked at the sight. 'People...come and have a look at this!' he said, summoning a group of students.

The students crowded round and peered into the dark hole that looked like a coal mine after an explosion – a few shards of black teeth sticking out here and there; her tongue gnarled with criss-crossing rivulets, the result of lifelong *kutha-choona* abuse.

Mortified, I had to explain to the shocked crowd what she had been chewing with the aid of her portable *paandan*, which now comprised a Tupperware plastic box with tiny jam jars and empty tic-tac containers. She almost got us arrested when she casually sat down in Harrods furniture department on the display sofas, took out her makeshift *paandan* and proceeded to make *paan*.

'Amma Ji, you are not allowed to sit on these sofas; they are for display,' I said, looking around in embarrassment.

'It won't do any harm if I sit here for a minute,' she said, unperturbed, as she proceeded to make her *paan*.

The staff called security, thinking she was doing drugs. Needless to say, I had a lot of explaining to do.

***

I adored Shama Khala, with her painted nails, stiletto heeled winkle pickers and tight Teddy outfits (designs adopted from her magazines), which so outraged Amma Ji. Shama Khala, in contrast to Baby Khala, was a very pretty, vivacious young lady. And she was a giggler. When she started giggling, she got us all going, and once we started there was no stopping us. We laughed at anything and everything, and the slightest thing set us off like chimes in the wind. Unable to stop, we had to leave the room with Ammi and Amma Ji glaring at us in disapproval.

Shama Khala once spent days sewing a black and red outfit, copying the design from a film poster. It had narrow *painchas* and an almost skin-tight shirt with tiny side slits, decorated with red appliqué triangles.

'Shama *baiti* no one wears black in our family. You would be struck by the evil eye!' warned Amma Ji.

Unperturbed, Shama Khala wore it to college. She looked stunning. When she returned home, she had a high temperature. Despite the fact that the doctor diagnosed typhoid, Amma Ji was adamant she had been struck by the 'evil eye'. She read prayers and burnt red chillies to ward off the evil. Abba Ji's friend, Altaf Uncle, was summoned to administer daily injections for the next ten days. To help her recover, extra fruit and Ovaltine was specially purchased and kept safe in the alcove beside Abba Ji's bed. But, whenever I got a chance, I sneaked a spoonful of Ovaltine.

***

Abba Ji didn't approve of music, especially Indian pop songs. As soon as he went out to the mosque to pray, Shama Khala would switch on the radio. On his return, without saying a word, Abba Ji would switch it off. No one dared to complain.

In the cold winter evenings, Shama, Baby Khala and Ammi, rushed to complete their chores and nestle with their knitting near the portable coal fire stove, their knitting needles clicking while they listened to *Shastri Ji*, a satirical play based on the then PM of India. I picked up the key phrase from the play *'Ji Guru Ji'* and repeated it, hands pressed together, humbly bowing, in front of Shama Khala, whenever she asked me to do anything. It set her off giggling.

We all helped with the household chores. Ammi took charge of the cooking and sat flushed, sweat running down her forehead and neck, making mounds of *chapattis* for the whole family, while one of us fanned her with the hand-held fan. Baji and I ran errands to the local shops and bought fresh rusks and hot *naans* from the bakery for breakfast. Shama Khala supervised the cleaning and Baby Khala tackled the laundry.

Shama and Baby Khala treated Baji as an equal, giving her the respect due a contemporary, but dismissed me as a little child, which I resented. They helped Baji with her homework, took her to meet their friends, to Moti Bazaar, and to the cinema. Despite my protests, they refused to take me, saying I was *too* young.

When a money order from Abbu arrived, Ammi treated Shama and Baby Khala and they sneaked off to the cinema with Baji, without asking Abba Ji's permission. He strongly disapproved of the cinema. I was so incensed I told him where they had gone – to see the film, *Naila*.

It began to rain and the cinema became flooded. Unable to find a *tonga*, they had to walk home. As they arrived back, Shama Khala holding her new jute sandals in her hand, I teased her saying she looked like the peasants who walk with their shoes in their hands so as not to spoil them. Fida Mamo told Ammi I had spilled the beans to Abba Ji. She gritted her teeth and thumped me. Had it not been for the fact that she didn't want to create a scene, I would have got a good hiding.

Shama Khala was a real tease. She teased me mercilessly. She teased her cousins Sajid and Tusneem, who came to stay while on leave from training at the Military Academy in Kakul. They loved to hear me speak in Punjabi and often used me as a go-between to send messages to Shama Khala, for although Shama and Baby Khala did not observe *purdah*, they did not speak to them directly, especially in front of Abba Ji, for everyone knew Tusneem Mamo fancied Shama Khala.

One morning, Tusneem Mamo went to wash at the big water drum fitted with a tap and propped up on wooden crates in the courtyard. The moss-covered wooden stool slipped beneath him and he went flying under the drum. He quickly stood up, checked to see if anyone was watching, pretending nothing had happened. He was unaware that Shama Khala and I had seen him fall. Later that evening, when we gathered round for tea, Shama Khala, giggling as usual, nudged me to ask him if he had hurt himself. He looked up startled. I continued to tease. He lunged forward to grab me but I retreated quickly and ran out into the *gali*. He chased after me through the bazaar, past the cobblers, the rows of stainless steel kitchen utensil shops, the tailors, the bakery, dyers and the whole row of goldsmiths. He finally caught me by Gamma *Hulvaie's* sweetmeat shop. As we walked back, panting breathlessly, with my hand firmly held in his, he paused to rest, leaning against a closed door. It flew open with his weight. Inside, some *Pathani* women were resting in the courtyard. They began shouting obscenities at him, calling him a *budmash* and a scoundrel. In the pandemonium, I made good my escape, running home bubbling with laughter, providing Shama Khala with further ammunition to tease him with.

13
SCHOOL IN PINDI

Baji, Shano and I attended Liaqat School in the nearby *gali*. Every morning Ammi combed our long coconut-oiled hair, etching a parting in the centre of our heads with the comb, from the front all the way to the back, so it appeared as if our heads had split down the middle. She braided our hair into two tight shining plaits, which were looped over and tied back with red ribbons. They hung down on either side of our faces like inverted outlines of rabbit's ears. As soon as I was out of her sight, I untied my plaits, fully aware of the consequences on my return.

When Ammi set eyes on me she clenched her teeth and gave me a smack if I was within striking distance and yelled, 'You will catch lice and be possessed by *Djinn!* You roam in such unearthly places with your hair loose!'

How she knew where I roamed has always been a mystery to me. She gripped me between her knees like a chicken ready to be plucked and combed my hair with her fingers. She intertwined the plaits, and criss-crossed them at the back of my head. Only then did she allow me to escape. 'If you catch lice, I will have your head shaved,' she threatened, waving her finger.

***

Shano hated school. She was never ready on time. Every morning she whined and squirmed in the corner of the room, refusing to go. Eventually, we left without her. Later, Ammi had to request our neighbour to drop her off on his scooter. But even before he returned from the main road, Shano herself was back, having taken shortcuts through the *galis*. Whenever possible, I sneaked her into the school through the rain drain that ran behind my class to save her from the wrath of Miss Nadra, our stern Headmistress, who stood at the main gate, cane in hand, in her stilettos and teddy outfits, force feeding quinine to latecomers as punishment.

I was a good student. Shama Khala taunted me

saying I only came first in class because Liaqat was such a crappy school.

'Urdu is my maternal language. English is my paternal language. Islamiat – I was born a Muslim, and maths I know,' she teased derisively. She persuaded Ammi to move us to the Muslim Girls High School, where she had studied. The fees were higher, but it was considered a better school.

I joined Muslim Girls in class two. It was far larger than my previous school and initially I found it rather daunting. I was terrified of the well in the courtyard because rumour had it that it contained the souls of the girls who had drowned in it, and their screams could still be heard at certain times. Unable to find my way through the maze of rooms and corridors, I often got lost. Baji tried to reassure me saying she would come and collect me from my class after school, but I wasn't convinced. I latched onto the beautiful Miss Safia, Shama Khala's friend, whom I adored. I shadowed her around the school, holding her hand, and eventually had to contend with vinegar-tongued, prune-faced Miss Zohra as my class teacher.

Miss Zohra had an ugly mole on her hairy upper lip that twitched when she spoke. It frightened me. She didn't speak but yelled in a piercing shrill voice, with such expressive gestures that they made me jump. Stooping down, she'd grab her victim firmly by the ear, moving closer, so her ugly face almost touched. Then she would narrow her fiery eyes so they almost met in the middle like a vulture's, and yell, 'Did your mother feed you crow's brain for breakfast?'

When I glibly imitated her at home, Shama Khala was furious. Despite my protests, she complained about Miss Zohra's behaviour to the Headmistress, Miss Nadra, who summoned me to an audience, along with Miss Zohra. Sheepishly I entered Miss Nadra's office. She was sitting behind her desk, gently rocking on her padded wicker chair. Shama Khala sat on one side of the huge desk, Miss Zohra on the other, her face more sour than usual. Her lips were pinched tight and her hairy chin twitching in irritation. I stood cowering between them, hands behind my back, swaying from side to side, trying not to look as nervous as I felt. I had to repeat in front of them what Miss Zohra had said. Of course, I couldn't imitate her as I had done at home. Miss Zohra tilted her head to one side, clenched her teeth, opened her eyes wide and raised her eyebrows as high as they would go, but said nothing.

Miss Nadra sat quietly with a grave expression and told me to return to my class. I feared the worst but on Miss Zohra's return, she only scolded me for being a tattle-tale. I was relieved at getting off lightly. I'm sure that had it not been for Shama Khala's friendship with Miss Nadra, she would have wrenched my ears off my head. I hated Miss Zohra, but she taught me my times tables and how to make pretty maps, outlining the continents with blue fringes to represent water.

In the fifth grade, the famously strict Miss Chunun Bibi was my class teacher. She had taught at the school for as long as anyone could remember and had even taught Shama Khala. She was a tiny old lady with a long silver-white plait, braided with a coloured *paranda*. She wore platform sandals and always dressed in a starched white *shalwar-kameez*. Despite her strictness, I liked her, and she liked me. Every morning she hollered out the names in the register, to which we replied, 'Present, Miss'. Then, suddenly she would point to a girl at random and say, 'Hey you *larki*, recite verse so and so from the *Quran*.'

The whole class chanted after the nervous leader. Everyone learnt the prescribed verses, in case they were picked. Then I, being the monitor, stood in front of the class and chanted the times table of the day and the rest of the class repeated it after me. By which time the class had settled, and I distributed packets of powdered milk – courtesy

American Aid to third world countries – and the regular lessons proceeded.

Our classroom was exceptionally hot since it was on the top floor and we had to keep the windows and the door open to let in the breeze, but that also meant we were constantly distracted by the PE lessons taking place on the flat roof. As the girls played *khoo* and *kora chupai* I chanted the rhymes in my head.

Kora chupai, kali jumairat aiee ai.

Jinai agai pechai dekha udi shamat aiee ai.

Drinking water was stored in each classroom in clay *mutkas*. The older girls helped themselves to water from our *mutka*, or sneakily exchanged their cracked *mutkas* with ours, and we were forced to knock on doors in the neighbourhood for water.

During the break, the gatekeeper allowed the younger girls to go out and purchase goods from the vendors that gathered by the main gate, but would not let the older girls out. They screamed their orders to the *Ayas* above the general din. Ignoring Ammi's warnings about the ill-prepared food covered with flies, we bought *aloo chana chaat*, *imli*-tamarind and *golgappas* from the hawkers, who chanted praise of their colourful merchandise in elaborate couplets:

Lai ja chatanki anai di,
(Take a portion for an anna)

Saveree uth pakai nai,
(Freshly prepared this morning)

Masalai gin kai pai nai
(Added special blend of spices)

Lai ja chatanki anai di
(Take a portion for an anna)

One afternoon, during the break, my friend Nelo and I were sitting on a windowsill eating fresh *imli*.

'Didn't you get some *masala* with the *imli?*' she asked.

'No, shall I get some?' As I jumped down, I slipped and fell with my legs astride on the tap under the window sill. I rushed in agony to the toilets behind Baji's class.

Nelo ran after me. 'Are you alright?' she shouted solicitously from outside the toilet.

'No, I am bleeding,' I sobbed.

'Bleeding? Shall I call Miss?'

'No, no, she will ask me to show her. Just get me the fabric from my bag.'

I placed the fabric I had for my needlework between my legs and holding back my tears hobbled back to the classroom. Nelo held my hand to comfort me. We sneaked in, grateful the teacher hadn't noticed we were late. By the time I got home, my *shalwar* was covered in blood. Petrified, I had no choice but to tell Baji. She called Ammi, who saw my soiled *shalwar* and grabbed me by the shoulders. A horrified expression on her face, she whispered, 'Who did this?'

'I fell on the tap and had to miss my art class. The teacher taught them how to draw a duck and I…'

'Don't tell me stories about your art class; tell me the truth – who did this?' she demanded.

Shama Khala pushed Ammi aside. Hugging me, she whispered, 'Don't be scared. Tell me the truth. Who did this?' In bewilderment, I told her the same story. She didn't believe me either.

Ammi was crying. She wrapped her shawl around me, dashed across the *gali* and called Uncle Bisharat, who rushed me to Holy Family Hospital on his motorbike. Ammi and Shama Khala followed by *tonga*. At the hospital, the nuns examined me and recorded my narrative and spoke to each other and Ammi in hushed tones. They tried to reassure me and continued to question me.

'Who did this? Here you are safe *baita*, take these sweets. Do you want a drink?'

'Yes, please.'

'Now, tell me *baita*. What happened? Don't be scared. No one will harm you here. Did some bad man touch you?'

'She is only nine!' everyone kept saying. I was mortified at being examined by so many people but couldn't understand why they kept asking me again and again *who had done this*. I repeated my story, emphasizing I had to miss my art class, and everyone else had learnt to draw a duck. I had to spoil my needlework fabric. I couldn't understand what the problem was, why they kept saying, 'She is only nine.' We often got hurt and Ammi never made such a big deal about it.

After this accident Baji and I were restricted from going out unaccompanied and we had to go to and from school with Shama and Baby Khala. On our way back, while we waited for our aunts outside Government College, we teased the girls in their stiletto heels and tight Teddy outfits, so tight that a girl fell into the drain as she tried to jump over it. I gathered white fragrant *Chambeli* flowers from the climbers that covered the walls and formed an arch above the gates, for Amma Ji; my frock improvised as a basket.

Amma Ji loved the flowers and placed them amongst her *paan* on the moist cloth in her *paandan*.

Closing the lid, she chided me for going near the *Chambeli* bushes with my hair loose. 'You will be possessed by *Djinns*. May *Allah* protect you,' she murmured, trying to stop the red betel juice from spilling out from the side of her mouth, and wiping the corners, just in case.

I watched her toothless red mouth open and close and asked, 'Why do *Djinns* live in *Chambeli* bushes?'

'I don't know; our elders have always said *Djinns* inhabit desolate places such as graveyards and they love fragrant bushes.' She smiled pensively, spitting into the spittoon and placing yet another *paan* in her mouth.

'Then why would they possess me if I go there with my hair loose?'

'They live in such places so they can pray undisturbed. If someone disturbs their abode, they get very angry and possess them. It's very hard to exorcise them. That's what they say...' She finished with a dismissive shrug and upraised brows.

In the sweltering heat we walked home along Murree Road, dotted with a few cars, *tongas* and the occasional double-decker bus, and a sea of bicycles. The tarmac glistened in the distance, so soft and squidgy underfoot that it spoiled Shama Khala's stilettoes.

We looked forward to Thursdays, when we

finished school at 11.30am, instead of 1.00pm. One such Thursday afternoon, Shama and Baby Khala were busy with college debates, so Baji and I hired a bicycle and tried to learn to ride it with Zareena, a girl with a bad reputation, whom we were forbidden to play with. In the *maidan*, the playground where the boys played cricket, I wobbled from side to side trying to remain in the saddle while Baji and Zareena held onto the oversized bike.

I spotted Amma Ji in the distance, recognisable by her distinctive walk, striding along in her black *burqa*, her right arm swinging back and forth. She was marching towards us in the mid-day heat. On seeing her, my laughter and sense of freedom congealed within me and I momentarily froze on the spot. Unfortunately she saw us before we could scamper off.

I jumped off the bike, ditching it immediately as if it was an abhorrent object I wanted nothing to do with it. She threw back the fine muslin *niqab* covering her face and gestured with her forefinger, indicating we were to come at once. Knowing what was to come, I kept what I thought was a safe distance, but Amma Ji moved swiftly forward and grabbed my ear firmly between forefinger and thumb. 'What are you doing out here in this heat?' she demanded.

I wanted to ask her the same question as I squirmed, trying to free my ear.

Without waiting for a reply, she let go. 'Haven't you caused enough anguish to us all? Get home this minute!' she ordered, annoyed. 'I will deal with you later.' She pointed the way home.

Abandoning our bike and Zareena alike, we ran home.

14
EID

Just before the festival of *Eid-ul-Adha*, the bleating of goats, sheep and cows is heard in almost every house in Pakistan. Those who can afford to, and even those who cannot, buy animals to sacrifice, emulating the story of Prophet Ibrahim in the *Quran*. The festival is a great excuse to gorge on *tikkas* and *kebabs*.

We were chasing our goat on our roof. Overwhelmed by the mob of children, he jumped off the balcony into the *gali* below. Miraculously, he got up and ran towards Raja Bazar. Tusneem Mamo chased after him, pursued by us and other children from the neighbourhood. He finally caught the goat near the *tonga* stand. Hearing about this escapade, Amma Ji gave fervent thanks that the animal remained unscathed, for it would not have been possible to sacrifice an injured animal.

Eid was always fun. Ammi and the aunts prepared a whole array of special dishes – *sheer khurma, pakoras, dahai-bhalas*, *choolai* and *kebabs*. We all had new outfits and accessories – new shoes, matching ribbons and bangles, even new vests. Massi came round with a jingling basket of bangles perched on her head. The women, young and old, gathered around amongst excited chatter. She ceremoniously lifted the gold trimmed cloth covering the basket and a whole array of glittering glass bangles winked at us. We chose dozens upon dozens of slender coloured circles of glass, arranging gold banded ones amongst silky, fluted ones and matching them with our *Eid* outfits. Massi, with her coarse fingers, somehow had no trouble in slipping the tiny fragile bangles onto fat or slim wrists alike.

On *Chand Raat,* the night before *Eid*, Ammi oiled our hair and Shama Khala applied henna in intricate designs on our hands, tying paper bags over them to protect the bedding. Inevitably the bags came off during the night and stained our clothes and the bedding. In the morning, we washed the henna, applied mustard oil to our shrunken wrinkled palms and compared designs. We then bathed; the men taking precedence as they had to go to the mosque to pray. The women prayed at home. The youngest were scrubbed raw by Ammi, and then we changed into our new outfits – all laid out neatly on our beds.

Surprisingly, the butcher kept his word and came early with his young assistant, carrying a selection of large knives and ropes in a hessian bag, just as the men were returning from the mosque. All of us, including many children from the neighbourhood, gathered around the goat. The butcher's assistant untied him from the railing and led him firmly by his horns to the open drain in the courtyard. Effortlessly, he tied the goat's hind legs and knocked him down onto his side. The goat bleeped and struggled helplessly, as if aware of his impending doom.

Ather cried, 'Don't kill my goat; please don't kill it!'

Fida Mamo deposited Ather with Ammi and called Abba Ji to recite the sacrificial prayers:

'*Bismillah, hir Rahman nir Raheem. Allah O Akbar, Allah O Akbar* (I begin with the Name of Allah the Greatest),' said the butcher and Abba Ji in unison.

With one sharp cut, he slit the goat's throat. We jumped back to avoid the squirting blood, shouting '*Aaahh!*' The goat bleated for the last time and then lay shaking and throbbing. The butcher severed the head, chopped off its feet and hung it up with its hind legs against the wall by the drain. He then pulled off the skin, pushing his fists against the steaming flesh, as if removing a tight garment. Soon the dismembered head, eyes wide open, teeth showing, lay on top of the sodden skin like a discarded woolly jumper. The butcher then slit the stomach and the intestines plopped out in a heap on the floor, still steaming. He cut out the liver and the heart, chopped them into small pieces and presented them to Fida Mamo on a platter like a trophy. It was immediately fried for brunch.

The butcher departed, leaving the carcass hanging to drain, saying, 'I am going next door to do their *qurbani* and will be back shortly.'

'Don't sacrifice my neighbour – just his goat!' joked Abba Ji with a smile.

Some of the children followed the butcher next door.

'Abba Ji, perhaps it was *Eid* when the rivers turned red in Egypt in the story of Moses,' I suggested, watching Hameeda, the cleaner, as she washed away the blood which had already congealed.

Abba Ji looked at me thoughtfully. Tapping my back gently, he said, 'No, no...that was a miracle because Moses cursed the Pharaoh.' A few minutes later I heard him repeat to Ammi and Amma Ji what

I had just said. 'She is a sharp cookie and has an incredible imagination. Mark my words, one day...' he left his sentence incomplete as I walked in.

By the time the butcher returned, Hameeda had already washed away the blood, got rid of the innards and left, well pleased with the head and trotters for her trouble. He cut the carcass into tiny pieces. It was unthinkable that this pile of meat in the steel trays had been a goat just a few hours earlier. Even before the butcher had finished his work, the ladies were enjoying the liver and the heart that Ammi had fried with crushed garlic and chillies. Ather continued to cry. Abba Ji paid the butcher and gave him the skin and some meat as an extra reward for his handiwork.

Portions of meat, draped with bright fabric, were distributed amongst family and friends, orphanages and servants amid shouts of *Eid Mubarak!* The poor little goat was quite forgotten in the festivities and feasting.

Commotion erupted as the transvestites, dressed in garish clothes, with ornate artificial jewellery, and dark make-up, appeared clapping and playing tambourines in the *gali*. They went from door to door, singing and dancing the *bhangra* with exaggerated gestures. When they came to our house, much to our disappointment, Fida Mamo handed them money and some meat and shooed them away.

They were never welcome in our house, though many other families happily enjoyed having them around to sing and dance, especially on joyous occasions such as childbirth or weddings.

We eagerly awaited our *Eiddi* (monetary gifts) from Abba Ji, who took out a wad of crisp notes as everyone, including the adults, stood in a line. As he walked past, keeping his thumb folded, he handed out one rupee notes to each of us, young and old alike. On receiving our *Eiddi*, we touched our foreheads, bowed in respect and said *Salaam Alaykum* with a smile, reiterating his greeting of *Eid Mubarak*. He blessed us, patting and ruffling our hair. The one rupee we were allowed to spend on the rides and stalls in the *gali*. The other *Eiddi* we received from our aunts and uncles, had to be given to Ammi without question.

'I too, have to give *Eiddi* to the children,' she informed us firmly if we protested.

Vendors gathered in the *gali* from early morning, selling all sorts of goodies. Plastic toys, *kugoo ghorai* (miniature clay pots and animals), elaborate birds and flowers, skilfully made by twisting coloured spun sugar wound around sticks, and long, thin balloons twisted into animal shapes. We moved from stall to stall, showing off our clothes, henna, shoes and bangles, and spending a few *paisas* here, a few *annas* there, counting our change repeatedly until we had spent all our money. Through the morning, friends and family dropped in, bringing meat. They were served tea, cold drinks and snacks.

***

Shama Khala showered and came to the roof with a towel draped around her shoulders, the cool, damp smell of almond soap lingering about her and her long hair dripping and soaking the back of her *qameez*. She sat on the *palung* in the sun, flicked her thick hair forward. Rubbing the ends with a towel, she began to untangle the strands with a comb. She and Baby Khalo chatted quietly, chewing *gandairi* and spitting out the spent husk to one side. I could not hear the whispered exchanges but knew it had something to do with the unexpected arrival of their cousin, Iqbal Khala, and her husband, Ayub Khalo, from Karachi. Ammi joined them with a basket of *cheeko* and they all chattered excitedly, giggling intermittently.

***

In the evening, Wazir Khala arrived with her family. Everyone was getting impatient to eat and there was no sign of Tauqeer Khala, who was notorious for being late. Eventually she arrived, grinning from ear to ear.

'Don't blame me, he came home late,' she said, nodding at her husband.

We all settled down on the spotless white floor around the *dusterkhan* laden with steaming food and enjoyed an extravagant meal amongst quiet chatter.

Abba Ji cleared his throat, adjusted his skull cap and running his fingers through his white beard, announced, 'I have some good news to share with you all. Your Amma Ji and I have decided to accept the proposal for Shama to marry Tusneem.'

We all cheered. Beaming, Iqbal Khala rose and retrieved a basket from the corner of the room and placed it in front of Shama Khala. She took out white fragrant *motia* garlands and placed them around Abba Ji and Amma Ji's necks amongst the customary polite protests, and another around Shama Khala's neck, who sat demurely, surrounded by joyous shouts and clapping. Iqbal Khala then fixed fresh floral ornaments on Shama Khala's wrists and hair, and a gold ring on her finger. Planting kisses on Shama Khala's forehead and cheeks, she congratulated her. Taking a tray of *methai*, she offered some to Abba Ji and Amma Ji, and then fed some *luddo* to Shama Khala. Tears in their eyes, the women hugged and congratulated Shama Khala, while we dived into the tray of *methai*.

'What happened to Abba Ji's thumb? Why does he always keep it folded like that?' I whispered to Farooq.

'I don't know. I asked him once. He told me off.'

The highlight of the evening was yet to come – a *kat-putli* show on the roof. The puppeteers operated the puppets from behind upturned *palungs* draped with bright sheets and illuminated with lanterns. The puppets danced and sang the latest pop songs. We all joined in, as did the neighbours, who initially watched from their roofs and then gradually climbed over the walls uninvited. The show went on late into the night, climaxing with a mock wedding ceremony with lewd, evocative wedding songs punctuated with rude jokes and an abusive exchange between the bride and her mother-in-law. Amma Ji served *paan* from her *paandan*, and Shama Khala served hot tea and cold drinks.

Ammi, Tauqeer Khala, and Wazir Khala continued to tease Shama Khala as she showed off her ring to the neighbours. Iqbal Khala and Ayub Khalo stayed for several days and left with demands not to delay the wedding. Amma Ji agreed to a date next year, after Shama Khala's graduation. We all joined in the festivities, blissfully unaware that we would not be present to witness the happy occasion.

15
UNEXPECTED VISITORS

A few days after *Eid*, the postman arrived with a parcel. It contained a cassette tape and the long awaited tickets for our flight to London. We all danced with joy, hugging each other in elation. We quickly played that tape. Out poured Abbu's voice, reciting a poetic reply to Ammi's letter in his melodious voice.

Jawabai Khut (Reply to Letter)

Reviving the world of wine and intoxication I am ruining my life wittingly	پھر جام ومے کی دنیا آباد کر رہا ہوں دانستہ زندگانی برباد کررہا ہوں!
Tell me, do you miss me at times? I think of you every step of the way	تم بھی کبھی بتا دو کرتی ہو یاد مجھ کو ہر ہر قدم پہ تم کو میں یاد کر رہا ہوں!
Our dilemmas preclude us from uniting Do not think I'm revoking you	مجبوریاں ہماری ملنے سے روکتی ہیں تم یہ سمجھ نہ لینا بیداد کر رہا ہوں!
The captor released me from the cage saying Go, for I free you from your prison today	صیاد نے یہ کہہ کر چھوڑا قفس سے مجھ کو جا میں بھی آج تجھ کو آزاد کر رہا ہوں!
You were right to keep me from leaving I regret today not listening to you	تم نے بجا کہا تھا پردیس میں نہ جاؤ کہنا تمہارا اب تو میں یاد کر رہا ہوں!
Unite the hearts that yearns to meet Oh Lord I make a plea, an earnest request within	بچھڑے ہوئے دلوں کو پھر سے ملا دے یا رب میں آج دست بستہ فریاد کر رہا ہوں!
Why are your eyes tearful Azhar? When I am reciting my tale of my woe	اظہر تمہاری آنکھیں نمناک ہوگئیں کیوں میں تو بیان اپنی روداد کر رہا ہوں!

Ammi was crying and laughing at the same time. Abba Ji patted her on the head and gave her his blessings. Amma Ji sat quietly on her *palung*, tears clouding her eyes. It had taken almost three years for Abbu to save up enough and organize our travel to London. Soon my initial joy and excitement turned into apprehensive trepidation as it dawned on me that we would be flying to a faraway place about which I knew nothing, leaving behind everyone I loved.

I was playing jacks with Baji outside our house, talking about our fears, when I spotted Abba Ji's friend, Uncle Altaf, approaching at the head of a large group of people. Uncle Altaf was a familiar figure who frequently visited Abba Ji, sometimes alone, at other times with Professor Ishtiaq Hussain Qureshi. But he had never come with such a large group before. There were several lanky boys, followed by a thin woman in a black *burqa* and two plump women in white shuttlecock *burqas*, each holding the hand of a young girl. I gave nervous smiles as I greeted the group and then rushed inside to inform Abba Ji about the unexpected guests while Baji led them to the drawing room.

Amma Ji quickly wrapped up the knitting she was unpicking and stood up, tidying the bedsheet and plumping up the pillows. She smoothed her hair and clothes with her hands and scrambled to search for her slippers under her *palung*. Abba Ji removed his glasses, shuffled his feet under the *palung* to find his slippers and, fixing his clothes, hurried to the drawing room, grooming his hair and beard with his fingers.

'*Assalam Alaykum,*' the group said almost in unison as he entered the room.

'*Walaikum-Assalam, Walaikum-Assalam,* good you have brought the family,' replied Abba Ji, as he embraced Uncle Altaf.

'We are going to a wedding in the neighbourhood so I thought we would pay our respects to Amma Ji.'

'Good, good,' Abba Ji replied smiling, gesturing for them to sit down. He asked Baji to take the ladies to Amma Ji.

Uncle Altaf introduced his sons, Khalid, Asim, Arif, Asif and Adnan. I became aware of the unflinching stare from one of the boys, Asif, a skinny boy with a multi-coloured tank top. Abba Ji and Uncle Altaf settled down on the sofa. The boys sat in a row on the divans. I followed the ladies and girls out.

Amma Ji greeted the group, extending her hand to take their *burqas*. Two overdressed, plump ladies in bright clothes emerged from under the shuttlecock *burqas* and a smart young woman, about Ammi's age, from the black *burqa*. The young woman awkwardly explained that they were overdressed because they were on their way to a wedding. The stern looking, larger of the two older ladies, with a dark complexion and prominent white patches around her tightly pursed lips and eyes, introduced herself as Khushi, Uncle Altaf's wife.

The smaller lady with bright smiling eyes was her sister, Raffian. Both had orange, henna-dyed, curly hair. The younger lady was Uncle Altaf's daughter, Khalida and she introduced her younger sisters as Furkhanda and Rukshanda.

'Gosh! That's a mouthful,' I exclaimed.

Ammi gave me a tight-lipped 'watch your tongue' look, her eyes flaring, as she made room for them to sit. 'Salmi, Najmi, take the girls to the roof to play,' she said firmly, pointing to the door.

'Yes, I know, call us Furri and Rukshi,' nodded Furkhanda, with an infectious chime-like laugh. Furri came with us but Rukshi clung to Khalida. We waited to see if she would change her mind but realised she didn't want to come, so we skipped away. Furri was cheerful and friendly and we opted to play hopscotch.

'We are going to London,' I boasted excitedly as I threw the disk.

'You lucky things! When?' she enquired.

'Soon. We've got our plane tickets,' I said, trying to sound casual.

'Okay okay, play the game,' said Baji impatiently. I gave her a sideways glance.

'Abba Jaan is going to Jeddah soon,' added Furri with a slight smile. 'Maybe he'll call us there?'

I didn't know where Jeddah was, but didn't like to ask, and continued with the game.

The aromas from the kitchen below were inviting. Shama Khala soon called us down for a lavish tea of *hulva, pakoras* and even *samosas* and biscuits. We found Khushi Auntie sitting quietly with a pained expression on her face, and Amma Ji struggling to make conversation. But Raffian Auntie chattered on joyously, answering on Khushi Auntie's behalf, with chuckles that caused her entire body to wobble. We knew the protocol. We had to wait for the guests to help themselves before Ammi indicated with her eyes that we could help ourselves.

Soon after tea, Asif came in said, 'Abba Jaan says we have to leave now.'

The ladies scrambled to put on their *burqas* and left, thanking Amma Ji for her hospitality. I stood on the *thara*, watching them walk down the *gali*. When Asif turned round and waved, I poked my tongue out at him and rushed back inside.

'Gosh, their names! Rukshanda, Furkhanda,' I said. 'Who'd name their daughters *Rukshanda, Furkhanda*? Hurts your mouth saying them, and that Khushi Auntie wasn't very happy was she?' I giggled.

Amma Ji suppressed a wry smile. Shama Khala chuckled as she continued to clear the dishes.

'And that boy, what was his name? Asif! He kept staring at me. I poked my tongue out at him. And Uncle Altaf is going to Jeddah,' I announced just as Abba Ji entered the room.

'Who needs newspapers when we have you, Salmi?' he laughed. 'You should become a journalist, when you grow up.'

'Ohh Abba Ji, then I could read the news on the radio'

'Journalists *write* the news, presenters read it,' corrected Shama Khala.

'Her...a journalist?' tittered Baji.

Shama Khala pinched my cheek. 'Yes Salmi, you should become a journalist, you are such a tattle-tale,' she taunted, imitating my expressive mimicry, reminding me of the Miss Zohra incident.

'That wasn't my fault. I told you not to come to school. You caused all the trouble,' I protested loudly.

'That wasn't my fault; you caused all the trouble!' she mimicked me in a high pitched voice, tears glistening on her long eyelashes from laughing so much.

'Don't encourage her, Shama. And you,' Ammi pointed at me and gave me 'the look', 'you go and tidy the drawing room.' She rolled her eyes in mock despair.

Baji enquired about Khushi Auntie's patchy skin and Amma Ji explained that it was a skin disease that happens from drinking milk after eating fish.

Little did I know that day in Pindi that fate had linked my destiny to this family.

16
DEPARTURE AT LAST

A melancholy gloom settled on the house as the date of our departure was fixed. Ammi snapped and burst into tears at the slightest provocation. She was excited and overjoyed to be finally leaving for London, something she had at times thought would never happen. Nevertheless, she was full of dread and apprehension at having to leave behind her family, with little hope of ever seeing them again.

After lengthy discussions with Abbu by mail, regarding what we should bring with us and what to do with our belongings (whether to bring bedding or not, what kind of clothes to make, etc.), Ammi sold our meagre possessions – the radio, pedestal fan, electric iron, and her most prized possession – the sewing machine she had purchased by collecting the pittance she got from knitting for various shops. She even sold the camera and the Grundig tape recorder Abbu had sent her. Her gold jewellery Abbu had already sold to finance his own trip. I cried when she burnt her purple velvet shirt to extract and then sell the silver from the *zari-karchobi* embroidery on it. With the meagre amount all this raised, she paid her outstanding rent, made new clothes for us all, bought shoes and sweaters. The crockery, pots, and pans, bedding, etc., were distributed amongst her sisters, Massi and Amma Ji.

My excitement about the imminent journey to a strange and alien land was palpable, yet I too, was sad and nervous about leaving behind everything that was familiar, things I had taken for granted – my home, friends, family and all the people I loved. An avalanche of thoughts and a million and one unvoiced questions bubbled up and burst in my little head. I hadn't known any other place. This was home. No doubt Ammi and my siblings were going through the same turmoil.

Finally, the day of departure arrived. The house buzzed with people. It was like *Eid*. Everyone, yes everyone – family and friends – gathered at Amma Ji's, to bid us farewell. They laughed and cried at the same time. Each of our teary-eyed aunts and uncles embraced us, kissing us repeatedly.

Farooq watched with a sad twisted grin, quiet and distant, while Rosy and I clung to each other in a lingering embraces. Our paths were parting, never to converge again, or so we thought. Now *we* were the 'lucky ones', harbouring secret conceit, dressed in completely new outfits, going to London by plane. No one we knew had ever travelled by air. Ammi said she had when they fled from Burma during the Second World War, but that was in a cargo plane, and she couldn't remember much about that flight. I didn't know whether I should be sad or happy. I just followed the motions with everyone else.

Tauqeer Khala was inconsolable. She shadowed Ammi, holding her hand, letting her tears flow. She was happy for us, yet heartbroken. She tearfully said, 'Jugnu, I am so happy for you, but I feel as if my umbilical cord is being cut. Look at you – going to England. Your children will study in English schools with the English. That's *kismet*. Make sure to write often.'

'*Haan*, you go off to London. What's here?' Wazir Khala said with a sigh. She too, seemed genuinely upset at our departure. Tauqeer Khala exchanged a quick glance with Ammi and a secret smile, sensing the resentment in her tone.

Ammi, not wanting to offend and sound egotistical, replied, 'Baji, don't bite the hand that feeds you.

Our country is paved with gold. What *don't* we have here? In England, they have to import everything. The only thing that grows there is potatoes. Our country is a gold mine. We have everything here. It's our leaders that have crippled us. I would never go if I didn't have to.'

'You are only saying that because you *are* going,' replied Wazir Khala.

'What's that saying? God gives you the leaders you deserve!' retorted Tauqeer Khala, not so reticent.

Ammi smiled a watery smile and changed the subject before she broke down, sobbing, 'Have you said good-bye to Khala Ji? Look, she has come all this way. She is going to miss you.'

I gave Khala Ji a long lingering embrace as she kissed me affectionately on the forehead and both cheeks. Other friends and family offered crumbs of sympathy to Amma Ji and Ammi. Fida Mamo finally announced the *tongas* were here to take us to the station.

'Are you going to London by train?' asked Khala Ji.

'No, no, you can't go to London by train. You have to fly in a plane, but you have to catch the plane from Karachi,' explained Amma Ji. 'Oh, may *Allah* protect you!' she said, blessing us with numerous verses from the *Quran*. When it was time to leave, she recited *Ayatul Kursi* and prayed for our safe journey. She ceremoniously produced a clutch of *Imam Zamins* from her *paandan* and began tying the tiny black amulets she had sewn, onto our upper arms.

Abba Ji held a copy of the *Holy Quran* aloft and patted our heads as we all passed under it. Everyone encircled us, crowding each other. Those closest, kissed us repeatedly until finally we left them teary-eyed amidst shouts of '*Khuda hafiz*, goodbye, safe journey!' and exhortations to write, and send a telegram as soon as we reached Karachi. Amma Ji reminded Ammi to throw the amulets into flowing water on reaching London and give alms to the poor.

I ran up and gave one last hug to Rosy and Farooq. Rosy kissed me and Farooq pinched my arm, trying to conceal his agitation, his hand trembling. 'Write as soon as you get there,' he said.

'*Khuda Hafiz*,' I replied, taking a deep breath and exhaling loudly.

As we settled into the *tongas*, Farooq ran up and squeezed in next to me. Rosy looked at her father, pleading for permission. Salahuddin Khalo shook his head but then smiled and relented. So Rosy too, jumped into the *tonga*. Ammi sighed from somewhere deep within, for her heart was breaking. Tauqeer Khala stood weeping; the bewildered look of a hen whose only chick had been snatched by a kite, on her face.

At the station, in the chaos of departing passengers and those who had come to see them off, and mulling of porters, we finally boarded the train. I watched the multitude but only Rosy and Farooq remained in the forefront of my vision. The rest dissolved into the background. Behind them, the sun was setting in a mild glow of gold.

As we finally embarked on our long awaited journey, I couldn't wait for the train to start moving. But the only thing I now remember about that journey was the nausea and headache we all suffered. The journey seemed never-ending and the carefully prepared minced meat, *parathas*, boiled eggs and *hulva* were left uneaten

17
KARACHI

———————~———————

*A*mmi's cousin, Iqbal Khala, and her son Suhail, and her driver, greeted us at Karachi railway station. We had to hire an additional taxi to transport us all home with our luggage. We must have looked like starving beggars after throwing up throughout the twenty-four hour journey. I was as shocked as she was when Iqbal Khala remarked in alarm, 'You will surely die on the plane if you are so sick in a train...' In my mind I had imagined a plane journey to be amazing and only realized the meaning of her remark much later.

Iqbal Khala lived in a huge house with her four children. Suhail and Fareeda were both older than Baji and me; Nadeem, a skinny little boy, was about my age, and Fauzia was three. They knew a lot about us from Iqbal Khala's brothers, Sajid

Mamo and Tusneem Mamo, who were regular visitors to our home in Pindi. We were all extremely impressed by their massive house, servants and garden with fruit trees – something no one we knew in Pindi had.

Life in Iqbal Khala's house was an entirely novel experience for us. Her cook, Islam, prepared food on demand, unlike in our house, where meal times were fixed and you ate whatever Ammi cooked, no questions asked! Occasionally Ammi asked us what we wanted to eat but didn't always comply with our requests. Islam was happy to cook fried eggs for one person, omelette for another and *parathas* for a third; and made all kinds of snacks throughout the day. The fruit basket was always full of fruit, some of which we had never seen in Pindi – custard apples, lychees, Sharon fruit – to which we could help ourselves whenever we wanted. In our house, Ammi shared whatever Abbu brought, and we ate it all at once. Initially, from politeness, we showed restraint but after a few days, the fruit basket emptied as soon as it was filled.

All day, Iqbal Khala lay propped up in a recliner, issuing instructions to the home-help and chatting with Ammi or reading her magazines. Occasionally, when she heard an exceptional clatter in the kitchen, she'd shout out, 'Islaaaam!

What have you broken?' 'Nooothing;' came a nonchalant reply. End of story.

Aya Amma looked after all of us, and Purveen cleaned the huge house, made beds, washed clothes and tidied up after us throughout the day. In Pindi, Ammi had done all the chores.

Suhail, Fareeda, and Nadeem were driven to their posh English school, the largest I had ever seen. They took sandwiches for lunch; only Nadeem took a kebab roll and his siblings teased him, calling him *desi*. I wonder what they thought of us! We had always walked to our Urdu medium school in the *gali*.

The children had their own rooms. We were given two guest rooms, but soon Baji and I moved in with Fareeda. She was very fussy about her appearance and looked voluptuous in her stylish, skin tight short shirts, without side slits. Her *shalwars* had tiny *painchas*, with elaborate designs spanning almost six inches on the bottom edges, stiffened with buckram, and her high stiletto heels made her walk funny. Although we were almost the same age as Fareeda, we still wore frocks and *shalwars* stitched by Ammi. Baji and I tried on her shoes when she was at school but didn't have the courage to try on her outfits.

Sohail Bhai had a radiogram on which he listened to English songs that we had never heard before.

The radio remained on all the time, even when he was out. He ignored us most of the time, unless we bothered him while we skipped, played hopscotch or *pithoo garam* and the ball landed in his path. He wore skin tight hipster trousers, with big buckled belts and bright shirts with huge pointy collars, buttons open almost to his navel, and pointed shoes. I blamed his swanky walk on his tight trousers and uncomfortable shoes. He was forever fixing his long hair, even after spending hours setting it with expensive creams.

Ammi, had always worn a *burqa* in Pindi but Iqbal Khala, who had been to London and was our sole source of information on life in England, stopped Ammi from wearing it in Karachi so that she would get used to it. Initially, Ammi was very self-conscious, but since we travelled in Iqbal Khala's car, she soon got used to it.

While Ammi visited the embassy or went shopping with Iqbal Khala, we played in the huge garden, climbed trees, chased birds, picked fruit and waited for Fareeda to return from school. I picked some tiny green bananas and custard apples and hid them in our suitcase. It was a lovely surprise to discover them ripe in London.

Iqbal Khala took us shopping for coats and woollens. There wasn't a great deal to choose from since it was hot throughout the year in Karachi.

Hence we all ended up with identical thin red coats, except for Ammi, who had a purple one. It was fun and exciting going out by car but we had to make frequent stops since we all suffered from travel sickness.

PART II

PRE-PARTITION INDIA

Yaari

Hafiz Shiraz

I see no friends around, whatever happened to every friend? I see no one I love, when did come to an end?	یـاری انـدر کـس نـمـی بینیم یـاران راچـه شد دوسـتـی کـی آخـر آمـد دوسـتـداران راچـه شد
Water of life has turned dark, where is glorious Elias? Flowers are all bleeding, whence the breeze which branches bend?	آب حیوان تیره گون شد خظر فرخ پی کجاست خـون چـکیـد از شـاخ گل بـادبهـاران راچـه شد
Thousands of flowers are in full bloom, yet not a song What happened to nightingales? Where did those thousands descend?	صد هزاران گل شـکفت و بانگ مرغی بر نخاست عـنـدلیبـان راچـه پیـش آمد هـزاران راچـه شد
For years no gem has been dug from the mine of loyalty What happened to sunshine? And what about wind and rain's trend?	لـعـلـی از کـان مروت برنیـامـد سـال هـاست تـابـش خـور شیـد و سعی بـاد و باران راچـه شد
Venous is not making music any more, did all her instruments burn? Nobody is in the mood, to whom do the wine-sellers tend?	زهره سـازی خـوش نـمـی سازد مگر عودش بسوخت کـس نـدارد ذوق مستی میگسـاران راچـه شد
Nobody says that a friend has got the right to befriend What has come of loyalty? Whatever happened to every friend?	کـس نـمـی گـویـد کـه یـاری داشت حق دوستی حق شنـاسـان راچـه حـال افتـاد یاران راچـه شد
This was the home of the Kings, and the land of the Kind-hearted When did kindness end, and since when Kings pretend?	شهـریـاران بـود و خـاک مهـربـانـان این دیـار مهـربـانـی کـی سـر آمـد شهر یـاران راچـه شد
Hafiz, secrets divine nobody knows, stay silent Whom do you ask, why isn't our turning fate now on the mend?	حـافـظ اسـرار الهـی کـس نـمـی دانـد خـموش از کـه مـی پـرسـی کـه دور روزگـاران راچـه شد

18
AMMI

I know quite a lot about Ammi's family history, having imbibed it first hand, mostly from Ammi and my maternal family. Ammi drip-fed us with the nectar of her idyllic childhood, which turned sour after the Partition of India. Unlike Wazir Khala, who could not let go of her past, Ammi accepted it as the bittersweet fruits of life.

Ammi's family was of Yemeni descent. They lived in Rohtak, seventy kilometres north-west of Delhi, in a fort perched high on a barren and bleak hill, overlooking the town. The fort must have been a grand imposing structure in its heyday, with tall towers and turrets, but as Wazir Khala remembered, when the family lived there, it only had one of its four towers intact. The massive metal studded gates hung loosely on their hinges. The approach road was a shallow slope to allow elephants to climb with provisions. The fort and the surrounding farmland were bestowed on Ammi's forefather, Qazi Qawam-uddin Siddiqui, by the Mughals, for the family's services to the throne.

By 1947, the clan had grown to over 500 extended families, all living together, with their residences interlinked, beehive fashion, sharing the bounty of the land, intermarrying and further populating the fort. The labourers who cultivated the farmland, lived at the foot of the hill and had served the occupants of the fort for generations. In return, they were rewarded in kind from the annual harvest.

In a rare flurry of nostalgia, for Amma Ji was not a lady of many words, told us why she was named Shehzadi by her father, Arshad Ali. Emulating the regal excesses of the Mughals, he lived a carefree existence, hunting deer and game and even an occasional tiger on his land, accompanied by an eager entourage. The prodigality of his bounty was such that he was nicknamed *Badshah*. Hence, it was only befitting that his firstborn be named Shehzadi. He couldn't foretell, of course, what fate had in store for his little princess.

My maternal grandmother was both Shehzadi by name and Shehzadi by nature. As was the custom of the times, the women seldom ventured out of the fort. Tutors and doctors, as well as vendors armed with their best wares – the latest printed silks, bangles and shoes – served the fort. When the women visited within the fort, they were carried in embellished palanquins.

Shehzadi grew up in the fort in the traditional manner. She was married in her late teens to Fallahuddin Siddiqui (Abba Ji), a respectable young man from within the family.

'He was a humble history graduate from St Stephen's College, Delhi, and the *only* graduate in the fort; also the *only* Muslim to attend St Stephen's College because he was an excellent cricketer. He was the first to work in an office,' emphasized Amma Ji with pride. 'He was a civil servant at the Survey of India, in Delhi.

There was always a carnival-like atmosphere at the fort whenever there was a special occasion such as a marriage, birth of a child, or *Eid*, with merchants clamouring with fabrics, jewellery, shoes and household goods. But my wedding was something else. The whole fort was engulfed in frenzied activity and the celebrations lasted for weeks. There was singing and dancing, henna nights and bangles and new colourful outfits for all, including the servants. Food and sweets were distributed amongst friends and family, as well the poor. My father spared no expense!' remembered

Amma Ji smiling. 'Trails of servants carried my dowry in a procession that was a spectacle in itself. Furniture, clothes, jewellery, kitchen utensils and several servants were dispatched to my new lodgings. There was *nothing* my father didn't provide.'

'Didn't you mind that Abba Ji was poor?' we asked.

'He wasn't exactly poor; he just wasn't as rich as my father. Besides, your Abba Ji was a caring pious man. His family name, breeding and education ensured security. My father had given me a generous dowry as well as the servants who had raised me, so my henna never faded and I never had to lift a finger. The annual harvest was distributed amongst all the inhabitants of the fort and the farmhands, so I continued to live in my accustomed lifestyle.'

'And Abba Ji didn't object to all the singing and dancing and the excesses?' we asked in amazement.

'He wasn't so religious then,' smiled Amma Ji. 'Besides, his mother and sister were very lively; they delighted in celebrating the first marriage in their family. And who would have dared question my father?'

Seeing Amma Ji in such a good mood, I plucked

up the courage to ask, 'Amma Ji, why does Abba Ji always hide his thumb?'

She laughed. Patting me gently she explained, 'Your Abba Ji was a brilliant cricketer. He broke his thumb while playing cricket. When it wouldn't heal, part of it was amputated and he had to give up cricket. He doesn't like to talk about it.'

Abba Ji was very appreciative of the fact that despite having come from a privileged background, Amma Ji never made any unreasonable demands. But, some years later, when Abba Ji was posted to Dalanwala, a hill station near Dehradun in northern India, Amma Ji was beside herself and Abba Ji at a loss to console her. Men from the fort seldom ventured beyond Delhi. Having heard the gossip about men cheating on their wives, and never returning from distant lands, Amma Ji feared that some local woman would entice her handsome, naïve husband and she would be left waiting at the fort with her little girl Wazir, and baby boy Zia.

Abba Ji left teary-eyed Amma Ji and the children with the extended family, promising to call for them when he found suitable accommodation. Amma Ji soon joined Abba Ji in Dehradun, where Jugnu (Ammi) and Tauqeer Khala, her non-identical twin sister, were born. Unable to feed the twins, Amma Ji employed a young widow as a wet nurse – *Aya Amma*. She was happy to help Amma Ji with the care of her children in return for board and lodging. The family continued to live an idyllic life in Dehradun, with the addition of three more sons – Saba, Zaka and Fida.

During World War II, the British in India forcibly enlisted local Indians into the British army to fuel the demand for manpower in Europe. All government employees were drafted into the military according to their rank, and Abba Ji became Major Fallahuddin Siddiqui. He was transferred to Maymyo in Burma, another lush, picturesque hill station, where he delivered maps to soldiers in the field, in a small plane.

Mamo Saba has vivid memories of the day the Japanese bombed Burma and the resulting trauma. Oblivious to war, he was playing with his siblings in the parade ground of the army barracks, when hundreds of planes appeared overhead, blocking out the bright daylight. Darkness descended, turning the sunny day into night. Unaware of their significance, the children chased the planes in excitement. Their screams of glee soon turned to terror and panic when the planes dropped napalm bombs, which set everything alight. The tranquillity of the afternoon was shattered by wailing sirens, fires, blood and gore. Just as Amma Ji dashed out of the house in search for her brood, a bomb fell on the house, engulfing it in flames. She gathered her terrified children and took shelter in a nearby trench.

When panic-stricken Abba Ji returned, making his way through the chaos and dodging the explosions, he was horrified at the spectacle. Stepping over corpses, burning bodies and debris, with tears soaking his beard, he frantically called for his children. 'Zia! Saba! Where are you?'

Kullo, the family dog, ran up to him, barking. Wagging her tail wildly, she pulled at his trousers. Initially, Abba Ji tried to shoo her away, but soon realized she was telling him something. The dog led him to her puppies. When Abba Ji picked up the pups, Kullo guided him to the trenches, where Abba Ji found his petrified family, huddled together amongst other survivors.

Wazir Khala remembers how the bewildered family fled Maymyo with just the clothes on their backs, with bombs falling left, right and centre, among chaos, death, and destruction. Little Saba continued to scream for his dog, Kullo, as they fled. They escaped with their lives watching beautiful lush Maymyo engulfed in flames and reduced to rubble. Baby Fida bit Amma Ji's shoulder each time a bomb fell. Ammi still blames hers and her sibling's hearing loss on the carpet-bombing of Burma. Wazir Khala still shudders at the memory, bringing back the stench of gunpowder and burning flesh.

In the following days, the family travelled by plane, truck, steamer and bullock cart, as well as on foot, to finally reach Lashio, where they moved from one refugee camp to another. After this macabre existence among the dead and the dying, Abba Ji ushered all the women and children, including his family, into a cargo plane. He got off at the last minute, remaining behind to oversee the safe evacuation of the remaining refugees. His traumatized family was left screaming as the aircraft took off without him.

The plane landed in Mandalay, where the camps were still worse. The squalid bamboo huts were dark, cold and damp, teeming with flies, mosquitoes and insects they had never seen before. It was rife with disease; bodies remained unburied for days, with no one to claim them or dispose of them. The food was appalling – thin *daal* served with thick stale *rotis*. But after turning up their noses for a day or two, the family was so hungry that they savoured whatever little was served.

At night, the darkness was absolute. Evening brought on an unnatural silence. One was lucky to find even a mouldy jute mat to sleep on. Amma Ji sat up all night, her knees drawn up to her chin, unable to sleep for fear of a snake or scorpion crawling out. Dread of the unknown and hunger gnawed her stomach like a demented demon. Left far behind was the sweet, carefree life of plenty. Ahead lay an uncertain future.

When the Nazim of Hyderabad visited the camp, he was struck by a group of beautiful children, huddled together. He picked up five-year-old Saba and sat him on his knee. Sobbing, Saba told him his Abba Ji and Kullo were left behind. Touched by the despair of the families, the Nazim gave a generous financial donation to the refugees but was unable to help locate Abba Ji.

Amma Ji was beside herself with grief. With no news of Abba Ji, she did what she could to protect her children. She feared for his life and felt totally helpless and alone. She had never before had to communicate with strangers, especially men; now she begged officials to write letters on her behalf to her family in Rohtak and to try to locate Abba Ji, hoping against hope that he was still alive. Touched by Abba Ji's valour and Amma Ji's despair, feisty Miss Walters, a bilingual English lady, helped her badger the officials and fight for food and water for the children.

The refugees were transported from camp to camp, finally arriving at a travellers' lodge in Calcutta, *Mosa Ji ka Musafir-Khana*, run by various political parties. After many desperate months, Taya Nasir, Abba Ji's elder brother located them and took them back to their ancestral home in Rohtak.

When Abba Ji was officially declared lost in action, the entire fort became engulfed in oppressive gloom. Everyone spoke in low hushed voices as if a baby was asleep nearby. Finally, the elders decided to carry out Abba Ji's funeral in absentia, hoping for closure. But Amma Ji refused to believe her husband was gone forever. She enlisted the help of her cousin, Razia, and embarked on a letter writing campaign. Secretly, Razia too, thought Abba Ji would never return, but indulged her cousin thinking she would soon grow tired. But she underestimated Amma Ji's resolve. Razia was surprised by the strength of her conviction as every day Amma Ji dictated a lengthy letter to her missing husband.

Dear Falah, Assalam Alaykum,

I am hoping against hope that you are safe and well and will receive this letter. I wish you had insisted that I continued my education. I feel so ashamed when I have to ask Razia to write on my behalf. She says she doesn't mind but nonetheless - I am practicing. Insha'Allah soon I will write to you myself.

It has now been 93 days since that dreaded day when you so cunningly put us on that plane. I know your reasoning, but we promised to stay together, come what may! Everyone is praying for your safe return. Nasir Bhai has taken to the mosque. He has vowed that he will never miss another namaz if Allah grants his prayers. Your sister also has been giving alms to the poor and has been of tremendous support to me.

I pray that you receive this letter and return home soon. Saba is constantly asking for you and Kullo. All the children miss you terribly though they are too frightened to say anything.

May Allah protect you and return you to us safely.

Your loving wife,

Shehzadi

Despite receiving no reply, Amma Ji continued her letter writing ritual. Nine months later, when everyone except Amma Ji had accepted Abba Ji's absence as a reality, Zaka Mamo was playing hide and seek with his friends when he saw a bedraggled figure climbing the long path towards the fort. Initially he ignored the emaciated, barefooted man covered in blisters and sores, with overgrown beard and nails, thinking he was a beggar, but noticing something familiar in his walk, he looked again. Suddenly he was running down the path screaming in elation, 'Abba Ji! Abba Ji! Abba Ji!'

Soon the whole fort was echoing with chants of, 'Abba Ji! Abba Ji!' Relatives emerged from every corner and smothered him, saying loud prayers of thanks to the Almighty. Amma Ji, Taya Nasir, and the children, sobbed with relief as they hugged him. He had made his way from war-torn Burma to Calcutta on foot, covering a distance of over 1,200 miles.

The overjoyed family gathered around him to celebrate his miraculous return from the dead. Goats were sacrificed; sweetmeats distributed amongst friends and family; generous alms donated to the servants. The celebrations lasted for days.

On his return to his office, he was awarded a medal for valour and was handed the wad of letters from his wife. When he read the heart-wrenching words, they became more valuable to him than the medal. His love and affection for Amma Ji were immeasurably enhanced.

Abbu's story began five hundred kilometres east of Rohtak, in Lucknow. He seldom spoke of his family, hence we knew little but the barebones of his background. What little I learnt was from the only surviving member of his family, his younger brother Nadir Chacha, and through Ammi's correspondence with Dadi Jaan, my paternal grandmother.

Abbu, Syed Azhar Ahmed was the second of ten children, born on 18 June 1925, in Lucknow, into an intellectual family. Of his two sisters and eight brothers, only one sister, Sultanat, and four brothers – Akhtar, Nadir, Asfahani and Ghazenfer – survived. The elder of the two daughters, Asif Jahan, died aged nine, when her *Aya* accidently gave her the wrong medicine, leading to complications.

Dadi Jaan never forgave herself for this tragedy. The other daughter, Sultanat, like her mother, was a stunning beauty and the centre of attention in the male dominated household.

Abbu inherited his height, physique and olive complexion from his father, Syed Afsar Ahmed, and his beautiful features from his elegant mother, Iqbal Jahan. She, with her fair complexion, delicate features and regal mannerisms, was considered a real beauty in the Lucknawi society. Iqbal Jahan was wealthy by birth, but Abbu's father Afsar, was an officer in the British India Steam Navigation Company. He acquired a vast amount of land in a curious manner. After saving a British officer's life, he was told to float a banana tree trunk in the nearby river. All the land from that spot to where the log came to rest, was bestowed on him. He named this vast expanse of land Barisal, Naul Chattay *Bashan Churr* (Floating Island). The acquisition of this land caused envy and enmity in the community and following an unsuccessful attempt to kill his family, he moved his wife and children to his in-laws in Lucknow, since he was often away.

According to my uncle, Nadir Chacha, Dadi Jaan's family lived amongst the elite in considerable style. There was no shortage of space in the house, which had many rooms, arched verandas with marble pillars and exquisite gardens. They even had a Cadillac, a rare privilege at the time. Although Dada Jaan had a sheltered, traditional upbringing, as was the custom at the time, she was schooled at home in etiquette and courtesy, Urdu, English, Persian and Quranic studies, by governesses. With her husband away working, and with plenty of servants at hand, she had very little to do. So she took charge of Shaukat Memorial Girls School, founded by her mother, Kokab Jehan.

I once asked Nadir Chacha how it was that Abbu was so well versed in English, and his handwriting so good.

'Lucknow was the cultural centre of India,' he told me, 'the capital of Uttar Pradesh. The *nawabi tehzeeb*, culture, music, poetry, paintings, architecture and Lucknow's beautiful parks and gardens were renowned throughout the sub-continent. The city was also famous for its elegance and poetic flamboyance. Its splendour and wealth bedazzled even the British. In the absence of television and modern day distractions, and with access to Nawab Sulaiman's library, we read extensively. We could all read Urdu, English, Hindi and even some Sanskrit. Our maternal grandfather, Mirza Ahmed, was a published author and a celebrated poet. He had superb command over Urdu, Farsi, and Arabic as well as English. He was celebrated for his incredible memory and could recite countless poems and couplets from prominent poets. It was through his friend, Nawab Sulaiman, Sheriff of Calcutta, and his foresight that we attended the best English school in the city. Our grandfather oversaw our education and encouraged us to practice handwriting and mental arithmetic and we competed as to who knew the most couplets. If we did as we were told, as a treat we were allowed to accompany our grandfather to the station where he was the station master and watch the trains go by, or to go to the cinema in Hazratganj.

Nadir Chacha described Dadi Jaan sitting, poised on an ivory inlaid *thukht,* propped up by patchwork bolsters, dressed in delicate hand embroidered, pastel coloured *ghararas,* in her hereditary jewellery, graciously receiving visitors. Maids carried silver trays laden with delicate imported china and tiny homemade delicacies – *shami kebabs, gulab jamans –* silently serving the ladies, as Dadi Jaan prepared *paan* from her *nuqsheen,* silver *paandan.*

I imagined Abbu and his brothers sitting in grand surroundings, with carved ornate furniture and fine paintings on the walls, having animated discussions, reciting poetry, like the *nawabi* lifestyle depicted in the Hindi film, *Devdas.* My elegant aunt Sultanat, dressed in exquisite silk saris, rustled about with feminine grace, like Indian film actress

Nargis in *Andaz*, laughing, gesticulating and teasing her brothers. Or perhaps, like the feisty, independent Abida Sultana, the rebel princess of Bhopal, who excelled over her male counterparts in sports, hunted tigers, played with and beat men at polo and even flew a glider.

Nadir Chacha reminisced about visiting the nearby Charbagh Lucknow railway station with his brothers and friends to take in the hustle and bustle of the busy city. He nostalgically recalled that Abbu preferred his grandfather's company to that of other kids his age. He accompanied his grandfather to *mushairas* where poets recited their verses in Urdu and Persian. Abbu began writing poetry at an early age, which he recited in his melodious voice to prominent poets of the day, who listened intently. Through their encouragement and appreciation, he became mature beyond his years. With his looks and excellent singing voice, Abbu's friends encouraged him to try his luck in the Indian film industry. Like any young man, he hankered for fame and fortune. So he sneaked off to Bombay, but before he got a chance to try his luck, he was summoned back by their father and severely reprimanded. Acting and singing were not considered respectable professions for a Syed (direct descendants of Prophet Mohammad [PBUH]). He returned home utterly dejected, his aspirations dashed, his yearnings unfulfilled. He couldn't possibly disobey his father!

Nadir Chacha found employment in Delhi and Abbu joined the British Army as a recruiting officer. With his exceptional stature, impeccable dress sense, confidence and sophistication he stood out among the Indians. He spoke fluent English as well as Urdu, Bengali and Hindi in the polished *Lucknawi* manner, peppered with flashes of wit and humour. His integrity gained him authority and recognition, and he was soon sought after as an interpreter by the British. He travelled with the British recruiting officers throughout Bengal, enlisting men to the war effort. He was paid two Rupees per recruit.

At this point I searched for the family albums and rummaged through old photographs. Among the images of many men no one could now identify, were pictures of Abbu in shorts, with his greyhound; looking dashing in his army uniform; enjoying a picnic with his friends; posing on a bicycle in his white toe-cap Oxfords, cigarette in hand. There is only one surviving faded sepia image of Dada Jaan, dressed in a short sleeved shirt and cotton khakis, casually standing by a chair in the garden. I found a sepia photograph of Dadi Jaan, looking very delicate and elegant in a sari. I can see the striking resemblance to Abbu, with his Assyrian profile, penetrating eyes outlined with thick lashes and a mass of curly hair which he tamed with perfumed oil. They all appeared as remote as the scenes in the miniature prints of Mughal indulgences of a bygone era hanging on our walls.

There were just two pre-partition photographs from Ammi's family – one of Abba Ji without his beard, in a fez, and the other of his brother Nasir, in a procession. The stark contrast of cultures between Lucknow and Rohtak is evident in the two photographs. Abba Ji and most of the men in the procession are dressed in *sherwanis,* wearing fez or turbans, whereas Dada Jaan and Abbu are in Western attire. I made a mental note to ask Ammi how these photographs had survived Partition and to message the family to send me other old photos for my for ever-expanding collection. I also discovered my school reports and exam results and smirked at the red stars I had added to my not-so-impressive B and C grades.

After riffling through the photographs, Nadir Chacha became even more reflective and continued, now in full flow. 'Those were hard times. We didn't have the kind of start in life that many young men have today. Jobs were hard to come by, especially for Muslims in Hindu dominated India under the British Raj. We had seen nobles laying their caps at the feet of the white *Sahibs* because they were high officials. A lot of bootlicking was required even for the most menial jobs, and bootlicking we were not prepared to do! After a lot of struggle, I finally found a job in Burma Shell in Delhi.'

Alarmed by the surge in Hindu-Muslim unrest in the country, Abbu decided to return home to Lucknow, to be with his family. On reaching Delhi railway station, he found the place eerily deserted. After a long uncomfortable wait, the train arrived. Not wanting to stand out in his usual Western clothing, he had decided to dress down. Feeling uneasy in his Muslim attire of white *kurta pyjama* and skull cap, he took a seat in an empty compartment. At the next station, a group of Hindu students boarded the train and Abbu quickly removed and hid his skullcap between his legs. As more Hindu passengers got on, they discussed the riots and killing of Muslims. Abbu, the lone Muslim in the compartment, sat nervously in one corner, listening to their excited chatter, trying not to attract attention.

'They are all bloody traitors, these Muslims! Why should they split our country? If they get to have a separate country, the Sikhs will demand an independent Sikhistan. We can't allow them to fragment India,' shouted one of the men.

'Let them have a separate country, then we'll be rid of them, and all this bloody violence will end,' piped up another young man dismissively.

'No, why let them? We should stay united. We have to re-establish ourselves after the *Angraiz* depart. First, the Muslim Mughals suppressed us, then the *Angraiz*. Let the bloody *Angraiz* leave, then we will teach the Muslims a lesson. The bastard A*ngraiz* have bled us dry, looted our wealth and packed it off to England,' shouted the agitated young man.

'Why blame the Mughals and the *Angraiz*? We allowed it to happen. They took advantage. Anybody would,' replied the first young man.

'Yes, but we all have to work together to get back on our feet once the *Angraiz* have gone.'

The discussion was getting heated. Abbu was relieved to reach Lucknow. He couldn't find a *tonga* to take him home, so he had no choice but to walk cautiously through Hindu Bazaar. As he neared home, he encountered a mob shouting anti-Muslim slogans, 'Leave before you're forced to leave!'

On reaching the main road, he observed a group of Sikhs, armed with *kirpans* and rifles, killing anyone who appeared to be Muslim. Several Hindu men had to prove they were not circumcised to confirm they were, in fact, non-Muslims. Abbu quickly turned into a side lane, where armed military personnel were shooting, throwing fire bombs and stones, while a lone fire engine stood idle.

Abbu turned towards Gole Market, where the Hindus were looting Muslim shops and businesses. Beleaguered Muslim families from the surrounding neighbourhoods were fleeing with whatever they could carry. The crazed mob surrounded an unarmed Muslim family. They shot the only man in the group and snatched the baby from its mother's arms. A burly Sikh forced a hosepipe into the baby's' mouth and drowned him, while another pinned a toddler to a tree with his *kirpan*. The terrified and helpless mother screamed hysterically for help, but no one dared intervene. Everyone rushed past, avoiding eye contact, scrambling to board the few trucks taking the refugees to safety. The men ripped off the woman's *burqa* and tore her clothes to shreds. Helpless and unable to watch the despair and grief in the woman's face, Abbu dashed into the nearby mosque on Mandir Marg. His senses heightened like a startled animal, he was halfway up the minaret before he realized he had omitted to remove his shoes. Breathlessly he pulled them off and shoved them under his armpit and then sat in the tower, from where he had a bird's eye view. Silently he watched from his vantage point.

The 'pack' moved on, leaving behind a river of blood and ripped bodies like meat in a butcher's shop.

Alone with his thoughts, Abbu couldn't get the woman's terrified face and blood-curdling screams out of his head. He cursed himself for not helping her, but knew they would have killed him had he intervened. He kept wondering if he had done something, whether others might have helped. Gritting his teeth, he held his head in his hands and waited for the violence to subside. When he sheepishly ventured out, an armoured car pulled up and Lord Ismay, Viceroy Mountbatten's Chief of Staff, dismounted. Men emerged from the lanes and surrounded him like ants around sweetmeat.

'What are you doing about our safe transit to Pakistan? Where is the army? What are you doing about this violence?' they shouted.

'Calm down, calm down, peace is restored, and there is no more violence,' announced Lord Ismay.

Abbu, still traumatized and enraged by what he had witnessed, boldly walked up to him and pointed to the bedraggled Muslims still arriving and shouted, 'What are you talking about? It's easy for you to say all is well, sitting in your armoured car. Are you blind to the violence and looting around you?'

There was a sudden silence as if cold water had been poured on a roaring fire. Shocked at a *native* speaking to him in such a manner, the irate Lord Ismay glared at Abbu and without another word, got back into his car and drove away, still staring at him with fiery eyes.

When Abbu finally reached home, he found that his childhood friend had been shot dead, and his younger brother Ghazenfer, had been shot in the leg by a Hindu sniper. Abbu was furious. He stormed out and shouted at his Muslim neighbour, 'You are sitting smug outside your house with a rifle while that bastard Bunya has killed Agha and shot Ghazenfer!'

He snatched the man's rifle and clambered up to the roof and scrambled down to the balcony, to a vantage point, and took out the Hindu gunman with a single shot. It was only after pulling the trigger that he realized what he had just done. Sweat prickled his skin and the roots of his hair. He was shocked by his own action. He was relieved that he did not know the man he had just killed and comforted himself thinking the gunman hadn't hesitated to kill his neighbour or injure his brother. Given half a chance, he would have killed him too. Encouraged by Abbu's actions, other

Muslims came out into the street, armed with whatever weapons they could find, and formed a self-appointed vigilante group to guard the neighbourhood.

Inwardly, Dadi Jaan was proud of her son for avenging Agha, who was like a son to her, but was worried about the consequences of his action. She was especially concerned about her niece, who lived in a particularly volatile part of the city. She begged Abbu to get news of her. Abbu changed into his army uniform and persuaded a driver, paying him 100 rupees, to take him and Nadir Chacha the distance of one kilometre. The driver dropped them off beside the *gali* to their cousin's house. Abbu didn't want to think about the unpleasant smell that entered his nostrils from the eerily quiet *gali*. Signs of looting were evident from the open doors and broken windows. The house had been ransacked and looted. Clothes, pots, pans and ornaments were strewn everywhere. Unable to pass by the open *Quran* lying face down on the floor, he picked it up, kissed it and touched it to his brow. Clutching it tightly and reciting prayers, he moved cautiously from the courtyard towards the bedrooms, looking for his cousin.

Drawn by the buzzing of a multitude of flies to the mess by the table, he moved closer. He flinched on seeing the naked, headless torso of his cousin's husband, in a pool of congealed blood. Abbu looked around. The severed head lay several feet away; eyes wide open, his circumcised penis sticking out of his mouth like a demonic, swollen tongue, his hair mangled with blood. Choked with hate, Abbu wondered where was God when his finest creation ran amuck.

Devoid of emotion, Abbu looked around for something to cover the body with. From the corner of his eye he noticed a slight movement in the stack of rolled up hessian mats standing on their ends. As he rushed towards it, his cousin Sadiqa emerged from one, pointing at the other mats. As Nadir Chacha moved the mats, his ten-year-old niece, Riffat, appeared from one and collapsed like a new born foal at his feet, and little Nadeem emerged from another. For a split second they stood terrified. In silence they stared at the mess on the floor. Abbu grabbed Sadiqa by the wrist, slung Riffat like a sack of potatoes over his shoulder; Nadir Chacha seized young Nadeem by the waist and they ran out of the house.

They dragged a dumbfounded Sadiqa, for the first time in her adult life without a *dupatta*, without a *burqa*, without her shoes, through the street with raging fires, dead bodies, and mayhem, dodging crowds of men. Men who harboured years of resentment and anger, embittered by the loss of family members and all their worldly possessions; they stood in groups, eyes darting from side to side, ready for revenge, ready to be ignited like dynamite awaiting a single spark. Sadiqa ran like a wide-eyed zombie until they reached home.

Dadi Jaan was pacing by the door. Relieved at their safe return, she raised her hands to the sky and exclaimed, *'Ya Allah tera shukar!'* She hugged them repeatedly, continuing to recite prayers of thanks to the Almighty. Sadiqa, who hadn't uttered a word, began to scream hysterically. While Dadi Jaan took care of her, Sultanat attended to the children. Young Nadeem, who had been such a little chatterbox, never spoke again.

No amount of prayer wiped from Abbu's mind the images whirling in his head. Whenever he closed his eyes, he saw the petrified face of the woman he had not helped. It mortified him that he and the others had watched and done nothing. The guilt and sense of complete helplessness remained with him. Those pleading eyes continued to haunt him whenever he closed his eyes. That day, something deep within him, perhaps humanity, died. Trying to shut the lid on his memories he instinctively began reciting verses from the *Quran*. He buried the incident deep within the depths of his being.

Locking up his guilt, he threw away the key. But he knew he would carry it with him always. The images churned in his mind like a restless worm which hibernated sometimes, but *never* left.

20
ABANDON FORT

After the harrowing departure from Burma, life gradually resumed near normalcy. Abba Ji finalised the marriage of his eldest daughter, Wazir, with Shahid, an educated and handsome young man within the family. Over the years Amma Ji had been accumulating gold and silver jewellery, furniture, brass and steel pots and pans, bedding and a vast array of outfits for her daughter's trousseau. She procured *ghee*, sugar and other provisions, rationed due to the war, from other family members, in preparation for the upcoming celebrations.

Suddenly things turned ugly and the political situation came to a head. The country began to descend towards sectarian civil war. Even before the exact border between India and Pakistan was disclosed, violent skirmishes between Hindus and Muslims escalated into daily occurrences. The patchwork of communities that had coexisted in harmony now became suspicious of each other, a bubbling cauldron of hate, ready to sear all who came within reach. Reports and stories of Hindus and Sikhs slaughtering entire Muslim families spread like Chinese whispers throughout India.

Beneath the veneer of calm was unnerving fear. The whole fort was astir, like the rest of the country. The lifelong *chowkidar,* who had guarded the gates; the maids who prepared and served the food, helped raise the children, and cleaned devotedly, all looked menacing. Everyone looked at each other with suspicious glances, watching for signs of anything untoward. How could one explain to a child the paranoia of a mother about sending him to school? Why he could no longer visit his childhood friends and why the *aya* that had cared for him more than his own mother, upped and left?

The doors and windows that were never locked, that had no locks, were barred and firmly shut, preventing the children who had always played outdoors, from venturing out; prohibiting them from playing with their lifelong friends. Neighbours who had popped in and out all the time to exchange gossip, food and sweetmeats, no longer did so. The happy, joyous community turned dull, hushed and spooky. Everything looked rundown as the home help departed. Fear fractured the society, leaving everyone suspicious of each other.

***

With the date for independence and Partition brought forward from June 1948 to August 1947, and the border lines declared, men congregated in segregated, secret meetings to exchange news and make plans to protect their families without alarming them more than was necessary. They gathered knives, swords, stones and whatever else they could find to defend themselves. They filled huge *mutkas* with water mixed with chilli powder to pour on anyone who tried to scale the walls of the fort. Abdullah, a lifelong, loyal servant, skimmed the gathering for news and kept Amma Ji abreast of the discussions taking place in the men's meetings, preparing her for any eventuality. But as the riots escalated, the men decided they had no choice but to abandon the fort and leave for Pakistan.

The women too, made plans. They exchanged stories in hushed tones and fretted over their menfolk, babies, sick mothers, young unmarried girls and pregnant daughters. They planned how best to hide their precious jewellery and what they could cook and take on the imminent journey. They used whatever provisions they had to prepare dry food, *channas, rotis,* to take with them.

Amma Ji's only sister was married to Syed Hamid Ali, son of one of the wealthiest constructors in Delhi – Syed Nawab Ali. He had built Connaught Place, Palam Airport and the Parliament House, among other prominent buildings in Delhi. She abandoned her home, Hamid Manzil on Connaught Place, and beseeched Abba Ji to leave India on the plane they had chartered to take the family and servants to Pakistan. Abba Ji refused to relinquish his official duties as he was involved in organising the evacuees' departure. Amma Ji, having almost lost her husband once before, declined to leave without him.

Till now, Amma Ji had only known the fruits of possession. She had no idea about the mechanics of family management. She had never had to worry about anything other than what food to prepare for the day, for even that was dictated by the sacks of seasonal fresh fruit and vegetables that were delivered to the house daily. Now she was suddenly left without servants and most importantly, the cook. Finding a replacement was out of the question. She scurried around trying to run her household as best she could, warning the children to stay close and look out for each other. Amma Ji was particularly concerned about her six-month-old sickly baby, Tauseef, who could only digest goat's milk. Handing Tauseef to her eldest daughter, Wazir, Amma Ji gathered a few possessions to take with her and buried her ancestral jewellery in a trunk under the old *peepal* tree, hoping to retrieve it someday.

Abba Ji organised travel plans for all the occupants of the fort, most of whom, barring a few servants, were relatives. On the day of the departure, the fort was as busy as a disturbed anthill. Abba Ji gathered the children, instructing them to wear another outfit on top and Wazir to don one of Amma Ji's *burqas*. Wazir had never worn a *burqa* but didn't have the nerve to protest to her father.

'I am not wearing a *burqa*,' she muttered under her breath to Amma Ji.

'Do as you're told or be ready to be abducted by the Sikhs,' replied Amma Ji curtly as she rushed off to usher the children into the waiting *tongas*, not giving Wazir a chance to respond.

'Take off those bangles and your earrings. The Sikhs have chopped off hands and ripped ears,' warned Abba Ji as Amma Ji was putting on her *burqa*.

Amma Ji removed her jewellery and handed it to Abdullah, who placed it in his skull cap and stuffed it into the bedding he was holding. Then they all boarded the *tongas* to go to the railway station.

Abba Ji had booked a train compartment for his immediate family in the specials that were taking migrants to Pakistan, guarded by the Frontier Force. Even before they reached the railway station, armed Sikhs looted the few belongings, including the food, milk and water they had brought with them. The railway station itself swarmed with people, littered with bundles and belongings. In the chaos it was impossible to prevent anyone from boarding the train and people piled in. Amongst anguished screams and shouts, gesticulating men stuffed their families into the packed train. Women clambered on, dragging their shrieking children. Male elders sat by the windows. The youngsters, especially the girls, sat hidden within, their faces blackened with mud and shoe polish. Boys clambered onto the roof. Finally the train left the station amongst shouts of *Allah O Akbar*. As it gathered speed, the overladen train, spilling the weak and unsteady, made its way towards Pakistan by night, and stopping in jungles by day.

Throughout that nightmarish journey, people peered nervously through the windows and watched Sikh soldiers brandishing severed heads on swords like trophies; the headless torsos mutilated by dogs and vultures. The elders tried to shield the youngsters from these atrocities but it was impossible. Countless families made their way on *tongas*, bullock cart and on foot, carrying the old and the feeble on their backs. Barefoot children, men and women, silently trudged on with deep despair and fear in their eyes. No one dared to leave the train, not even to relieve themselves. With the passengers sitting in absolute silence in their own waste, with only the occasional muffled cry of a baby, unable to dispose of the bodies of the weak who had succumbed to heat, hunger and thirst, the train sped past stations, snaking through jungles.

Having lost the goat's milk to the looters and unable to breastfeed baby Tauseef, Amma Ji clung to the whimpering infant, who was now too weak even to cry out loud. Helplessly she looked at her baby's tiny fingers clinging to her thumb for dear life. She pressed her shrivelled breast to her lips, hoping against hope, praying for just a few drops of milk. Eventually, the baby's whimpering too, stopped. Amma Ji continued to cling to her lifeless baby.

Abba Ji forced his way out at a station and asked a Sikh to allow him to fill a pot with water for the children. The response was, 'Our children had to drink urine; you do the same.' 'We would rather let them die than give them urine!' Abba Ji replied helplessly.

Wazir Khala tried to peep out of the window. A

soldier called out, 'Oh you daughter of *Huwa*, hide your beautiful face before the Sikhs grab you!'

Fortunately the train had stopped in the jungle when Afshan went into labour. Her mother, a brave sister and her brother, helped her out of the train and accompanied her into the pitch darkness of the jungle for some space, but were unable to save her. She bled to death after giving birth to a dead baby. Unable to bury them, they had no choice but to leave them under the bushes.

The twenty-four hour journey from Delhi to Lahore took three days and four nights. It was when the train finally reached the Wagah-Attari border that the young boys dared to shout *Allah-O-Akbar, Pakistan Zindabad!* The petrified passengers were helped out of the train at Lahore. They had made it alive to Pakistan.

Pakistan *zindabad* indeed!

21
FAMILY SPLIT

Dadi Jaan was a wise old lady. She had great misgivings about migrating to an alien land and was not in favour of moving, preferring to accept her lot in her familiar surroundings. She valued Abbu and Nadir Chacha's opinions since they were wordly and well informed about current affairs, and judging from what was happening around her, she feared anarchy after the British departed. She was particularly worried about her grandchildren, Bulbul and Ahsen, her daughter-in-law, and her beautiful daughter, Sultanat, for reports of kidnapping and rape were rife.

Abbu and his brother, Nadir Chacha, were actively involved with the Muslim League (the political party founded by Muhammad Ali Jinnah, that led to the demand for Partition, resulting in the creation of East and West Pakistan). They believed they would have a more secure future amongst Muslims in Pakistan. Their siblings, Akhtar and Asfahani Chacha, were against the move. They harboured great resentment against the British for two hundred years of colonial oppression and blamed them for the 'divide and rule' policy and for inciting hatred amongst Hindu, Muslims, and Sikhs, who had happily coexisted for centuries. They refused to uproot themselves and leave behind all that was dear and familiar, preferring to be buried in the land of their forefathers.

Having witnessed the heated, polemical discussions between her sons for months, Dadi Jaan knew deep down that it was futile to try to make her sons agree to stay. Still, she tried in vain to persuade them to remain together and united in these uncertain times. Gone were the happy, poetic exchanges between her sons; of teasing and laughter, where conversation was treated as a fine art, and verbal prowess and dexterity regarded as scintillating. No one seemed to talk anymore. Everyone argued. Every gibe, every remark pierced like a dart. Every mealtime ended in a verbal eruption. The conflicting ideals of her headstrong sons created a febrile atmosphere in the house and left Dadi Jaan sobbing speechlessly. Every day there was an angry explosion of some kind as if someone had lit an ammunition dump to inflict deliberate wounds.

Like everyone else throughout India, on 3rd June 1947, Abbu too, sat glued to the radio along with the whole family, to listen to the live broadcast by the Muslim and Hindu political leaders on All India Radio, about the decision to partition India.

Jinnah said: *The statement of Government, embodying the plan for the transfer of power to the peoples of India, has already been broadcast and will be released to the press and will be published here and abroad tomorrow morning. It gives the outline of the plan for us to give it our most earnest consideration. We have to examine it coolly, calmly and dispassionately. We must remember that we have to take the most momentous decisions and handle grave issues facing us in the solution of the complex political problem of this great sub-continent inhabited by 400,000,000 people.*

The world has no parallel of the most onerous and difficult task which His Excellency had to perform. Grave responsibility lies particularly on the shoulders of Indian leaders. Therefore we must galvanise and concentrate all our energies to see that the transfer of power is assisted in a peaceful and orderly manner. I most earnestly appeal to every community and particularly to Moslems in India to maintain peace and order. We must examine the plan, its letters and spirit and come to our conclusions and take our decisions. I pray to God that at this critical moment he may guide us to enable us to discharge our responsibilities in a wise and as statesmanlike manner having regard to the sum total of the plan as a whole.

It is clear the plan does not meet in some important respects our point of view, and we cannot say or feel that we are satisfied or that we agree with some of the matters dealt with by the plan. It is for us to consider whether the plan as presented to us by His Majesty's Government should be accepted by us as a compromise or a settlement. On this point I do not wish to prejudge. The decision of the Council of the All India Moslem League which has been summoned to meet on Monday, 9th June, and its final decisions can only be taken by the conference according to our constitution, precedence and practice....

I cannot but express my appreciation of the sufferings and sacrifices made by all classes of the Mussalmans, and particularly the great part that the women of the Frontier played in the fight for our civil liberties. Without a personal bias, and this is hardly the moment to do so, I deeply sympathise with all those who have suffered and those who died and whose properties were subjected to destruction, and I fervently hope the Frontier will go through this referendum in a peaceful manner, and it should be the anxiety of everyone to obtain a fair, free and clean verdict of the people of the Frontier.

Once more I most earnestly appeal to all to maintain peace and order.

Pakistan Zindabad!

Nehru said: *Today, I am speaking to you on another historic occasion when a vital change affecting the future of India is proposed. You have just heard an announcement on behalf of the British Government. This announcement lays down a procedure for self-determination in certain areas of India. It envisages on the one hand the possibility of these areas seceding from*

India; on the other it promises a big advance towards complete independence. It is with no joy in my heart that I commend these proposals to you, though I have no doubt in my mind that this is the right course. For generations we have dreamt and struggled for a free and independent united India. The proposals to allow certain parts to secede, if they so will, is painful for any of us to contemplate. Nevertheless, I am convinced that our present decision is the right one even from the larger viewpoint.

The formal date of independence was set as15th August 1947.

Dadi Jaan wept as she listened to the broadcast.

'Why are you crying Ammi *Hazoor?* We should be celebrating that we will *finally* be free – free from being ruled over by foreigners who treat us worse than animals,' said Abbu.

'I *am* happy, but also frightened of what this means for our family and millions like us. I am with Akhtar on what he says – this is where we were all born. This is *our* country, *our* land. This is our home but…'

'How will we know where Pakistan is?' interrupted Sultanat.

'I suppose they will print maps in the newspapers,' Abbu said, shrugging his shoulders.

'But so many people can't get newspapers, can't even read, especially in the villages.'

'They'll announce it on the radio too.' Turning to his mother. 'Ammi *Hazoor*, I don't know how to say this to you, so I will say it as is: I have been given a choice to remain in the Indian army or move to Pakistan and join the Pakistani army. I have decided to join the Pakistani army.'

'You have made that decision?' asked Dadi Jaan, rather sternly.

Abbu nodded without making eye contact, then said haltingly, 'I think it's in our interests that we *all* move to Pakistan... I have said I will join the Pakistani army.'

'Why should we leave our ancestral homeland and move to God knows where?' shouted Akhtar Taya. 'Have you forgotten who you are? Speaking English and dressing like the *goras* doesn't make you an *Angraiz*. The *goras* will never consider a *kala Angrez* their equal!'

Abbu knew his announcement would result in fireworks, and he had vowed to be polite and respectful to his elder brother.

'You are all as different as the fingers of this hand,' implored Dadi Jaan, waving her bejewelled slender hand dramatically. 'But still you must stay united, for individually these fingers are useless, utterly useless,' she emphasized, shaking her head. Tears rolled down her cheeks. 'You *must not* let them divide us like our country. We *must* stay together.'

'Ammi *Hazoor*, Ghazenfer and I too, have decided to move to Pakistan. We have to pay a price for freedom,' added Nadir, patting Dadi Jaan's hand gently and wiping her tears.

'Freedom nurtured on the blood of innocents,' Dadi Jaan sobbed.

'Ammi *Hazoor*, please don't cry. I hate to see you cry,' pleaded Abbu, supplicating the woman he adored.

'God knows what we have to face in the coming days. At least stay united for now.' Dadi Jaan continued to sob, blowing her nose in her handkerchief.

'The British have ruled for over two hundred years; once they leave our very existence will be threatened. How can you expect to live with the Hindus, when even our shadows defile them?' pleaded Abbu.

'How can *you* walk away from what has been ours for centuries? Everything we have is *here*, Abba Jaan's grave is *here*, *all* our forefathers' graves are *here*,' Akhtar Taya stood up and shouted.

'Bhai Sahib, our forefathers will not rise out of their graves to help us when the Hindus annihilate the Muslims once the British have gone,' snapped Nadir. 'They haven't forgotten or forgiven us for having ruled over them for hundreds of years. They *will* take revenge. You are blind to their prejudices that are destroying our culture and religion. You sit cocooned in the mosque praying for a miracle. We have witnessed first-hand the nature and effect of violence and self-preservation on seemingly rational, humble human beings. We have watched the most timorous of men turn into demons, pushed to desperation and rage when it concerned their loved ones. You have not seen...'

'Yes, yes, I don't know anything! *You* know what is best for us all. It was fine for you to live amongst them yesterday; why so different today?' asked Akhtar Taya.

'Yesterday we were asleep. Today we have woken up! Have you forgotten our lifelong neighbour killed Agha and injured Ghazenfer? He wouldn't have hesitated to shoot us all! Have you already forgotten what they did to poor Riffat's husband? She and her children will never be normal after what they witnessed. Can't you see what is happening around you? If we don't go now, we will be mired.' Abbu tried not to raise his voice amongst his elders.

'It was better to have the British ruling over us

than the Hindus,' Dadi Jaan added, sighing deeply as she passed *paan* to her quarrelling sons.

'We have long burnt that boat, Ammi *Hazoor*. That's no longer an option. We have to prepare for sacrifice. Our mere existence is threatened,' Abbu said with a forced smile.

'Have you forgotten how Dyer ordered his men to open fire on unarmed women and children in Jallianwala Bagh, killing more than a thousand innocent people? The *goras* don't consider us human. They crush us underfoot like vermin,' yelled Nadir.

'Do you have to bring that up?' asked Asfahani. 'Dyer was an arrogant fool.'

'Yes, but I don't expect them to be sympathetic to us now,' added Nadir. 'They have milked us dry and now that we have nothing left, they are running away with their tails between their legs, without a care for what happens to us after they leave. This Mountbatten they have sent – he's no different from Dyer. He has brought forward the date of Partition from June 1948 to August 1947, knowing it will cause chaos. He's scared he will lose his wife to Nehru if he doesn't leave India soon!'

'What do you mean?' asked Sultanat, intrigued.

'Haven't you noticed Edwina and Nehru's pictures in the papers? She appears more with

Nehru than with Mountbatten. They say they are inseparable,' Asfahani replied with a snide grin.

'Speculation, that's all it is,' said Abbu. 'Don't believe everything they print in the papers. They make a mountain out of a molehill.'

'There's no smoke without fire,' smiled Asfahani.

'They make a Mountbatten out of a molehill!' Sultanat said, sniggering.

Dadi Jaan gave them a stern look of disapproval. The boys felt the force of their mother's frown all the way across the room and changed the topic.

'If the Congress is willing to give Muslims twenty-five per cent representation in parliament, why should we separate?' asked Sultanat.

'The Muslims in Congress are being duped to give a secular appearance. Do you know what Nehru said to Jinnah in parliament? "We will see about that after the British have left." He has already made his intentions clear,' replied Abbu, shaking his head.

'*Bhai*, why don't you wait till after the British have gone before you decide?' said Sultanat, putting an arm round her brother's neck.

'No, we have to make our intentions clear now.'

'Perhaps you can return to Lucknow after the British have departed.'

'You are hopelessly sanguine. Don't you see, it will be a different country? We'll need documents to travel from Pakistan to Lucknow and from Calcutta to Dhaka, perhaps even visas?'

'Don't be ridiculous...visas indeed!' Akhtar Taya laughed, mocking the idea.

Abbu frowned at his brother, 'Bhai Sahib, with respect, I don't know in which fairyland you are living. *Yes,* even visas. It will be a *different* country, a *different* nationality.'

'Whatever! I have my family to think of. I have a *wife,* children, Ammi *Hazoor and* Sultanat to think of. You have been given an option with safeguards. You go. I am not prepared to give up my patrimony.'

'You and your children have no future here. Your family is *not* safe here. I am willing to take Ammi *Hazoor* and Sultanate with me,' Abbu pleaded.

'You are *not* taking Ammi and Sultanate anywhere. You don't even know where you'll be. At least, we'll be safe in our home *here,*' Akhtar Taya scoffed.

'Safe? Safety is our only concern...' Abbu replied.

'Nonsense!' Akhtar Taya interrupted. 'This is my country, my home. This is where I was born, and this is where I will die. And that's the end of it!' He violently banged his fist on the table and stormed out of the room, slamming the door behind him, cursing the British under his breath. The abruptness of his action silenced his brothers.

Dadi Jaan remained vehemently opposed to splitting the family she had so painstakingly kept united. She tried to reason with both parties. Despite her pleas she could not persuade Akhtar Taya and Asfahani Chacha to move or Abbu, Nadir and Ghazenfer Chacha to stay. She found her family torn apart even before Partition. Much to Abbu's anguish and chagrin, Dadi Jaan refused to be parted from her grandchildren and opted to remain in India, along with her daughter Sultanat and sons Asfahani and Akhtar and his family.

After days of feverish activity, Abbu and Nadir Chacha finally managed to obtain papers to move to Pakistan. Despite lengthy arguments, Akhtar Taya and Asfahani Chacha refused to leave India. Abbu begged his mother to come with him, but she resolved to remain. Abbu felt he was betraying his beloved mother and sister but had no choice but to leave them behind, hoping they would soon see sense and follow. Failing to suppress her grief and amongst tears, lingering embraces and protective prayers, Dadi Jaan bade farewell to her three sons. Sultanat's hysterical cries as they departed haunted Abbu for a long time.

Abbu, Nadir and Ghazenfer Chacha moved to Pakistan. In the days that followed, they helplessly watched the upheaval and destruction of their generation, their continent, their world. Abbu lamented his decision for the rest of his life, for no man should ever have to witness what he did. Just as he had predicted, it was easier for them to visit the whole wide world than the land they once called home, the land of their forefathers – India. He remained bitter about it to the end.

22
ABDUCTED

A fter Partition, contact with those across the border became near impossible. Unable to get news of the family, Abbu feared the worst for his loved ones back home in India. He ceased to live, merely existing. It was the hope of seeing his family, his beloved mother and sister, that kept him alive. Meanwhile, the situation for Muslims in India worsened. Akhtar Taya and Asfahani Chacha realized their mistake in ignoring their brothers' warnings and began making arrangements to abandon their ancestral home and move to Pakistan.

One day when Akhtar Taya returned home, he found his mother unconscious and his wife and children tied up in the store. There was no sign of his sister, Sultanat. Amongst hysterical tears, his wife told him about the gang of armed men who had ransacked and looted the house and abducted Sultanat. Akhtar Taya was left holding his head in his hands in despair. During the following days, the brothers tried every possible means to locate their sister.

Night after night, Dadi Jaan watched helplessly as her glassy-eyed and unshaven sons returned home with no news. She sat on the prayer mat and prayed for the safe return of her precious daughter. At times she prayed that she was dead. She couldn't bear to think what torments her innocent little girl must be enduring. Initially, she faced her ordeal as the will of God, but gradually she began to question God.

She no longer knew what to pray for, or if to pray at all, for she couldn't see any outcome of her prayers. 'Dear Lord, are You testing my faith? Why have You abandoned us so? Why do You not call me? What sin did my innocent child and I commit that You have punished us so? Why did You leave me to witness this torture?' Exhausted, she prayed for her own death.

'This not knowing is unbearable. Had I buried her, I would have died in peace. I hope she is dead. Yes, it is better that she is dead,' she cried.

Dadi Jaan strictly forbade them from informing Abbu, Nadir and Ghazenfer Chacha across the border, hoping against hope that her beautiful daughter would somehow return. Akhtar Taya blamed himself for the disaster. Their world had changed forever; now they could never leave. In the dead of night, he found his mother sitting on her prayer mat, palms upturned, sobbing. Seeing the state of his heartbroken mother, he became totally withdrawn. Had he decided to side with the living and move with his brothers instead of siding with the dead, perhaps none of this would have happened. Helpless and not knowing which way to turn, he turned to God. His devoutness took on an internal meditative form and he withdrew from the world altogether, submerging himself in the *Quran* and a life of prayer.

When Asfahani Chacha visited refugee camps trying to locate his sister, Dadi Jaan insisted on accompanying him. They visited camp after camp, witnessing the squalor and the countless women and children separated from their families. Dadi Jaan began to hate the country of her birth with the zeal of a convert. Unable to locate her precious daughter, she selected some destitute girls, initially as potential teachers in her school. Soon, the few became many and her school turned into a women's refuge.

After Partition, the border between India and

Pakistan remained closed and the postal system was in shambles. When postal communication was finally restored, Abbu managed to get in touch with his mother and brothers. Dadi Jaan continued to write loving letters to her sons in Pakistan, pretending all was as well as could be.

All the Muslims who had left for Pakistan were declared 'evacuees' and their properties declared 'evacuees' properties' and confiscated by the Indian government. As Abbu, Nadir and Ghazenfer had gone to Pakistan, their share of the property was taken away and what little was left, after harassment by petty officials and lengthy cross examinations, was not safe.

Abbu seldom talked about the traumatic move to Pakistan, about his home, his garden with peacocks and fountains, servants and carriages, his friends and family, his past. He had chosen to leave it behind and there he left it. It was almost as if he had blotted it out. Perhaps it was easier that way. He wasn't alone; there were thousands like him. Every family had a tale of woe. Unaware of what had happened with his sister, he felt lucky they had come through it alive. Most people had lost many members of their family; some had lost all. He locked the memories away and sealed his heart, burying his love for his family in the deepest recesses of his being. He had his own demons to fight and expressed his pain and sorrow only in his poetry, dreaming of a world without borders, a world without manmade lines on maps, where men could live and be free to roam the earth, truly free and liberated.

23
PARTITION

On the eve of 14th August 1947, the 27th of *Ramzan*, the holiest of holy nights in the Islamic calendar, when Muslims all over the world pray for peace and forgiveness, India was dissected into three: East Pakistan, West Pakistan, and India. Overnight, nearly twenty million people found themselves on the wrong side of the border. The religious fury and violence Partition unleashed resulted in the biggest exodus of mankind in human history. More than one million Hindus, Muslims and Sikhs died, and countless were wounded. Seventy-five thousand women were abducted, raped or separated from their families.

As the demand for independence from the British came to a head, the political situation in India deteriorated. War-weary and desperate to get out without too much blood on their hands, the British government dispatched Louis Mountbatten to India as Viceroy, with a clear mandate for the transfer of British sovereignty in India to a single independent nation within the Commonwealth, by June 1948.

Mountbatten gathered the four top Indian leaders – Muhammad Ali Jinnah, leader of the All-India Muslim League, Jawaharlal Nehru and Sardar Vallabhbhai Patel, leaders of the Indian independence movement; and Mohandas Gandhi, the religious leader who became an iconic figure for civil rights and the freedom movement in India. Mountbatten listened to their views on a feasible exit strategy and the formation of a united country. Having failed to garner agreement, and with increasing unrest in the country, Mountbatten reluctantly agreed to the partition of India along sectarian lines, by 14-15th August 1947 – dates picked out of thin air by Nehru; the same date as Japan's surrender after World War II. The decision was made public by national radio on 3rd June 1947.

British Prime Minister Atlee summoned a British lawyer, Sir Cyril Radcliffe, from the court where he was a presiding judge, to draw the line on the map of the sub-continent, a place he had never before visited, to segregate it into Pakistan and India. Radcliffe had just five weeks to complete the mammoth task of carving up a land of over 350 million inhabitants, with a multitude of religions and opposing beliefs, languages, and cultures.

Without knowing anything about the land he was segregating and having only out-dated maps and census materials; with no expert support or knowledge of cartography; ignoring its long history and culture; he followed the advice of the Boundary Commission, spilling blood with every stroke. The Golden Bird was carved up like a butcher, as carelessly as a child tearing paper. Brutally segregating railway lines and cities, separating people from their burial grounds, and excising lifelong ties between families and friends, he severed the lives, the past and the future of millions. That line may well have been drawn in human blood since it destroyed so many innocent lives. The greatest impact of this random act was felt in Punjab and Bengal, which were dissected in half, but the effect of Partition in other areas, though it didn't register on the Richter scale, was just as devastating.

Passion ignited by religious fervour sparked an outburst of violence, setting the sub-continent ablaze. Hindus and Sikhs killed Muslims, and Muslims killed Sikhs and Hindus. Divided by religious belief, men fought with swords, knives, metal bars, sticks, spears and axes – almost anything they could find to annihilate each other. Ordinary men turned into monsters and went on frenzied rampages, looting, maiming, raping and killing women of other faiths.

Men chose where to go and the women and children had to follow without question – to an uncertain future. People were deprived of their inheritance and history, mothers were deprived of showing their daughters where they had played as children; fathers of showing their sons the trees they had climbed and the streams they had learned to swim in. They left behind their past, their roots, their identity – the things that made them who they were.

Women blackened their faces and huddled with their children, hiding their terrified daughters. Women whose voices had never been heard outside their homes shouted the names of their husbands; names they had never before uttered. They smothered their children's whimpering. Terror silenced their wails. The men ushered them forward and onwards.

The Grand Trunk Road, built many years before by Sher Shah Suri to unite the country, was now used to segregate it. The Grand Trunk Road had never before been pounded by so many feet in its entire history. Dragging the young, the old and the feeble on overladen bullock carts, wheelbarrows, *ekkas*, bicycles, or on anything that moved, but the majority on foot, carrying bedding rolls, pots, and pans, boxes, sacks, suitcases spilling their contents, destitute humanity jostled forward to unknown destinations with desperate eyes, fearing for their lives. Looking over their shoulders at their lives, their dreams, their past; not knowing what lay ahead, Muslims moved west, and Hindus and Sikhs moved east. They all kept moving, moving, moving...in opposite directions. Young men and boys clung desperately to carts, *tongas*; sat atop trains stuffed with people, animals and luggage.

Unarmed men watched helplessly as their wives, mothers and sisters were raped by armed manic mobs moving from caravan to caravan. Sikhs ripped apart babies and young toddlers like roast chickens in front of their mothers, slashed open pregnant women's bellies with *kirpans*, spilling guts and unborn babies. Women's bodies were desecrated by cutting off their breasts and raped to implant their seed in the 'enemy womb' in the hope of wiping out the 'opposing religion.' As women became the battleground, some set fire to themselves, other jumped into wells. Brothers and fathers slaughtered their own women to save them from humiliation and dishonour.

Might was right for now. A land and its cosmopolitan inhabitants, who had coexisted like the strands in a plait, with centuries of shared culture that had taken even longer to take root, were violently uprooted overnight by the British, who had arrived in India unburdened by conscience. They planted the seeds of segregation with their 'divide and rule' policy, raped India over three centuries and departed in haste without a care for the outcome.

The police and the border security force stood and watched helplessly. The ill-prepared Gurkhas, under inexperienced British command, had no chance against the suppressed lifelong hatred, anger and carnage that ensued. Endless caravans of destitute migrants crossed the north Indian peninsula, disposing the dead on the way. In death there was no distinction between Hindu, Muslim and Sikh. Torn and broken, their lives in tatters, their dreams shattered, caught in land grab and territorial battles, men became demonic beasts, killing for the sake of killing. Their God, in whose name a new nation was being formed, looked on at *Ashraf-ul Mukhlooqat*, His finest creation, transformed into the devil himself. The inescapable, unbearable stench of rotting or burning flesh remained with these people for years to come, sometimes forever.

It wasn't just the living that were desecrated and destroyed; mosques, gurdwaras and temples were set ablaze. The roads, railways and bridges that the British had so meticulously built, the lifelines on which the economic prosperity of India was built, were gashed by explosions. As blood filled craters, it ran over the lawless roads like veins in an old woman's hand. The blood-soaked land was covered with human carcasses, limbs strewn everywhere like autumn leaves, uncaring about laws of proximity in death. The smell of death was tangible. Bloated, purple bodies covered in flies lay strewn on the roadside, in fields and rivers, pecked by vultures, and devoured by dogs, leaving the carcasses for hyenas to pick – like the India the British were leaving behind.

Abbu was part of the border force that was to oversee the safe transit of migrants. What he witnessed in the next few days no man should ever have to see. It remained with him for the rest of his life. As children, we couldn't fathom why Abbu, a lover of good food, so vehemently abhorred the smell of barbeque.

No one, not even the perpetrators and key players of Partition – Mohammad Ali Jinnah, Nehru, Gandhi and Mountbatten – had envisaged the carnage that ensued and the chasm that developed between the two new countries that threatened to destroy the soul of both nations. What for? For a dream to be free of the British and a Muslim country ruled by Muslims for Muslims?

The seeds of Pakistan were sewn in blood-soaked soil. Both Pakistan and India still bear the scars of separatism and the resulting polarity exists to this day. Pakistanis are an emotionally volatile people. Having acquired Pakistan on the grounds of religion, after so much bloodletting, they go crazy when provoked, like a disturbed beehive. They defend their homeland without considering their own safety. Unfortunately, nearly 70 years later, violence remains the answer to political differences and is the dominant currency today. Having fought three wars, both the countries are still reeling from the aftershocks.

British rule in India was marked by violent revolts and brutal suppressions but the British Army marched out of the country with barely a shot fired and just seven casualties. However, injuries inflicted on Mother Earth left gaping wounds that have not yet healed, and may never heal. The wounds continue to bleed. The real tragedy is that despite the sacrifice and enormous loss of life, it was futile. The crowning glory of the British Empire, the Golden Bird, once known as the land on which 'the sun never set', turned into a sunset on which the blood never dried.

Part III

POST-PARTITION PAKISTAN

After 1947

POETRY IS MADE OF LINES, SOME BLACK, SOME WHITE
~ MALINDA

Tell me of lines, mother;
those entities made of countless dots
traced by a mind-finger, inked with blood,
things that say 'this far and no further,'
tell me about the we-they thing,
show it on a map,
point it on the ground.

Tell me, mother,
about tectonic movement,
of earthslips and landslides,
of cartography and carving.
And will you tell me, mother,
if the sepulchral tears that spilled upon your breasts
in the name of freedom,
or upon pain of annexure,
if they were less or more salty
on account of source?
And the blood,
was it less precious, more sacred
because it fell here, or there?

And mother, tell me this as well:
Did it hurt when history's pen was drawn across your
bosom, was it a suturing, is that what you think? And
if so, is it one that itches, or one that adorns, a perfect
blemish that punctuates humanity? An imperfect
something that happened for reasons that will not get
written?

24
PAKISTAN ZINDABAD

Abba Ji was relieved to note that Amma Ji was unconscious as he carried her off the train in Lahore, still clinging to her dead baby. His silent tears soaked into his beard. The train station was hot and airless, unnervingly quiet, with only wild dogs darting amongst corpses buzzing with flies, which littered the platform. The stench was unbearable. The traumatized family held their breath and had no choice but to walk over the slain, blood-soaked bodies. The previous train had arrived in Lahore with every single person mutilated and slaughtered. They silently made their way to Amma Ji's cousin Razia's house, where not surprisingly, they stayed as unwelcome guests in a home already packed with other desperate relatives.

Amma Ji regained consciousness several hours later but continued to have fainting spells. While Abba Ji went about trying to secure permanent accommodation legally, other families occupied the best properties vacated by outgoing Hindus and defended what they had grabbed by force. They knew it was morally indefensible but for now might was right. Overnight, princes became paupers and paupers became princes. The original Muslim residents of the area felt angry about how the newcomers had come and taken over land and property by force, causing further bitterness and uncertainty.

Abba Ji finally managed to get a small house till his 'claim' to the property they had left behind was settled. Shehzadi the princess, and her family, arrived in Pakistan with just the clothes on their backs and began their new life in a house no bigger than their servants' quarters in India. Ammi recalls, 'We only had the clothes we were wearing. When we went to bathe, we washed our clothes and had to wait in the bathroom till they dried. Amma Ji would sob as she traced our ribs and vertebrae.'

One day Zia Mamo said to Abba Ji, 'This wall in the store sounds hollow. Can I knock it down and see what's behind it?'

'Don't do anything so foolish. We are here temporarily.'

'But Abba Ji...'

'No *baita*, I said no,' Abba Ji said decisively as he left for work.

When they later moved to more permanent accommodations, the new occupants did knock down the wall and discovered a safe that had been walled in by the Hindu jeweller to whom the place had belonged.

'Abba Ji wouldn't have kept the treasure had we found it,' remarked Wazir Khala resentfully.

Abba Ji was transferred to the Survey of Pakistan Office in Murree Hills in northern Pakistan, where he was allotted a house in Sunny Bank as part of his claim for compensation for the property left behind. Murree had been a summer retreat for the British and had minimal amenities. Ammi reminisces about playing in the snow, rolling down Sunny Bank and burying pots of sweetened milk that turned to ice cream. But she also remembers the arduous existence in near arctic conditions, with inadequate clothing, without gas and electricity, and firewood expensive and scarce; of having to cook mounds of *chapattis* to feed the large family with eyes burning from the smoke from the damp wood that refused to ignite.

After five long gruelling years, Abba Ji was finally transferred to Rawalpindi, where he was able to claim another house in Bhabra Bazaar, and some agricultural land in Multan, as compensation for the estates they had left behind in India. Meanwhile, Wazir Khala's fiancé in India moved to England and broke off the engagement. There was, however, no shortage of offers of marriage for Wazir Khala, and she finally married Salahuddin Khalo.

Ammi and Tauqeer Khala were forced to drop out from school after the eighth grade since there were no high schools for girls nearby, and because of Amma Ji's constant ill health following the birth of baby Shama. To help finance the education of their brothers, the girls knitted sweaters for the local shops in Moti Bazaar in the evenings. Their financial situation improved a little when Zia Mamo secured a job with the nascent country's newly formed airline, PIA.

25
ABBU AND JUGNO

How Abbu's life panned out in Pakistan and how he got married is a strange story. To avoid living in army barracks, Abbu gave his status as married. He wished to live in private accommodations and participate in the late night *mushairas*. Someone reported him. He faced court martial if he didn't present his wife within the month.

He turned to his friend Ejaz for help. Ejaz gave him the address of someone called Salahuddin, who had several marriageable daughters. Abbu went to the given address. He asked a little girl in the street for directions. She escorted him to her brother-in-law's house. On meeting Salahuddin, Abbu was puzzled as the handsome young man didn't look old enough to have grown-up daughters. Nevertheless, he narrated his predicament.

When the young man heard why Abbu was at his door, he laughed. 'Mr. Azhar, you are at the wrong address. There is another Salahuddin down the road. But it is a blessing indeed that you have landed at my door. I don't have daughters, but I *do* have beautiful eligible sisters-in-law. As for our family, we are Urdu-speaking, as are you. You are from Lucknow. Who can raise an eyebrow regarding your background? As for Salahuddin down the road, he is Punjabi,' he added with a wry smile.

Salahuddin Khalo was immediately taken by Abbu's charm and personality and overwhelmed with his poetry. And Abbu, having met the gorgeous young girl Shama, with her beautiful buttermilk, china doll complexion, and brown curls, decided any sister of this pretty girl couldn't be at all bad. On his way out he asked Shama, 'Can your sisters cook *chapattis*?'

'Of course, they can,' was the quick response.

'Are they as pretty as you?'

The little girl blushed and said, 'Prettier.'

Without setting eyes on his bride-to-be, Abbu decided on the spot to marry into this household. He made it clear to the family from the outset that he lived on his meagre army salary and was unable to afford a lavish wedding. As luck would have it, just before the wedding, he won 2,600 rupees in a crossword competition, which was sufficient to pay for gold jewellery and several fancy outfits, as well as a respectable reception. Within days, he had a wife to present to the army.

On their wedding day, Ammi's sisters and friends continued their teasing late into the night, refusing to let Abbu leave with his wife. Eventually, he whisked the bride off her feet, slung the coy bundle over his shoulder like a sack of potatoes, and dashed out of the house so fast that the women were left aghast. On breathlessly reaching home, he dumped his shocked wife on the bed. She gaped at her abductor, horrified yet bemused. They looked at each other and burst into uncontrollable laughter.

Ammi liked what she saw – a tall handsome man, elegantly dressed in a beige *sherwani*, with olive skin, a mass of dark curls, large sensuous eyes, towering above her. Her porcelain face turned scarlet as he looked tenderly at the petite bundle wrapped in red velvet, adorned with the gold jewellery he had sent her. 'Jugnu!' he exclaimed – the name he uttered with every breath till his last.

Ammi was small in stature but huge in personality. Strangely, she and most of her siblings could have passed off as Mongolian, due to their short height and Chinese features. Compared to Wazir Khala or Shama Khala, Ammi was plain, but she had a very pure face with clear eyes and skin that had an unexplainable allure. Her high fleshy cheekbones and smiling eyes under puffy eyelids, were overshadowed by thick eyebrows. She was totally transformed by her radiant smile into something utterly charming. When she laughed, which was often, her eyes became mere slits. Her flawless fair complexion and petite girly figure belies her age to this day.

Abbu and Ammi made an odd couple. Ammi was fair and tiny, all of five feet. Abbu was dark and appeared taller than his six feet due to his muscular physique. He was well educated, whereas Ammi had not even finished high school. When they went out together, he walked so fast that he frequently had to stop to allow her to catch up. Despite the fact that Abbu was twelve years her senior, and they were as different as can be, they were inseparable; they merged like mercury. The lucky day he accidently stumbled into her home was, he believed, *kismet*, and that his mother's blessings had landed him the most beautiful prize – his beloved Jugnu. His gamble had paid off.

When Abbu informed his mother of his marriage, she was saddened at not being present to bless the union, but happy for them. She gave her consent and on seeing Ammi's photograph commented, '*Eik rung sow dhang!* (A fair complexion is worth a hundred virtues.)

Ammi was deft with her fingers and she could do anything she put her mind to. Unafraid of hard work, she sewed our clothes, knitted our jumpers and did all the laundry. She made her clay stove and the *mutka* stand that housed three clay *mutkas* beside the floor level tap. Most households, even the poorest, had at least part-time help to clean and wash the dishes and clothes, but the only help in our house was Massi, who helped with the most arduous tasks.

Before winter set in, Ammi laboriously unpicked the old quilts. Massi took the cotton to be re-spun. The washed covers would then be refilled with the fluffy cotton. While everyone slept during the afternoon siesta, Ammi and Massi, chattering happily, spent long afternoons stitching intricate designs into the thick pile to hold the cotton in place. In the cold winter evenings, we snuggled in our beds, cocooned in the warmth of the cosy quilts, eating the monkey nuts, pine needles, walnuts and *ravris* that Abbu brought on his way home from work, individually portioned into paper bags for each of us.

Like most traditional Asian wives, Ammi never called Abbu by name. She never called him anything. Instead, she would start her sentences with *sunyai* (listen...). Ammi, like Amma Ji, who at times seemed cold, always appeared composed and in control. She did not show outward displays of affection to anyone, not even to us as children. She was rarely tactile and stiffened if we hugged or kissed her, but we knew she loved us just the same. I have never witnessed any show of affection between my parents – something still not done in public in Asian families, not even an innocent hug, holding hands, or a peck on the cheek. But we knew they loved each other very much.

'Jugnu, Jugnu, Jugnu!' Abbu would repeat, getting louder each time.

'Whaaaaat? I am coming!' Ammi would shout, dropping whatever she was doing and go immediately.

I never heard them argue or quarrel; they always spoke to each other with love and respect. They went everywhere together, and our house echoed with happy chatter and laughter since they both loved to entertain. Visitors were never allowed to leave before downing endless cups of tea and being fed, for Ammi loved to cook. 'Stay, have some tea,' she would insist. 'What's a cup of tea...just hot water.' As she prepared mouth-watering food, she effortlessly dipped into her bottomless well of memories, narrating one anecdote after another.

She had the habit of tilting her head upwards when she spoke, perhaps as a consequence of being so tiny and being married to a tall man. As soon as one story ended, another began, giving no time to the listener to get a word in edgeways or get away. Abbu enjoyed the gaiety of these gatherings, when he took centre stage and recited his poetry to demands for more and more.

With increasing hostilities between India and Pakistan, travel between the countries became impossible. Dadi Jaan continued to write to Ammi and Abbu. When the children were born, her longing to see her daughter-in-law and grandchildren turned to despair. In each letter, she besieged Abbu to send more photographs and somehow arrange to let her see his family just once. *Allah has blessed me with grandchildren, why then does He torment me with separation? I cannot imagine what sin I have committed that He punishes me so*, she wrote.

Time and again Abbu made plans to take his family to meet his mother but due to the unfavourable political situation and financial constraints, the plans never materialised. When the borders were eventually declared open in 1963, Abbu immediately had passports made for the family and Ammi began preparations for the long-awaited trip to India. Unfortunately, Dadi Jaan fell gravely ill and wrote her last aerogram to her son from her deathbed, telling him the secret that had been gnawing away at her heart. When Abbu reached India sixteen years after Partition, all he could do was fall on his knees and weep at his mother's grave.

26
BUD KISMAT

That fateful morning, when Humaira's friends called out to her to join them as they walked to the well to fetch water, she was still cocooned in her quilt and didn't feel like getting out of her cosy bed.

'Go on without me. I'll come later,' she replied.

'Get up, you lazy girl! It's going to rain,' shouted Shamsa, as she walked past the window.

Humaira peeped out at the rain clouds in the sky and stretched lazily, tinkling her bangles. 'No, you go on. I'm still in bed,' she shouted back. Enjoying the morning serenity, she nuzzled into her soft pillow.

Yawning, Humaira finally got out of bed, shuffling her feet absentmindedly till she found her slippers.

She hummed a happy song before making her bed: *Suyyan phir sai aana ray; Aa kai phir na jaana rai…..*

Her mother smiled as Humaira handed her a comb and plonked herself against her knees, placing her breakfast of *hulva*, *parathas* and tea in front of her. Inhaling the fragrance of her hair, her mother couldn't resist kissing her. 'Sit still,' she admonished. Plucking the hairpins from between her teeth she flattened and braided her daughter's thick hair, sticking the hairpins here and there. She adored her daughter's long hair and loved combing it, and Humaira enjoyed being pampered by her mother.

Now, the young girl smiled and looked up fondly at her mother saying, 'Amma, tell me my favourite story.'

'Humaira, when *will* you grow up?' her mother chided in mock annoyance.

Taking a big sip of tea from her favourite bowl, Humaira replied 'Never Maa, never...' and hugged her. A gentle smile played on her mischievous face.

Her mother wondered whether it was the shape of her lips or her sunny disposition that made her appear to be always smiling. 'Ouch! Easy *baita*, you'll crack my ribs.' she said, shaking her head. Once again she began the story... After seven years of marriage, I was still childless. I made the arduous daily pilgrimage, barefoot, *all* the way down the valley to the shrine of *Pir* Haroon Rasheed, for forty days. I lit oil lamps, gave alms to the poor and fed hundreds of orphans, praying for a healthy child. One dark moonless night, there was a loud knock at our door. I was shocked to see the *malung* from the shrine clutching a wriggling bundle. He asked to come in. Startled, I let him in.

He thrust the parcel into my hands saying, '*Allah* has answered your prayers. Someone has left this baby at the shrine. I have no idea what to do with it... God moves in mysterious ways.'

'We can't take this baby!' your father said, shocked. 'Whose is it?'

'I don't know,' the *malung* replied "All I know is that if its mother wanted it, she wouldn't have left it at the shrine in the middle of the night.'

'Take it to the police station,' your father suggested. 'We don't want any trouble.'

'What would the police do?' said the *malung*. 'If you don't take her, she will die.'

As soon as you were in my arms I knew *Allah* had answered my prayers. It was a miracle! Tucked deep within the folds of your shawl was a piece of paper with just one word on it: Humaira.'

Now, looking adoringly into Humaira's beautiful brown eyes, her mother planted a kiss on her dimpled cheek and whispered, '*Baiti* does it bother you that I am not your real mother?'

'No Amma no, *you* are my mother, and that's all I know. No one could have loved me more than you and Abba.' She hugged her mother. 'I just like hearing the loving way you tell the story.' Humaira threw her long plait over her shoulder as she picked up her *mutka*, and mockingly grumbled, 'It's such a long way back with this heavy *mutka*.'

'I know, but…'

'I know Amma, I know,' Humaira giggled, interrupting her mother and playfully imitating the water diviner, with the strange collection of beads round his neck, who had failed to find water in the village, having tried for days, walking up and down all around the village. His stick outstretched and eyes closed, he was reciting verses from the *Quran*. Humaira now kissed her mother and left to fetch water.

At the well beyond the village, Humaira twisted her plait into a loose bun at the nape of her neck, secured her *dupatta*, pulled up her *shalwar* and hummed as she worked the hand pump. Cold silvery-white water gushed out in spurts with each motion, splashing in all directions. She could feel the large mass of her hair uncoil and slide to the ground. Unconcerned with the ends of her long plait getting soaked, she continued to operate the pump.

She heard the sound of hooves before she saw the distant dust cloud. Startled, she stopped humming and looked up. She saw a large group of riders galloping towards the cluster of houses that formed her village, their *kirpans* flashing like twinkling stars as they caught the sunlight. Instinctively, she left the *mutka* and ran as fast as she could towards her home.

Long before she reached her house, the mob arrived in the village. She could hear screams and shouts for help and pleading; she smelt fire and could see flames and smoke spiralling like serpents from burning homes even from a distance. She stopped dead in her tracks and crouched in the long grass, watching the jubilant mob appear from the village with screaming and writhing girls flung across their saddles. She recognized Shamsa from the bright print of her *kameez,* on one of the horses, kicking and shouting obscenities at the burly Sikh who was trying to subdue her by smacking her on her head and face. Amid jubilant shouts of *Waheguru Ji ki Fateh,* and waving their blooded *kirpans* in the air, the mob charged in her direction like a furious whirlwind, raising a cloud of dust.

Petrified they might have seen her, Humaira hid in the grass, numb with fear. When the riders got nearer, she stuffed her *dupatta* into her mouth and lay motionless as the horses rode past. Only when they were out of sight did she dare to look up. She ran towards the village, now a raging furnace. Terrified dogs, goats, and chickens darted in all directions. Unable to enter her burning house, she collapsed in a heap and continued to scream, '*Amma*! *Amma*!' until she could scream no more.

***

Nadir was cycling back from work, hurrying to reach home before the rain, when he saw the smoke and flames rising in the distance. He instinctively turned his bicycle towards the village. The smoke and charred stench were unbearable. He threw his bicycle aside and ran wildly to see if he could help someone, but found it impossible to enter the hellhole because of the intense heat. Right in front of his eyes the village was being reduced to a charred, desolate heap of smoke and ash.

Desolated, he picked up his bicycle and headed home. It began to rain. Large fat drops pelted down on the parched earth, turning into a downpour and sending up the smell of fresh wet earth. The rain fell in slanting sheets, the first rain of the monsoon. Even in the pouring rain Nadir could hear the whimpering coming from the paddy field. He thought it was an injured animal and stepped into the knee-deep grass to take a closer look. To his surprise, it was a beautiful girl! On careful examination, he couldn't find any visible sign of injuries, but her bare feet were cut and bleeding. He carefully picked up the limp body, surprised at how light it was. Her long, wet plait touched the ground. He had no choice but to abandon his bicycle and carry her home in his arms.

As he reached the vicinity of his modest home, he called out to his brother, 'Ghazenfer! Ghazenfer!'

A young boy rushed out, hearing the urgency in his brother's voice. Ghazenfer looked at the spectacle in confusion but opened the door wide without a word. 'Who is this, Nadir Bhai?' he questioned, wide-eyed, once Nadir and his burden were inside.

Nadir briefly explained how he had found the girl. He put her on the bed and asked his brother to fetch hot milk and a bowl of warm water and towels. As the brothers cleaned up the girl, they discussed the dire implications of having a young girl in the house, especially in the absence of a woman. Ghazenfer suggested they hand her over to the police.

'No, no...God knows what the police will do to her.'

Together, they cleaned her wounds as best they could, bandaged her feet and covered her with a blanket. 'Hello…,hello… hello,' Nadir said desperately, getting louder each time.

The girl stirred, opened her eyes. Startled, she sat up, recoiled and hugged her knees. Pulling the blanket close, she winced. She looked at them, her eyes darting in all directions like a wild animal in danger. She remembered what had happened and felt the pain of her wounds. Shrinking deep under the blanket, she began to sob uncontrollably.

'Don't be scared; you are safe here,' Nadir whispered kindly. 'Please don't cry. Can I get you something to eat…drink?'

But the girl shook her head and continued to cry. Ghazenfer pushed the cup of milk towards her, keeping his eyes on the floor.

Nadir said softly, as if speaking to a baby, 'Look sister, you are safe here. I found you in the field near the burning village.' The girl cried even harder. 'Please, please don't cry. Drink this milk and when you feel better, I will take you to your family,' Nadir murmured.

She looked up at him with her doe-like, red-rimmed eyes, tears rolling down her pale cheeks like a broken string of pearls. 'My name is Humaira', she sobbed. 'I was at the well. I am *budh kismet*. My mother abandoned me at birth and now the only two people who loved me in the world were at the village. Now I have…nowhere to go.'

Nadir looked bewildered and said haltingly, 'I don't know what to do. We are two *muhajir* brothers. We only moved here from Lucknow recently. We live alone. We can't keep you here. There must be someone. We have to take you somewhere…we can't take you to the police. Let me think what to do…'

'Please don't take me to the police. I won't be any trouble, please… please let me stay here. I will cook and clean for you… anything… anything,' she pleaded.

They didn't have to explain to her about keeping a strange, young girl without a woman in the house. They looked at each other, confused. Next morning, Nadir called a *Molvi* and married her.

27
NADIR AND HUMAIRA

Nadir Chacha, his wife Humaira Chachi, and Ghazenfer Chacha, moved to Dhaka in East Pakistan. After struggling initially, both brothers joined Pakistan International Airways. Ghazenfer Chacha had a good voice and loved music, and in his spare time he sang on national radio.

The physical separation of a thousand miles between the two wings of Pakistan, without a common border, was problematic from the inception of the country in 1947. Mohammad Ali Jinnah, Pakistan's first Governor-General, chose Karachi in West Pakistan as the capital of Pakistan, declaring Urdu as the national language for the new nation. But Urdu was only spoken in West Pakistan and some parts of India. East Pakistanis spoke Bengali. This decision proved to be highly controversial since Karachi, being the capital, attracted wealthy industrialists, politicians, doctors and professionals, who then exerted influence on national and regional affairs. This created a significant economic imbalance and an uneven distribution of national wealth and privileges. The people in East Pakistan believed that it was due to local prejudice that the West Pakistanis took all the white-collar jobs. East Pakistan claimed that as their population (fifty-five per cent as compared to forty-five per cent in the West), was greater and that, democratically speaking, the federal capital should be Dhaka in East Pakistan.

They also resented the vast sums of foreign exchange earned from the sale of jute from East Pakistan, which was then spent on defence when it could otherwise have been used to improve the infrastructure of East Pakistan and eradicate poverty, illiteracy, and supply food and shelter to the ever-growing population. Anti-West Pakistan feelings grew to such an extent that in 1949, Bengali nationalists formed the Awami League as an alternative to the Muslim League.

By 1971, the political situation had become so volatile in East Pakistan that civil war became imminent. People fled from the east wing to the west. Nadir Chacha too, made arrangements to move his family from Dhaka to Karachi.

On 21st March 1971, he left his wife and children with his brother, Ghazenfer, and flew to Karachi to secure accommodation for the family. Meanwhile, the Awami League launched a non-cooperation movement which paralyzed the civil administration and all government institutions. The transport system came to a standstill and factories and shops shut down. All governmental interaction between the two wings of Pakistan ceased. Gangs of Awami League freedom fighters, known as Mukti Bahini, led violent demonstrations and howled racial and anti-West Pakistan slogans, inciting more violence. The failure of the military regime to resolve the political problem resulted in civil war.

Unfortunately, General Yahya Khan chose to use force to bring law and order to the country. The borders between East and West Pakistan closed and Nadir Chacha's family were marooned in Dhaka. Unable to locate his family and fearing the worst, he wrote to the Red Cross and Abbu in London, for help to trace them.

India seized the opportunity to dismember its enemy. On 22nd November 1971, India attacked East Pakistan. With the supply of modern Soviet missiles to the Mukti Bahini by the Indian army; geographical separation of thousand miles across hostile Indian territory; and assisted by fifteen million Hindus in East Pakistan, defeat for the Pakistan's military was inevitable. On 17th December 1971, Pakistan surrendered, which resulted in the brutal and violent amputation of Pakistan's eastern wing. East Pakistan declared itself an independent country, renamed Bangladesh. India took forty-five thousand Pakistani troops and an almost equal number of civilians as prisoners-of-war.

India was the first to recognize Bangladesh as an independent nation. Indira Gandhi, the then Prime Minister of India, voiced her resentment of Muslims, stating in Parliament on 18th December 1971: *'We have sunk the idea of two nations theory in the Bay of Bengal and have avenged the thousand years of Muslim rule in India.'*

After a nightmarish few months, Nadir Chacha finally received word through the Red Cross that his family was amongst the prisoners-of-war in Dhaka. Meanwhile, in London, each evening, Abbu and Ammi nervously retuned the already tuned television to BBC, adjusted the antenna and huddled close to the TV, anxiously watched the news and peered at the screen as if they would spot their lost family, most of whom they had never met. We were hushed into silence and severely reprimanded if we as much as shuffled our feet. In silence, we too, watched the distant war, with tanks rolling into a lush green, war-torn city, the only buildings not yet demolished, barricaded. Thousands of emaciated refugees, in appalling conditions, cowered together, begging for food. Initially, BBC broadcast reports on the war as headlines but within days it had diminished to a brief mention at the end of the news. Eventually, the reports dwindled to just the final death toll and the world forgot about the plight of the people of Bangladesh. Abbu and Ammi agonised over every word in the censored Asian newspaper, *Jang*, and the World Service on the radio.

Ammi cursed the leaders of both Pakistan and Bangladesh as she prepared *chapattis* for our evening meal. 'That idiot Yahya Khan – how could he send the army to kill his own people? What would that drunkard know of the plight of the people?' She continued to pray for the safety of Nadir Chacha's family as she tossed the *chapattis* on the *tuva*, rotating it as it ballooned. 'They have embroiled us all in it. If they lost their loved ones, then they would know. And that *kutti* Indira Gandhi, she is behind it all. India is supplying them with arms. Where else would they get all those guns and grenades?'

'You don't have to swear. Why are you cursing her?' Abbu too, was worried, but he tried to appease Ammi.

'Because it makes me feel better. It's our corrupt

leaders who have landed us in this mess. It's Nadir I feel for. God knows how he must be coping. He has no one in Karachi. I'll write to Abba Ji to go and comfort him.' She continued praying out loud for the miraculous survival of Nadir Chacha's family as she cooked.

One day, Nafeesa Momani observed that Abbu was looking thin and unwell.

'It's all this worry about Nadir's family. I don't know what sin we committed to have to go through this *again*,' Ammi sighed with despair. 'His nightmares have returned.'

'Why don't you persuade him to see a doctor?'

'He doesn't even speak to *me* about it; he would never speak to a stranger. It's all this pent-up anger and stress that's killing him.'

Ammi narrated Maasi's story about the Pathani and Humaira to Nafeesa Momani.

Momani stared at Ammi in disbelief. 'You don't think...no, it can't be.'

Ammi looked up with a quizzical smile and shrugged her shoulders. 'I have wondered but never had a chance to ask Nadir. Sometimes I wonder if she is *nemul-badel,*- a substitute for his sister Saltanat.'

'Have you told Bhai Azhar?'

'No, I don't want to remind him.'

Throughout this period, Pakistanis in the UK organised fairs and events to raise funds to help their brothers back home. Ammi, together with both Momanis and their friends, formed the 'Pakistan Women's Organisation,' which exists to this day. They organized *meena bazaars*, jumble sales, music shows and *mushairas*, for which Baji and I made huge batches of *gulab jammans*, paper flowers and soft toys. Ammi and her friends cooked mounds of food and made items to sell to raise money to help the refugees.

Abbu sent money to Nadir Chacha's family. They paid brokers to assist them to cross the border to India. Trudging on foot, blistered and bleeding, they shared stale bread and scavenged for food along the way. When the children begged their mother for food, Ghazenfer offered to give them his share of bread. Humaira snatched it back, reminding him that it was he who had to get them to Calcutta. During their nightmarish journey, the Mukti Bahini robbed them of the little money they had, and the children contracted chickenpox. In desperation, Humaira covered them with the shawl Ammi had once sent her from London, and gave her gold earrings to some men to carry the children. Unable to get proper medication, food or rest, her youngest son died. They finally crossed the border at Jaisoor, and headed for Calcutta, where they had family. It was many months before they recovered from their ordeal and Taya Akhtar arranged to smuggle them across the Indian border to Kathmandu in Nepal, from where they flew to Karachi by Pan Am.

On seeing the family, Nadir Chacha's eyes filled with tears as he hugged his wife. 'I am sorry...I am sorry,' was all he could say.

'I must be paying for the deeds of my parents, for I have never wronged anyone,' Humaira sighed bitterly.

'Nothing justifies this,' Nadir sobbed. '*Nothing!*' He looked at his frail, emaciated brother. His teeth protruded and his vacant eyes bulged in his skeletal face. His clothes hung on him like a puppet on strings. The tremendous responsibility Ghazenfer had carried and the atrocities he had witnessed along the way, took their toll, and he soon suffered a nervous breakdown. He was never the same again.

It pained Nadir to remember the carefree young man who used to sing like a lark.

Along with other refugees from East Pakistan, Nadir Chacha settled in Karachi with his family and engrossed himself in his work. Humaira Chachi, already suspicious of strangers, became even more reclusive, keeping to herself. The locals, however, were not welcoming of the Bengali refugees, who were very different both physically and culturally. They were short, with dark complexions, and spoke only Bengali. Even their diet was different as they preferred fish and rice to meat and *chapattis*.

As Nadir Chacha's boys grew up, they got involved in the Muhajir Quami Movement (MQM), a political party established by the refugees in Karachi. Despite their parents' objections, the hot-headed boys became zealously patriotic, demonstrating on the streets, resulting in violent clashes with both police and locals.

One night, the family woke up to find their house and car ablaze. Once again losing all their possessions, they fled to a new neighbourhood. The boys had learnt their lesson, and they settled into a civil, more cautious life, making efforts to blend in with the people of Karachi, where they live today.

PART IV

A NEW BEGINNING

LONDON 1966

STILL I RISE (Abridged)

~ MAYA ANGELOU

You may write me down in history
With your bitter, twisted lies,
You may tread me in the very dirt
But still, like dust, I'll rise.

Did you want to see me broken?
Bowed head and lowered eyes?
Shoulders falling down like teardrops.
Weakened by my soulful cries.

You may shoot me with your words,
You may cut me with your eyes,
You may kill me with your hatefulness,
But still, like air, I'll rise.

Out of the huts of history's shame
I rise
Up from a past that's rooted in pain
I rise
I'm a black ocean, leaping and wide,
Welling and swelling I bear in the tide.
Leaving behind nights of terror and fear
I rise
Into a daybreak that's wondrously clear
I rise
Bringing the gifts that my ancestors gave,
I am the dream and the hope of the slave.
I rise
I rise
I rise.

28
NEW BEGINNINGS

W e travelled to London on 27th November 1966, on Garuda Airlines. The whole trip is now a blur except for the cute little Indonesian air hostesses in skirts, with dark hair tied in high buns, and beautiful make-up. They welcomed us on board, manicured hands outstretched with sweets, as we were ushered in and strapped into our seats. They distributed little black and white jute boxes that contained a toothbrush, toothpaste, a pair of socks and an eye mask. When I finally worked out what the elasticated black strip of fabric was, I couldn't fathom why anyone would want to sit blindfolded on a *plane*. We treasured the little jute boxes for a long time.

The excitement of the flight and the precious gifts soon evaporated, for as soon as the plane took off, nausea set in. All of us, including Ammi, threw up non-stop from Karachi to London, and we didn't as much as look at the exotic food served throughout that lengthy journey. So the long awaited voyage remains a sickly blur.

On reaching London, immigration officers detained us for what seemed like an eternity, convinced that the clutch of pallid children, still heaving and vomiting, were not the offspring of the tiny little lady. The fact that none of us spoke English didn't help. Finally, they called Abbu over the intercom.

As soon as we saw him, we all ran up and grabbed his long legs, clinging on for dear life. 'Abbu!' we screamed with glee when he entered the interview room. He seemed much taller than I remembered. He hugged each of us, observing how much we had grown in three years, while Ammi looked at him self-consciously, embarrassed without her *burqa*. He tried to pick up Muzher, but unable to recognize him, Muzher began to cry. Abbu turned to Ather, who shyly put his tiny hand in his; Abbu showered him with kisses. He spoke at length with the immigration officer, and we were finally allowed entry into the UK.

Our uncle, Zia Mamo, was waiting to take us to his house in Wimbledon, where my aunt Nafeesa Momani had prepared a lavish meal. It was a day of firsts. After our first ever flight and first time abroad, we saw our first television, which was just as disappointing as the flight – rather like watching a foreign film, since we couldn't understand anything. Without as much as looking at the food, we dropped to sleep like flies in the heat. Later, Zia Mamo took us to our flat in Stockwell, where we slept through the whole night and most of the following day.

I woke to find myself on the second floor of a huge house on Stockwell High Road. The spacious, pleasant room spanned the width of the house. It had large bay windows overlooking the main road. The room was light; a faint glimmer of sunlight, piercing through the morning mist, quivered on the floor and the wall. There was a lot of furniture in that little flat, more than all the furniture in Wazir Khala's and our house put together, yet it was still spacious. In the silence, the tick-tock of the clock seemed exceptionally loud.

The room was furnished with two double beds with plush peacock blue velvet bedcovers; separated by an enormous television, which had an inbuilt gramophone and radio in a drawer below. Swathed in mahogany double doors, concealing its function, it looked like a little closet. Ammi duly draped this dwarf cabinet in a crochet lace cover which did nothing to protect it from dust. In fact, it made it necessary to bring out Mr. Sheen every evening at the unveiling. I surreptitiously stroked the cabinet and wished I could show it to Farooq and Rosy. There was also a three-piece suite and two large maroon velvet armchairs, so snug and comfy that once you sank into them, you didn't want to get up. I tucked my feet between the cushions to keep them warm. The long dining table was big enough to seat all eight of us.

Baji and I were assigned one of the double beds and Shano and Nunni the other. The only other room also had two double beds, where Ammi and Abbu slept with Ather and Muz. Abbu's snoring was reassuring and as soothing as a lullaby.

The hand basin in the recess made gurgling sounds like a stomach rumbling, followed by burps. There was a sturdy, oval dressing table with three panelled mirrors. A suedette lion and a tiger stood guarding the mirrors. A lace doily, adorned with a silver-backed hairbrush with a comb in it, a large bottle of 4711 cologne and a red tub of Brylcreem, decorated the dressing table. Beside the little lion stood a framed black and white photograph of Abbu outside the British School of Homeopathy, dressed in a striped double-breasted three-piece suit, the tip of a white handkerchief, folded into a triangle, peeping out of the breast pocket. He held a bundle of books casually in his hands. On his feet he wore polished Oxfords. His curly hair was slicked back, and he had a bemused, slightly lopsided smile. He looked pleased with himself and his triumphant grin seemed to say: I have arrived! Everything is possible!

Our flat was one of four in a tall Victorian building. It was an odd living arrangement. An old English lady lived in the top flat. We called her *Buddhi*. She didn't have a toilet in her flat and shared our Lilly of the Valley smelling toilet situated on the landing beside the entrance to our flat. Abbu had acquired the apartment through his friend, Aftab Uncle, as no one was willing to rent property to a coloured man with six children. Aftab Uncle lived with his wife Musarrat Auntie and their son Salman, in the flat below. Their flat didn't have a bathtub, so they came to our flat to use ours, *in the kitchen*.

We kept our home in immaculate condition, especially as we had to share the key facilities with our neighbours. Besides, Mussarrat Auntie had warned Ammi that the landlord could drop in anytime. We later learnt that this was a ploy to keep us on our toes, since no one ever came.

Those early days were a very sharp learning curve – bonding with Abbu after three years of separation; learning English; learning to use knives and forks; eating all kinds of new foods like porridge, cornflakes, fish and chips, sweets and biscuits, the likes of which we had never before seen. We had to adapt to the cold winter of England, a new home, a new school, and new friends. Within days my skin felt dry and taut as if it had shrunk. My chapped lips cracked and my numb toes became sore and itchy. Ammi massaged my feet with salt and mustard oil. Abbu bought thick woollen socks and made us wear them twenty-four seven.

I loathed being trapped within the confines of our flat in the ubiquitous fog. I paced the room like a caged animal, longing to be free. Treacherous draughts came down the chimney and the insidious cold wind found its way under doors and even keyholes. There was nowhere to go and play, and even if I did venture out, I had to put on so much clothing – coat, gloves, hat and scarf – that the fun and spontaneity of it was lost. My whole existence had dulled and faded like a sodden garment. London seemed almost monochrome in comparison to vibrant Pindi.

Everything was different. Even the sky here was different. Somehow it seemed oppressively lower than in Pakistan, grey for the most part, and forever changing with black and violet clouds, whereas in Pakistan, there wasn't much variation from the usual azure. Only during the monsoon did it momentarily turn dark and menacing, and immediately after the downpour, it resumed its reassuring bright cerulean colour again.

I found time keeping awkward. Back home, all reference to time revolved around prayer times. We woke up after *Fajr*, came home from school before *Zohar*, and in the evenings, we had to be home before *Maghreb*. If we had an invitation to lunch, it was taken for granted it would be after *Zohar*, when the sun's heat had diminished, and before *Assar*. All evening festivities began after *Maghreb*. The *Azan* call to prayer reminded us of the passage of time, replacing watches and clocks. Here, there was nothing to tell you what time of day it was, and the fact that it got dark so early was really disconcerting.

We felt most awkward in mixed company, especially Ammi, who had worn a *burqa* for most of her married life. We were used to segregated gatherings. Even when we had family dinners, men and women automatically sat in separate groups. Here, everyone sat higgledy-piggledy. For a long time Ammi remained completely silent, and everyone thought she was very shy, unaware of her real personality. It was a long time before Ammi could voice her opinion in a mixed group.

The clothes we had brought from Pakistan were wholly inadequate and out of place. Our brightly coloured cotton *shalwar-kameeze were* too bright and too thin, the red coats utterly useless in the chilly November winds of London. Abbu took us shopping and bought us new coats, hats, shoes and warm clothes. Dressed in my new clothes I tried to walk with poise. The upturned collar of my coat and scarf chaffed my neck and prevented me from moving my head. I shielded my sensitive ears with my hands from the freezing wind that threatened to lift me up and toss me about like a leaf and go right in one ear and out the other. I walked stiffly on as the wind snatched the breath from my mouth and stung and nipped every pore of my face and hands.

The paving stones sent a pang to my heart – they were perfect for playing hopscotch, I thought. And the smell of autumn leaves took me back to a place I so loved. I had never before seen so many leaves, plastered on the wet pavement almost as if someone had glued them on in a collage.

We went sightseeing to witness the Changing of the Guards, Madame Tussaud's, London Bridge, Oxford Circus and Piccadilly Circus. We loved travelling on the underground. Abbu had to stock up with extra change to buy chocolates for us from the vending machines at the stations. On the bus, he climbed to the upper deck while Ammi scuttled behind, herding Muz and Nunni.

'Do you have to climb to the top?' she asked, much more loudly than she intended in public.

'The children enjoy the view,' replied Abbu.

Ather, Shano and I rushed to find window seats. The bus conductor handed a yard long ticket to Abbu. Nunni and Muz began squabbling for it so Abbu tore it in half and gave one piece to each. Muz threw away his ticket and buried his head in Ammi's lap, sniffling.

Mortified, Baji said, 'No one has so many children. Everybody is looking at us,' getting up to move to the back of the bus.

'No one is looking at us. Come, sit next to me.' Abbu tried to appease her, but she sat alone at the back.

One Sunday morning we marched off to Speakers' Corner at Hyde Park. While Abbu listened to the fiery speech by Tariq Ali, we ran off to the swings and slides. Later, Abbu took us on the paddle boat in the Serpentine. Despite Ammi's protests, we fed our sandwiches and crisps to the ducks in the pond. On our return home, Abbu wrote a poem and recorded it on our spool tape recorder:

The king, the crown, the power,

The castle, the garden, the tower,

We all joined in the chorus.

Will not remain for ever

Will not remain for ever....

I wrote long letters to Abba Ji and Farooq, telling them about the places we had visited. I felt a great sense of pride. For once I was better informed than Farooq. I had never realised that all those places on my Monopoly board were 'real places' in London. It left me wondering why Coventry and Leicester Square were yellow and Piccadilly and Bond Street blue.

In a dressing table drawer I found the amulets Amma Ji had tied on our arms at departure. I unpicked one to see what was inside and was surprised to find Arabic numerals written in black Indian ink. I showed it to Ammi, asking what they meant, and was duly ticked off for opening the amulet. But she explained the numbers represented verses from the *Quran*, probably protective prayers. Abbu and Ammi made a special journey to South Bank to throw the amulets in the Thames and donate money in the charity box at Woolworths.

On Saturday mornings we marched to the cinema in Brixton, where we watched cartoons for sixpence and later elbowed our way through the crowd with Abbu, in Brixton market, for the weekly shopping. We helped to carry home the vast amount of provisions we consumed. When Abbu bought me an ice cream in a cone from Woolworths, I wondered if the cone was edible and didn't bite into it until I saw someone else do so.

Baji and I dragged all the laundry to the public launderette in our shopping trolley. We took turns to feed the dryer with shilling coins. Ammi cooked, Baji and I cleaned with an enormous, cumbersome vacuum cleaner that had a huge fabric bag which billowed up like a sail. It was so noisy that all conversation ceased, and everyone sat up on the sofas to keep out of the way. The stairs had to be cleaned with a hand brush.

The *Buddhi* was very impressed with us children and remarked to Abbu that we were angels since we rushed to help her with her shopping and cleaned her stairs despite her protests. It was unthinkable in our culture to allow an old lady to carry her shopping up three flights of stairs and clean while we watched. She bought us ice cream and chocolates in gratitude.

We were intrigued by this old lady's solitary existence. In Pakistan, women her age are highly revered and pampered. Ammi was concerned that no one ever visited her and that she lived by herself. On Ammi's insistence, Abbu asked the old lady about her family. She told him that she lost her husband in the war, and her only son was found mysteriously dead in bed at twenty. Ammi became even more sympathetic and insisted on sending her food, especially when she cooked something she thought was not too spicy.

Buddhi's flat was a dark Aladdin's cave, with the musky smell unaired rooms have. She kept the thick damask curtains drawn at all times. Large paintings depicting scenes from the Bible adorned the walls. A very gruesome image of Christ on the cross, surrounded by cherubs and beautiful women, remains vivid in my mind to this day. Vases, plates, pots and a vast array of ceramic trinkets, were carefully arranged in groups of three on the dark furniture.

Buddhi spent most of her time in the back bedroom, with the oven on to keep the room warm. She sat silently in her thick towelling dressing gown, in a faded, gold damask recliner, which like her and the rest of her furniture, had seen better days. Head resting on a lace antimacassar, her deformed toes curling inwards in her slippers and her arthritic hands in her lap, she sat squinting with watery grey eyes at the black and white television, even when there was no programme on. Head tilted to one side, drool on her prickly chin, she would doze off. She reminded me of the crazy old lady we called *Pugli* in Pindi.

'Yuck! *Buddhi* keeps her teeth in a glass when she's at home,' I reported to my siblings.

'What? She doesn't have her own teeth?'

'No, she has plastic teeth.'

'Why?'

'I don't know.'

Abbu and Ammi looked at each other and chuckled.

Aftab Uncle and Mussarrat Auntie made a handsome, trendy couple. She wore hipster saris and tiny sleeveless blouses, her bare midriff accentuated by her small waist, and stiletto heels. Intrigued by the vast collection of cosmetics on her dressing table, I would watch as she backcombed her long hair and inserted a sausage shaped hairpiece to make it even higher. The rest of her long hair she tied into a bun. She spent hours filing and painting her nails. Ammi never used any make-up; at most she put *kajal* in her eyes. And she wore her hair in a simple braid.

Salman, Aftab Uncle and Mussarrat Auntie's three-year-old son, was terribly spoilt. He threw tantrums, kicking and screaming, if he didn't get his way. Once, when Ammi was taking an afternoon nap, he struck her with a hammer, bang in the middle of her forehead (she still has the bump). She woke up startled and threw him face down on the bed and smacked him till he made his escape, yelling at the top of his voice all the way home.

The basement flat was empty when we first moved in but soon a newly married couple, Safia Auntie and Iftekhar Uncle, moved in. Both were jolly people and Safia Auntie often burst into infectious fits of girly giggles. As soon as Ammi heard that the new arrivals were Siddiqui, she was intrigued to find out if they were related to us. Ammi's quest for genealogy proved time and time again that we were all descendants of Adam and that the world was round. With her encyclopaedic knowledge of our family, we inevitably unearthed another relative. After interrogating Iftekhar Uncle, she found him to be a not-so-distant relative. Safia Auntie burst into giggles.

'We moved to England to get away from our relatives, and now they have found us here,' chuckled Iftekhar Uncle.

Safia Auntie enjoyed my chatter. I spent a lot of my spare time with her, especially since she was pregnant and was ordered bed rest. She lay in bed, arms outstretched above her head, cracking her knuckles and instructing me to carry out her household chores and run errands from the local shops. I didn't mind.

Safia Auntie was instrumental in teaching me English. She sent me to the store, telling me precisely what to say, and I went down the road, avoiding the slab that squelched muddy water if you stepped on it even when it wasn't raining, repeating the words in my head: 'Two pounds of onions please, two pounds of onions please.' If anyone said anything else to me, I blurted out, 'Sorry, I can't speak English.' One day the greengrocer answered my admission with a smile, putting up his thumb. I returned home mortified and told Safia Auntie about his offensive gesture.

She went into one of her giggling fits and said, 'He wasn't being rude; it means thank you here.' Pinching both my cheeks affectionately, she kissed me.

Every evening I stood at the bay window waiting for Abbu to return from work. I could see him approaching in the distance, laden with bags of shopping. I stood melancholically observing the pigeons in their nest atop the window in the adjacent flat, the parents flying back and forth, feeding their chicks. Their freedom momentarily lifted my spirits, but my pensive mood persisted. I felt caged in behind the misty window in the cold, wet and windy winter of London. The lace curtain flickered in the window, forming patterns on the walls, like my flitting thoughts of past and present. I watched through the gloom the desolate streets, picturing in my mind's eye Farooq and Rosy back home in sunny Pindi. Like a time traveller I was transported back to the past, a cheerful carefree child, playing in our *gali*.

As memories glowed more and more vividly,

I had the sudden realization that it wasn't just Farooq I missed. I missed roaming in our *galis*. I missed Pindi. Back home, I knew everyone in our neighbourhood, and they knew me. Here I was a total stranger amongst strangers. Our parents had lifted us out of our niche and moved us to a foreign environment, like a gardener whips out seedlings from the ground and moves them to wherever he likes. We had no choice or say in the matter – Abbu knew best! The *gali*, the house and the people around me had been my whole life – the only thing I knew, my little universe. We had left them all behind and moved to London, to an alien land, alien roads and alien people, with nowhere to play.

Rain poured down softly from the dark grey sky like the hissing sound of silence. Rain in London was so serene and quiet, like the people, going about silently in the dark, gloomy city. When it rained in Pindi, after the sun had been breathing fire for a few days, hot steam rose from the ground. Rain, almost always accompanied by thunder and lightning, pelted down violently, causing torrents that washed the streets clean, and the *galies* turned to noisy playgrounds as we dashed out and played in the downpour, screaming and chasing each other like demented demons. Sometimes the sun shone through the rain, with a cool breeze. The rain was no relief from the heat. Even after it rained it was seldom cool for long; instead, it became sultry and muggy, and soon the sulphur sun shone brightly in the azure sky once again, and the stifling heat returned.

Here it was cold and quiet even with so much traffic whizzing past. There were no hoots and horns, or shouts of street hawkers mingling with the noise of music from neighbouring homes, and of course, no sound of the *Muezzin* calling the faithful to the local mosque five times a day. In Pindi, even at night, it was never quiet. The watchman banged his stick and blew his whistle intermittently to let potential troublemakers know he was around.

I wondered where children played in London, for there were none in the streets. My heart ached to be back in Pindi, playing hopscotch with Farooq in our *gali*. No doubt he had found a new companion. My heart wrenched with anguish at the thought of Farooq roaming *our* haunts with Rosy, and quickly dismissed the idea.

As I pressed my face against the cold, misty windowpane, my nose made a mark in the condensation. I pressed my lips against the glass and drew a face with tears streaking down the cheeks. Vicarious memories flooded back. I swallowed hard, striving to hold back and hide the emotions, even from myself. Suppressing the tears that welled up and wiping my stinging eyes,

I looked around to see if someone had seen or overheard my thoughts. I moved quickly to the kitchen to get a cheer-me-up snack.

Night after night I lay in bed, longing to be home. I wondered with whom Farooq was gallivanting. I prayed hard, just like Abbu had taught us. He said that if you wanted something badly enough, you always got it if you made your declaration of faith by reading the *Kalima,* and prayed. And when you woke up the following morning, before opening your eyes, you should recite the *Kalima* again. Then your prayers would be granted. I believed this to be a fact, for I had prayed to come first in my class, and to come to London, and both things had happened. Now, each night, with my hands clenched, my eyes shut tight, I prayed hard to be back in Pindi with Farooq. Each night in my dreams I was there, hopping and skipping down the *gali*, on the rooftop, by the stream in the park, beating the water with palm leaves, chasing the frogs. When I awoke in the morning, I made sure I kept my eyes shut tight, focusing my mind, I prevented it from drifting from my prayers. I prayed hard.

Later, I asked Abbu, 'Where do children play in London?'

'In the park,' he replied, confused by my question.

The following weekend, Abbu took us to the park. Baji refused to come with us. On that cold windy day, the park was as devoid of people as the trees of leaves. Ather, Shano and Nunni chased each other; no doubt overjoyed to be outdoors. Thinking a multitude of thoughts, I stood alone, mesmerized by my reflection in the pond, watching the distorted face swaying to and fro amongst floating leaves. Suddenly, a frog jumped out, shattering the image. Startled, I jumped aside. Muddy water splashed my new boots. My boots felt heavy, as heavy as my heart. I jumped aside, trying to shake the distorted image from my mind and the mud from my boots, but neither would leave me. I watched the frog disappear into the bushes.

It annoyed me that Ammi, who had cried for days before we left, never mentioned Amma Ji or Shama Khala, though she eagerly awaited Abba Ji's blue aerograms. She read his letters out loud, savouring each word and replied to each point, and our progress, omitting to mention that we missed them all. Abba Ji was satisfied that she was now in her rightful place, with her husband. Ammi wrote to Tauqeer Khala, but writing letters not being her forte, she often didn't reply for weeks.

Ammi busied herself with setting up our new home and cooking Abbu's favourite meals. Perhaps grown-ups were different, I thought. My torturous memories roiled within me, but I never voiced them, not even to Baji. She seemed happy enough; a quiet loner. Perhaps there was something wrong with me then? Everyone said we were so lucky to be in London. So why did I feel so homesick?

I did not see Ammi cry until the invitation to Shama Khala's wedding arrived. She bought shimmering black and gold cardigans and sent them with Zia Mamo and Nafeesa Momani, who were going to attend the wedding. It was nearly forty years before Ammi voiced how desperate she had felt on leaving behind her family, without any hope of ever seeing them again.

And it was a long time – too long – before my prayers were finally answered. By which time everything had changed. I had changed.

29
CORONATION

———————————

Abbu's move to London was harder than he
had ever anticipated. On his first visit to
Britain in 1953, during the Queen's coronation,
accommodation, food and transport had all been
provided for him. He never really met the general
public. Now, here he was eleven years later, having
to fend for himself. Initially, he stayed with Zia
Mamo, in Wimbledon. Being a proud man he didn't
wish to overstay his welcome and immediately set
about looking for a job. He acquired a copy of
the Yellow Pages and sent applications and letters
to many companies, applying for jobs he thought
he could do. He answered vacancies advertised
in the papers, but when he enquired about his
application, he sensed hostility and was awkwardly
informed the position had already been filled.

It was the same when he went to enquire about rooms advertised to let. Many advertisements blatantly stated 'No coloured, Irish or dogs.' He had never before encountered prejudice and had been treated with great respect because of his qualifications and army background. Nevertheless, he had no choice but to persist with his quest and finally landed a job in a mattress factory. He was fit and healthy but had never worked so hard since his army days. He worked there until he found a less arduous job. After many menial jobs he took up a post in Decca Television Company. It was better paid and more interesting *and* less gruelling. He soon made his way up as an accountant.

Meanwhile, Zia Mamo managed to secure a room on his behalf. Because of his fair complexion he was mistaken as European. But once Zia Mamo had secured the place, the landlord had no choice but to allow Abbu to stay.

***

Abbu was the only person I knew who wore tie pins long after they were no longer fashionable. He also loved perfume. His scent announced his arrival before he appeared and lingered long after he had left. He had countless shirts, many brand new and unopened; just as many suits; shoes in every colour, including black patent leather with white-toed oxfords; cufflinks in various shapes and colours with matching tiepins, all arranged neatly in labelled display sections in his wall to wall wardrobe.

Abbu dressed in one of his many three-piece, double-breasted suits, a gold tie pin holding his tie in place, freshly polished shoes on his feet and the waft of cologne about his person, he strutted downstairs adjusting his cufflinks.

'*Ufffoooo*, did you empty the whole bottle? Have you an appointment with the Queen?' asked Ammi.

He just smiled his lopsided grin and asked, 'Is it too strong? I only dabbed a little.'

'That rose perfume is for women. Even I don't use it because it gives me a headache,' Ammi retorted, wrinkling her nose.

'Salmi *baiti*, perfume is perfume isn't it? I love this rose smell.' He turned to me, asking for affirmation.

'Abbu it's nice, but it *is* for women.'

'Does it smell nice or not? Answer me that,' he said resolutely.

'It's nice but...'

'Settled!'

He did meet the Queen as it happens. He was selected as one of the *jawans* to represent Pakistan at the Queen's coronation in 1953. He wrote a poem in her honour and sent it to the palace and later recited it on BBC radio. It earned him an invitation to a tea party at St James Palace during the celebrations, and he was awarded a coronation medal and letter of thanks along with a silver cup, of which he was very proud.

That fateful journey to Europe, one he could never have dreamt of or afforded had he not been selected, opened his eyes and he decided back in 1953, that London was where he wanted to live. After the birth of his sixth child, he thought it was time to make his dream come true for the betterment of the whole family. It took him many years of hard work and great sacrifices to turn his dream into reality.

***

Besides Ammi, the love of Abbu's life was poetry. A stream of Asian artists visited the UK from the sub-continent, nurturing the Asians starved of their culture. Setting aside their conflicts and differences, Hindus, Muslims and Sikhs all came together to these gatherings, *mushairas* and concerts. Abbu was a regular participant. With time, our parents became an integral part the Asian social circle and their lives revolved around work, home, and elaborate dinner parties.

Abbu presided over *mushairas* as far afield as Glasgow and Edinburgh. His poetry was highly appreciated for it was simple and touched a chord in people's hearts. Once he started to recite in his melodious voice, breathing life into every *ghazal*, there was always a demand for more. Head thrown back, without the aid of a microphone, he recited one *ghazal* after another. When he had finished, people rose in rapturous applause, calling for more.

At one such gathering, a poet who had travelled a good distance to recite his poetry, became impatient and said sourly, 'If you only wanted to hear Dr. Azhar, why did you bother to invite us?' Abbu spontaneously came up with a couplet in response:

جاۓ جم چاہیۓ، نہ ارم چاہیۓ
با ترنم بھری بزم میں دوستو
شعر پڑھنے کو سینے میں دم چاہیۓ

Jamai jum chaheyai, na erum chaheyai
(Need neither wine nor false heaven)

Ba-turunnum bhree buzm main dostoo
(To recite in verse in a gathering dear friends)

Sheer purnai ko seenai main dum chaheyai,
(You need a courageous heart.)

He received a standing ovation.

As children we didn't appreciate renowned Urdu poets such as Faiz Ahmed Faiz, Josh Malihabadi, Hafeez Jalandhari, Ahmed Fraz, Kosar Niazi, Raees Amrohvi, Iftekhar Arif, Ahsan Sultan Farooq, Ahsan Danish, Habib Hyderabadi, Akbar Hyderabadi, Noori, Shubnum Hyderabadi and Aqeel Danish, who frequented our house. These poets were well known in the Urdu-speaking community in England, as well as in India and Pakistan, and were famed for their vivid descriptions of valour, vicissitudes of life and powerful similes. Hankering to express themselves in their mother tongue, they gathered together to recite their latest poems to each other, exchanged *dewans* (poetry collections), over tea and heated discussions about Pakistani politics, in which Ammi was always very vocal.

Once, when Aqeel Danish Sahib came to our house, I answered the door. Escorting him inside, I politely said, 'Please come in; take a seat.'

'You are the daughter of such a renowned poet, and you don't speak Urdu?' he asked.

'Oh... sorry,' was my feeble, embarrassed response.

Abbu spent months organising his lifetime of poetry into five volumes, which were published and sold at various *mushairas,* along with cassettes of his recitations. This was a matter of great pride to him as well as the rest of the family. How delighted he would have been to know that his poetry is taught as part of the course on 'Post-Partition Contemporary Poets of Asia', at Harvard University today!

It wasn't just Abbu's poetry people loved. He was a highly respected member of the community. Unlike Ammi, who was garrulous, Abbu wasn't a man of many words. What he said was important. People gravitated towards him and his presence made them feel at peace. He listened intently, making you feel you were the centre of the universe. He was present in the moment and you felt his presence. You could confide in him, tell him anything; your most intimate, deepest thoughts; he would keep everything to himself and not judge, merely, advise, for he was wise. His measured words were like warm honey. You felt at peace with yourself, your existence, your family, the world. He soothed your troubled soul.

Despite great demands on his time and income from his large family, he was incredibly generous and never refused anyone help. His wallet was always bulging with cash. He regularly sent money to his family in India. He helped people in the community spiritually, socially and financially. He persuaded people to settle their debts, mediated in arranged marriages and feuding families. He often helped those less able with official correspondence. Before the construction of the Balham Mosque, he was instrumental in gathering funds to purchase the house on 42 Childebert Road, which was used by Muslim men to pray. His unpretentious lifestyle, intense look and presence commanded respect. He reminded me of Mario Puzo's Godfather.

Abbu was a gentle soul but didn't stand for any nonsense. A local Pakistani boy kept pestering Baji and me as we walked home from school. He had somehow got hold of my telephone number and kept calling. Initially, I tried to brush him off, but when he continued to annoy me, I asked him to meet me outside the Balham Baths and told Abbu. Like a true patriarch, Abbu went armed with a cricket bat to sort him out. He grabbed the young man by the collar and dragged him to his father, who apologised profusely for his son's behaviour and dispatched him to Pakistan.

The only vice Abbu had was smoking. Even that he gave up the day he asked Ather to fetch some matches while they were fixing the car together. Ather absentmindedly pulled a match box from his pocket. Abbu didn't say anything but never smoked again.

Abbu should have studied engineering, for his dexterity was astounding. He could fix almost anything. We never called anyone to do any handiwork in our house. Whatever needed fixing or repairing, Abbu did it. He painted and decorated the house, replaced kitchen units, installed a new bathroom, changed the carpets and even installed our central heating.

He repaired household gadgets in our home as well as for family and friends. When our long serving washing machine broke down, he took the broken timer to the spare parts shop to get a replacement, only to be told that particular model was no longer made. There was nothing to be done but get a new machine. Abbu came home, acquired a lump of Perspex and painstakingly made the offending part with his handsaw and files. When he got it working, he showed it to the shopkeeper, who was utterly astounded that Abbu had made the part by hand. Our washing machine continued to give service for years to come.

Late in life Abbu took a mistress. When he learned to drive and bought a car, he was overjoyed, like a child with a new toy. He treated it like his pet, referring to it as 'Vauxhall Viva 64'. Our car never went to the garage. He bought the car manual from *Loot* and took the car apart; including the gearbox, and reassembled it part by part. Much to Ammi's annoyance, various car parts sat in our front room for months while he lay under the car covered in grease.

When Zia Mamo came to visit, he'd call out, peeping under the car, 'Bhai Azhar, are you in your bedroom?'

Abbu would emerge covered in grease, laughing his hearty laugh. Besides his routine work he had a private homeopathy practice, but never charged his patients. He even handed out free medicines. 'How can I charge the poor man? He's off work as it is,' he'd say.

Unfortunately, the abiding tragedy of his life was one of the people who mattered most to him, but to whom Abbu could not get through – Muz, his younger son.

30
SCHOOL IN STOCKWELL

Abbu had registered us at the local school before our arrival. Within days of our arrival, a woman came to the house from the local education authority to assess us. My paperwork was sorted before anyone else's, so I was the first one to go to school. Abbu took us to Morley's in Brixton and bought us our uniforms. I was delighted, though a little self-conscious, in my navy blue pleated skirt, white blouse, red jumper and tie.

Unable to speak a word of English, I joined Stockwell Girls' School. A few days later, Baji joined me. Although she was older than me, we were put in the same class so we wouldn't feel totally isolated. Abbu taught us a few useful English words such as 'please', 'sorry', 'excuse me' and 'thank you'. Initially, in school, we got by on these and gradually increased our vocabulary. Every day we came home with new words we had learnt and exchanged experiences. During a fire drill, we rushed out and lined up in the playground with the rest of the class. I was cold without my coat, clasping my hands and shivering. Jacky, a ginger-head with freckles, thought I was praying. She tried to reassure me saying, 'Don't worry, it's only a drill.'

I didn't understand what she said but learnt the phrase. At home, Abbu explained what it meant. Everything was new and exciting. Unlike Pakistan, we didn't have to lug huge bags loaded with school books. All textbooks, notebooks, and even stationery, was provided. During the morning break, we bought chocolate fingers or chocolate digestives for tuppence from our class teacher, Miss Carey, which we ate along with the half pint of milk distributed to every child. On Fridays, Miss Carey sold two shilling stamps, which I purchased from my pocket money of half a crown and carefully stuck it in the little red post office saving book. When completed, I got five pounds in redemption.

Baji and I kept each other company and despite the language barrier, we managed to make friends with the red-headed Jacky with Chinese features and freckles, and with Valery, a black girl with tight worm-like hair sticking out of her head. I was intrigued by the intricate, cubed designs on her head, the likes of which I had never seen. I wondered how long it took her mother to braid her hair. Jacky and Valery often stopped over at our house after school and enjoyed Ammi's snacks. We played hopscotch in the back alley. We even taught them the Pakistani version, which is much harder.

Shirley, a tall girl at school, looked much older than the rest of us. She had breasts, wore a bra and had ginger pubic hair. I stared at her in amazement when she and the other girls undressed without hesitation for PE. I came to hate PE and swimming because I was too shy to change in front of others. I devised a meticulous method of changing without revealing any part of my body, my skinny chest in particular, on which tiny pumps had emerged like little plums, that hurt when touched; a bittersweet pain which I secretly enjoyed, like scratching chilblains.

Miss Carey wrote to Abbu asking for an explanation for our absences from school on PE days. We explained to him about the lack of privacy in the changing rooms and the curtain-less shower cubicles. He was horrified and complained to the school. Soon shower curtains were installed.

I loved school dinners, especially the puddings, which were a real treat since we only had curry at home and Ammi only made desserts on special occasions. Initially, we stuck to vegetarian food, but much to Ammi's chagrin, started eating meat as long as it was not pork, even though it was not *halal*. In class, the first few students to finish their classwork were rewarded with a helping of the leftover cakes from lunch. Since I was far advanced in maths as compared to the rest of our class, I always managed to get some. Sometimes, during maths class, I was sent to Mrs. Wassi to learn English.

For some odd reason, our school was affiliated to a school in Bangladesh, for which we helped raise funds. We had to say *namaskar*, putting our hands together, after saying good morning each day. Miss Carey had learned to make and play bamboo pipes from her visiting counterpart in Bangladesh, and we spent numerous music lessons making bamboo pipes, decorating them with marker pens and embroidering cases for them. We played Lord of the Dance for Blue Peter on TV and at a concert in Westminster Hall. I treasured the Blue Peter badge for many years.

The credit for teaching me English goes to my teacher, plump little Miss Carey, who loved the colour green. She wore green right down to her shoes. She even wrote with green ink. When she saw Ammi for the first time, she jumped up with delight, held her green tartan skirt on both sides and curtsied, 'Oh Mrs. Ahmed, at last someone as small as me!' she exclaimed. She kept me behind after school, and we read together, made jigsaw puzzles and played board games. Somehow, during this period, I learnt English. She taught me manners too. When she saw me yawning in assembly, she gave me a serious look, gently tapping her mouth. She waved her finger from side to side, gesticulating with her eyes when she caught me licking my knife at lunch. I loved Miss Carey.

When Valery messed up her classwork yet again and asked if she could tear out another page, Miss Carey smacked her on the back of her leg with a ruler and yelled, 'When you tear out a page, you lose another at the back. Soon you will be left with just the cover!' I told Miss Carey through gestures and my limited English that she could cut the page out leaving an inch margin and stick that down with glue in order to avoid losing the back page. Miss Carey was delighted. She hugged and kissed me. At dinner in the evening, I proudly told the whole family that Miss Carey had kissed *me*. I continued to write to and exchange Christmas cards with Miss Carey until 1980, when I stopped getting a reply.

Our English progressed in leaps and bounds. As Ammi dished out food, Baji said, 'I don't want too much.' Muzher piped up, 'I want three much!' hoping to get the lion's share. I was sitting at the dining table with animal pictures in front of me and said to Abbu, 'Baby chicken!'

'Chick - c-h-i-c-k,' he replied.

'Baby cow.'

'*Caff* - c-a-l-f, the l is silent.'

'Baby dog.'

'Puppy. P-u-p-p-y,' Abbu said.

Ammi too, repeated the words, as if humouring a child. Abbu glanced up, smiling. 'They have specific names for baby animals, for males and females of animals, and yet they don't have individual names for specific members of the family,' Ammi told him.

'What?'

'They call everyone Auntie and Uncle. You can't tell from which side of the family they're from. They care more about animals than their family,' Ammi said, shaking her head.

Abbu laughed his hearty laugh. 'You've hit the nail on the head.'

By the end of the school year I could understand

oral English, though writing was still a problem. Our end of the year exams were oral. I understood the questions but was unable to write down the answers. Frustrated, I wrote my responses in Urdu. Miss Carey got me to explain what I had written by drawing on the blackboard, which was successful in most part. The answer to one question was 'dates'. Well, dates drawn on the board didn't look like much so I drew a box of dates and wrote 'Eat Me' on it. My fellow students recognized this instantly. I got good marks too, better than Baji, except for spelling. I still can't spell. Within the year I was competing with my contemporaries and by the time I left junior school a year later, I was awarded the book, Man on the Moon, as prize for excellent progress, having topped my class.

Every week Abbu took us to the library, and we came back laden with our selection of six books each and fought with each other to read them with him. We were not allowed to watch TV until we had finished all the work he had assigned to each of us. Then the TV was ceremoniously switched on and we all sat on the carpet in a semicircle, hugging our knees, with Abbu between us. His long legs stretched out in front, hands clasped behind his head, he watched wrestling, Come Dancing, The Lucy Show and the Black and White Minstrel Show on our huge Grundig television. The TV was switched off after the National Anthem at midnight. On Sunday morning we woke up early to watch the only Asian programme on TV: *Naie Zindagi-Naya Jeevan,* with Mahendra Kaul, Saleem Shahid and Robert, who taught English to Asians. We especially looked forward to the song at the end, willing it to be in Urdu, since sometimes it was in Bengali, Gujarati, Sindhi or any of the many languages of the sub-continent. We listened to Abbu's collection of music – Adam Faith, Dionne Warwick, Dusty Springfield and Sandy Shaw. His favourite was *Walk On By,* which we played so often that the record developed a deep groove and got stuck.

As Ammi dropped us to school, she met Mrs. Sharma and Mrs. Sethi, who worked at a TV manufacturing factory. With all of us at school, for the first time, Ammi was alone at home with time on her hands. Mrs. Sharma and Mrs. Sethi persuaded Ammi to come to work with them, assuring her that not being able to speak English was not a problem for they could teach her all she needed to know. Getting a job in the 60s wasn't difficult, even for Asian women. Unlike some of their British counterparts, often unaware of their rights, these women worked hard, had nimble fingers, seldom complained, and made no demands, feeling grateful for being given a job, especially since they couldn't speak English. Ammi, who had never before ventured out alone, had little formal education and spoke no English, was now working in a factory manufacturing TVs in London. For the first time in her life she felt empowered and financially independent.

I can't imagine how Ammi, who had lived such a sheltered life in Pakistan, felt being so liberated as to earn and contribute to the household income. But unlike many Asian men, Abbu was very appreciative and helped her with domestic duties. He changed his day shift to the night shift for better pay and with Ammi's income, they could finally think about buying a house. However, the change meant Ammi had already left for work before Abbu arrived home in the morning and when Ammi returned in the evening, Abbu was about to leave. Baji and I had to grow up fast to help with the chores and get everyone off to school in the morning and escort them home after school. Baji adopted the matriarchal role, which she maintains even today.

Abbu slept till about two o'clock, then got up and prepared dinner. We all did the chores assigned to us. Baji and I took turns to clean and tidy the house and wash the dishes. Ather emptied the bins and ran errands to the shop. Muz was in charge of bringing six pints of milk in and putting out the empties in the evening. Shano and Nunni were supposed to make the beds, but they never did, so

I ended up making them. It was a hard job fixing the bedsheets, two or three thick blankets, and the bedcover. Baji made sure this we did with military precision. On weekends, Abbu and Ammi went to the Cash and Carry and got the groceries. Baji and I took the laundry to the laundrette and did the weekly wash.

As Christmas approached, with all the hype at school and on TV, we waited in anticipation for the big day. I expected a great hustle and bustle in the streets, like *Eid* in Pakistan. I woke up early to look out of the blurred and misty window. Much to my dismay, the streets were deserted; there wasn't a soul on the road. The only joy of the day was that the *Buddhi* gave each of us individually wrapped presents – the first we had ever had – and Ammi made a special meal.

31
MOVE TO BALHAM

Abbu had told us what an uphill task it had been for a coloured man with six children to find accommodation to rent. Ammi was petrified that any day there'd be a knock at the door and we would have to leave. It was, therefore, imperative to buy their *own* house. Having learned how a mortgage works, Ammi's resolve to buy a home strengthened. She could think of nothing more important than a sanctuary for herself and her children. She dreamt that she was standing in front of Prophet Mohammad's (PBUH) tomb praying, 'Dear Lord, everyone has a home of their own. Only I and Baji Wazir are still homeless. Please grant my prayers for a home of our own.' She took this dream as a sign from God and began saving in earnest. Within the year we moved to 29 Cheriton

Square in Balham – a four-bedroom house, our very own, with a garden – which no one could ask us to vacate.

Everyone was extremely impressed that Abbu had bought such a large house.

'Bhai Azhar, what a great location! Five minutes to the Underground and British Rail, two minutes to the main road, with so many buses; and look at the size of the rooms!' Mamo Zia saw the potential straight away despite the house being gloomy. The fact that Pak Food Store was around the corner was a bonus. People came from miles to the store for *halal* meat and Pakistani groceries and dropped in for a cup of tea on the weekends, which helped lessen Ammi's homesickness.

Ammi once tried to light the ancient geyser in our bathroom with four-year-old Muz standing beside her. There was a massive explosion. Years of soot and ash exploded like an erupting volcano. The bathroom window shattered. Ammi and Muz's faces were scorched. Muz, being lower, bore the brunt of it. He ran screaming, 'I can't see anything, I can't see, I can't see!' He was so traumatized he wouldn't let anyone near him, nor open his eyes. I dialled 999 for an ambulance. Despite a thorough washing of his eyes in the Emergency Room, Muz still couldn't see. It was agonizing not knowing if the explosion had caused permanent damage.

Ammi forgot her own scorched face and blamed herself.

'It was an accident, Jugnu. *Inshallah*, he will be all right.' Abbu tried to comfort her but she knew he too, was worried. Eventually, to our relief, Muz opened his swollen red eyes and was able to see. Ammi and Abbu thanked the Lord, vowing to give alms to the poor.

One of the first tasks Abbu took on was to replace the ancient geyser that had nearly killed Ammi and Muz. All the rooms in our new home had huge fireplaces and black or navy blue wallpaper with ships, seagulls and nautical images. Abbu transformed the house by removing the large fireplaces and built much-needed cupboards. He stripped the dark paper, replacing it with lighter, brighter themes, and bought second-hand furniture. He spotted a real bargain in Loot for enough Axminster carpet to cover the whole house. The catch was that he had to remove it himself and transport it to Balham. He spent every free minute he had, painstakingly fitting the house with the blood-red carpet.

Both Abbu and Ammi were very proud of their achievements. We were required to keep the house spotless. Ammi would start tidying up even before she took off her coat when she returned home from work. Shaking her head, she would sigh, 'Even a dog wags his tail before it sits down.'

By now, Baji had progressed to Ensham Grammar School in Tooting Broadway, and Shano, Nunni, Ather and later Muz, enrolled at Ravenstone, down the road. My teachers advised Abbu not to change my school since I only had another year before starting secondary school. I continued to travel to my school in Stockwell by Underground by myself (it was safe then).

Our new house was in a predominantly white neighbourhood. It was fortunate that Ammi was so friendly. Despite her limited English, she made friends with our neighbours. There was just one other Asian lady in the neighbourhood. Watching her from a distance, Ammi said, 'I'd like to talk to her one day.' Mrs. Khan soon became her best friend.

Cheriton Square was a cul-de-sac, secluded and quiet since hardly anyone had a car. The front door remained open for most of the day and we played on the street. It was so safe that Abbu absentmindedly left his keys in the front door or his car door as he manipulated his way in, laden with groceries. The postman rang the bell the following morning to tell us.

As we played outside, we got to know everyone on the street and the people, on the whole, didn't mind us playing outdoors. However, one day when I was trying to learn to ride Muz's bike, which was far too high for me, we annoyed the crazy old lady we called 'The Witch'. Whenever we negotiated the bend, I fell off, and the whole gang of us squealed with laughter. 'The Witch' came out and threw a bucket of water over me. We laughed even harder, tears running down our faces, but we didn't say anything to her. I gave up my quest to learn to ride a bike, for whenever I attempted to learn, I got into trouble. I still can't ride.

Once, a drunk man walked into our house when we were playing outside and made his way upstairs. He was walking back down with Ammi's handbag when I caught him. Snatching the bag from him I shooed him out. But we didn't realize until much later that he had also ventured into our bedroom and pocketed my gold rings from the dressing table. We never thought to inform the police but were severely reprimanded by Abbu and Ammi.

Another untoward incident occurred in December 1971, during the India-Pakistan conflict. A Bengali man came to the house asking for Abbu. Baji escorted him to the front room and went to get Abbu, thinking nothing of it since many people called on him for homeopathic medicine, advice, or just to listen to his poetry.

'*Assalam Alaykum,*' Abbu greeted the man cheerfully. 'How can I help you?'

'*Walaikum Assalam.* I am looking for a room to rent,' said the man.

'I am sorry, I don't rent out rooms,' Abbu replied.

After a cup of tea, Abbu sent him on his way. It was late. He closed the doors and went upstairs to bed. A little later I happened to come downstairs and saw smoke coming from under the front room door. As I called the fire brigade I screamed, 'Fire! Fire! Fire!'

Abbu quickly ushered us all out of the house. We stood outside in our pyjamas, along with our horrified neighbours and watched the firemen smash the front room window to put out the fire. As soon as they broke the window, the gently smouldering sofa burst into flames and engulfed the room. Mr. Hudson, our neighbour, tried to usher us to his home, but none of us would budge from the action.

'We have made this house into our home like a bird builds her nest, stick by stick. We are going to be left homeless again,' Ammi sobbed into her *dupatta*, while the neighbours tried to console her. It was *déjà vu* she thought.

Luckily the damage was confined to the front

room, and we were able to go back in once the fire was put out. The front room was black with smoke and sopping wet. The beautiful sofa, our first ever furniture acquisition, and the expensive maroon floral wallpaper that Abbu had so lovingly hung only weeks earlier were totally ruined.

'Don't worry Jugno, thank the Lord we are all okay. That's *all* that matters. As long as we are safe... I'll soon have it even better than before.'

'*Nazar lug gaie* (Someone has cast an evil eye),' remarked Mrs. Kalbai Ali.

'Who could be so envious?' Ammi snapped. She wouldn't stop crying. 'We've only just finished decorating it. I've never wasted money on make-up and jewellery like other women. For the first time in my life I bought new furniture.'

Within days Abbu redecorated the room and surprised Ammi with our new green velvet sofa suite.

32
MAMO MOMANI

———— ∿ ————

Zia Mamo moved to London with his wife Nafeesa Momani and his three children, Subohi, Attia and Yusuf, a few years before Abbu. By the time we arrived he was already settled in his house in Wimbledon. Being the entrepreneur that he was, he left his job in PIA and opened his own travel agency in the heart of London, in Haymarket, and later in Burlington Arcade, Piccadilly. He was the eldest son and was expected to support his parents. Having done well financially, he sent expensive gifts – televisions, cassette players, clothes and money – for the dowry of his younger siblings Shama, Baby and Fida Mamo. He secured a job for Zaka Mamo in PIA and helped finance his move to London, with his four children. After Shama, Baby and Fida Mamo were married, Zia Mamo funded Abba Ji and Amma Ji's Hajj trip, and they came to stay with him for a long awaited visit to London.

Our aunts and uncles were amongst many visitors who came to our house every weekend after shopping for *halal* meat and Asian groceries at Pak Food Store in Balham. Those carefree early days in London were a joyous time. Our three families were like the corners of a triangle. Zia Mamo and Nafeesa Momani were more like friends to Baji and me than aunt and uncle, and we accompanied them to Asian concerts, films, picnics, poetry recitals and had elaborate meals together. Any Asian artist who came to perform in London from India or Pakistan, we were sure to attend the concert. We had such a loving relationship with our family that unlike other Asian families, we were never homesick.

As children, my younger siblings got on well with their cousins and were an insignificant nuisance to Baji and me as they played out in the garden and got up to mischief together. The most memorable of which was when they got hold of a box of plasters and cut each other with a blade so that they could be used. Yusuf, the youngest, cut himself rather too deeply and needed assistance when his plasters wouldn't stick on his bleeding finger. They got into trouble with the police too, when they shot at the streetlights and the flowerpots in a neighbour's garden, from a bedroom window, using Muz's air rifle. The poor old lady in the house across from us went hysterical thinking war had broken out. As the youngsters grew up, the dynamics of our home changed as it buzzed with the hum of teenagers and the house suddenly began to feel small and crowded.

Zia Mamo loved gadgetry of any kind. He was the first to buy the latest model of car, television, phone, etc. Once he acquired a mobile phone, he called before reaching our house to say: 'Salmi put the kettle on.'

He loved Ammi's cooking and she loved to cook and lapped up his praise. She stood in her tiny steam-filled kitchen amongst large pots, surrounded by mounds of meat, sliced onions, ginger, garlic, coriander, and jars upon jars of her unique selection of spices, chillies, turmeric, cumin, nutmeg and cardamom, happily cooking his favourite dishes. Baji and I hovered in the background opening windows, clearing up, washing the dishes, preparing salad, and laying the table while *Jagjit* and *Chitra* blared in the background from my music centre amongst the din of all the cousins playing and squabbling.

Ammi occasionally shouted out instructions. 'Najmi make the salad. *You* should be making the *chapattis*. I was only eight when I started making *chapattis*.'

'No, one can make *chapattis* like you Jugno, not even Baji Wazir,' Zia Mamo would praise Ammi, wolfing down her paper-thin *chapattis* as they ballooned off the *tava*, with steaming *koftas*. 'You should learn to make *chapattis* from Jugno. Your *chapattis* are...' he shook his head at his wife as he took another mouthful. 'Of course, you will never be able to cook like Jugno,' he teased, '...you have killed too many *chipkalis* (geckos). You have no taste in your hands.'

Ammi tried to appease Nafeesa Momani. '*Bhai Jaan*, give over now. She is such a good cook! I don't know how she manages to make so many dishes so quickly.'

'Oh she is fast,' Zia Mamo added in an offhand way, 'she just forgets to add one primary ingredient.'

'And what's that?' Ammi enquired absent mindedly.

'Flavour!' Eyes shut, head thrown back, Zia Mamo doubled over with laughter.

Nafeesa Momani gave him a hard look; her face pinched with humourless pain. 'You've got *saalun* all over your tie.'

'*Nafeesa*, why don't you eat while it's still hot? Try the *bhindi*,' Ammi said hastily.

'No, no Baji, I'll wait for you to finish cooking.'

Zia Mamo teased Abbu mercilessly too, and Baji and I joined in. He told tall tales, not entirely fabricated but highly spiced. One story he often repeated was about Abbu selling his black and white TV before our arrival in London: 'Bhai Azhar rushed home from work, switched on the television and drew the curtains when it was still early afternoon. "What're you doing?" we asked. "Someone is coming to buy the television." It took over ten minutes for the TV to warm up and even then you could only see the image with the curtains drawn,' Zia Mamo went on to explain, chuckling.

Nafeesa Momani, siding with Abbu said, 'Cut it out. Don't exaggerate or so. It wasn't that bad!'

He repeated this story often and each time we laughed just as hard and Abbu never once denied it nor was he offended by it.

'You know when I asked Khala (Nafeesa Momani's mother), your Momani's date of birth, she said: She was born the day my beloved Cutto (her favourite water buffalo) died.' Eyes closed, he roared with laughter. We joined in.

He reminisced with Ammi, recalling anecdotes from their past. 'Jugno when I think of Pindi, I remember the smoky aroma of *chapattis* and do you remember Khala Chanda?'

'Of course I do. I'm not surprised you remember the smoky aroma. We had to cook on a damp wood fire that wouldn't stay lit.' Ammi went on to explain abo ut their elderly neighbour who had never ventured further afield than her neighbourhood. She would sit by the fire chatting with Amma Ji, hanging around for a free meal. When she finally got up to leave after eating, Amma Ji offered her food for her sons as well. Initially, she declined but then finally accepted when Amma Ji insisted.

She once said to Zia Mamo: 'Zia, my Kamal is educated; he passed his matric exam. He will soon find a good job. But I am worried about Jamal. He is a duffer and has dropped out from school. Will you look out and see if you can get him a job as a plane driver? You have connections in PIA.'

Mamo, being Mamo, replied, 'Sure Khala, I'll keep my eyes open for a position for him.' He kept his word too, and got him a job at the airport canteen.

As soon as we had cleared away the dishes, there were demands for tea. Zia Mamo was very fussy about his tea. The bone china teapot had to be rinsed with boiling water and just the right amount of tea leaves added to the warmed teapot and brewed for just the right length of time and served with hot milk. Only then was the tea acceptable. Baji took pride in making tea for him, just as he liked it, so I was spared the task. After tea, or sometimes even before, Zia Mamo asked Abbu to recite poetry. We always sat on the carpet, knowing we would have to vacate the sofas for our elders.

'Bhai Azhar, *ho jai, ho jai* your new *gazal*.'

Abbu happily obliged. One *gazal* followed another. Ammi, Zia and Nafeesa Momani listened intently, praising each couplet.

'*Wah, wah*, bravo, bravo Bhai Azhar!' Zia Mamo exclaimed, eyes closed. 'You have outdone yourself this time, *wah, wah!*' He genuinely loved Abbu's poetry and the sittings continued late, with most of us disappearing upstairs.

Zia Mamo and Nafeesa Momani continued to play a pivotal role in my life. They have been present at every momentous occasion. They witnessed my marriage and were amongst the first visitors after my children were born. There I was, hobbling along in agony from the stitches after Kashif's birth, when Zia Mamo and Nafeesa Momani came strolling down the long corridor with Abba Ji. I immediately straightened up.

'He will be a *duss numberia* (size ten),' beamed Zia Mamo as he kissed Kashif's tiny feet. Abba Ji recited the *Azan* in Kashif's ear.

When Nimra was born in the freezing winter of 1987, the snow was knee deep, and there was no way Asif could move the car to take me to the hospital at 2am. I had to go alone by ambulance while Asif stayed behind with baby Kashif. But Zia Mamo and Nafeesa Momani braved the snowstorm and walked over a mile to the main road and were the first visitors the next morning.

When they visited after Samirah's birth, Nafeesa Momani looked at my baby adoringly. Hugging and kissing me affectionately, she commented, 'Darling what a doll you have produced! Just one more and your family will be complete.'

'Mommaaaani!' I yelled in horror. 'You only have three so why are you asking me to have *another* one?'

'We didn't know any better when we were young,' she replied, smiling affectionately. 'Look at us now, *Budha, burya* and all alone,' she said with touching simplicity.

Zia Mamo grinned at her impishly, saying. 'Why? Do you want another one? We can still try!'

She looked up in amused shock. 'Look at him! He has no shame, talking like this in front of the children,' she remarked, blushing.

33
TUZZY

———— ～ ————

After finishing junior school in Stockwell, I joined Baji at Ensham Grammar School in Tooting Broadway. On my very first day at Ensham, amongst all the newcomers in the hall, I spotted Tuzzy from a distance, sitting on the freshly polished wooden floor. She too, recognized me and gave me a half smile. I smiled back and sat a few rows behind her. We ended up in the same class and became friends instantly, as if it had been destined.

I first met Tuzzy at Ravenstone School, when I had locked myself out of the house. I went to Ravenstone to collect the keys from my sister, Shano. As I strolled into the school hall (there were no security issues), morning assembly was just coming to an end. Girls and boys sat row upon row on the floor, heads tilted upwards towards the head teacher. Realizing I was an intruder, the teacher looked at me questioningly. I explained why I was there. She pointed to a girl and called, 'Taazy, please take this young lady to Class three B.' A tall, long-legged, graceful girl with striking eyes stood up, tossing back a mass of long, raven black hair. With a gentle nod of her head, she led me out of the hall.

'Tu-zzy,' she emphasized as she glided towards me.

'Salma,' I replied with a fleeting smile, following her down a long corridor and admiring the student artwork on the walls. We went up some stairs and then down another hallway, with classrooms on either side.

'That beauty spot on your cheek… is it real?' she asked.

'Of course, it is.' I flushed, touching the mole on my cheek.

'I thought you might have put it on with *kajal* to ward off *nazar*, you know, like Noor Jehan.'

I liked her frankness. She stopped in front of a door clearly labelled Class III B.

'All right?' she asked with a smile.

'Thanks,' I winked, knocking on the door.

Tuzzy and I became best friends from day one at Ensham. Coincidently, she lived on Foxbourne Road, just a couple of roads away. Every morning she walked to our house and we took the bus from Balham High Road outside Noel Studio together. As we waited for our bus, we mocked and giggled, running a commentary on everything – Anil's long hair; the old lady with the hairy upper lip; the black man with the white, short-sleeved polyester shirt, always in a hurry, as if late for an appointment; his earnest expression and bizarre shoes with black rubber soles.

Tuzzy was tall and slim like her mum, but while her mum had hard masculine features, she was feminine and as graceful as if she had just stepped out of a Botticelli painting. The little groove on her upper lip, below her well-proportioned diamond-studded nose, was wider than normal, giving prominence to her full lips. She had the hint of dimples in her cheeks, which became accentuated when she laughed. Her sharp collar bones arched like the wings of a soaring eagle from the base of her neck to the ends of her shoulders, above her small breasts. Although her tiny waist and shapely hips were suited to her slim petite figure, she envied my larger breasts. Her striking dark eyes, emphasized with eyeliner, were fringed with long lashes. When she glided down the road in her hipster chiffon sari and tiny sleeveless blouse, her long black hair flying behind her, heads turned. She looked stunning in whatever she wore – maxi skirts, bell-bottoms or *shalwar-kameez*. She was an enchanting mix of East and West.

She moved with grace, self-aware and unapologetic. In response to the wolf whistles she received, she turned around, stood with her weight on one leg, holding the long strap of her handbag, dangling from one shoulder. Lips pursed and without a word, she gazed at the teaser for a fraction of a second longer than normal, with sparkling killer eyes. She sent the boys scampering off with their tails between their legs. Tuzzy expected and accepted attention, while I was embarrassed by it.

At school, Tuzzy and I sat together for all our lessons. We ate lunch together and sometimes school dinners, if we could afford it, a takeaway from Deen's, a Wimpy burger or Kentucky Chicken from the High Street. We shared everything – food, secrets, hopes, desires, joys and sorrows. We laughed uncontrollably – not the kind of laughter when you are obliged to laugh at a joke but the painful, belly-aching kind when you just can't stop. When we got the giggles, it was infectious and we just couldn't stop. On one such occasion, we laughed so hard that Baji wet herself, and then we laughed even harder. Tuzzy and I had a bond of genuine affection and a naïve, unconditional love that one only lavished on very close friends.

In summer, heavy school bags chaffing our shoulders, having blown our bus fare on fish and chips, Baji, Tuzzy and I walked home barefoot through Tooting Common. The ink of the newsprint smudged and mingled with the oil and vinegar of the hot chips, making them taste even better. When we had any money left, we splashed out on coconut mushrooms, humbugs and cherry drops, while flirting with the boys in the park.

Baji and I had to let our siblings in, so Tuzzy came over to our house instead of us going to her empty house, since her mother and her elder sister Tammy, didn't get home till late. We fried *pakoras*, fish fingers and Cassava chips, and made spiced tea – Tuzzy's input from Kenya. Our cellar was like Aladdin's cave, a treasure trove of food. Occasionally, Baji and I stopped at Tuzzy's to listen to her vast collection of Indian film songs, as well as Elvis Presley, Cliff Richard and Marc Bolan, on her radiogram – record player and radio housed in one large oak cabinet.

Tuzzy was a carefree soul and didn't conform to rules. She was both sensitive and temperamental, a real hippy by nature. She got very upset if I spent time with other friends, and at times was even jealous of Baji. The slightest remark by anyone and she would complain that they hated her and had it in for her. She was like that. If she didn't like something, she made no bones about it.

At school, right from the start, she clashed with our Head of Year, Mrs. Strong. When Mrs. Strong reprimanded Tuzzy for skipping lessons or being out of uniform or for smoking, Tuzzy glared at her and sulked. 'I hate that stupid bitch. She always picks on me,' she would complain.

'No, she doesn't. She's just doing her job.' I'd say.

'You never see any fault in anybody. The entire world is right and agreeable in your eyes.'

'Not true, I hate Sharon Ahern and Stinky. They're a pain in the arse.'

She didn't take up science because she hated Mrs. Strong, who was also our Head of Sciences. Instead, she took up English, because she liked Mr. Spencer, the dashing new English teacher. Little did she know that he was already having an affair with lovely little Miss Tatum and soon had to leave when she got pregnant.

Tuzzy had a dysfunctional family that had a detrimental effect on her. At first she did not confide in me about her abusive, ill-tempered father, of whom she was petrified. I had taken a dislike to the bold little man with a flabby face, at first sight. Once, when I stopped over after school, I saw him smash things and lash out at his wife, screaming such abuse that I ran home. I had never witnessed anything like it, not even on TV. I didn't tell anyone at home, fearing Abbu wouldn't allow me to go to her house again. Eventually, Tuzzy's uncles kicked her father out and said they'd break every bone in his body if he came back. Her mother took out an injunction against him, and they divorced.

Tuzzy's mother and aunts were superstitious, believing in astrology, black magic, and the occult. Her mum frequently visited *molvies* and held séances with her sisters. She recited *vazeefas*, ritualistic prayers, locked away in her bedroom for days. After her father left, her mother spent most of her free time at the cinema, with her sisters or her elder daughter Tammy, even though they were forever quarrelling. Tammy was five years older than Tuzzy and engrossed in her career at Barclays Bank or brooding over her own failed relationships.

Tuzzy felt left out and unloved. She came home to an empty house and often had to cook for herself and her mother and sister. Her family dynamics affected her terribly, especially when she witnessed the warmth, support and wealth of love in our family.

'Why can't my family be like yours? Everyone is so bitchy in ours,' she sighed.

I pointed out the confinement and restrictions of Abbu's rules but failed to convince her.

Initially, Abbu didn't allow us to visit Tuzzy since her family had a bad reputation amongst the Asians. Pakistanis in the neighbourhood considered her African-Asian mother too westernized. And being divorced, driving her own car, and visiting the cinema every weekend, didn't help her reputation. Everyone considered her a loose cannon. Tuzzy's aunt, who happened to work in the same company as Abbu, was going out with a *gora* – a real taboo! Even Ammi initially objected to our friendship, but when she got to know Tuzzy and her mother's circumstances, she began to sympathize, though she never visited their house or invited Tuzzy's mother to ours in all the years of our friendship.

I confronted Abbu on one occasion. 'Why don't you like her? Why can't I go to her house?'

He became reticent, then haltingly said, welling up, 'She reminds me of Sultanat, my little sister.'

Abbu hardly ever mentioned his family. We only heard about them from Ammi. Seeing him so emotional unnerved me and I asked him no more. In time, Abbu relaxed and became more lenient. Tuzzy and I began spending most weekends together, completing our schoolwork, even attending each other's family events.

Tuzzy didn't lack attention from the opposite sex; she turned to her boyfriends for the love and care that was lacking at home. Like a butterfly she flitted from one boyfriend to the next in search of romance and 'true love', the kind we read about in Mills and Boon and Jackie magazine. In trying hard to please them, she frightened them off. With each boyfriend she thought herself madly in love. She overwhelmed the poor young man with expensive gifts and constant phone calls, made from the call box at the corner of Tooting Common; eventually driving him away. She was left desperate and depressed. Initially, she thought of all her defeats as the will of God, but gradually she began to question the will of God and lost faith altogether. When her inner turmoil turned to despair and bitterness, she started smoking and drinking, which resulted in heated arguments and rows with her mother. She became bitter and cocooned herself like a thorn tree.

After O' Levels, Tuzzy and I drifted apart since I opted for science and she for arts. We made other friends. I noticed she became distant and moody. Unable to understand why she was behaving so, I initially reacted by ignoring her in my anger.

When I finally confronted her, she whispered, 'I was raped.'

'What!' I thought she had just said it to shock me.

'I was raped. Now I've said it!'

I stared at her, trying to work out if I had understood what she had just said. I believed her. A storm gathered beneath her eyelids, then her beautiful eyes clouded and there was an unstoppable downpour. Stunned, I was left speechless.

'Do you want to talk about it?' I whispered sympathetically.

'No, I fucking don't!'

I tried to hug her. She stiffened and pushed me away. We both knew the consequences of telling our parents would mean the imposition of more restrictions on us. Riddled with the guilt of her secret, she felt worthless, insignificant and unworthy. She never voiced this to me but she didn't have to. I knew from the sadness in her eyes and her painful smile. She spiralled into the black hole of depression. She blamed herself, not realizing that fate had dealt her a dud hand.

Despite all her problems, Tuzzy finished school with exceptional grades; one of the few of us with 'A' in Art and English. After A' Levels, I went to

University to study Biochemistry and Tuzzy joined Teachers' Training College. Though our friendship had stagnated, the affection we felt for each other had in no way diminished. We promised each other that we would remain friends forever. At the invincible age of eighteen, who knew what life had in store for us?

34
SECONDARY SCHOOL

Eager to please my parents, I was a good student, at the top of my class. Abbu was proud of my achievements and boasted to family and friends about my results: 'Salmi is Head of Austin House and Deputy Head Girl. She has come top in her class. In fact, top of her year. Show your report Salmi *baita*. Show Auntie the curtains you have printed; the tie-and-dye shirt; the tablecloth you batiked. You must see the paper roses she made for the school fair.'

Proud but embarrassed, I reluctantly obliged and would be rewarded with a fiver, which after some polite reluctance I happily accepted.

'The teachers are so prejudiced in Ensham School they are making Mumtaz sit for CSE

(Certificate of Secondary Education) instead of O' Levels,' remarked Mrs. Raheem.

'Mrs. Strong is insisting Salmi do an extra Urdu O' Level,' Ammi piped up tactlessly. Abbu gave her a look to keep her quiet.

All this praise boosted my ego and self-confidence no end. Unknown to me (and I'm sure to Abbu), Baji, who was very reserved and mute by nature, felt eclipsed by my fairer complexion, outgoing personality, and achievements. She did not show any outward signs of resentment, except when it was time for her to sit for her O' Level exams. She defiantly refused to study for her exams, resulting in heated arguments with Abbu.

We shared a bedroom, and I heard her babbling in her sleep. For the first time I realized her feelings. I confided in Abbu and stopped bringing my work home. He took time off from work and tried to help Baji with her revision. He even arranged for private tuition, which was unheard of at the time, at least within our circles. He took her to each of her exams. Thankfully, she passed them all with good grades.

In the 70s, when Idi Amin expelled Asians from Uganda, it appeared as if they all came to south-west London. Before their arrival, this area of London had been predominantly white. The newcomers came with ready cash and bought up all the local shops. They were hard workers. By opening early and closing late, they drove away local businesses. It changed the dynamics of the whole area as well as of our school. Until their arrival, I was amongst the top students in my class. Once the expelled Asians arrived, I had competition. The new arrivals were intelligent and formed tight cliques. They looked down their noses at the white girls and didn't mix, resulting in name-calling, segregation and the formation of gangs.

Abbu had told us from an early age, 'Don't ever start a fight, but if someone hits you, never come home beaten. If you do, I'll give you a good hiding.'

So if anyone called me a 'Paki', unperturbed, I called them 'honky' or 'stinky'. When my white friends referred to Asians as 'Paki', I reminded them 'Paki' meant pious and I too, was a 'Paki', and proud of it. They responded saying: 'But you are different.'

One day I saw Shano coming out of Mrs. Cooper's office crying. 'What happened?' I enquired.

'She told me off because I don't have the right jumper,' she sobbed.

'Did you tell her it's out of stock?' I asked.

'She didn't give me a chance.'

I barged into Mrs. Cooper's office and told her, 'It's not our fault if the jumpers are out of stock!' The news spread like wildfire through the school that I had shouted at Mrs. Cooper.

I stood up for Tuzzy too, and never allowed anyone to bully us. When the school bully, snotty Sharon Ahern, tried to stop me from entering the library, I asked her to let me pass.

'Nope,' she replied firmly.

'Why?' I asked, unafraid.

'Because I said so!'

I pushed past. She fell and grazed her arm. We were both summoned to Mrs. Cooper's office. After listening to our explanations, Mrs. Cooper narrowed her azure-blue eyes and asked me to leave, and gave Sharon detention. From that day onwards, Sharon and I became arch enemies. While others crouched in awe as they slunk past Sharon, I made myself several inches taller and glared at her when our paths crossed in the corridor; she did the same.

No one ever intimidated me again. My sisters too, were immune. Everyone knew they were *my* sisters, and there were three of us.

35
CULTURE CLASH

Once settled, Abbu embraced England as a man embraces his new bride. Being a product of colonialism and an orderly man, he loved the infrastructure, the education system, and the welfare system. Having no family in Pakistan, he wasn't compelled to return, though he would say in winter, 'Jugnu, when the girls are married and we are free of our responsibilities, we'll spend the winters in Pakistan and the summers in London.' Unfortunately, by the time he was 'free', age, ill health and the draw of his grandchildren, intervened and his dream remained unfulfilled.

Ammi, on the other hand, though happy and content with her husband and enjoying the comforts and the security of her adopted country, missed her family and yearned to return 'home'.

Pakistan was in her heart and soul. She listened to and discussed the news and politics of her homeland as if her life depended on it. She had carried her roots into exile and tried to replant them in an alien environment. Curiously, she succeeded. Like all migrants, she regarded herself as Pakistani, talked about 'home' with longing and nostalgia, and thought of her stay in England as a brief stopover. She dreamt of returning home one day.

Winter thawed into spring and spring bloomed into summer. It took Ammi and Abbu more than seven long years before they could finally afford to go back 'home'. It wasn't just the cost of the air tickets that deterred Ammi from returning, but the obligatory purchase of gifts for every single person in the family. She had been buying presents for years before she finally managed to accumulate the funds and gifts for the long awaited trip.

Thankfully, it was the airline weight allowance that deterred her from taking gifts for all the neighbours and their families too, by which time my parents had totally forgotten about the intensity of the heat, the flies, and the mosquitoes. And if the constant stomach upset after visiting one relative after another was not enough, the lack of law and order, the erratic comings and goings of water, and fluctuation in electric supply that damaged appliances, left them flabbergasted. After several such visits back 'home', Ammi finally began to refer to England as home, though the hankering to go back to Pakistan never ceased; if only to criticize it.

Being an ex-army man, Abbu was conservative and authoritarian. He laid down rules and his decrees were immutable. The boys in our family were permitted some liberties and allowed out, but the girls were expected to follow tradition and live a sheltered life. We went out with our parents or not at all. The world of pubs, clubs and music festivals remained forbidden territory. Even going to school we chaperoned each other and had to be home by seven without question, a rule I had to comply with even at university. I had to accompany Baji to her French tuition and the dentist. When Ammi and Abbu went out, even shopping, both Baji and I stayed behind to look after each other and our siblings. Baji, being a recluse, didn't like going anywhere, so she didn't mind, whereas I wanted to go out – anywhere and everywhere.

Our friends were welcome in our home, but we were not allowed to visit them. If we wanted to go anywhere we had to beg and give so many explanations as to why and where, that we didn't bother to ask. We knew the answer. It was just as well we had each other and our cousins. At most, after school, we hung out in Chelsea Girl at the corner of Tooting Broadway, trying out clothes we wouldn't be allowed to wear, or in Woolworth record booths, listening to Marc Bolan, the Beatles, Elvis Presley, Led Zeppelin and Pink Floyd, records we couldn't afford to buy.

In school, we mixed with girls of diverse ethnicity and formed a congenial group. Although Tuzzy and Samia, my best friends, were Asians, I was an intrinsic part of the larger 'top' group. Stephanie, Dawn, Sharon and Beverly were English, and Barbara and Victoria were Afro-Caribbean. Like our English friends, we lived to watch *Dallas, Top of the Pops, Starsky and Hutch*, and rushed home to watch 'Lost in Space' and devoured *Jackie* and *Look-In* magazines. Unable to afford the latest records, we recorded the top 40 from the radio on our spool tape recorder, later substituted by our cassette player. Our friends had boyfriends went out shopping, visited each other and had sleepovers. Having been brought up in a patriarchal society, where a woman's place was in the home, we knew our limits. We, as did our friends, accepted that we couldn't join them in these activities. Although restricted, I never considered myself a lesser being and while my friends occasionally teased me for my academic achievements, they accepted me as an equal.

There was a strange dichotomy in our upbringing. Ethics, morals, culture and the importance of education were things our parents instilled into us. At home, we spoke Urdu, ate Pakistani food, socialized with Asians, wore Asian clothes, practiced liberal Islam and were brought up as Pakistani. We were expected to dress modestly. Wearing fashionable skirts, sleeveless dresses or tight jeans was out of the question. Even at school we had to wear trousers under our skirts, which was embarrassing because it looked ridiculous. While on the one hand Ammi and Abbu wanted for us the metropolitan culture and ambitions they had been unable to realize for themselves, on the other they feared the pernicious effect of such exposure.

Our parents wanted us to fit in with Western society but only as much as was necessary without betraying our upbringing and culture. They wanted us to be exemplary children and grow up to become doctors or engineers, have respectable white collar jobs, and above all, fit into Pakistani society when we went back 'home'. They were ambitious and wanted us to excel in school, but our education was merely a tool to earn a respectable living and probably to lure a good partner.

They allowed us to step out of the confines of our culture and propriety a little, but when we began to evolve and morph, sprouting wings, they tried to hold us back, fearful of the consequences and dreading losing us all together. They feared, in fact, were petrified, we would no longer recognise them or be recognised. They didn't want us to ape 'foreign' ways and lose our identity. They were terrified that, imbued with Western culture, we would start smoking, drinking, and worse still, reject arranged marriage and marry 'foreigners'. Perhaps it was because they had remained unchanged, or because they had witnessed first-hand the Anglo-Indians who were social outcasts in both societies. They were trapped in the 1960s Pakistani culture they had left behind. Little did they know that our contemporaries 'back home' had moved on as well.

'You must remember who you are and the family you come from. You are not *Angraiz*, you are Pakistani! Honour and virtue are all a respectable girl has. If you want to succeed in life, you have to be better than the *Angraiz*,' were constant chants that echoed in our home as well as in the homes of our Asian friends.

Our family was not overly religious. But religion was a constant hum in the background, and *Allah* was forever present in our daily lives, for Islam is a way of life. Abbu and Ammi read *namaz*, but they never forced us to perform the obligatory five prayers of the day. Instead, they gently coaxed us to pray, at least on Friday, and fast in the month of *Ramzan*. Baji and I had read the *Quran* in Pakistan. We could read *namaz* and knew countless prayers by rote, mostly taught by Ammi and our *Quran* teacher, Khala Ji, in Pakistan. Ammi and Abbu arranged for a teacher to come and teach our siblings to read the *Quran* at home. A teacher also came to school to teach the Muslim girls the basis of Islam and Islamic history.

In my mind, I questioned the existence of God, and wondered why He would record our five daily prayers and punish us for not praying. But I didn't have the courage to voice my heathen thoughts for fear of hurting my parents. These questions niggled at me so much that I thought about writing to Abba Ji in Pakistan (with whom I communicated by post), but didn't for fear of upsetting him. I didn't mind praying but found the obligatory ablution a real nuisance because it spoilt my carefully applied eye make-up.

During *Ramzan*, the routine in our home changed totally. We were all expected to fast from sunrise to sunset and on the whole, did so voluntarily. We woke up for *sehri*, to eat before dawn. Getting back to sleep for an hour or so before getting up again for school was almost impossible, so we became sleep deprived. In the evening, Ammi prepared our favourite foods for *iftari*, to break the fast at sunset and we enjoyed a lavish feast.

We celebrated the end of *Ramzan* with the festival of *Eid*. Our parents made a concerted effort to keep with tradition and had special outfits made for us. For some odd reason, Ammi dressed us in pairs. Baji and I had identical outfits, Shano and Nunni the same. Since Baji and I were the same size, we soon realised it made sense to have different outfits so we could share them and double our wardrobe. Abbu insisted we took the day off from school. Dressed in our new *Eid* attire, we travelled to the mosque in Baker Street by Underground. During the late 60s and early 70s, foreigners seldom ventured out in traditional clothing. *Eid* was a rare occasion when we dressed up and strutted out like peacocks in our Asian outfits, irrespective of the sideways glances from the locals. At the mosque there was a carnival-like atmosphere, with traditional food, bangles and henna stalls. It felt like *Eid*. In the absence of Indian restaurants, Asian snacks at the mosque were a rare treat. Later, we met up with our uncles' families for a celebratory feast and were given *Eidee*.

We adopted many aspects of the West with wild abandon. There were Easter eggs at Easter, birthdays were celebrated with great gusto, and every year at Christmas, we'd have Christmas dinner, turkey and all. Stirred by our liberal Western education and the ideas of freedom and independence we observed in our English friends, as opposed to the restrictions imposed on us by our Eastern values, we were torn between two cultures. We accepted it on the whole, as we were conditioned to do so, but at times it cultivated deceit, as we had no choice. Many of our Asian friends lived double lives – one open and seen, the other secret and closeted. In their homes they dressed and behaved as was expected of them. As soon as they were out, they changed into miniskirts and sleeveless tops, often smoking and drinking to fit in with their friends, who pretended to treat them as equals to their faces, but called them 'ethnic', 'Indian', or worse still, '*Pakis*', behind their backs.

We were no different. We referred to the whites as *goras* and knew in our heart of hearts that we would never be accepted as equals. The colour of our skin defined who we were, both in and out of our homes. Those who dared to smoke or drink had to do it in complete secrecy from their parents and the prying eyes of the extended army of 'aunts' and 'uncles', who felt it their duty to keep an eye on us. Hence one's personal life rested on complete and utter secrecy and lies.

***

Ammi called me into a private audience. Looking stern, she said, 'Who were you with in Tooting?' From her cold scowl, her brow scrunched up in wrath, I knew it was serious.

'No one. Who said what?' I demanded.

'Bano Auntie wouldn't lie to me.'

'Well, she is, 'cause I wasn't with any boy. And besides, if I wanted to meet a boy, I wouldn't do so in my backyard!' I yelled. 'She should mind her own business and look out for her own daughters instead of spreading false rumours about others.'

'Why what are her daughters up to?'

'I am not in the habit of telling on people.'

Ammi gave me a sideways glance and sort of believed me. A couple of days later, I remembered I had bumped into Asif in Tooting, and we had exchanged greetings. I realized Bano Auntie must have seen me talking to him.

Ammi said, '*Baita* she only told me because she cares.'

'Like hell, she cares! If she cared enough, she would have spoken to me and not snitched on me. She is just a stirrer. I'm going to talk to her.'

'Your elders are your well-wishers and guides. They want what is best for you. Remember, good manners is a sign of good breeding. I don't want anyone pointing fingers at my girls. It will be a sign of my failure as a mother. Besides, *izzat*, honour and good reputation are all a girl has.'

Some families opted to ape their white contemporaries and were so proud of their Western culture that they were more Western than the *goras*, and more critical of Eastern culture than the English. They were mocked behind their backs.

Mrs. Sheikh reported to Ammi in horror, 'Jugnu, I visited Saira the other day and when I said *salaam* to her daughter, she replied, "Auntie I don't speak *that* language". She didn't even say Urdu!' She shook her head and commented mournfully, 'Those who live in a borrowed culture will fall flat on their faces one day. She will learn when no *gora* gives her a second glance, and Pakistanis refuse to piss at her door!'

'Let it be. Those who live in glass houses shouldn't throw stones at others. We too, have daughters. God knows what's in store for us,' responded Ammi ruefully.

Mrs. Sheikh looked at me sitting at the dining table reading a book. 'Get your head out of your books *baiti*. Those books will only give you thick glasses. Learn to cook, clean and sew. A man's heart is through his stomach. Then women will fight to choose you for their daughter-in-law.'

'I'd rather remain a spinster than marry a man who only needs me to cook and clean for him,' I said without looking up.

'Your duty is to your husband *baiti*. It is through service to your family that you fulfil that duty. It isn't what you say but what you do for others that they remember,' she advised.

After she left, Ammi chided me saying, 'Salmi, you should know better than to be so outspoken and rude in front of guests. You'll get a bad reputation and besmirch the good name of the family. Two ruling concepts in our culture are...'

'*Izzat* and *sharam*...' I completed. 'Yes, and who will marry me then? Who wants a wife who can think for herself? The ghosts of our ancestors are left behind in Pakistan, Ammi. No one here cares about our manners, breeding and culture!' I said in exasperation, half expecting a clout.

'Salmi, watch your tongue. Green leaves don't sprout from thorns, and no one can take shelter under such a tree,' Ammi scolded.

I looked at her in annoyance, not fully grasping what she meant.

Baji added her bit. 'Yes Sal, you should only speak when spoken to, cook *chapattis*, pray and *only* read the *Quran*, if you wish to get a good husband. All these books are corrupting you.'

'That tongue of yours will get you into trouble one day,' Ammi warned both of us, a smile twitching at the corners of her mouth.

Baji and I knew enough about our culture to listen and obey Abbu most of the time. When we were reprimanded we kept quiet and did not question or answer back. My siblings Shano and Ather were passive by nature and went with the flow. Shano seldom objected to anything. She accepted whatever came her way. Ather had always been a gentle soul. He preferred to maintain the peace and never argued. It was pointless yelling at him for he never disagreed with anyone.

As I grew up I began to question and debate with Abbu. Nunni and Muz too, refused to abide by Abbu's rules, especially the seven o'clock curfew, resulting in arguments and rows. Who wants to hold back when one can fly? We wanted to wear jeans, get a Saturday job, and visit our English friends. Ammi pacified Abbu but had no choice but to side with him.

It took many arguments and Nafeesa Momani and Zia Mamo's support, before Abbu eventually relaxed his austere rules somewhat and we were allowed to wear jeans – which Abbu considered to be the uniform of the working class. Curiously, he didn't object to us wearing make-up. Like Tuzzy, Baji and I were fond of make-up and we painted our faces as if we had just stepped out of Mary Quant's catalogue – thin plucked eyebrows, blue and green eye shadow, black eyeliner, and long nails painted outlandish shades of blue and green. Baji even painted white dots on her black nails to match her polka dot outfit.

Later, when Abbu relaxed a little, we, unable to afford the clothes we craved, learned to sew and made our own outfits. We dressed in bright purple, turquoise, green and maroon velvet or crimplene bellbottoms, maxi dresses with mutton sleeves, and flared, lace trimmed gypsy skirts, which we wore with psychedelic twin sets and high heels or wedge espadrilles or boots. With our long hair tied in a high ponytail, we thought we looked ultra-trendy.

Despite the fact that our parents made every effort to shield us from Western culture, the effects of the environment were quite evident within our family. Eventually, TV and radio invaded our home and jeans replaced the *shalwar kameez*, and **curries and chapattis were often substituted** with burgers and pizzas. And we all spoke a colourful patois of English peppered with Urdu. Our Eastern culture remains diluted but forever present. Baji and I, who were older when we came to London, were more Pakistani and religious compared to our siblings. Understandably, our Urdu is much better, and we can still read and write it fluently. Our siblings understand and speak Urdu though their vocabulary is limited. Nunni and Muz are more westernised than the rest of us, and I think only Muslim in name. They listen to English music, most of their friends are English and Muz most definitely shuns Asians. In jest, we call Nunni and Muz *Kalai Angraiz* (Black British) or coconut.

36
MUZ

After Ather came back from a school trip wheezing and with a broken arm, Abbu refused Muz permission to go on his school trip. One day, we returned from school to find a note for Ammi:

Dear Ammi,

Run away. See you soon.

Love Muz XXX

Baji phoned Abbu at work. He was furious. He came home and called Muz's friends, but was unable to locate him. His friend Richard was also missing. Abbu refused to call the police. 'He will be home soon enough when he is hungry,' he snapped.

We could do nothing but wait. Muz didn't come back. Ammi didn't sleep all night. Next morning, Abbu and Ammi didn't go to work and I didn't go to college. Mid-afternoon, the police called from Wales. Muz and Richard were in a police station in Bangor.

Abbu was beside himself, particularly as he had not reported his eleven-year-old son as missing. He refused to go to collect him, so I volunteered to go. Driving me to King's Cross, Abbu was so agitated that he had an accident. I had no choice but to leave him to deal with it and rushed off to catch my train.

At Bangor police station, I found Muz and Richard sitting in a police cell eating fish and chips without a care in the world. They had jumped on a train to Bangor in the hope of meeting up with their friends in Wales. When they got to Wales, they had no idea where their friends might be. Hungry and confused, they stole milk and bread from a doorstep and knocked on another door, asking for odd jobs. The elderly lady who answered the door, saw two schoolboys, with London accents, in school uniforms on a week day, and realized something was amiss. She asked them to clean her garden and called the police.

As Muz grew up, he shot up to over six feet, taller than both Ather and Abbu. Being slim, he seemed even taller. He had grown up in Britain and was a typical Western teenager. He enjoyed his friends' company, preferring to play snooker, ride his bicycle or play football in the park to being cooped up at home or nagged by his four sisters and parents.

If Ather came home late, he apologised and gave a plausible explanation. It's hard to argue with someone who doesn't talk back. But when Muz came home late, he didn't see why he should apologise. He was stubborn and had always had a fiery temper. With the angularity of inexperienced youth, he was bold and unafraid, had a total disregard for Abbu's rules and worse still, argued defiantly – something that was totally unacceptable in our household. Muz went out when he wanted to and came back late, which resulted in fiery exchanges between him and Abbu.

'Why the hell should I be home by seven? All my friends go out at seven!' he yelled.

Abbu resorted to locking the door when he wasn't home on time. Ammi lacked the skill to curb her wayward son or get through to her stubborn husband. She found herself torn between the two. All she could do was cry. I waited up for Muz, to let him in. I tip-toed down fearfully, knowing which creaking steps to avoid, or slid down the banister, sneaking him in after

Abbu went to bed. This caused fierce arguments the next day.

We all tried in vain to pacify Abbu and Muz, but Abbu wasn't nicknamed *Junno* (stubborn) for nothing, and Muz was his son! The more Abbu tried to control Muz, the worse he behaved. When reprimanded, he went into a rage, his body tensed like a coiled spring. He argued. Muz possessed a sharp wit and could hold his own. Fists clenched, fiery red-rimmed eyes screwed up, teeth clenched, he shouted back at Abbu, his thick hair dancing. He would emphasize his point so forcefully, it was as if his life depended on it. Initially, these arguments were upsetting and painful to us all, but in time it seemed as if he enjoyed the confrontations and they no longer pained him. When he was convinced he had won the argument, he departed triumphantly, leaving Abbu irrate and the rest of us crying and bewildered. Abbu considered Muz's behaviour to be insolent and utterly intolerable. At times their conflicts became so fraught that Abbu raised his hand against his rebellious son.

In Muz, Abbu saw a stubborn young man, unafraid of authority. He didn't like what he saw, for he feared his son was heading for disaster. Abbu considered Muz a thorn in his flesh; the more he tried to remove it, the more it hurt. Unable to get through to his delinquent son, Abbu stopped talking to Muz.

What Muz needed was tender love and understanding. What he got was harsh regimental discipline. He appeared not to care what anyone said to him, yet deep down we knew how much it all mattered to him. Not getting the attention he craved, Muz resorted to seeking negative attention and became even more cantankerous.

Restless by nature, like a rudderless ship, he headed for disaster. He skipped school, didn't do his schoolwork and failed his exams. To impress his compatriots, he became an excellent snooker player, beating everyone at the local club. He played the guitar like a pro and performed incredibly daring stunts on his bicycles that no one in the neighbourhood could match, leaving his friends, and us, gasping and awestruck. Much to Abbu's consternation, he began to smoke and drink openly, which antagonized Abbu even more. Blaming bad company, and despite Ammi and Muz's pleas, Abbu changed his school. But Muz found like-minded friends at his new school and continued to shun his studies.

Muz blamed everyone, criticized everything except himself, for the conflict and his failings. At times Muz lamented that Abbu favoured Ather and picked on him unfairly. He may well have had a point. Ather was Abbu's much awaited *first* son, with whom he had bonded before his move to London. Muz was seven months old when Abbu left for London, and three years later, when we arrived in London, they never really bonded. Ather was submissive and gentle by nature; Muz argumentative and fiery. The scenario that played out in our household was exactly the one depicted in *Rebel Without a Cause* and in *East of Eden*. He did things to himself to hurt Abbu, in the process he was destroying himself.

'What do they say in English...cut your nose to?' asked Ammi.

'...spite your face,' Baji added.

Neither Abbu nor Muz would relent despite Ammi's misgivings and dismay. As soon as Muz was old enough, he moved out.

'If you knew what your father and I have been through to bring you this far, you wouldn't do this to us,' sobbed Ammi. She cried for days, grieved and mortified.

True to his nature, Abbu remained silent. Initially, it appeared that the incident would be too much even for his spirit. Thankfully he was resilient. How he felt he never said.

When Muz left, the jocularity in our home went with him. He seldom visited, and when he did, he came during Abbu's absence. Although Ammi worried about him, she accepted that it was better for him and Abbu that he stayed away. She secretly helped Muz financially, and Ather kept us informed of his wellbeing.

The fact that Muz had left home was kept hush-hush from all neighbours and friends, and especially our extended family. In Asian culture, boys are expected to live with their parents even after they marry, and take care of them in old age. Like all mothers, all Ammi wanted was to be proud of her children and boast of their successes to relatives and neighbours. Ammi never allowed it to be known, not even to her brothers, that Muz had left home. Whenever anyone asked about him, she pretended that he was out. 'You know what kids are like these days...' she said dismissively, changing the subject. She was ashamed to admit that things were not as perfect as she made out.

After Muz's departure, Abbu became very subdued and gradually relaxed his rules a little. But the changes were too little too late.

37
FIRST CRUSH

Baji's plain looks underwent a transformation as she grew older and she blossomed into a beautiful young woman with a dark complexion and bright eyes with long eyelashes. Her long dark hair with soft curls hung loosely, framing her round face. She was very photogenic. Our local hairdresser and Noel Studios had her portrait displayed in their windows. Compared to Tuzzy and Baji, I never thought of myself as remotely beautiful, quite plain in fact. My nose was too long, my lips too fat, my legs too short. I wished I was slender and at least two inches taller, like Tuzzy. Teasing me, my sisters called me 'Busty Bertha' and wondered why I didn't topple forward. I responded the only way I knew, saying: 'Just 'cause you have fried eggs, quail eggs at that...' But I fretted all the same.

When Ajai sent me a message through some girls to meet him outside the school gate, I was very surprised and told them to tell him to get lost. When he persisted, I marched outside to give him a piece of my mind. On reaching the gate, I found a most adorable young man with gorgeous blue-grey eyes, waiting for me with a beaming smile on his face. Forgetting my resolve, I said, 'Oh hello,' grinning foolishly from ear to ear. I blushed, aware of the awakening of new feelings that made me tremble within. I walked with him to the park, feeling shy and ashamed of my weakness.

Rizwan sent me a Valentine card with a profound comment, so deep that I couldn't figure out what it meant: *'The cure for pain is in the pain'*. I wondered if he thought I was a pain and if so, why send me a Valentine card? Nonetheless, I was surprised and flattered. Unfortunately, I found him too serious and we remained platonic friends.

I flirted gaily with young men but by and large I wasn't interested in anyone in particular. It was Khalid's interest in me that awakened the sleeping tiger within. Till then I was happy to muse over Tuzzy's latest crush, for she was forever swooning over one boy or another. Khalid was my very first crush. He was Nafeesa Momani's nephew and had come to London in the late sixties from Pakistan, to study. He passed me a love letter right under

Abbu's nose, hidden in the book he had borrowed.

When I first read it, I was scared. Then I reread it. It released a bucketful of butterflies in my stomach. I panicked and tore it up. It was an unwritten rule: to keep away from the opposite sex. 'Don't forget the family into which you are born. A girl's *izzat* is all she has,' echoed in my head.

Unable to keep my secret to myself, feeling very smug of his interest in *me*, I told Tuzzy and Baji. 'Khalid sent me a *love* letter.'

'What! Where is it?'

'I tore it up.'

'Whaaat! Why?'

'Abbu will kill us both if he sees it.'

'At least you could have shown it to us.'

Full of curiosity, they painstakingly taped the letter together and we set about writing a reply. I copied each sentence Khalid had written, in black, and my idiotic response in red. Where he had written *'I really like you'*, I replied, *'People like monkeys too'*. To *'Can I meet you after school? I will wait for you in the park'*, I replied, *'Sure, I'll come with Abbu. We can have a romantic lunch'*.

At the time we thought it hilarious. In hindsight, I realize how hurt and humiliated he must have felt by my rude and indignant response to his carefully drafted letter. But I was young and foolish, devoid of emotional insight about how others would feel about my thoughtless actions.

But I was excited and flattered by his attention and soon began having long, secret chats with him on the phone and later lunchtime rendezvous. He began to spend even more time at our house and phoned as soon as he left. We teased each other. A new kind of intimacy developed between us. Being surrounded by family when we met, we managed to exchange only a few meaningful glances, or surreptitiously brushed past each other, or he tugged my ponytail on the landing – the lightest contact detonated a conflagration of nerves. I guess it was a form of flirtation, but it was impossible to take it further. It was enough that he was near.

Perhaps because of his persistent phone calls, and the fact that he spent so much time at our house, I lost interest and became bored. He became an unwelcome guest and I began to ignore him. But he pursued me like a man possessed. The more I turned him away, the more he chased me, and the greater was my annoyance. The most annoying thing was that he was a compulsive liar. I could never fathom why he lied so outrageously when he didn't need to, *especially when he didn't need to.*

He'd arrived in an expensive smart car and say it belonged to his friend, when it was perfectly obvious it was a hired vehicle.

I felt embarrassed and mortified for him when Zia Mamo mocked him to his face about his outrageous lies. I could never marry anyone who was not respected, especially by Zia Mamo, whom I adored. He had no real need to impress my family or me for he was exceptional – not conventionally handsome, but good looking all the same. He was from a respectable, prosperous family and was studying medicine at Oxford University. Had I wanted to, Abbu and Ammi would have had no objections to my marrying him.

With time he became possessive and obsessive. He constantly phoned, full of confidence and vanity, and showered me with expensive gifts – gold chains, rings, a suede jacket, clothes, and records. I refused to accept them, especially since I had no way of explaining them to Ammi. Worse still, he began stalking me. He would drive down all the way from Oxford, arriving at our doorstep as soon as Ammi left for work in the morning, demanding that I see him at lunch time. Or he would stand outside the school gate, sending girls in to find me. He knew exactly where I had been, who I had met on my way from school, and where I had eaten lunch. As soon as I got home from school he called to ask why I was hanging around on the common. Who was that boy I was talking to?

One day, outside my school, he grabbed my arm and refused to let me go until I made various promises. I begged him to release me. Eventually, Tuzzy called Mrs. Strong. She wrote to my parents despite the fact that I told her my father would stop me coming to school altogether if he found out. But she did not understand. I intercepted the letter and used it to blackmail Khalid. He knew how Abbu would react and kept out of my way for some time.

On Baji and Tuzzy's advice, I finally plucked up the courage to confide in Nafeesa Momani. She spoke to Khalid firmly and wrote to her sister in Pakistan.

Asif too, came to London to study at about the same time as Khalid. Before his arrival, Abba Ji had given him a list of contacts of family members in London, which of course, included our family. He contacted both the Mamos and Ammi and found her most welcoming and warm. He occasionally visited our house. Khalid, Asif, and Tariq, Ammi's friend's nephew, met at a charity fete. The three boys became friends and shared a house.

Khalid stole my photo album, painted my portrait and displayed it in his room. He told his friends I was his fiancé. Asif had no reason not to believe him. During the summer holidays, both Baji and I were working at the factory where Ammi worked. Tariq too, was working there. Unaware of Khalid's interest in me, he boasted to Asif that I was his girlfriend. Rumours spread like Chinese whispers in a close-knit society such as ours, embellished on the way. Asif told Khalid his fiancé was two-timing him. Khalid phoned to accuse me of going out with Tariq. I had no idea what was going on.

I phoned Asif in a rage. 'What's your problem?' I yelled. 'How dare you go around spreading rumours about me?' Without giving him a chance to explain, I hung up, resolving not to speak to all three of them.

People began to ask Ammi and me why my engagement to Khalid was being kept so quiet.

Ammi confronted me. 'Salmi, what is this? Irshad Auntie was asking me for *mithai* to celebrate your engagement with Khalid.'

'What!' I exclaimed, horrified.

'Yes, don't act so innocent. There is no smoke without fire.' When I protested vehemently, she believed me. 'You must remember *izzat* is all a girl has. It's as fragile as glass. Once damaged, it can never be mended. The slightest blemish on your reputation would not only harm you but your sisters too.'

However, Ammi realized I was not entirely to blame. She spoke to Nafeesa Momani and told her as politely as possible that Khalid was no longer welcome in our house. Nafeesa Momani phoned Khalid's parents and told them that he was embarrassing her with her in-laws. Realizing the seriousness of the situation, his parents flew to London and on Khalid's insistence, they formally asked my parents for my hand in marriage. Ammi did not wish to offend them and asked Nafeesa Momani to ask me directly. As expected, I refused. She didn't try to persuade me otherwise. Khalid's parents had been told about his behaviour and they decided to take him back to Pakistan.

'Salmi, wait for me. I will change. I want to share my life with you...I'll make something of myself,' he begged. For once I was speechless.

Khalid joined King Edward Medical University in Lahore. He continued to write to Ammi and me, pleading with me to reconsider. I thought it better not to respond.

During the summer holidays, after my A' Levels, I was looking for a summer job. Asif worked in Harrods. He told me they were recruiting summer sales staff. I applied and got a job as a sales assistant in the crystal department. Initially I was little curt with Asif because of the Khalid-Tariq saga, but he reminded me of our brief encounter in Pindi, when he had visited Abba Ji with his family, which I had totally forgotten. He also explained that he genuinely thought he was being a friend to Khalid by telling him his fiancé was cheating on him. I realized his innocence and forgave him, and we became friends. I often met him in the Tube on the way to work, and we came home together.

Later that summer, while having lunch in Hyde Park, on the Serpentine, Asif proposed to me. I was totally taken aback. I didn't refuse him outright but said, 'I am going to university and have no idea what I will be doing in three years' time, so I don't want to commit to anything.'

I could see from his expression that his vanity was wounded. He had not expected a refusal. But he didn't pursue it any further.

38
GROWING UP

As we grew up, the foremost concern of our parents was to get us girls married. They believed it was their duty and responsibility to ensure that we were settled in our 'own homes' as soon as possible. Abbu firmly believed that it was better to get married young so you could learn to adjust with each other before you got too set in your ways.

In the patriarchal Asian society, girls are groomed from an early age to be tolerant and obey elders, especially men. We were expected to have arranged marriages and were frequently reminded that a girl *has* to 'fit' into her marital home. Respectable girls listened to their parents, husbands, mothers-in-law, never answered back and only left their husbands' homes in a casket. There were restrictions even amongst our own kind. The right match had to be Muslim, Urdu speaking, and in our case, a Syed was a strong preference, since Abbu was a Syed. It was inconceivable that we would marry *goras*. Hindu or Sikh was equally unthinkable! Those who didn't conform often became outcasts from their families and were sneered at openly.

Ammi repeatedly reminded us that when she went to her parental home after a row with Abbu, Abba Ji firmly told her, 'You are welcome in this house always, but if you come here after fighting with your husband, the doors to this house are firmly shut.'

'Hmm...yes, that's it! God must be a man! In your father's house, you have to listen and obey him. In your husband's house, you have to be subservient to him. From one prison to another! Why bother to send us to school and get an education if we are not allowed to think for ourselves?' I retorted.

Ammi glared at me. I knew the meaning of that glare.

In Asian society, the family name and respect are of utmost importance. Hence we could relate first hand to the texts we were studying for O' Levels English – *Pride and Prejudice* and *Romeo and Juliet*. We understood the intrigues and subliminal dynamics of the concerned families. We compared Ammi and the 'aunties' to Mrs. Bennet, with her primary concern about finding suitors for her daughters.

The 'aunties' were the eyes and ears of society. They scoured around for obedient daughters-in-law, brazenly marketing their sons in search of the best catch. They avidly looked for a daughter-in-law they could show off to their friends and family, who would produce a healthy male grandchild before the first wedding anniversary and go on to produce a clutch of grandchildren for them to spoil and pamper. And most important of all, a daughter-in-law who would look after their son, and of course them, in their old age. Wherever we went, smiling aunties eyed us for their sons, brothers, cousins and friend's sons. They formed a network of matchmakers in the community, and some attended Asian gatherings for this sole purpose, considering it a good deed.

'Ohh...you are Dr. Azhar's daughter. Hmmm... how old are you, *baita?* What are you studying?' We could almost see their brains ticking away, pairing us up with one boy or the other. Soon they came round with a young man in tow, who was interviewed by Ammi and Abbu over an elaborate tea and formal conversation, only to be rejected for he didn't fit the criteria.

There were many things to take into consideration in a suitor, most important being religion, family background, education, job, age and, of course, they *had* to be Urdu speaking (Urdu-speaking communities think of themselves as being more cultured and sophisticated than their Punjabi counterparts), in that order in our family. Preferences differed from family to family. Some gave priority to looks, others to education or wealth to improve their financial standing. A girl from a wealthy family was likely to bring a handsome dowry, and maybe a car and even property. Hence pretty, educated girls from well-to-do families got snapped up early. Any scandals, illnesses or bad habits were fiercely guarded as family secrets, for fear of driving away good proposals. Why marry someone who could be potential trouble and a liability?

The girl's side too, had similar requirements and considerations. The prospective son-in-law had to be accomplished *and* financially stable, preferably with his own house and a car. The boy's family set-up was also crucial. In our joint family system, a young man with many sisters would have added responsibilities, while a domineering, interfering mother-in-law would make trouble for their daughter.

We belonged to a Syed family and Ammi was from a Siddiqui family with a published *Shijra* (family tree, dating back to Abu Baker Siddiq, the Holy

Prophet's best friend and the first Caliph of Islam). Many spurious Syed families had also emerged but our pedigree was undisputed. Our families hailed from the most cultured part of India and were highly respected amongst the community, enhanced by Abbu's fame as a poet and Ammi's friendly nature. With the Indian class system still firmly engrained into the core of Asian society, this lineage gave us an almost nobility status. Besides, we sisters were considered pretty, trendy, respectable girls and the aunties knew us to be polite, educated, and we could cook, clean and sew. We were considered accomplished and good catches. Hence we were bombarded with *rishtas*, proposals of marriage, many of which were laughable and rejected by Abbu and Ammi outright. But occasionally they gave serious consideration to some proposal. After the initial research into the family background, they would discuss it with both the Mamos. Since Nafeesa Momani was close to us girls, Ammi would ask her to put the proposal to us.

At Nitin Mukesh's concert, eyeing handsome Nitin, I said to Nafeesa Momani, 'Momani, if you bring someone like him, I might even say yes!'

'Darling, if someone like him came, your Momani might slip up!' she smirked.

There were several families in the neighbourhood who had sons of marriageable age. Auntie Shedi affectionately said, 'Salmi, if Bobby was older, I would have fought to have you for my daughter-in-law. I wouldn't have cared that you are Sunni and we are Shia.' Several young men in the community broached us directly, secretly, only to be laughed at.

Much to our annoyance, embarrassing parties were organised at great expense for 'the viewing', and we were forced to parade like prized cows and interrogated and inspected in our Sunday best by the prospective party, shamelessly hawking their son. Since Baji and I were both of marriageable age, we were both 'presented'.

It was most awkward to meet somewhere a candidate we had rejected. Worse still, when Ammi and Abbu got excited over a proposal, but on investigation an abhorrent fact about the other party emerged – that he was an illegal immigrant or he drank or his sister had run away with an English boy, or that his father/brother was a convict, or his parents divorced, or he was on the wanted list by MQM in Pakistan...

One such candidate came to our house with his parents. His mouthy, hawk-eyed mother sat eyeballing Baji and me as she sat stiffly on the sofa. She was a broad-shouldered heavy woman, with a faintly perceptible moustache, large protruding eyes under thick black eyebrows. Her centre parting glistening in her oiled head and her peppered hair was drawn tightly away from her square forehead, making her appear severe and matronly. Her dark eyes surveyed the room with secret satisfaction and then rested on me. The woman's scrutiny impaled me like an X-ray passing through me. Unnerved by her stare, I looked at Baji.

Without takings her eyes off me the mother patted the sofa and said, 'Come sit here *baiti*...what's your name?'

'Salmi,' I replied, obediently sitting beside her.

She did most of the talking, praising her son to the hilt, while her submissive husband and son sat sheepishly quiet. 'I have brought up my children to be *proper* Muslims,' she said, waving her bejewelled fingers, adorned with diamonds, rubies and emeralds, her voice oozing with pride and virtue; a satisfied smile on her face that didn't quite reach her eyes.

Ammi blinked at her bling with distaste. 'Well, all mothers do their best to bring up their children to the best of their abilities,' she replied, trying to sound civil.

When Ammi mentioned we were still studying and hoped to go to university, the lady leaned forward and declared, 'I don't believe in educating girls beyond what is necessary in this forsaken country. It gives them ideas beyond their station.'

Ammi glared at her and their eyes locked momentarily. 'Whatever do you mean? I think all children should have a sound education, *especially* girls. You can't hand over your girls like cattle – to the highest bidder. A good education is just as important as culture and family, if *not more* in this day and age. An educated girl can hold her own. Otherwise, the boys think they can kick her, and she will have to put up with it.'

'All the customs are upside down in this country. Co-education in schools and colleges; girls and boys should never be allowed to mix. It leads to trouble,' the Auntie croaked with a self-satisfied expression, thinking things were going her way.

'Mrs. Nabbi, that depends on their upbringing. It is important for girls and boys to learn to mix and accept each other as equals if we are to succeed in life and progress,' Ammi said obliquely.

'Mrs. Ahmed, it's all this business of thinking they are equal that causes trouble. I am totally against this modern education and career girls. It gives girls ideas above their station. A woman's place is in her home, looking after her husband's family and her children.' She wiped her mouth with the back of her fist.

I wanted to put *her* in her place and stick pins into her body, but as protocol demanded, Baji and I sat morose and mute.

Ammi's face flushed a dusky red, her eyes flaming with an inward fire as she tried to keep her voice low and steady. 'Mrs. Nabbi, in this country one income is just not enough to give you a good standard of living, unless one is born with a silver spoon in your mouth. *I work*. If you are organized and hardworking, you can work to support your husband *and* look after your family. Ask anyone about my children and my household. And why should a girl remain cooped up at home if she can pursue a career? Children don't want to live with their ageing parents these days. They can't be expected to…'

'Oh no…no, no, no…my daughter-in-law will not need to work. She will live with us. We have our *own* house. My family is not short of *money*,' Mrs. Nabbi interrupted, rubbing her middle finger and thumb together to emphasize the point. 'It isn't right that the children abandon their parents in their old age. It is their *duty* to look after them. Isn't that why we have brought them up?' she said with a solemn, serious face.

Ammi clenched her teeth in frustration. We knew Mr. Nabbi had inherited a large estate which they were now squandering. A life of luxurious incarceration, I thought.

Mr. Nabbi, a little man with a nervous disposition, sat with his red face twitching, picking at an invisible speck of dust on his suit. Having realized that this was not going in their favour, he took off his glasses and began polishing them vigorously, then putting them back on, he knitted his brows, cast down his eyes and with a polite tip of his head and a conciliatory little wave of his hand, he turned to me and tried to change the subject, saying, 'And what do you like doing *baita*? What are your interests?'

By now I was bursting to give Mrs. Nabbi a piece of my mind and couldn't bear to look at her indignant face. But my upbringing had taught me to keep my mouth shut and to honour our guests so I replied as politely as I could. The conversation turned to prejudice.

'Do you go back home?' asked Mrs. Nabbi.

'We don't have a home in Pakistan. Our home is here,' I replied politely.

'Our children have never known any other place but England as their home. Pakistan is a place they go to for holidays,' replied Ammi.

'In the eyes of the British, we are foreigners. We will always remain so. They will never consider us as one of them, as *Ingglish*.'

'There are Asian men *and* women in the houses of Parliament these days. And if *they* are foreigners, where is their home? Some of our children have never been back. They don't belong in Pakistan. They may not belong in real British society, but they are British Pakistanis nonetheless,' Ammi tried to explain.

Exhausted by this mercurial conversation, and looking at the young man slumped on the sofa with his starched cuffs spilling out of his shiny suit, while he gazed vacantly at the wall, Abbu shook his head. 'I fear for the younger generation. They are lost. They are neither fish nor fowl.' Exhorting the young man to speak he said, 'You are silent; what do you think?'

For a brief second the young man didn't realize Abbu was addressing him, then he jerked up as if he'd been poked and said, 'The *goras* are so prejudiced, they don't even like us visiting their pubs,' came the gruff reply.

His parents glared at him in horror while Ammi glanced at Abbu with laughing eyes. Abbu suppressed a smile, looked at the young suitor thoughtfully for a few moments and then replied, 'Now why would any decent Muslim want to go to the pub?'

I rose and with an air of studied dignity, strolled

out of the room, smiling. His mother had dug a hole for the poor fellow and he had jumped right in! End of interview, end of proposal.

'Who on earth referred this lot?' chuckled Abbu after they left. 'What a waste of *methai!*' He helped himself to a *gulab jamman*.

'Where there are fruit trees there will be stones. You have to remove the chaff from the wheat,' Ammi said, taking the plate of *methai* from him.

'I was waiting for her to ask what we would give as dowry.'

'Wish she had, then I would've happily kicked her out of my home!' Ammi said wistfully.

39
NASIMA

Nasima was Baji's classmate and lived next door. She hailed from a very conservative *Pathan* family from northern Pakistan. Her parents were illiterate. Her father, Ibrahim Khan, was a bus driver, and very strict with Nasima and her mother. They were forbidden to go out without his permission, even to the local shops. Nasima and her mother sometimes sneaked out to our house when Ibrahim Khan was out. Nasima's mother complained to Ammi about her husband's draconian rules but made sure to get home before he returned home from work. Occasionally, Ibrahim Khan came to Abbu for help with his correspondence, and Nasima came for help with her homework.

Baji and I knew that though Nasima had been

betrothed since birth to her cousin in Peshawar, twelve years her senior, she was secretly going out with Moed, a handsome young man from the neighbourhood. After doing well in her O' Levels, she begged Abbu to persuade her father to let her stay on at school, to study for her A' Levels. Ibrahim Khan argued that she was already more educated than her prospective husband, in fact, more educated than anyone in his family, and he didn't see the need for her to go to school anymore since she would soon be married. But Ibrahim Khan had great respect for Abbu and at Abbu's insistence, agreed to allow Nasima to go to school until the arrangements for her wedding were finalized.

One day, on the pretext of studying in the library, Nasima was out with Moed. Someone spotted Nasima and informed Ibrahim Khan, warning him to protect his daughter's *izzat*. Ibrahim Khan couldn't believe his daughter could defy him. He came to ask us if we knew where she was. Baji and I denied any knowledge of her whereabouts. Outraged, he began pacing the corridor, like a wounded animal, up and down, up and down, agonizing over the insolence of his disobedient daughter.

When Nasima finally returned home, she found her father waiting by the front door. 'Where have you been?' he roared as she turned the key in the door.

Seeing the fire in her father's eyes and her mother sobbing in the corner, Nasima instinctively knew the game was up. She could no longer brazen it out. 'Library,' she said in a small voice.

Ibrahim Khan's eyes flashed and a muscle throbbed in his clenched jaw. 'You dare to lie to me!' he screamed as he slapped his daughter across her face, knocking her against the wall.

Nasima's mother shot up like an uncoiled spring, putting her hand to her horrified, tear-stricken face, and gasped, *'Yaa Allah!'*

Red welts appeared on Nasima's pink cheek. Her face began to throb, stinging as if a thousand bees had stung her. She ran up to her room and locked the door.

'Where were you?' Ibrahim Khan shouted from below, cursing the day she was born.

Nasima's mother stood outside her door, coaxing her to open it. Eventually, Nasima did so. With swollen, red-rimmed eyes, breathless and wretched with grief, Nasima told her mother about Moed.

Her mother looked at her daughter in wide-eyed horror, thinking of the consequences of what she had heard. 'You know you are betrothed to Kamal,' she pleaded with a bewildered expression. '*Putter*, your father will kill you *and* your *yaar-boyfriend*.'

'I want to marry Moed. I love him,' Nasima sobbed.

Her mother stared at her in stunned disbelief, but it was a momentary silence, like the tense pause before thunder. 'You shameless hussy! How can you talk about marrying another man when you are engaged to Kamal?' she yelled.

'I won't be treated like an animal and be handed over to anyone *he* likes,' sobbed Nasima.

'Your father will kill you. You have ruined our name, our *izzat*. You have no *sharam* or *haya*. Have some shame, you insolent girl. *Love!*' She spat out the word with venom, shaking her head in disgust. 'It's this Western education I blame. You are a fool to allow your heart to rule your head; dreaming impossible dreams. What has *love* got to do with marriage? *Love indeed!*' She shook her head. 'Life is not one of those stories you always have your head stuck in. Life is hard. A man's love is no different from an animal. He takes what he wants, and the woman is left to bear the consequences. Your father will kill you!' She shook her head. 'You have ruined us. You have blackened your face and left us nowhere. How will we ever face our family?'

When Ibrahim Khan heard his daughter's decision, he slumped in his armchair, his head in his hands, a broken man. He cursed his only daughter and the day he had come to this country. 'I wish you had died the day you were born! You have ruined me. What am I to do now? I will call your uncle today; take you to Pakistan and get you married. I blame this schooling. Girls in Pakistan are good obedient girls. They have no need to go to school. It's given you fancy ideas!'

He continued to sob, shaking his fists. Nasima covered her ears but his words continued to boom in her ears through the closed door of her room: 'That's why they lament the birth of a daughter! That's why they marry girls young, so they don't go blackening their father's faces. You have ruined my good name. What else does a man have beside his *izzat?*' He cursed and screamed till his voice became a hoarse whisper.

Nasima remained locked in her room, unable to face her parents. She was surprised her father hadn't killed her. Ibrahim Khan sat and stared blankly at the wall, tears soaking his white beard. His wife sat at his feet, sobbing and swaying to and fro, praying quietly to Allah to resolve this crisis. She had seen the determination in her daughter's face and knew her to be just as stubborn as her husband.

The next day Ibrahim Khan came to Abbu. In tears, he told him his tale of woe. Abbu calmly listened to what he had to say, pushed his spectacles up onto his forehead and sighed deeply. Assuming his most impassive and judicial expression, he said, 'You cannot force your daughter to marry an illiterate boy in Pakistan, even if he is your nephew.'

Ibrahim Khan looked at Abbu in bewilderment.

'Ibrahim Khan, I know about your people but in Islam, *and* in this country, a woman has the right to choose her husband. Your daughter was brought up here in England. Her husband would never understand her. She would not be happy. She would hate you for the rest of her life. Will you be happy if she is unhappy? You will lose your only daughter.'

Ibrahim Khan continued to stare at Abbu. 'But I have given my word to my brother. In my community, a man's word is a *man's* word. If I turn on my word, my family would never speak to me.'

'What would be worse – to lose your only daughter or your family in Pakistan, who you haven't seen in twenty years? The best thing to do is to get her married off *here* respectably. No one need know…'

'*If* that boy will marry her! Who would want to marry a girl who has no *sharam or haya?*' said Ibrahim Khan, with an air of resignation.

'I know Moed. Let me talk to him. He seems like a respectable young man.'

Ibrahim Khan smiled wanly, but nodded.

Moed was from an affluent, elite family of Karachi. His father was a banker, and his mother owned and ran a successful chain of schools in Pakistan. Abbu feared that the two families were poles apart, but he promised to talk to Moed nonetheless. Moed told Abbu his parents were expecting him to complete his studies and return home to take charge of the schools, but he agreed to talk to them.

Within days Moed's parents flew to England. His mother, an elegant lady with penetrating dark eyes, dressed in an expensive silk sari, sat very erect on our green sofa. While Moed sat nervously tapping his fingers on his thigh, she told Ammi she had selected at least half a dozen girls amongst the elite of Karachi for her son. She was counting the days before she could show them to him on his return home. She was vehemently opposed to meeting Nasima and her family.

'It is out of the question. Young men are often foolish and credulous at this age. He cannot marry into this backward family,' the lady told Ammi and Abbu with determination. 'We are from an educated family with background and culture. Moed is the apple of our eye. He's been schooled in the best institutions since the age of five. Nasima would never fit into our family. Can you imagine these turbaned *Pathans* amongst our crowd? No, it cannot be.' She whispered to Moed, 'How could you get involved with her? What were you thinking? Brigadier Sadiq's wife has been pestering me for months, asking when you are returning. They are hoping I will ask for Saiqa's hand for you. Mrs. Qureshi has said she would kill to have you as a son-in-law…'

Moed took a deep breath and in a flat tone whispered, 'Ammi, I am not interested. I like Nasima,'

'*Not interested?* Not interested in making your life? This isn't child's play. You are talking about a lifelong commitment. *You* are our future. Come to Karachi now and you will soon forget this crush,' cried his mother.

When Moed's mother asked Ammi to talk sense into him, Abbu ruefully asked, 'Mrs. Wahab, what would you say if Nasima was your daughter?'

Mrs. Wahab's look would have curdled milk. 'But she is *not* my daughter. If she were, she too, would have had the best education,' she snapped.

Ammi gestured to Abbu to keep quiet. Gently patting her guest's arm, she said, 'Mrs. Wahab, I know Moed is your only son. You must have many dreams and expectations for him. But look at it this way, by educating our children we have brought them up to think for themselves. Sometimes they have different expectations from us. They are not cattle that we can tether them to any post and they'll stay put. They are intelligent and know what they want. Besides, even if you *did* bring a bride from a wealthy, influential family, what would you gain if Moed did not care for her? *Alhamdulillah* you are blessed financially with more than anyone could want. A young socialite would think only of herself, flitting from beauty parlours to parties. She wouldn't appreciate you, your family or your son.

Unlike this girl from a humble background, who cares deeply for Moed. Nasima is from a respectable family. Have you seen her? She is stunning, and her hair! She has such lovely hair. She is bright and intelligent and is studying for her A' Levels. She is an excellent cook, and with your guidance and love, she will pick up your ways in no time. She *will* fit in your society before you know it. Unlike many girls from Karachi, she will respect you, look after your son, his home and his children.' Ammi ticked off Nasima's virtues on her fingers before asking, 'What more can one ask for? Besides, if they get married here, who would know about her background?'

'I have family and friends. What will I tell them?'

'Your family will understand, and besides, the wedding day is just a wedding day! These two have to spend the rest of their lives together. Wealth is like dirt on your hands; it washes away in no time. It's good character, respect, and love that count. Moed must have seen something in Nasima to like her. And I assure you it can't have been easy for Nasima to stand up to her father. Respect and honour in a *Pathan* family – you know they'd kill for it! She has risked her life to be with your son. Surely that counts for something.'

Mrs. Wahab listened silently to Ammi's speech in sullen silence. But the following day, when she returned after meeting Nasima and her family, she hugged Ammi, saying, 'You opened my eyes Mrs. Ahmed. All this time I was worried about what my friends in society would think of a 'nobody' as my daughter-in-law and how odd this uneducated family would look mingling with our crowd. But you were right, she is a lovely girl, and her parents are so humble. Moed is my only son. His happiness is all that matters.

'Call me Jugno,' Ammi said, chuckling in relief.

'Well, well...this calls for *methai*,' beamed Mr. Wahab, who had kept out of the altercation till now. He hugged his son. 'Call Mr. and Mrs. Ibrahim... and Nasima too,' he added nonchalantly.

Moed had been sitting silently out of respect for his elders. Now he took a deep breath and put his arm around his mother. 'Ammi *Jaan*, thank you, thank you,' was all he said, his face flushed, his voice vibrating with emotion and excitement.

Soon Ibrahim Khan and his wife joined the group. Nasima was too shy and embarrassed to come face to face with her elders just yet.

Moed bent to touch Ibrahim Khan's feet and stammered, 'U-uncle, please forgive me for giving you so much grief. I have the greatest respect for your daughter and you. I didn't mean to...I need your blessings.'

With tears in his eyes, Ibrahim Khan raised up the young man, his features convulsed with emotion. He kissed Moed on the forehead and said, 'Son, may Allah grant you a long, happy life. You have saved an old man from ruin.'

Ammi giggled and said to Mrs. Wahab, 'Thank the Lord you will have such a pretty daughter-in-law. She is like a fragrant rose. She will be the talk of the town when they see her. At least you won't have to pander to the air and graces of a socialite!'

Everyone joined in the laughter and *methai* was passed around the room. If ever there was a fusion of two souls, it was in the union of Nasim and Moed.

40
BAJI'S ENGAGEMENT

Baji left school after her 'O' Levels and started working at Coutts and Co. Bank. With her education complete, there was an avalanche of proposals for her. Amongst all the suitors, Aamer Bhai was vetted by Abbu and Ammi as being a suitable candidate.

Abbu, who was also quite a bit older than Ammi, was happy with the match, preferring a mature, settled person with a secure job. Besides, Aamer Bhai didn't drink or smoke, was from a respectable family, *and* he didn't have any family living in London. This was a definitely plus since Baji was very fussy and pernickety and would be spared the ordeal of having to put up with interfering in-laws.

After several formal meetings over elaborate teas

and dinners, where both parties checked each other out, Ammi wrote to Abba Ji in Pakistan, to make the necessary inquiries about Aamer Bhai's family in Karachi. No doubt Aamer Bhai did the same. After receiving a glowing report from Abba Ji, Ammi invited both the Mamos to meet Aamer Bhai for their approval. The only objection was that he was twelve years older than Baji. *Mithai*, gifts and rings were exchanged. *Mithai* was distributed amongst friends and family, and Baji and Aamer Bhai were formally engaged.

Aamer Bhai's cousin saw me during these meetings and proposed for me. Ammi and Abbu were delighted and thought it was an excellent idea to have a double wedding and save on expense. We were groomed from an early age to accept our elders' decisions as final, but rebellion began to feed my thoughts. Eventually, I plucked up courage and refused.

'But why?' they asked. 'He's from a good family; he is good looking; with a respectable job. He said he would allow you to continue with your studies after marriage. What more do you want? What is wrong with you? Why can't you be like Najmi?' demanded Ammi.

'A fish that flows with the flow is common; one that flows against the flow is rare. *I am that fish!*'

'Stop showing off and think seriously,' said Baji.

'Do not go gently into the good night,

Rage, rage against the dying of the light,' I chanted.

'He is asking to marry you not bury you!'

'Might as well bury me if I need permission from my husband to study! *Allow* me to continue indeed! And anyway why would I want to share *my wedding day* with *you?*'

'Cause it would save Abbu a packet!'

'Well, I'll give him a chance to save up.'

Inwardly, I too, wondered what was wrong with me. Why was I so different? Why couldn't I be like Baji? But how could she marry a person she didn't know? I sobbed into my pillow. Having read all the Mills and Boon novels, Baji was in love with the idea of getting married, dreaming of a life of luxury and gaiety, or perhaps she was happy to get out of the confines of our home. Maybe she accepted it as her fate. Finally, after many heated discussions, Abbu realised my resolve and accepted my excuse that I was going to university and didn't want any distractions.

After Baji's engagement, our home was entirely taken over by the wedding preparations. Nothing else in an Asian woman's life reaches the sheer ecstasy of arranging her daughter's wedding. Even the bride is often sidelined, and the parents and family take over the entire arrangements. In most cases the bride doesn't even get to choose what she wants to wear on the day. It is chosen and sent by the groom's family. Ammi had been collecting our trousseaux for years. Fabric, saris, electrical equipment, crockery, cutlery, pots and pans, bed linen, etc. had been purchased in sales and accumulated in the loft. Abbu and Ammi made meticulous shopping lists of items to complete the collection, as well as for gifts for Aamer Bhai and each member of his family.

Endless discussions about venues, menus, and the in-laws, amid the snipping of scissors, the rattle of sewing-machines and the smell of hot curries, amongst Ammi's friends who had gathered to help, became the norm. Abbu continued to leaf through the Yellow Pages for a suitable, affordable venue.

The biggest problem was the all-important gold jewellery and the tailoring (there were few Asian jewellers and boutiques in London and those that did exist, were far too expensive). Abbu's cousin, Zameer Chacha, happened to be visiting from Lahore. He suggested Baji and I go to Lahore, where his wife and dress designer daughter would be happy to help. So Baji and I were dispatched to Pakistan.

41
RETURN TO PINDI

Baji and I were returning to Pindi after years of yearning. As the plane made its descent, I watched the fields of the Punjab plains from the window, appear like an exquisite patchwork quilt in hues of green, from emerald to almost yellow. When the whir of the engines finally subsided, the buzz of chatter amongst the passengers escalated as they rushed to collect their belongings from the overhead lockers, ignoring the advice of the flight attendant to remain seated till the plane came to a complete stop. I too, wanted to rush out and kiss the ground like the Pope, on landing.

As I clambered down the metal stairs, weighed down by my heavy bags, I cursed myself for wearing such high heels. The heat and bright sunshine hit me like a physical force. An overpowering whiff of fuel mixed with fresh clay hit me like a physical force. We boarded the bus that took us to the terminal, passed the chaotic immigration, waited for what seemed like an eternity for our luggage, loaded our suitcases onto the trolley, and finally made our way out of the airport.

Squinting in the dazzling sunlight, fighting off the throngs of porters, taxi drivers, and smelly beggars, I spotted Salahuddin Khalo and Wazir Khala amongst the swarm of people leaning over the metal barriers. Salahuddin Khalo removed his dark glasses, rushed forward and squeezed me tight like a precious gift from God. He held my face between his soft hands and examined it affectionately. He tenderly planted kisses on my cheeks and forehead before relieving me of my bags. Wazir Khala, beaming from ear to ear, embraced Baji, her voice inaudible in the cacophony of porters and drivers milling amongst the bewildered passengers. She appeared a little fragile but had aged well.

After haggling with several taxi drivers, Salahuddin Khalo finally opened the door to one and ushered us into the dilapidated taxi. While we settled in, the driver loaded our luggage in the back. The yellow and black taxi began to edge forward through the crowd, honking and billowing thick smoke. I breathed a sigh of relief, and we greeted our aunt and uncle properly, exchanging news of the family.

The taxi wormed its way through chaotic traffic and unruly people, eventually arriving at Murree Road. I was excited to be back in Pindi but had forgotten the chaos. The *tongas* had been replaced by rickshaws, and there were far more cars, people, dust and noise than I remembered. Baji noticed the absence of what we used to call double decker buses. Murree Road had also spawned a host of new shops all along the road.

Finally the taxi stopped at the main road outside Qamar Bakery, the *gali* being too narrow for vehicles. Both the bakery and the *gali* seemed much smaller than I remembered, but I had forgotten nothing of the aroma in either. On entering the *gali*, I imbibed the essence of my surroundings as if inhaling oxygen after a deep dive. The nostalgia I felt in returning to the old familiar surroundings I cannot describe in words. As we walked through our neighbourhood, my haunts were as recognizable as my sister's features. I was engulfed in a nostalgic gloom that stifled my soul. It was the same *gali* and the same sun shone down just as it had always had, but everything seemed drab and dirty, as if the colours from a watercolour painting had faded or been washed away. We knew Wazir Khala had moved within the same neighbourhood.

I momentarily stood outside what used to be our home before reluctantly rushing on, aware of the burden of our luggage on the driver carrying it.

Wazir Khala had moved from our big house to an apartment nearby, after Bader went to the States to study engineering. Misbah had moved to Dubai, where he worked for an airline. Farooq became a political activist during Bhutto's election campaign, and after his photographs appeared in the national newspapers, leading political rallies and marches, Salahuddin Khalo feared for his life. With his contacts at GHQ, he secured a medical scholarship for him in Tashkent and banished him to the Soviet Union. Rosy was studying medicine in Lahore.

My thoughts buzzed like bees in a disturbed beehive. Who would have thought in the age of innocence, when one doesn't think past the next day or the next adventure, that we, peas in a pod, would be scattered so far and wide and put down roots across the world? I, who had longed to travel by *tonga* and envied Rosy for travelling by train to Gujranwala, now lived in London. My childhood seemed tangible yet incredibly distant.

As we entered Wazir Khala's apartment, we were greeted by my over-smiling cousin, Ruby. She wore a muslin outfit with a blue zig-zag design running vertically, making her appear scrawny.

Her dark hair was cut into a stylish bob and her bright eyes beamed an effusive welcome. It pained me to note that Wazir Khala's financial situation appeared to have worsened. Her tiny flat, dark and damp, was crammed with furniture and paraphernalia from her old home. The only addition seemed to be an old television. Three single beds were squeezed into one room and the only other room housed her three-seater wicker suite, sagging and in need of repair. It had been pushed to one side to make room for us to sleep on a rug laid out with bedding. Salahuddin Kahlo's paintings were unceremoniously stacked in a corner, his collection of art books dusty and unused. It was evident he hadn't painted in years. His passion had been killed by contempt and disuse.

Ruby excused herself and reappeared carrying a tray with a jug of lemonade and jingling glasses. We made room for our luggage and settled on the floor with our backs against the wall, freeing our swollen feet from our shoes. Feeling awkward, Baji took out the gifts Ammi had sent for Wazir Khala and handed over the large illustrated book on Michelangelo we had bought for Salahuddin Khalo. He was overjoyed. He hugged and kissed us repeatedly as he leafed through the book. He reluctantly put it away when Wazir Khala handed out *samosas* and tea.

Lighting a fragrant coil, Salahuddin Khalo said, 'I did spray the room, but I'll light this coil or the mosquitoes will devour you.' A baby began to cry next door. Raising his eyebrows, shaking his head, he said, 'I hope he doesn't scream all night.'

Outside, it began to rain. Baji fell asleep as soon as the lights were out. Despite being sleepy, I couldn't sleep. My mind wandered in all directions, remembering various incidence and my childhood companions. I wondered if Khala Ji was still alive. I realized I had a headache. Suddenly the ticking of the clock seemed to be hammering within my head with each stroke. In the dark I fumbled through my handbag for some painkillers, carefully stepping over Baji to get some water. When I finally fell asleep, I was disturbed by intangible dreams, and throughout the night I remained aware of the traffic, neighbours talking in animated voices, and the sentry patrolling the street. I woke with heavy lids and a slight headache, to the sound of the *muezzin* calling for the dawn prayer. Baji was still fast asleep.

We decided to surprise Tauqeer Khala. Accompanied by Ruby, we walked into her home without knocking. She still lived in her old house, but it felt strange, unpeopled and mute. Tauqeer Khala was sitting on a *palung*, her oedema-swollen feet dangling like a child's, watching television, the remains of her unfinished *paratha* and fried egg beside her. She looked up with a bewildered expression. When she saw us, her eyes lit up and it was like sunshine had broken out from behind the clouds. She jumped off the *palung* and ran towards us, arms outstretched to embrace us, saying, 'I was just thinking of coming over to see you!' She kissed us again and again.

It was a shock to see her. Although she was Ammi's twin, she looked much older and was now gaunt. The freshness and naïve expression in her eyes had vanished.

Wiping away egg yolk from her floral shirt, she told us, 'You know, since the day Jugnu left, I have never been the same. I miss her every single day.'

She kept hugging and kissing us amidst tears of joy as we exchanged news of relatives and relived past anecdotes. With genuine simplicity she cursed the invention of the aeroplane that had taken her beloved sister so far away. Tears welled up in her eyes and flowed unashamedly. She paused to wipe her cheeks.

'But I am glad she is happy,' she added softly with a wan smile. 'Things have never been the same since you all left. Abba Ji and Amma Ji moved to Karachi after Shama, Baby and Fida got married. All the children have moved abroad.'

Following Ruby with her eyes as she walked away with her tray to the kitchen to make some tea, she whispered, 'and you know Baji Wazir!' Her sadness and loneliness were palpable as she continued to reminisce nostalgically about old times.

I had not laughed or cried so much or so freely, for a long time. I found a rope lying in her courtyard. Wrapping the free ends around my hands and adjusting the length against the back of my calves, I began to skip, slowly at first and then speeding up, chanting the rhymes I used to sing as a child with great vivacity. I was surprised I could still remember them. Baji joined in. We giggled like little girls, singing and skipping till we were breathless.

Outside, I heard the *doog-doogi walla* rattling his tiny hand-held drum, chanting a song. Baji and I rushed out. The melancholy cry of kites circling in the cobalt sky, sounded from above. We saw a man selling spiced chickpeas in paper cones. His trained monkey danced as he wrapped the chickpeas in twists of pages torn out of children's notebooks while continuing to encourage the monkey to dance and perform tricks. A group of children stood watching the performance. A couple of stragglers stood with their hands in their pockets.

Ruby offered to buy some chickpeas as we didn't have any local currency. As she handed over the money, the man looked at his pet, expecting her to tip the monkey.

I said firmly, 'It's cruel keeping a wild animal tied up like this.'

The man gave me a sideways glance, picked up his wicker basket and moved on, his monkey trailing behind him.

As we walked back, we pointed out to Ruby the imprint of my foot, made as a child on the wet cement outside our house. Mirza Sahib Grocery Shop was now a laundry, and Bashir's sweet shop was not as vibrant as I remembered. The balconies of our house had been walled in, giving our house the appearance of a block of flats. Abbu's nameplate on our house had been replaced by that of Jamal Khan, the dairy owner from across the street. A tall multi storied house had sprung up on the empty plot where Aslum's *tandoor* used to be.

Memories burst forth like fireworks and bloomed like flowers in the sun. There was a delicious intoxication about wandering through those familiar *galis*. For the first time I was conscious that all of these houses had stories of reinvention embedded in them, a sort of breathing in and out, of visibility and invisibility. Everyone who inhabited them had started somewhere else. We relived the past but we were only partially satiated since most of the people we knew had moved or died. I felt like a stranger in this place, which till now, in my mind, I had still called 'home'.

As we looked nostalgically at our house, Jamal appeared, dressed in a baggy white *shalwar* with a grey waistcoat, his hair as white as Father Christmas, sporting a long white beard, with gaps in his teeth like missing books in a public library. When I explained to him who we were, he was flabbergasted! We exchanged news of our families and neighbours. His wife had passed away. Khala Ji's family had moved away after she departed this world. Jamal's daughter, my friend Naz, lived in Pindi. I eagerly exchanged telephone numbers and promised to call her. I so wanted him to invite us in, but he never did. Later, I regretted not asking him to let us see our old home.

We knocked on the seamstress Phama's door. She was stunned when she realised who we were! Phama was sitting oiling her grey hair under the shade of the *Sukh Chain* tree in her courtyard. She was even bigger than I remembered. I nearly suffocated between her breasts as she hugged me.

'I can't sew any longer. My shoulders hurt too much,' she explained when she saw me eyeing her sewing machine perched on a high shelf.

'I was hoping you'd sew our clothes for Baji's wedding,' I teased.

'I still remember making your doll's trousseau and now you are making your own!'

'No, not mine, Baji's,' I corrected.

'Soon it'll be your turn,' she smiled and called to a girl to bring us cold drinks, despite our protests.

The magnificent *huldi* yellow building that had once been the Liaqat School, was now a ramshackle ruin, the moss covered walls swollen and crumbling with damp. The intricately carved woodwork, once so beautiful, was rotting and looked menacing. Muslim Girls School was still going strong, though closed for the summer. We explained to the caretaker that we had studied there many moons ago. He let us in with a wry smile. Excitedly recalling our time there, we walked from classroom to classroom, taking photographs. I traced my name, still etched inside the cupboard door, with my finger.

On Murree Road things we had never before noticed seemed to loom large – the cyclist holding onto the truck for an effortless ride; street urchins roaming aimlessly in all directions; the unruly traffic; the rubbish and rubble; entangled electrical wires; crazy couplets and the black fabrics and shoes tied on the backs of buses and rickshaws, to ward off evil. The cacophony of noise – vendors selling shawls, cardigans, coconuts, fruit, vegetables and even carpets, to passing cars and pedestrians, yelling 'Baji *daikh tu lain'* – just have a look – appeared bizarre. And everything looked so dusty; even the leaves were covered with a thick layer of fine clay.

We elbowed our way through the throng, jostling amongst the bargaining folk amidst the shrill litanies of vendors. We returned home exhausted in the suffused dusk as the cicadas chirped in chorus. In Wazir Khala's courtyard, insects roasted with a sharp zap on the electrical bug killer, sending a charred smell into the air; the crisp incinerated corpses accumulating in the holder below. Geckos gathered around the lights and snatched flying insects.

A week later, we flew to Lahore, where Zameer Chacha's family greeted us warmly – too warmly as it happened. Their car and the driver were at our disposal. His wife and daughter took us shopping and helped us prepare Baji's trousseau. But unknown to us, they had an ulterior motive. Zameer Chacha had briefed his wife Chachi Jaan, to check me out for their son Rashid.

Just as all our preparations were nearing completion, the gold jewellery made, Baji and Aamer's wedding outfits done, and the dresses for Ammi and us sisters ordered, and the invitation cards printed, the Soviet Union invaded Afghanistan. Everyone feared Pakistan was next.

There was a frantic call from Abbu. 'Najmi, Salmi *baita*, get on the next flight. I don't want you stranded in Pakistan.'

'Abbu everything is fine here. Nothing is happening,' I said. 'We are coming in a few days. We haven't got everything done yet.'

'No, no...change your flight. Don't worry about the cost. Come right away!' Abbu shouted down the phone.

'Abbu, the clothes are still with the tailor!'

Chachi Jaan, who had the phone on speaker, with her family sitting around, now said, 'Bhai Azar, don't worry, everything is fine here. I am not sending Salmi without a ring on her finger. I want her for my son Rashid.'

Baji and I looked at each other and then at Rashid, in astonishment. Abbu too, was taken aback. He went silent and then, after a long pause, finally said, 'Send the girls back. I have to discuss it with Salmi and the rest of the family.'

'Oh no, I am not letting Salmi leave without a ring!' insisted Chachi Jaan, going on to elaborate on how much she liked me and how I was the perfect match for Rashid. She then listed all his attributes.

Abbu used my line: 'Salmi is going to university. She isn't ready to get married just yet.'

'No problem, we will wait. Get them engaged now and the wedding can take place after Salmi completes her studies.'

I had no intention of marrying Rashid or anyone else for that matter. After some very awkward conversations with Chachi Jaan, and repeating again and again that I wanted to go to university, we finally made our escape, promising to talk to our parents and think it over.

On our return journey to London, we stopped over in Karachi to meet the rest of the family. Amma Ji and Abba Ji were to accompany us to London, to attend Baji's wedding. I had strained my back lifting our luggage. Asif's mum, Khushi Auntie, Uncle Altaf's wife came to visit Amma Ji. On hearing about my back problem, she brought along a teenage boy and insisted I allow him to tie a black thread on my wrist.

'It may be an old wives' tale,' she said, 'but if a breach born child ties the thread, it will cure your backache.'

Baji and I giggled, but realising her good intentions, indulged her. Meanwhile, Fida Mamo got me to stand back to back with, put his arms under my arm and suddenly bent forward. This stretch did the trick and sorted out my back.

As our sojourn ended, we returned home, laden with shopping, accompanied by Amma Ji and Abba Ji.

42
BAJI'S WEDDING

—————————⌣—————————

By the time we returned to England, Abbu had found a venue for the wedding. Ammi wanted to invite everyone she had ever encountered in her life. Fortunately, due to the limitations of the size of the venue selected, the final guest list was curtailed to five hundred. Financial cost aside, the problem lay in remembering everyone whom the social code made it obligatory to invite. The fact that Aamer Bhai had very few friends in England and his family was in Pakistan and unable to attend, was of great help.

Abbu's search for Asian caterers was still on going as they were few and far between and extremely expensive. Ammi decided to cook for all the five hundred wedding guests herself, with the help of her friends. She was a brilliant cook and regularly helped to cater large parties, but she had never before cooked for more than a hundred people, so this was a mammoth task, even for her.

As the wedding date approached, Ammi was in terrible turmoil, worrying over the trousseau, the festivities, making phone calls and meeting with the in-laws to be. Endless editing of the guest lists and shopping trips were the order of the day. Ammi and her friends, and both Momanis, gathered each evening in the front room, and our house buzzed with their chatter. The aroma of fresh *chapattis* and curry filled the air. Surrounded by suitcases and piles of clothes, drinking cups of tea, with wedding songs playing in the background, they packed colourful fabric with matching *dupattas* for the ladies and pinned ties to shirts for the gents, to give as gifts to Aamer Bhai and his family.

As the ladies got on with their chores and Baji sat coyly to one side, us sleep-deprived sisters, cousins and friends choreographed and practiced dances to wedding songs, the lyrics of which I had scribbled down by repeatedly rewinding our spool tape recorder, to the beat of a *dholki*, for the *mehndi* party. The boys practiced their dances elsewhere. While the women were busy with these joyous activities, the men sat around the dining table imbibing the happy atmosphere and putting the world to rights till the early hours.

The jewellery and gifts that had been sent by the bridegroom's family were laid out for all to see. The women assessed the value of the jewellery and the gifts, and estimated the worth of the groom's family. Baji's outfits, shoes, handbags and jewellery were packed in attractive plastic bags. Her bedding, cutlery, crockery, pots and pans, sewing machine, electric kettle, toaster, and other gadgets, were itemized, packed and dispatched to her new home. This orgy of sociability culminated in a gigantic *mehndi* party a couple of nights before the wedding, when all the girls applied *henna* in intricate design on Baji's and each other's hands.

Nadir Chacha worked for PIA (Pakistan International Airlines) and air travel was free for him and his family. He arrived from Pakistan with his wife and six children, bringing gold jewellery and fragrant garlands and flowers as wedding gifts. His family, Amma Ji and Abba Ji were accommodated in our house. Farooq and Tariq arrived from Russia and Germany respectively. We hadn't met them since our departure from Pindi over a decade earlier, so it was a most memorable reunion. We had all done well, and none of us was the same person anymore. But it saddened me to note that despite his success, Farooq had lost his fizz and become a melancholy dark character. The only time his eyes lit up and became animated was when we reminisced about our childhood. We knew Farooq had married a Greek girl in Russia and asked him why Katia wasn't with him.

'I have chopped my own feet!' he said thoughtfully.

We looked at him confused.

'Katia doesn't speak English or Urdu, so she would have been overwhelmed,' he said with a wry smile. He went on to explain that she was pregnant.

Later, when their baby son Arif was born, they sent him to Greece, to Katia's mother, while they finished their education. Having done so, they no longer wanted to live in Russia. Katia couldn't work in Pakistan as she didn't speak Urdu or English. Farooq spoke Urdu, English and Russian, but no Greek, so he couldn't work in Greece. Sadly, when they met, Farooq could not speak to his Greek-speaking son. Eventually, Farooq compromised and moved to Greece, where he managed to get a job because of his good English. He learnt to speak Greek to bond with his son and his in-laws. But when he took his family to Pakistan, Salahuddin Khalo, his father, said in frustration, 'What are *we* to do; admire their beautiful faces? We can't even speak to our daughter-in-law and grandchild!'

A few days before the wedding, our house turned into a *mundi*. Huge gas stoves and pans were hired from Southall. Abbu and Uncle Ajaz purchased bags of rice, spices, sugar, saffron, almonds, pistachios, drinks, paper napkins and rolls of disposable table covers and crockery and cutlery to feed five hundred guests, from Raam Chund's wholesale warehouse. Abbu calculated it was cheaper to purchase the crockery and cutlery once and for all than to hire it for each of his six children's weddings. (These plates and cutlery were stored in our cellar and loaned to the entire Asian community for years to come, till Ammi got fed up of keeping track and donated them to charity after we were all married.)

Ammi and Auntie Shedi opted to cook *biryani* in our back garden. Mrs. Iqbal was nominated to make *zarda* (sweet rice) and Mrs. Farooq the *korma*. Auntie Shedi carefully weighed out the required ingredients, ready to be dispatched to each of Ammi's friends who had volunteered to cook. Our next door neighbours, Tom and Barbara, were used to our eccentric family and knew what was going on, but even they couldn't believe their eyes when they saw Ammi standing on a wooden crate, stirring the huge cauldron of curry with an oar. They stood taking photographs. Had social media been what it is today, the images would certainly have circled the globe.

As the cooking extravaganza began, confused phone calls from Mrs. Iqbal, a very experienced cook, alarmed Ammi. She complained there wasn't enough sugar for the *zarda*. Ammi despatched more sugar. Mrs. Iqbal called back to say there wasn't enough *ghee* and dry fruit. Ammi insisted they had weighed out the ingredients carefully, and they were sufficient. Puzzled, she decided to pay Mrs Iqbal a quick visit. When she got there and saw the mountain of orange rice Mrs. Iqbal had boiled, Ammi realized that the boys doing the delivery had delivered the rice meant for the *biryani*. Fortunately, the error was rectified without further waste, and the excess rice buried in her garden.

Abbu, Baji and I had planned the wedding day with military precision. All of our friends, cousins and friends were recruited to help – to decorate and organize the hall; fetch and carry from various shops and houses, to and from the venue, and finally serve at the tables. Although we hadn't seen some of these relatives and friends for many years, they all rallied round and mechanically executed our carefully worked out plan.

While my beautician friend Toula, and Tuzzy, took charge of dressing Baji, Abbu, Asif and I supervised the arrangements at the hall. We decorated the hall, placed two ornate chairs under a red and gold canopy supported by slender gold poles, on the stage for the bride and the groom, behind which we used the fresh flowers and garlands Nadir Chacha had brought from Karachi, as decoration. Having satisfied ourselves that everything was set, we left to go home to dress.

When we got home, the house was locked. Ammi had been told that our English guests had started to arrive punctually (it is quite expected in Asian weddings for guests to be at least an hour late), and in the last minute panic, she had departed for the venue with Zaka Mamo, *with our clothes*. Abbu had no choice but to break into his bedroom from the garden and wear a different suit from the one he had intended to. I was furious and had to dress in the toilet in the hall. My friends thought I was crying because I was losing my sister!

The *Maulvi* and most of our guests arrived, but there was no sign of the *baraat*, the bridegroom's procession. After the initial wait, our guests began asking questions and whispering amongst themselves. Abbu too, began to worry. He phoned the various telephone numbers he had but there was no reply. The worry turned to panic. Had the groom changed his mind? Was he coming at all? There was nothing we could do but wait. Baji sat in her heavy embellished red outfit, decked in jewellery, head bowed and face veiled.

'Why is she looking so glum?' asked Fay.

'She is supposed to look demure.'

'Demure is one thing, but miserable is another!'

'My grandmother has warned her that she will kill her if she doesn't behave like a Pakistani bride.'

'She is probably wondering how she is going to spend the rest of her life with a man who can't even come to his wedding on time!' taunted Rabia.

Finally the *baraat* arrived, three hours late. We all breathed a sigh of relief, and rushed to scatter rose petals over the arriving guests and place the withering garlands around the groom's neck, and hand the rest to the ladies. Without further ado, the guests were ushered to their reserved seats and the wedding ceremony proceeded. We learned later that on the way to the venue, Aamer Bhai had an accident, hence the delay.

Fortunately, the rest of the programme went according to plan. After all the guests had been fed, Abbu relaxed and tearfully recited a farewell poem he had written for Baji. It was so moving that all the women sobbed and hugged each other while praying for their blessed union. Ammi, who had been rushing around, now sat beside Abbu, tears dripping onto and wetting her sari blouse, hiding the ache in her heart under a forced smile. Huge baskets of fresh fruit and *mithai* were piled into the departing cars and amongst tears and prayers for a long and happy life, Baji was dispatched with Aamer Bhai and his entourage, under the *Quran* held aloft. I felt devastated and cried bitterly. I had lost my sister and my best friend.

As was the tradition, the following morning all of us youngsters took a lavish breakfast for the bride and groom and brought Baji and Aamer Bhai back home for the day. Ammi gifted Baji yet more jewellery, and the close relatives gave monetary gifts to Aamer Bhai.

The partying continued for many weeks as Aamer Bhai and Baji were welcomed into each other's families. I felt depressed and excluded. But I soon joined university and became engrossed in my studies.

43
COLLEGE

I went to university in East London, which was a good hour's journey by Underground. It offered me a great opportunity to catch up on my reading. Till then, I had barely had enough time to read the prescribed textbooks. Now I greedily devoured the comics, magazines and books I should have read in my childhood. Going to college was my first taste of freedom, my first experience of mixed company, and I had more fun than I had ever had.

I soon made friends and became part of a group of seven. Ken, Sheni, Maj, Jash, John and I were all studying sciences, but somehow Cliff, a Clint Eastwood clone and math student, became an integral part of our group as well. Cliff and Ken were talented guitarists. Cliff loved Flamenco music and we all enjoyed our free time together as they sat and entertained us. I joined in the activities during the day, but when my friends went out in the evening, I initially made excuses, and then later confessed to my seven o'clock curfew. I spent a lot of time on the phone with them, to catch up on what I had missed. This resulted in hefty phone bills. In an attempt to curb our phone calls Abbu had a coin box installed, which needed to be fed with 10p coins. This too failed, as we inevitably found the keys and continued to phone undeterred.

On my birthday, my friends organized a party at Maj's, who lived in digs. There, Cliff told me he liked me.

'But Maj likes you!' I replied, flabbergasted.

'I know, and John has told me he fancies you. But I am crazy about you.'

I tried to explain to him about our culture, my father…

'You look gorgeous in this black sari…' he murmured. Putting his arms around me, he lifted me into the air and kissed me.

Feeling weightless and adored, delirious with ecstasy, I let him. Cliff and I soon started seeing each other secretly. I felt very guilty because of Maj and John but couldn't help myself. They noticed our absence from the group but didn't say anything. I became the envy of all the girls in our group.

I knew that if Abbu found out I was seeing Cliff, he would be disappointed in me and perhaps stop me from going to college altogether. I had seen his reaction first hand when my cousin Rohi, Zaka Mamo's only daughter fell in love with Charles, a Catholic, and announced she wanted to marry him. I remembered the turmoil and heartache it had caused in our family. The whole family was horrified. Fearing she would stoke the fires of hell, Zaka Mamo and Asma Momani pleaded with Rohi to reconsider. They pointed out that unless Charles accepted Islam, she could not have the *nika,* the Muslim religious service, and they would be living in sin, and their children would be illegitimate (Muslim males are allowed to marry Christians or Jews, but girls can only marry Muslims as any children take the father's name). Marrying someone who was not a Pakistani Muslim was the very worst thing one could do.

The whole family tried to dissuade Rohi from her decision reminding her of the blot she was putting on the family name and its consequences on other unmarried girls. But, despite tumultuous rows, she remained adamant. Defeated, Zaka Mamo and Asma Momani broke all ties with her and Rohi was ostracised from the family. Zaka Mamo forbade her to even attend his funeral. She sacrificed her family for Charles. No one from our family attended her wedding or was allowed to see her.

I knew I couldn't do that to Abbu. I saw myself as the dutiful daughter and wasn't ready to go from being the family favourite to family outcast. I couldn't give up my family for anyone. I continued to see Cliff secretly while I was in college, carrying the guilt I felt about deceiving my family and what I was doing to him. Each day I resolved to break it off, but couldn't go through with it.

After graduating, I joined St George's Hospital in South West London, as a Biochemist, and Cliff found a job in Chelmsford, where he lived. It became almost impossible for us to see each other. Hard as it was, we gradually drifted apart and broke up.

44
INDEPENDENCE

My first job interview was at a brewery in Stratford. I was offered the job of biochemist on the spot but I declined it. 'I can't bear the smell,' I told the Director. 'Besides it's too far from home.'

He very kindly said, 'Why don't you sleep on it? I assure you, you'll get used to the smell within days. We can pay for your travel if that's a problem.'

I promised to think it over but had no intention of joining the brewery. The following week I went to St George's Hospital, a stone's throw from home, for another interview. The job, as biochemist, was interesting and my immediate boss and colleagues to be seemed friendly. I was temporarily working in the Central Hall at Harrods when Professor Armstrong, Head of Biochemistry at St George's called to offer me the position. I put my hand on the receiver and whispered in disbelief to my friend Pradeep. 'It's Prof from St George's. He's offered me the job!'

'What are they paying?' he asked pedantically.

'£ 5,000 per annum.'

'Is there a pension plan?'

'What? I guess so.' A pension plan at twenty-two was as comical as false teeth and glasses.

'Are you crazy? Say yes! Just say yes,' he urged, thumping me on the back.

'I was hoping to go on holiday to Pakistan before starting a permanent job,' I said into the receiver.

'How long do you want to go for?'

'A month,' I blurted without thinking.

'Well, that's fine. You can join us when you get back. Peter and I think you will be perfect for the job.'

I put the phone down and screamed, 'Bingo!' I had just landed my first job – a ten-minute bus ride from home, without even trying.

When I joined, Peter, my twenty-nine-year-old boss, put me in the highly experienced and most patient, capable hands of Lilliana, Professor Armstrong's technician. She was old enough to be my grandmother and happily took me under her wing. She not only trained me to work in the lab but gave me valuable life lessons.

'Marriage is like a sapling which needs utmost dedication and care to begin with, but once established and rooted, it can withstand many storms,' she once told me as I listened intently. Another time she advised, 'If you want a man to do something, put it to him in such a way that he thinks it was his idea. And when he does it, praise him,' Unfortunately, being tactless by nature, I never quite mastered this trick!

I was most impressed by Peter. He was one the most well-read people I had ever met. His messy home was strewn with books on every topic under the sun, and he could have an in-depth intellectual conversation on any subject. He played the piano like a pro and practiced on the grand piano in St George's Monckton's Theatre. He introduced me to classical music and a wide range of literature. I envied his knowledge and was embarrassed by my ignorance.

Peter was the first atheist I had met and I found this totally unfathomable. 'What do you do when you are in trouble?' I asked in confusion. 'I pray.'

Being a true scientist, he replied. 'I solve the problem or try to.'

'Who do you thank when you have good luck or have done well?'

'Myself or my hands!' he replied, smiling.

'I thank the Maker of those hands.'

I was one of only a handful of women in the department and soon became the centre of attention. Peter and my friends at St George's had never before had close contact with an Asian. They were complimentary about my looks and clothes and boosted my confidence no end by referring to me as 'Oriental Beauty'. John Graham called me 'Sultan's Delight' and Patrick blatantly flirted with me. Such comments would be considered sexual harassment nowadays, but I didn't mind. I relished it and rustled around in my flared skirts with what I thought was masculine determination and feminine grace.

I would like to think that Peter and my friends learnt something from me too. He had never before heard Asian music or tasted Asian food. But he got so used to hearing my Indian songs in the lab that he asked me to record them for him. One day I bought a *kebab* roll from Dean Take Away but was too embarrassed to eat it in the staff room, fearing to offend someone because of the strong smell. Asian food was not totally accepted then. I knew better than to eat it in the lab so I ate it in Peter's office while he was out.

'*Woo*! What are you eating? It stinks!' he said when he returned with his sandwiches.

'Just take a bite,' I said, pushing it towards him.

Reluctantly, he took a small bite, then another, and another. For the next few days, every day he bought a *kebab* roll for himself and one for me, until I introduced him to other Asian delights. Soon he was informing me about Indian restaurants I hadn't visited.

One day he told me, 'Oh Salma, you will *never* guess what happened yesterday. I bought an Indian takeaway and was happily eating my curry when I found this black thing in it. I was convinced it was a cockroach. Irate, I thought of reporting them to the food and health people. Then I started to dissect it, tufts and all. Out popped black seeds! I then realised it was some kind of spice!'

'Black cardamom!' I said, doubling over with laughter.

With time Abbu and Ammi had mellowed, and if I was working late, they didn't object to Peter dropping me home.

'Stay for dinner, Peter. You don't want to be

cooking when you get home. It's already so late,' Ammi would invariably say.

'Are you sure? Do you have enough, Mrs. Ahmed?' Peter would ask.

'What's a couple more *chapattis*?' Ammi would answer nonchalantly, showing him her vat of curry.

Peter was amazed at how we interchanged languages. We started a sentence in one language and ended it in another. He was so taken with the unity of our family that he contacted his brother and mother, whom he hadn't bothered to communicate with for years. When he saw my photographs from Karachi, he couldn't believe how well developed and beautiful Pakistan was.

'Did you think we lived in a tree house before we came here?' I asked, rolling my eyes in mock annoyance.

So impressed was he that it didn't take much to persuade him to visit Pakistan. When he returned from a trip which started in Karachi and ended in Peshawar, he was so taken by Pakistani hospitality that he said to me, 'Salma, your family wouldn't even let me pay for my laundry.'

When my three-year contract with Peter ended, I managed to find a job with Mark Wansbrough-Jones and later with David Grant. I loved working at St George's and only left due to complications when I was pregnant with Nimra.

45
SHAADI

After completing my studies, the pressure on me to marry intensified. I was presented with a photograph of Imran, who had been vetted by Abbu and Ammi, and they awaited my decision.

The man in question was handsome, from a respectable family, educated and had a well-paid job. As far as Abbu and Ammi were concerned, he ticked all the boxes and was the perfect match for me. He was invited to tea along with his father (his mother had passed away recently), to meet our extended family. During the meeting, his father questioned me on the nature of my work and was interested to know if I could cook, and how tired I was when I returned home from work.

'They are looking for a cook to replace the woman in their vacant kitchen,' I whispered to Ammi,

Ammi glared at me. The meeting ended with an invitation to their home in Birmingham. Abbu said he would give his final decision after our visit.

The following day I came home from work with a high temperature, my mouth on fire. Blood-filled blisters formed in my mouth and all over my body, then burst; to the point that I sat with a bin under my chin to catch the bloody drool. Dr. Akbar, our family doctor, was called. She immediately sent me to St George's. I was hospitalized and diagnosed with Steven Johnson Syndrome on account of my purple palms and soles. I had developed an allergic reaction to Phenylbutazone, earlier prescribed for my backache by Dr. Akbar.

The burning in my mouth was so severe that I was unable to eat or drink and lost weight rapidly. Within days, my nails peeled away and my hair started to fall out by the handful. Every day, Abbu and the doctors tried all sorts of juices to try and find one that I could drink, while the hospital dietician and Ammi prepared their concoctions. A feeding tube was inserted through my nose and, much to the delight of the medical students, I vomited it out all over the Professor on rounds as he tried to examine me. Finally, the doctors prescribed an anaesthetic spray which gave a twenty-minute respite from pain, during which time I was fed.

I was unaware of the prayer meetings taking place at home and amongst friends and family for my speedy recovery. I was in the flush of youth, never doubting my ability to survive.

'Look at the state of her, but she still won't stop talking,' smiled Zia Mamo.

'Mamo, you will have to bury me six feet under to stop me talking.'

'Hush, don't utter such things!' Nafeesa Momani said, giving me a stern look and blowing me a kiss.

Gradually, I began to recover. I had lost two stone and couldn't stand unaided. The doctors were unable to say whether the dark patches on my skin would fade, or what lasting damage may have been done internally. I was lucky to have survived, due to my youth and good health. Others with this illness had had lasting damage or died. Scientific research papers were published regarding my condition. Channel 4 made the documentary *Kill or Cure* on my illness, which was instrumental in getting Phenylbutazone banned. My hair and nails did grow back, but there were scars all over my body.

While I was hospitalized, Abbu rejected the

proposal from Imran's family. He decided it wasn't meant to be – *nuzzer luggai* (curse of the evil eye). He said he didn't have good vibes about the proposal.

Asif, whom I had got to know at Harrods, visited me in hospital. Post recovery, I began to think of him as more than just a friend. We started to meet secretly and fell in love. I teased him that the illness must have affected my brain. On Valentine's Day 1980, I proposed to him. He happily accepted. I give him credit for agreeing to marry me not knowing if the dark patches on my skin would ever disappear, and being aware that the doctors had warned me the illness may have affected my chances of conceiving. Fortunately, within the year, the scars faded, and there was no lasting damage, though my hair texture and volume were never the same again.

On Patrick and Peter's insistence, I sued my doctor. She decided to settle out of court, leaving me with a windfall which I used for the deposit on a flat, and a lavish wedding.

Much to Abbu and Ammi's delight, like Baji, Ather and Shano agreed to arranged marriages. On our parent's discretion and never having met their partners, they took a leap of faith. Shano married Mohammed Ali and Ather married Hina, partners vetted and selected for them. Fortunately, Hina turned out to be the perfect match for Ather and an Asian mother's dream daughter-in-law. To this day we all say she must be a reward for my parent's good deeds for she not only turned out to be Ather's soul mate, but also raised three wonderful children. She has been a godsend for our family. As in any marriage, Baji and Shano had their ups and downs but accept their lot as fate.

However, true to character, Nunni, who was radically opposed to the concept of arranged marriages and a real romantic at heart, defied convention and told Abbu she *liked* Osman (using the word 'love' would have been unthinkable). Though Osman was from a respectable Siddiqui family, and educated, while his late father had been an Ambassador and his brother was a senior executive, it wasn't the done thing to admit to your parents that you had been seeing someone. We were all relieved that Abbu didn't hit the roof. Instead, he calmly asked her to tell Osman to visit.

After meeting Osman, Abbu said, 'Nunni *baita*, I don't like his temperament.'

But Nunni couldn't see the thorn amongst the roses. 'Abbu I have been working with him for a long time and I know him well,' she pleaded.

'Have you thought this through?'

'Yes!'

'Okay *baita*; it is your *kismet*,' Abbu said with a deep sigh.

'And you have decided without consulting those who made you fit to do so!' Ammi added sternly, a hint of sadness in her voice.

Despite Abbu's objections, Nunni married Osman. Even on her wedding day, Abbu said to her, 'Nunni *baita*, think it over. I don't think he is the right boy for you. There is still time. You just say the word, and I will take care of everything.'

But Nunni was blinded by love. When the blossoms withered, only the barbs remained and Nunni realized her mistake. After Osman lost his well-paid job, he refused to take anything less prestigious. Unable to keep up with the mortgage payments, their home was repossessed. Osman spiralled into depression, began to drink and, exploded at the slightest thing, becoming abusive. Nunni tried hard to keep their marriage together as the sole breadwinner with two children, but eventually, after seventeen years, could take it no longer and she divorced him. Unfortunately Asians behave as if humans are biologically monogamous, and changing a mate is tantamount to defiance of nature, hence she never remarried.

Muz went a step further. He had left home as soon as was old enough to do so. One day he told Ather that his girlfriend Shirley, with whom he had been living, was pregnant. We didn't even know he had a girlfriend, let alone that he was *living* with her. Ather told Baji and me. We were dumbfounded. We knew how Abbu and Ammi would react to this bombshell. We spoke to Shirley and persuaded her to accept Islam and marry Muz. She agreed to convert.

But, for all of Abbu's sophistication and veneer of modernity, below the surface was an orthodox Muslim. He was furious and refused to attend the *nikah* ceremony, as did Aamer Bhai, who feared it would influence his girls. We implored Muz to speak to Abbu and the Mamos, and invite them to the *nikah* personally, but he was his father's son! Abbu, however, did not stop Ammi from attending. Baji too, came without Aamer Bhai and her children. Asif, Mohammad Ali and I were of the opinion that if there was the slightest chance that Muz's children would be Muslim, it was a chance worth taking.

One day, Muz came home unexpectedly with his baby, Aysha, and with a pervading sense of shame and imposed humiliation, dumped her in Abbu's lap. Abbu began to cry, hugging the child.

Ammi seized the opportunity to unite father and son saying, 'That's it! You hug your granddaughter when her mother is not welcome in this house?'

Abbu leaned back in his chair, pushed his spectacles up on his forehead and with an air of resignation, looked into baby Ayesha's eyes. Then he said to Muz, 'Bring your wife home.'

Shirley attended family functions, ate Asian food and even wore Asian clothes at family functions, but we felt she never considered us as family. Despite our best efforts to include her, she remained standoffish. As Muz became an insulin dependent diabetic, he grew irritable, capricious and quarrelsome. He and Shirley finally divorced. The divorce was a nasty affair that nearly killed Muz. Thankfully, as time passed and he became reunited with his two teenage children, he finally came to terms with it.

46
A WOMAN OF SUBSTANCE

Ammi has always been talkative and opinionated, and like Amma Ji, says it how it is, without thought or fear of offending. She has an incredible memory and surprisingly, even now, after a lifetime in London, she has kept up with her extended family back in Pakistan, and knows who married whom and how many children they have. She has a tale to tell about every topic under the sun and a proverb for every occasion. Her stock of preserved memories is endless.

Ammi loves to narrate our childhood misdemeanours, punctuated with numerous travesties, proverbs, humour and wit, causing us to retreat scarlet faced in embarrassment. Many of her tales have become as familiar as fairy tales, worn smooth with years of repetition, for she loves to talk – loudly. When we say, 'Ammi, you have already told us this story,' she ignores the remark with genuine simplicity and continues to tell it to the very end. I like the way repetition has worn things smooth. We are used to it, as is everyone else who knows her. Despite her chatter, or perhaps because of it, she is much loved by young and old.

Ammi's conversation can take strange turns. One minute she is animatedly talking about her childhood in Rohtak, the next she is describing how she had to cook mounds of *chapattis* in Murree on damp wood fires that threatened to go out any minute, producing dense smoke that blinded her with tears. Suddenly she would be climbing fruit trees in Burma; then just as suddenly she would be telling us of her obese Aunt Khalda, who had a strange way of asking for food: 'Amma Ji, Bubbly says she would love some *halva*.' 'Who the hell is Aunt Khalda, or Bubbly for that matter?' we asked in exasperation.

Ammi's achievements in life are monumental. Despite having little formal education, she is far more intelligent than many educated people. It must have been difficult for her to move to London, leaving behind her large family, without hope of ever seeing them again. Having moved to an entirely alien culture where she couldn't speak the language, she adjusted to the new way of life without complaining. The only fear in her heart was the fear of that dead of night call from Pakistan bearing bad news about her parents, and not having a chance to say goodbye. She panicked when there was a call at odd hours and fretted that calls to Pakistan were so expensive. As it happened, she *was* able to go to Pakistan to say her final good-byes to both Abba Ji and Amma Ji.

'There is nothing I can't do if I put my mind to it; except father a child!' was something Ammi liked to say. And she proved time and again that she could! After being made redundant from several factories during the three-day week policy in the early 70s, Ammi joined Wandsworth College to learn English.

Poor Ather was embarrassed by this since he also studied there. 'You go to the common room for a fag and your mum's sitting there with her mates. It's enough to make you jump out of the nearest window!' he complained.

Having completed her course, she started child-minding Catherine, Edward and Alex. When Sue came to pick up Catherine, Ammi insisted she stop for a cup of tea and take home the *biryani* she had just cooked. I think it was then that her attitude towards the *Angrez* (as she referred to the British), changed.   Edward's parents, Tom and

Kate, were often found drinking tea, and chatting and laughing with Ammi.

Having raised six children, Ammi readily gave advice on child care and the parents often called her for advice rather than take the children to the doctor for minor ailments.

'Oh Mrs. Ahmed, is this rash serious? Is it chicken pox? Shall I stay home from work with Edward today?'

'No, it's not chicken pox it's measles. But don't worry. Better he gets it now than later. You can leave him with me; Catherine has already had them.'

'Mrs. Ahmed, Catherine was crying for you in the middle of the night! You spoil her so much she doesn't want to go home!'

'Mrs. Ahmed, Catherine screams to be washed whenever she sits on the loo,' chuckled Sue.

While Sue explained the reasons for Catholic-Protestant disputes in Ireland, Ammi enlightened her about the similar Shia-Sunni conflicts in Islam. She expounded the reasons for the conflict between India and Pakistan over Kashmir. She didn't hesitate to say what she thought or that she might offend anyone; she called a spade a spade.

'The British left India and Pakistan unresolved

deliberately so that we would continue to fight amongst ourselves and they could sell arms to both sides,' she confidently informed Sue. Abbu looked up startled at this undiplomatic statement, but Ammi went on unperturbed. 'They have done the same throughout the world. Look at Palestine!'

Ammi became fearful about the racial hatred that flared up after the 'Rivers of Blood' speech by Enoch Powell. 'Can they really send us back home?' she asked Abbu.

'We were migrants in Pakistan, we are migrants here. Where would they send us?' Abbu asked laughing.

No, the NHS and London transport would grind to a halt if they kick the foreigners out,' Abbu replied, trying to appease her.

'That's what the Asians thought in Africa. It didn't stop Idi Amin from kicking them out,' Ammi retorted, raising her eyebrows.

Despite her size, she was a feisty little lady. One day, as we were cleaning our front garden, a group of Skinheads passing by, called out, 'Pakis go home!' Ammi took off her sandal and aimed it at them. Like a missile it struck the culprit on the back of his head. I ran after them with my broom. They scampered as Ammi got ready to throw her other sandal, leaving us in fits of laughter.

But, having witnessed the Asian invasion from Africa and the changes it brought in London, Ammi said, 'I don't blame them for being prejudiced. How many people can this tiny island hold? It's already bursting at the seams.'

During the 1971 war between India and Pakistan, Ammi and her friends formed the Pakistan Women's Organization. The organization continues to this day, supporting good causes in Pakistan and the UK.

Ammi has always been very vocal about Indo-Pak politics. When Lord Mountbatten was assassinated by the IRA on his boat in 1979, her immediate reaction was, 'He's got his comeuppance. His scheming and plotting have come to a bitter end. Allah punishes you for your deeds in this world, for all to see.'

'Jugnu, he was someone's husband and father; and he was doing a job. He did what he thought was best for the British at the time,' said Abbu.

'He colluded with Nehru. It resulted in countless unnecessary deaths and a bad deal for Pakistan,' Ammi spat. Try as he might, Abbu could not get her to change her mind.

Ammi loves the Royal family. When Princess Diana was killed, she was heartbroken, crying and cursing Camilla as if she had personally killed Diana. 'Hope you are satisfied now! Now that she is dead,' she yelled at the TV. To this day, whenever she remembers Diana, she tut-tuts and sighs. 'What a waste of a good life! What a beautiful, graceful Queen she would have been,' she laments. 'This is what you call bad *kismet*. He chucked that beautiful diamond for this hag! It runs in the family; his uncle was just as foolish.'

She disliked Benazir Bhutto, but when she was assassinated, Ammi was really upset and shouted abuse at the screen, cursing Zardari, as she watched the footage on TV. 'He was plotting to have her killed all the time he was behind bars. I can't bear to look at his *manhoos*, cursed face. How can anyone have the mother of their own children killed? I don't know!'

'Ammi, you don't know he had her killed,' I said.

'You don't have to be told the sun is out, you can feel it. The whole family is cursed! Her father was hanged, her brothers murdered, and now *her*. Just like the Kennedys and Gandhi.'

'Why, what happened to Gandhi's family?'

'Not him, her...Indira Gandhi. She was assassinated; her son Sanjay killed in a plane crash; and then Rajiv too, was assassinated. You get your comeuppance in this world. What good is all that power and wealth if you end up getting shot like a stray dog?'

Abbu shook his head but thought it best to keep quiet.

Ammi cannot walk down the street without saying *salaam* and exchanging greetings with every second person. But one day, when she pulled back the curtains and saw a hearse outside Jean's door and her coffin being carried out, she was furious. 'They didn't even inform us of her death. We have known her for thirty years! Admittedly they were not our best friends but they knew us well enough to send Christmas cards and exchange greetings on the street. They are like the flowers in this country, beautiful to look at but without any fragrance. Even wildflowers in Pakistan have a scent,' she muttered.

'What are you talking about?' asked Abbu.

'If someone dies in our community, everyone is informed. Look at this...Jean lived across the road... we knew her for years, and no one has bothered to tell us she is gone. They didn't have to invite us to the funeral. If they had only told us, I would have sent some flowers and prayed for her.' Ammi stood watching solemnly, shaking her head in disbelief.

Abbu looked out of the window and said, 'You can still send flowers and pray for her.'

47
BLACK MAGIC

———————⌇———————

After college, Tuzzy and I were rarely in touch. She didn't even come to my wedding, which was painful. I thought she might just turn up but she never did. I finally had to accept that we had drifted apart and changed. One day, out of the blue, I got a frantic call.

'Salma! You have to come over *immediately*.'

'Why? I've just had a baby. I can't drive, and Asif is abroad,' I stammered.

'It's a matter of life and death. I can't talk on the phone. You have to come,' she said, without bothering to congratulate me on the birth of my first baby.

Despite Ammi's protests I left baby Kashif with her and called Peter to take me to Tuzzy's. She lived by herself in a flat in Streatham. When we got there she was smoking a joint and the air in her neat little apartment was thick with smoke. I introduced her to Peter. She wasn't quite sure if she should let him in. After I explained I couldn't have come without him, and she could trust him, she finally did. Although fragile, she was immaculately dressed, with flawless make-up and manicured nails. She had retained her smooth olive skin and pitch black hair but lost her freshness. The fearful look in her eyes unnerved me – that of an animal caught in a snare. She was very agitated. She moved cautiously, feline-like, with sudden sideways glances, as if expecting someone or something to appear from thin air. She drew on her joint and then leaned in towards me. In a low secretive tone, as if someone might be listening, she said, 'Salma, the *Shadow* is upon me. You *have* to help me!'

'What shadow?' I asked, louder than I had intended, looking at Peter in confusion.

'The shadow of *death*,' she emphasized, looking sharply at me, irritated by my ignorance. She stubbed out her joint and immediately lit a cigarette.

On further questioning, she told me she was part of a cult and had participated in black magic rituals.

'What do you mean? What kind of rituals?' I interrupted. Peter gestured to let her continue.

'*Muti*...it gives you power, wealth, prosperity and *eternal peace*...whatever you wish,' she said. 'I was frightened by the last orgy at the altar when the priest gave me a drink that paralyzed me. I could see what was happening but couldn't move.'

She went on to describe the ritual in which members of the cult danced around her in long cloaks, chanting incantations and prayers recited backwards. The chants got louder and louder and the priest first penetrated her with a cross and then raped her on the altar. She feared that next time she would be used as a human sacrifice.

I looked at Peter. He was listening intently, a horrified expression on his face. I wondered if she was under the influence of whatever she was smoking or if she had totally lost it.

She went on, 'Body parts are used as medicine. The blood boosts your vitality when it's taken raw; the skull placed in the foundation of new buildings brings success and good luck to business; eating brains guarantees political power and success in business; hands built into shop entrances attracts customers. Human ash mixed into a paste cures strokes. Bodies buried on a farm secure big harvests, and genitals, breasts and uteri cure infertility and bring good luck. Virgin girls and children are particularly potent. Next time it's my turn,' she said with resignation.

'But you're *not* a virgin,' I blurted tactlessly.

'But *they* think I am.'

I was taken aback and stared at Peter in astonishment.

Taking a long deliberate drag, she pulled out a sealed envelope from her handbag, 'I want to give you this. Give it to the police when I am killed.' She took a deep breath. She was so sure she would be killed that she said *when*, not *if*. When I reluctantly took the envelope, she said, 'Now I am liberated.'

'Why did you get involved?' I asked.

'I didn't think it was going to be *me*, did I?' came the sharp response.

Peter and I asked her lots of questions. Finally I said, 'Tuzzy, I am not convinced. You have to give me proof. I am a scientist; I don't believe in all this... to me it is all mumbo jumbo!'

She looked annoyed...more than annoyed. She stubbed out her cigarette in irritation and asked me to meet her at her mother's house the following afternoon.

On our way back, sitting in Peter's sports car, I

couldn't believe what had just happened. He asked me many questions and I tried to convey the transcendental atmosphere in Tuzzy's home and her family's fascination with the supernatural. As kids, she got me hooked into reading our horoscopes. Tuzzy talked about black magic in Africa. On her return from a trip to Kenya, she told me she had been in touch with her dead cousin in a séance.

The following day I went to her mothers' house as agreed. Tuzzy was waiting for me. There was no one else at home. She took me to her old bedroom, which was as dark and sad as I remembered. She opened her wardrobe and showed me dresses on hangers which had crosses hanging by strings.

'See, what did I tell you?' she said, pointing. 'They are going to kill me and Auntie Saeeda and mum are in on it.'

Realizing I still didn't believe her, she became agitated. Her mood changed dramatically from moment to moment. She appeared highly excited and animated one minute, then suddenly reticent and sad. I looked at her dubiously and continued my questioning. In my mind, an Indian song repeated itself like a worm: *Likhne wale ne likh di meri taqdeer mein barbadi* (He who has written my fate has transcribed doom).

Her mother returned from work. On seeing her, Tuzzy suddenly transgressed into someone I didn't know or recognize. She looked vicious. She snarled and began swearing at us both, accusing me of being in on it, the plot to kill her. She cursed and swore; using foul language of a kind I had never heard her use before. Then she stormed out of the house.

By now I was crying, while her mum stood to one side, watching silently. After Tuzzy had left, her mother said, 'I am sorry, Salma, she's schizophrenic.'

'What? Since when? Auntie, why didn't you tell me before? Is she being treated? Getting help?' I blurted all at once.

'Yes, she's been in Springfield, and needs regular medication, but she won't take it. I can't keep her at home. Her doctors tell me *I* bring out the worst in her.' She too, was now crying.

Flabbergasted, I returned home really disturbed, believing her mother. I kept wondering if Tuzzy's schizophrenia was a reaction to her abuse. The following day I spoke to my medic friends at St George's to try and get her some help. They told me there wasn't anything I could do unless I could force her to take her medication.

I tried to contact Tuzzy on several occasions, but was unsuccessful. Soon, preoccupied with my hectic life, I accepted she was ill. I put her out of my thoughts.

48
WEDDING ANNIVERSARY

For Amma Ji and Abba Ji's fiftieth wedding anniversary, we organised a surprise party at Raavi, our favourite Indian restaurant in Euston. Everyone was already present and seated, anxiously awaiting their arrival with Zia Mamo and Nafeesa Momani. Ather, our lookout, informed us of their arrival and hushed us into silence, ready to shout 'Surprise!' when they entered.

After the initial exchange of happy greetings, when she was seated, Amma Ji saw the Sikh proprietor. Stiffening, she shot up, looking at Zia Mamo with steely eyes. 'You have brought me to eat at a Sikh's place?' she asked her wise old expressive face screwed up in a tortuous expression. She stood leaning on the table, blinking in the strong light, glaring at the *Sardar Ji*.

We had never heard her speak to Zia Mamo so sharply before. An uncomfortable hush descended on the gathering, which had been buzzing with excitement just a few minutes ago.

'You think I will eat in a Sikh's place? Have you forgotten what they did to us? *They killed your baby sister!*' Amma Ji shrieked through gritted teeth.

Mamo Zia flushed. He looked up at the proprietor with a nervous, sheepish half smile. 'Amma Ji, it wasn't his fault... and, and it was a long time ago,' he murmured.

'I remember it like yesterday,' she said firmly through gritted teeth, tears running down her wrinkled cheeks like streams in a valley. 'Take me home. *I won't eat here*,' she stated resolutely. Her voice took on a chilling edge as she glared with narrowed eyes.

'*Bhain Ji, please* take a seat for a minute,' said *Sardar Ji*, bowing humbly before Amma Ji, a tremor in his voice. Until then I had never really noticed that the friendly owner of Raavi was a Sikh. Suddenly his bright turban and beard were all I could see.

Amma Ji, once so erect and graceful, looked fragile, a hunched bag of skin and bones crushed by the weight of her memories, her face creased like scrunched-up tissue paper, each line etched by a specific moment in her past. This stooped little figure had borne many children, had seen some of them die. Afraid of nothing, she had stared death in the face many times. Nothing unnerved her. She had lived.

Her once bright eyes were now dull and sorrowful, sunken in caverns, lost in the ruins of a once-beautiful face. Although her cheek bones were prominent and her lips had disappeared into a thin slit, she still had an incredibly expressive face. Her disfigured ears, weighed down by the lifelong wearing of heavy earrings, seemed too large for her face; her once thick plait was now reduced to a thin white rat's tail; and her toothless profile and pale skin gave her an almost angelic appearance. Her skin gleamed with perspiration even though it was autumn. The indescribable despair and grief in her ancient face now seemed to capture the pain and suffering of all humanity. From her voice it was evident that she was utterly exhausted.

Abba Ji's white Father Christmas beard bobbed up and down, and his lips twitched as he tried to suppress his tears. He looked affectionately at the wrinkled face that still caused something to stir within him. He appeared confused and worried for he recognised that look – a look she had just before she had a fit. He stood beside her, combing his beard with his fingers, something he did when he was nervous. Fortunately, the moment passed and Amma Ji slumped into her chair sobbing into her *dupatta*. The death of her baby had left a deep wound in her heart, one that had never healed, like the pain of a phantom amputated limb. It still ached.

'We lost our baby *gurya* during that harrowing journey from Delhi to Lahore, and have never forgotten her,' Abba Ji tried to explain as he wiped his eyes with his fists, his lips trembling.

Putting his hands together, *Sardar Ji* bowed before Amma Ji. Taking a deep breath, as if trying to gather strength, he said with a mournful smile, *'Bhain Ji meri bhi gul aaj sun lou, phir tusi joo dil chahai karna* (Sister, just listen to what I have to say, then you can do as you please).' He paused, took another shuddering breath and then continued. 'You are so lucky to have such a large family.' Eyebrows raised, he cast a nervous glance at the assembled guests. 'Are these your sons, your daughters...your grandchildren?' he asked, trying to hold back the tears welling in his large eyes. 'You are so lucky to have such a lovely family... Listen to my story...I have never told this to anyone in my life...'

He paused and breathed deeply. *'Bhain Ji*, we too, migrated during Partition. My entire family was killed. I am the sole survivor of a family of nine.' Tears now ran down his cheeks, disappearing into his dense silver-streaked beard. He made no attempt to wipe them away. 'We had a jewellery shop in Anarkali, Lahore. I grew up playing in Shalimar Gardens and studied at Aitchison College on the Mall... We migrated to Amritsar with nothing except memories of our beautiful life in Lahore. Of the nine of us, I alone made it.' He swallowed. 'My father and eldest brother pushed our ma... ma... mother and sisters into a well when a mob came to our neighbourhood, dowsing Sikhs with kerosene and setting them on fire.'

We gasped in unison. Suddenly I saw *Sardar Ji* in an entirely new light. Shoulders slumped, he sobbed into his handkerchief. 'My brother was killed trying to save my father...then they killed him too.' He shook his head and whispered, 'They never even had *antim sanskar* (last rites), or a funeral. I was the unlucky one to make it out alive, to tell you this today. I have lived with this nightmare all my life.'

Abbu, who had been listening to this story along with the rest of us, rose and abruptly left the restaurant. By now, Amma Ji was holding her head in her hands and sobbing, trembling as if ready to drop. Nafeesa Momani and Ammi stood holding onto her.

Abba Ji moved forward and awkwardly half embraced *Sardar Ji*, patting him on his arm. 'May

Allah give you peace, *Sardar Ji*,' he said, a flutter in his voice. 'We all went through a terrible time. It wasn't our fault; we were just pawns in the hands of the politicians. They played with *our* lives and shuffled us about like chess pieces... I hope...I hope...the youngsters of today appreciate the sacrifices we made for our countries.' He patted his broad forehead with a crisp, white handkerchief, pursing his lips.

Sardar Ji composed himself, put his hands together and bent a fraction towards Amma Ji, saying respectfully, '*Bhain Ji*, forgive me for reminding you of that *manhoos*, cursed time on this auspicious day. It will give me great pleasure if you could find it in your heart to forgive and you and your family celebrate in my restaurant today. It will be a great honour for me if you forget the past and think of me as your brother, your son... and have this party on me.'

Everyone sat in pin drop silence, sniffling. I wondered where Abbu had gone.

'Of course, of course, let us all forget the past and enjoy the present. May Allah never let anyone experience what we went through,' said Abba Ji, forcing a faint smile as he tenderly patted Amma Ji's hand.

Sardar Ji disappeared to the back and then re-emerged with a tray of drinks for everyone.

'Where did Bhai Azhar go?' asked Zia Mamo, raising an eyebrow at Ammi.

Ammi rose, gave *Sardar Ji* a look of sad resignation, and stood biting the inside of her cheek. I watched her pained expression with a dry mouth, wondering what was to come. It was her turn to drop a bombshell.

'Sultanat, his only sister...was abducted during Partition. His mother kept it secret from him, only telling him when she was on her deathbed, always hoping that one day she would return,' Ammi said haltingly, crying noiselessly. 'But she never did.'

I had a sudden flashback to that day in Pindi, when that blue airmail letter had arrived from India and Abbu had sobbed like a baby. For the first time I comprehended the enormity of it all. Suddenly it was all clear, as if a fog had just lifted. That was why Abbu could never bring himself to talk about his family; why this great man who feared nothing, woke in the night shouting incoherently; why he was so strict with us; why he was so tormented when Muz left home; why he refused to go to Lucknow when Ammi forced him to visit India.

I observed the tortured expression on Ammi's face, realizing that for Abbu and his Syed family, it must have been a fate *far* worse than death. For the first time in my life I appreciated what they had all gone through to bring us here. I had heard many of their stories but never before felt their pain.

I ran out of the restaurant, followed by Zia Mamo, in search of Abbu.

PART V

FINALLY

Do not go gentle into that good night

~ Dylan Thomas

Do not go gentle into that good night,
Old age should burn and rave at close of day;
Rage, rage against the dying of the light.

Though wise men at their end know dark is right,
Because their words had forked no lightning they
Do not go gentle into that good night.

Good men, the last wave by, crying how bright
Their frail deeds might have danced in a green bay,
Rage, rage against the dying of the light.

Wild men who caught and sang the sun in flight,
And learn, too late, they grieved it on its way,
Do not go gentle into that good night.

Grave men, near death, who see with blinding sight
Blind eyes could blaze like meteors and be gay,
Rage, rage against the dying of the light.

And you, my father, there on the sad height,
Curse, bless, me now with your fierce tears, I pray.
Do not go gentle into that good night.
Rage, rage against the dying of the light.

49
TUZZY'S DEMISE

One hot summer's day in June, I was sitting in the garden with Asif and the children. Kashif and Nimra were in the paddling pool when Ammi called. 'Tammy just came round. Tuzzy was found dead in her flat,' she sobbed. 'She asked me to tell you.'

For a moment I was dumbstruck, as if someone had punched me hard in the stomach and knocked the wind out of me. 'What? She told me they'd kill her...I didn't believe her!' I howled and cried as I'd never done before.

I rushed round to Tuzzy's house, expecting to find it full of mourning relatives. Tammy, her sister, answered the door. The house was empty, quiet and sad as always. Tammy looked gaunt, her large eyes vacant with deep dark half-moons under her eyes, her skin loose and pigmented, especially around the eyes. Her chiselled features, once so attractive, now made her look masculine. 'Hello Salma,' she murmured, without any expression of grief, not at all like someone who had just lost her only sister.

'What happened?' I asked, hugging her to steady myself as I sobbed.

'We don't know. The police found her, 'she said in a matter-of-fact voice. She paused and then added, 'Apparently she had been dead for several days. The neighbours noticed the smell and called the police. They had to break down the door.'

I collapsed into a chair. 'When did you last see her?'

'Sometime last year,' Tammy said. Noticing the surprised look on my face she added, 'I live in Bournemouth; I only came when I found out.'

She didn't have answers to any of my questions. I asked her about the funeral. She told me it wouldn't be for a while because of the circumstances of her death and that she would let me know.

'Where's Auntie?' I enquired.

'She's out with Saeeda Auntie, sorting out the paperwork.'

I felt awkward and bewildered, at a loss for words.

'Mum doesn't want anyone coming around,' she told me flatly. 'What's the point?'

I left immediately, crying all the way home, unaware what passers-by thought.

Later, at the funeral in the mosque, there were just a handful of people. There were none of the usual embracing or hysterical crying. Tuzzy's mum sat in a corner. Head covered, gently swaying back and forth, she read the *Quran*. She had aged and now appeared scrawny and dark. Her prominent crooked nose was even more noticeable than I remembered. A persistent fly made several attempts to sit on her sticky face. She whisked it away, beating the air around her head with her free hand.

Tammy, Auntie Saeeda and Auntie Shamim sat to one side, whispering in the African dialect of Urdu, Punjabi and Swahili. They were talking about self-immolation. Other women I didn't recognize were gorging on gossip to pass on to those who were not present. I recognized Tuzzy's grandmother, a hunched bag of bones, draped in a thick shawl, too thick for this time of year, sitting on one side, praying with a rosary in her hands. Even at such a time, the family seemed divided.

I sat next to Samia, a school friend I had informed of Tuzzy's death. She asked me questions to which I had no answers. I tried to read the *Quran*, but my head was whirling with thoughts. What difference does it make, I thought, whether you decompose before you are buried or after, whether the birds pick your flesh or you are gobbled up by worms or the fish in the sea? The result is the same. We all return to the soil and are recycled. I made a mental note to plant some beautiful yellow fragrant roses – Tuzzy's favourite – on her grave. The strong, overpowering smell of incense and rose water and my suppressed emotions, brought on a throbbing headache.

The coffin was in the male section of the mosque during the final prayer. A group of men carried it into the segregated female part of the mosque. I wondered if Tuzzy's father was amongst them. I didn't recognize him. The coffin was sealed; the body had decomposed, so no one was allowed to see her. It was just as well; I couldn't bear to see my friend like this.

We gathered around the casket and prayed for her soul. One woman, dressed in pale silk, annoyed me in particular as she continued to whisper to her companion, shielding her mouth with her hand and stifling giggles. Tuzzy's mother sobbed as she walked round the casket, gently stroking it, her lips trembling, repeating, 'Tuzzy forgive me...forgive me.' It reminded me of the episode on *National Geographic* of the cheetah, or was it a leopard... crying for the cub a python had swallowed. The mother had paced, crying, for days.

The same men who had brought in the coffin now carried Tuzzy away, high on their shoulders.

I wanted to scream:

کیا ہے دستور دنیا خدارا

مرتے دم تک کسی نے نہ پوچھا

بعد مرنے کے میت کو میری

لوگ سر پے اٹھائے ہوئے ہیں

Kya hai dustoor duniya khudaara
(What a way of the world dear Lord)

Marte dum tak kisi ne na pucha
(No one cared till death)

Baad murnai kai mayyat ko meri
(After death my body)

Loog sur pay uthai huway hain
(They carry high above their heads.)

I stood and watched helplessly, mourning the passing of an unfulfilled life; my best friend carried away in the prime of her life, at thirty-two, by people who didn't give her the love she craved, the love she deserved. I continued to pray quietly, tears streaming down my face, regretting not having made more of an effort to see her, pondering about what she had told me, questioning myself if there was anything I could have done, wishing she had contacted me. At least she was now free from worldly woes. She had occupied such a small place in the world, yet suffered so greatly. I prayed that she be at peace at last. I wondered what she would have thought about this little gathering. I wondered if she was watching and smiling her lopsided quizzical smile that had sent men reeling.

I went up and hugged Tuzzy's mum. She smiled sadly and asked if I had any photographs of Tuzzy.

'Yes,' I replied, looking at her enquiringly.

'Could you give me some?'

I nodded, confused.

Later, when I went to give her the photographs, she explained that Tuzzy had torn all the pictures of herself, so she had none.

'Why didn't you call me?' I sobbed.

'She didn't want to see anyone. She wouldn't even see me. The doctors at Springfield said *I, yes I,* triggered her attacks, so it was better I didn't see her... When I did try, she wouldn't answer the door, so I stopped.'

We hugged, cried, talked, looked at her photographs, cried some more.

Finally she said, 'You know, sometimes I think all those *vazeefas* (ritualistic prayers) I used to read, backfired. Tuzzy suffered because...because... never mind.'

I came away wondering if there was anything I could have done. I couldn't face going home so I went to Ammi's. I went straight to my collection of records that I hadn't touched for years, found what I was looking for and placed the vinyl on the record player. *Jagjit's* melancholy voice poured from the speaker:

> *Ye daulat bhi le lo, ye shohrat bhi le lo*
> (Take away my wealth, take away my fame)
>
> *Bhale chhin lo mujh sai meri javani*
> (You may even take away my youth)
>
> *Magar mujh ko lauta do buchpan ka saavan*
> (But please return the monsoon of my childhood)

As soon as I heard the first notes I went into a trance, transported to a different world, anxious to hear the next note. The soft soothing words of the song bubbled up in my head, filling my mind like an empty vessel. It completely changed my mood, my demeanour, transporting me to a carefree existence, a different era. I sang the next couplet before hearing it:

> *Bhulaaye nahin bhuul sakta hai koi*
> (Even if one tries, one cannot forget)

> *Vo chhooti si raatein vo lumbi kahani*
> (Those seemingly short nights and lengthy stories')

Incarnate images of a world locked away in the depths of my subconscious poured out, opening folders, downloading sounds, visions and smells of my childhood. Memories whirled up, not in any chronological order, but haphazardly. Distorted images; incidents churned around in my head like in a dream, crashing against the walls of my mind, where there is no concept of space, sequence or reality; initially in a great gush then calmly, like water in a gentle stream; some crystal clear as the present, others skeletal and fragmented, faded and moth-eaten.

I sat listening to the song, tears streaming down my cheeks until Ammi came and hugged me. We cried together. Tuzzy's death wounded my soul – a wound that has healed with time but has nevertheless left a permanent scar. Tuzzy was gone, gone forever, never to return. But she does return, frequently, in my dreams.

The woman in the black *burqa* trudged up the long winding path. She wasn't as erect as she used to be. She had lost the sharp jerk in the swing of her right arm that she had once had, but she still had that determined distinct walk. Sidestepping graves, she reached the last one under the *peepal* tree and stood solemnly at the foot of the beautifully tended grave, covered with dry rose petals. She carefully scattered the fragrant jasmines from a small wicker basket she had brought with her. Then, putting her palms together, she stood at the foot of the grave, lips trembling, and prayed.

She threw back her chiffon veil, revealing a wrinkled face and then settled herself on a rock beside the marble headstone inscribed with *Quranic* verses. Wiping her eyes with her lace trimmed handkerchief, she began talking in a soft voice, occasionally smiling or laughing. She removed stray leaves and withered flowers while narrating the trivialities of the previous day to her silent companion. She brought food with her and placed it beside the grave, but called out to the graveyard keeper as she departed: 'Bukhsho, I've brought *koftas* for Abba Ji, his favourite.' She used to call him *your* Abba Ji, now she merely said Abba Ji.

***

It had hurt her children to see her gradually withdraw from the world as she cared for their ailing father like one tends a premature baby, talking to him in soothing, gentle tones as she carefully spooned the broth she had so lovingly prepared, into his mouth. After his death, when she began her daily ritualistic visits to the graveyard at dawn, they tried to reason with her.

'Amma Ji, it's a sin to grieve past three days. What will people say? It was Allah's will. We have to accept it as such. He is in a better place now.'

She didn't respond, just looked at them with a mute, benign smile. It is hard to argue with someone so reticent. They gave up eventually.

Amma Ji was the oldest person in the community. She was a living relic, still walking about though her soul seemed dead. She was well respected for who she was. Now, the woman who had given so much of herself to others, had become irritable and capricious, parasitic. She remained cocooned in her loss, unmindful of day to day worldly concerns. Her children and grandchildren showed grudging affection for the woman that time refused to obliterate into oblivion. Some mocked her devotion, but most understood her commitment and admired her dedication to the pious man in the grave. Mothers pointed her out as an example when teaching their daughters about real love.

***

Abba Ji's body, shrouded in white sheets, draped with a green velvet sheet embroidered with verses from the *Holy Quran* in gold thread, was laid out on a wooden cot in the courtyard under a marquee. His jaw was bandaged to stop it falling open. With his iridescent white skin and eyes closed, he appeared serene. Huge slabs of ice formed puddles around the cot with pedestal fans kept away flies while blowing cool air over the body.Putrefaction sets in quickly in the heat. Relatives continued to arrive, murmuring condolences and prayers for the departed and those left behind.

'May Allah make his journey forth easy and grant him a place amongst His chosen and comfort those whom He has bereaved.'

Men joined the congregation in the courtyard while the women retreated to the segregated women's section inside the house. Adjusting the *dupatta* on my head, I wormed my way through the crowd to get to the foot of the cot. Sobbing, I paid my respects, praying silently. Images of the gentle pious man he had been flickered in my mind like doves fluttering in an azure sky.

The house reeked of camphor and incense. I stepped over the mound of shoes and entered the courtyard. It was abuzz with women dressed in white, sitting in groups on white sheets on the floor. Heads covered, they gently, rhythmically rocked to and fro, like eggs boiling in a pan, reading the *Quran* and praying with rosaries or mounds of date seeds, which they used as counters. I saw Ammi with my aunts, Shama and Wazir Khala, huddled together, praying. Shama Khala was sobbing and mumbling, trying to contain herself. 'Read the *Quran*; pray Allah makes his journey to the next life easier,' advised a well-wisher, patting her gently.

My eyes skimmed the crowd. I spotted Amma Ji, sitting silently amongst a group of women, propped up with bolster cushions, dressed in pure white. Apologizing profusely while stepping over the seeds and the women, I made my way over to her. On reaching her I fell to my knees and hugged her, sobbing bitterly. She clung to me for several minutes. Affectionately adjusting the *dupatta* on my head, she wiped my tears, hushing me. I was surprised to see she wasn't crying. She continued to comfort me as I held her cold, bony hand and sat down beside her. Feeling awkward, unable to find appropriate words, I picked up the *Quran* and began reading it silently. My head throbbed with the overpowering smell of incense and pent-up grief. Unable to concentrate, my mind flickered through memories of my beloved grandfather and concern for Amma Ji, and the effect of the loss on the whole family.

There was a sudden commotion as the men carried the body into the women's section. The women moved aside, adjusting their *dupattas,* with a chorus of the *Kalima: La illa ha-ill lul-la ho*....(there is no god but Allah). Shama Khala began wailing. Ammi and Wazir Khala rushed to hush her. Women helped Amma Ji to the cot. She slumped down beside it, holding tightly to the rail with both hands. She didn't cry. Women walked past sobbing, saying their last farewells and reciting the *Kalima*. Ammi and Wazir Khala tried to persuade Shama Khala to approach the cot, but arms outstretched, she fell to the ground with a heart rending cry: 'Abba

Jieeee...' she buried her face in Ammi's breasts, howling.

Head bowed, the men humbly asked Amma Ji for permission to proceed. She didn't respond and sat mute. Women urged her to move aside. She sat speechless. Iqbal Khala prized her fingers one by one from the cot and the men lifted the cot, joining in with the recitation: *Ash-hado-un-la-illaha ill lallahu, wa shahdouna Muhammadun Abduhu wa rasulu hu* I bear witness that there is no deity besides Allah, And I bear witness that Muhammad is His servant and messenger. Amma Ji did not cry, she passed out.

My uncles looked helplessly at their mother and sisters and carried the cot on their shoulders, leaving the women fanning and sprinkling water on Amma Ji's face. I followed Ammi and Wazir Khala, looking vulnerable and helpless, muffling their mouths with their hands, mouthing the *Kalima*, out into the courtyard amongst relatives and friends. I searched for my slippers amongst the pile by the door but could not find them. Barefoot, I ran out, ready to run alongside the procession. Ammi held me back. One of the women reminded me: 'Women don't go to the graveyard for the burial.'

'Why not? I want to go,' I protested, trying to free my hand.

'It's a hard job, burying someone you love. Best left to the men,' Ammi said, forcing a little smile and trying to suppress her tears. She hugged me hard and burst into another bout of sobbing.

A lady trying to comfort her baby, who had woken in the commotion, nodded sympathetically in agreement. Upset, I stepped over a little girl who had paired up all the shoes and was now strutting about in high heels. Outside, the men who had been sitting on chairs under the multi-coloured marquee, now trailed the procession carrying the body, to the graveyard, like a convoy of ants carrying food.

Out in the street, arrangements were being made to cook *pulao* and curry in huge cauldrons set on makeshift brick stoves over a log fire. A group of grubby children squatted amongst mounds of rice, ghee tins, and meat, peeling onions, garlic and ginger as the sweaty cook, with a huge potbelly, barked orders to his young assistants while feeding wood into the stove. A boy stood fanning away flies from the meat piled high on a steel tray, while also keeping at bay cats and crows, and the kites circling expectantly overhead. I watched sobbing, with my siblings, cousins and relatives, till the procession disappeared into the distance.

***

I was glad I was able to accompany Ammi to Karachi when it became apparent that Abba Ji was not going to recover from pneumonia and had taken a turn for the worst. Zia Mamo and Zaka Mamo had already arrived. Everyone was concerned for Saba Mamo, who was delayed in Dubai as his passport needed renewing. Unfortunately, he arrived too late to see his father breathe his last but was there to bury him.

Within days Amma Ji's flawless fair complexion turned dark, as if scorched, and she lost the sparkle in her eye. She seemed to age not from day to day, but by the hour. Even the chime-like tinkle in her voice was replaced by a dull low tone. On the third day after Abba Ji's passing, she asked Zia Mamo, her eldest son, to take her to the graveyard.

She laughed when she saw the grave. 'Ah, you're sheltered under a tree. Good...you never could stand the heat! Hmm...Zia tells me there were hundreds of people for your final send-off...as far as the eye could see. They are still praying for you...they have read the *Quran* countless times, and still they read... It should be you sitting here, *not me*. I have had enough near misses. How many times did the doctors give up on me? Four...five? It was *you* who always called me back from death's door. I guess He knows best!' Smiling, she raised her eyes to the heavens.

Zia Mamo looked at his mother curiously but said nothing.

51
ABBU'S FINAL DEPARTURE

Both Ammi and Abbu were blessed with good health. I don't remember them being ill when we were young. But in later life, their health began to deteriorate. Ammi suffered from hypothyroidism and gradually put on weight, after which she turned into the Michelin Man, constantly battling fat – a battle she never won. Being so petite, it resulted in problems with her knees. But even in later life, her hair never turned snow white like Abbu's, and she continued to have a glowing complexion, a good set of teeth and she never lost the sparkle in her eyes.

Abbu had always been lean and fit in his younger days. In old age, diabetes gnawed away the flesh from his bones, resulting in a stroke in 1987, and he became an austere, frail figure.

His complexion turned dark; his teeth, once so even and white, became yellow and prominent in his thin, stroke-affected face, though he always retained a lopsided smile. His mahogany skin lost its sheen and hung like melted wax on his frail form. His gaunt Lowry figure looked insignificant and emaciated on the green velvet sofa. His white hair, dyed jet black, stained his forehead grey, giving it a shadowy second hairline.

'Bhai Azhar, every dark cloud has a silver lining,' chuckled Zia Mamo, as he strolled in one Saturday afternoon. Abbu looked up, confused. 'You either have a dark stain outlining your hairline or a silver halo as your hair grows out.' Abbu laughed his raucous laugh, throwing his head back.

Ammi and Abbu lived happily with Ather and his family. Abbu retained his pride and sense of humour to the end. He refused to use a stick or a Zimmer frame. When I took him for a routine check-up to St George's Hospital, he refused to use a wheelchair and insisted on walking all the way to the clinic unaided. At the clinic, I could have cried on seeing the corns and calluses on his feet due to his diabetes. It was no wonder he walked with a limp. When we returned home, I stood holding the car door open, waiting for him to step out.

He looked up at me helplessly. '*Susri*, damn leg won't obey me.'

His smile brought tears to my eyes. It wasn't that it was an old man's smile but that it held something apologetic, as if *apologising* for inconveniencing *me*. He had had another stroke on the way home. I began to cry. He had always prayed, '*Allah chultai hath pair oathana (Allah* please call me back fully functional). He squeezed my hand affectionately and said, '*Baita* I have had a good life. I have reached an age when the majority of my friends have already met their Maker. I am ready to meet Him.' I rushed him back to the hospital.

Abbu was in and out of hospital with minor ailments complicated by his diabetes and strokes, and his health continued to deteriorate. As his illness progressed, he became confined to his bedroom, where we all congregated, with Abbu as the centrepiece, reclining in bed. All his meals were brought to the bedroom, and one of us kept up a constant supply of tea. With time, he became more and more frail, thin and fragile, as if made of some ethereal substance. He looked older than his years.

In the winter of 1996, Abbu's health took a turn for the worse. I had always dreaded that late night call that would make me leap out of bed, my heart thudding. Despite being on antibiotics, Abbu had a high temperature that would not go down. He stopped eating. He sat propped up by pillows, his food uneaten, his tea undrunk, the newspapers untouched, looking helplessly at his food. Doctors diagnosed hepatitis. Abbu went into a coma.

All six of us siblings, our spouses and children, and Ammi, sat silently around him, praying. Ammi held his hand, reading the *Yaseen Shareef* and other verses from the *Quran*, her tea and food untouched. I held his hand and said, 'Abbu, it's me, Salmi. Squeeze my hand if you can hear me.' He gently squeezed my hand as tears rolled down his face. Immediately one of his couplets came to my lips:

بہتے ہوئے اشکوں کا سمجھ لیجے مفہوم

بیمار میں اب طاقتِ گفتار نہیں ہے

Behtai hoai ashkon ka samujh lijiyae mafhoom
(Grasp the meaning of my flowing tears)

Bemaar main ub taqatai guftar nahin hai
(For the indisposed has no strength to speak)

Everyone looked on helplessly, tears streaming down their faces. Baji's lipstick was visible only at the edges of her lips, and her eyeliner had accumulated at the corners of her eyes. We continued to read the *Quran*, intermittently talking to Abbu amid a continuous stream of visitors, not knowing if he could still hear us.

Surprised by the many visitors, one of the nurses asked, 'Who is he? Is he a VIP?'

'He is a famous poet; a celebrity in the Asian community,' replied Ather.

They moved Abbu to a separate room during visiting hours.

'Abbu, we've been reciting verses from the *Quran*. I will now recite some of your poetry.' I sang one of his poems out loud, the way he used to, unaware of the crowd congregated at the door.

'That was beautiful,' said one of the nurses as she hugged me.

I fumbled with the glass of milk that spilled from my trembling hands.

'You have been sitting here since Wednesday. Go home and get some rest,' Asif coaxed.

I refused but joined the rest of family in the waiting room. Ammi, Ather and Muz remained with Abbu.

At 2 O'clock in the morning, Muz came rushing over to us. 'Come quick! Abbu has come round.'

We all ran to his bedside. Abbu opened his eyes, took a deep breath, almost like a sigh, looked round the room with sad, searching eyes that fixed upon Ammi. With his lopsided smile, he whispered, 'Ammi *hazoor*, *this* is my *Jugnu*,' and with that he closed his eyes forever.

Breaking free of the tangle of trivialities of which human relations are woven, Abbu joined his mother in a place he could no longer be reached. In my mind I screamed '*Rage, rage against the dying of the light!*' but I think he was happy to go and meet his Maker. Reluctantly, we had to leave him behind and go home.

We reached home just as the sun was shedding its cloak of darkness. There was a mound of shoes in the porch. The house reeked of incense. Even at this unearthly hour it was packed with relatives and neighbours, including Zia Mamo and Nafeesa Momani, who had turned back from New York airport when they heard of Abbu's critical condition. The whole place was in turmoil. The furniture in the front room had been removed and the carpet was covered with white sheets, ready to seat the mourners. Copies of the *Quran*, bags of date seeds and prayer books, had already arrived from the mosque. More neighbours and friends were still coming from near and far. People came from all over – people we hadn't seen in years, some of whom we did not recognize or know. Leaving their shoes on the threshold, they entered the living room, awkwardly walking up to Ammi and us, whispering a few words of condolence, then sitting on the floor reading the *Quran* and praying, using the date seeds as counters.

Mamo Zia accompanied Ather and Muz to get the death certificate to release the body from the hospital. They purchased land for the grave and made arrangements for the burial as it was a religious requirement to bury the body as quickly as possible. An announcement was made in the Urdu newspapers and on Asian radio stations, to notify Abbu's fans of the date and time of the funeral. It was a surreal experience.

An oppressive dread of what was to come engulfed me. The events of the day had been heavy on my heart and stunned my mind into silence. I found it difficult to even utter the words that Abbu was no longer with us. Our cousins and the Momanis informed friends and relatives in England and abroad.

An invisible automation took over our home. Omelette, toast and *hulva* appeared from somewhere, and our cousins scurried around preparing tea and serving breakfast to the assembled mourners. Nafeesa Momani sat with Ammi, coaxing her to have some tea. Other friends and family tried to persuade us to eat. At lunchtime, big pots of chicken curry, *biryani*, salad and *naan* appeared in the kitchen.

Ammi sat in tearless immobility on the floor, propped up by cushions and pillows, receiving relatives and neighbours, her friends, our friends and their parents. Some gave welcome, others unwelcome, advice on how we ought to pray and behave.

'You mustn't cry. His life was a gift from God, and to Him he has returned. His soul is still in the house, and it would pain him to see you grieving like this.'

Another helpfully suggested to Ammi, 'You should take off your bangles and all your jewellery, change into white clothes; you are a widow now.'

Ammi was about to oblige when Ather stepped in. 'Ammi, that's a Hindu tradition. Abbu loved you wearing bright colours. We are still alive.'

Another lady informed us that it was forbidden to light a fire in the house for three days, so we shouldn't be cooking. Someone else explained to her that it means that those who are grieving should not have to worry about cooking for themselves and the other mourners.

I went about like a zombie, following instructions, reading the *Quran* and praying. I continued to pray like a woman possessed, without rest or food, ensuring that all the prayers were conducted and performed as prescribed, to make my beloved

Abbu's path to the next life as painless as possible. I was annoyed if anyone so much as smiled or chatted. I realized much later how therapeutic it was to pray in this manner. I would have lost my mind had I realised the enormity of my loss.

The doorbell rang. I opened it and came face to face with Khalid. We looked at each other in silence.

'I am so sorry, Salmi.' He whispered my name in his usual caressing way, his face grave and thoughtful, trying to conceal his agitation. 'I haven't uttered this name in a long time.' After a long uncomfortable pause, he said with a sad lopsided smile, 'He was a great man.'

'The best,' I replied, tears running down my cheeks.

He wiped my cheek with the tips of his fingers and placed them to his lips, his hand trembling. I wanted to hug him and cry, but just stood there staring at him. He hadn't changed much. He seemed a little darker; his hair streaked with silver. He had become slightly stouter, but overall he had aged well.

He gently lifted my lowered head by the chin and, smiling only with his eyes, hesitatingly asked, curiosity clouding his better judgement, 'Are you well? Are you happy? I looked at him questioningly. 'With life, I mean...' he stammered, his upper lip twitching as it always did when he was nervous. I nodded. 'That's good; I am happy for you,' he said.

I wanted to ask him a million and one questions but didn't. Instead, I showed him into the sitting room. He went over to Ammi and lowered his head in front of her to accept her blessing. She got up and hugged him affectionately. As he spoke with her, I sat beside Baji, reading the *Quran*. That was the last time I saw Khalid. A year later he passed away from a massive heart attack. I wish I had asked him if *he* was happy.

The funeral prayer was to follow the afternoon *Zohar* prayers at Balham Mosque. The *Maulvi* advised Ather to take the body straight to the mosque because the house was not big enough to accommodate the numbers expected. He said it was a waste of money preparing food to feed the mourners as most people did not return from the graveyard. It was better to donate the money to charity. Ather agreed.

The mosque was packed with people. Ammi sat silently with her hands folded in her lap, doing nothing, seeing nothing, staring vacantly ahead, while all around her people rushed backward and forward. The men said their final farewells to Abbu and carried the coffin to the segregated ladies section so that the women could say goodbye. Baji and I were worried about Nunni, but it was Shano who became hysterical when she saw Abbu. Baji grabbed her. 'Read the *Kalima*, read the *Kalima*,' I coaxed.

I looked at Abbu. He looked so peaceful, as if in deep slumber. Tears streaming down my face, I clung to Nunni, murmuring prayers. Men came and carried my Abbu away. I was left thinking, there goes the man who gave it his all, working night and day for *us*. There he goes to meet his Maker; empty-handed, in a single shroud. The ambulance drove away; other cars followed it to the cemetery. The women made their way to our house and automatically sat on the floor, picking up the *Quran* and reading silently.

When I opened the door to the men returning from the cemetery, Zia Mamo hugged me as I sobbed into his chest. 'Think about me; who will I tease now?' he said. 'He was my best friend. I knew Bhai Azhar since before you were born.'

For the first time, I realized another's grief. I hugged Ather and Muz, wondering how they must have laid Abbu to rest, leaving him behind in the cold cemetery under so much dirt. With diminishing daylight, Ather became extremely restless and agitated. He confided to me that he had left a Mars bar in the grave. 'I always used to take it away from him,' he said, sobbing. 'He's out there in the cold. He always felt the cold so...so much!' We hugged and cried.

I went up to Abbu's bedroom and sat on his side of the bed. Hugging his pillow, I rocked back and forth, my knees to my chest, taking in the scent, Abbu's scent, sobbing, my tears rolling into my ears. I continued to cry until I had no more tears left. Tired out, I rubbed my swollen eyes and thought about Ammi, who had shared his bed for so many years and decided to sleep alongside her for the next few days.

I had lost the person I loved the most in this world. Now that he was gone I felt how little I had learnt from him. How I wish I had paid more attention when there was time. Melancholy nostalgia crept in. Unlike Asian parents who expect to be paid back for raising their children, our parents had openly declared that they expected nothing from us except respect, and success in our lives. Abbu had asked for nothing except that we came now and then to let him know how we were, maybe ask his advice, to make him feel useful, needed.

I opened Abbu's wardrobe and looked at the neat row upon row of shoes, shirts and suits. Kashif and Nimra came into the room. In this surreal setting, I had forgotten my husband and children.

'Mama, Nana Jaan didn't take his clothes?'

He doesn't need these clothes where he has gone!' I said, shutting the wardrobe and hugging my children.

I picked up the glass from Abbu's bedside table, poured myself a glass of water from the crystal decanter and drank it down in one go. As I replaced the glass, I saw the writing pad that had always been by his bed side and began reading his morbid nocturnal scribblings. His frustrations and helplessness were expressed in an almost illegible scrawl, in verse.

لگتا نہیں ہے دل میرا اجاڑے دیار میں

کس کی بنی ہے عالم ناپائدار میں

کتنا ہے بدنصیب اظہر دفن کے لیے

دو گز زمین بھی نہ ملی کوئے یار میں

Lagta nahin hai dil mera ujray dayaar main
(What pleasure can the heart know in this derelict city)

kis ki bani hai aalam-e-naa paaye-daar mein
(who has found fulfilment in this mortal world)

kitnaa hai bad-naseeb "Azher" dafn key liye
(how ill-fated is Azhar even for his burial)

do guz zamin bhi na mili kuu-e yaar main-e-yaar mein
(was not granted two yards of land in the land of my beloved.)

Those few lines said all he had suppressed while he was alive. He had penned down his lifelong pent-up anguish in a few couplets. He had substituted 'Azhar' for 'Zafar' in the poem by the last Mughal Emperor, Zafar, who wrote it during his exile and incarceration in Rangoon (now Myanmar), where he died.

Abbu's last lament had been for his motherland. I wondered what his brother Akhtar would have thought of Abbu's burial in a foreign land, surrounded by *goras*, so far away from his father, mother and brothers; Akhtar who had mocked Abbu, calling him a *kala angrez;* Akhtar who had refused to move to Pakistan and sacrificed everything – his life, his mother and his family's lives – for the privilege of being buried next to his father in his homeland. I wondered if he thought it had been worth it. All I could think was:

Ask not how he died, ask how he lived

He left the world knowing he was loved

The song has ended but the melody lives on.

52
HUSH

Ammi, who seldom stopped talking, now spent most of the day sitting silently as people milled around her. She found solace in reading the *Quran* and took comfort in knowing it was recited over a hundred and fifty times in London alone. Family and friends in Pakistan too, gathered in their homes to pray for Abbu's soul. The praying continued non-stop for three days, then intermittently for another forty days.

With Abbu's death, a strange sadness crept into our house, settling like a fine dust on every available surface, slithering under the carpet, lying on furniture, inhabiting the bric-a-brac that he had so lovingly collected from the Thursday market. An invisible, morose sorrow clung to the house like a dying lover, casting a melancholic gloom on our hearts and souls. Our vibrant colourful house, that was always buzzing with people and filled with joyous laughter, took on a lazy hush, a sepia tone, overcast with dark shadow, like a passing cloud on a sunny day. The TV, which had been almost always on, was now silent. We didn't speak in our typically loud, animated 'Ahmed' manner but crept about quietly, silently, or whispered, as if afraid to wake someone. Our house was never the same again.

An almighty tree had fallen...a tree that had sheltered me and so many others. But it left many saplings. I prayed that they would flourish and continue to produce shade and seeds that are even more special. Abbu was the pole star of the family. He had steered us across continents for a better life. Now we were left rudderless, with lifelong memories of a man who lived for his family, his children. There was so much that we never knew, that he had kept unvoiced, deep within the recesses of his heart. Now it was all lost to oblivion. He had excelled way beyond his duty as a husband and father. He could now go and claim the eternal life to which he was so entitled, with the knowledge that he had achieved what he had set out to do – provide for his family and see them progress.

***

We took Ammi to the graveyard. It gave her solace to note that Abbu was buried under a huge oak tree. We stood solemnly at his feet and prayed. After planting fragrant roses on his grave, we left Ammi alone as we cleaned around other untended graves.

For many months after Abbu's death, Ammi remained in the large bedroom she had always shared with him. She tethered herself to the same routine, doing the same things at the same time, day after day. Everything in Ammi's bedroom remained unchanged. As usual, the water decanter beside the bed with an upturned glass, sat on his bedside table; Abbu's blue and maroon striped dressing gown hung behind the door; his brown leather slippers remained neatly tucked under his bed. All his clothes hung in the wardrobe as if he would appear dressed in one of his three-piece suits, smelling of roses, at any minute.

We left it to Ammi to dispose of his belongings in her own time, but when she made no effort to do so, I spoke to her and persuaded her to give his clothes to Oxfam. At a family dinner she finally announced that she was giving Abbu's things to charity and anyone who wished to take a memento was welcome to do so. I laid claim to all of Abbu's handwritten poetry and his vast collection of books. Asif said he'd have one of

Abbu's many watches; Osman took some of his shoes, and Kashif a couple of suits, hoping he'd grow into them. Ammi saved a few suits to send to Abbu's brother Nadir and his sons in Pakistan, and then finally disposed of the rest. She moved to a smaller bedroom and gave up the bedroom she had shared with Abbu since the first day we had moved into the house.

When I think of Ammi in my childhood, when Abbu was alive, she seems invisible. I can't seem to see her. I know she must have been around, but when I had that terrible earache, it was to Abbu I went to in the middle of the night. He put drops in my ear, tied a muffler round my head and I snuggled up beside him. When I woke up at night, my heart thudding after a nightmare, it was always Abbu who gave me homeopathic drops and tucked me back in bed. When I fainted, it was Abbu I found standing over me calling, 'Salmi, Salmi *baitai*, are you alright?' Abbu took us to the library, read with us, helped us with our homework and told us bedtime stories. Even during my wedding preparations, I remember shopping with Abbu. Ammi must have been there too, because Abbu never went anywhere without her, but it was he who sent Nafeesa Momani back to buy the beautiful sari I had loved but didn't buy because it was too expensive. Even after Kashif was born,

I remember Abbu pacing, cradling the baby in his arms as he screamed with colic.

I remember Ammi eyeballing us to correct our manners, Urdu pronunciation or in photographs and family videos. She even corrected Abbu's pronunciation and etiquette, irritated when he soiled his hands beyond the tips of his fingers while eating rice. Even after Abbu's stroke, when he found it difficult to eat and spilled his food, she couldn't resist constantly cleaning him though it embarrassed him and annoyed us to see the pained, helpless expression on his face.

After Abbu's stroke, Ammi withdrew from social life and gave up many of her friends, devoting her life to taking caring of him. Her close friends, Auntie Shedi, Najma Auntie and Mrs. Farooq, continued to visit her, though due to their own age-related ailments, less frequently than she liked. When they got together, they exchanged details of their aches and pains, operations and number of stitches, even the extent of their incontinence, competing to see who was in greater pain – a perfect sketch for Meera Sayal, I thought.

Ammi changed after Abbu's death. Like Amma Ji, she had always been brusque and undemonstrative with us children, but after Abbu's death, she began to hug us, awkwardly at first. But a little pat or a kiss on the cheek as we departed became the norm. She lost the sparkle in her eyes and even stopped talking as much, becoming more and more withdrawn as if she had nothing to look forward to. She ventured out less frequently, especially after her knee replacement surgery. At times she even neglected her personal hygiene, about which she had always been so very particular. She sat in her crumpled nighty in silence, knitting.

They say time is a great healer and with time Ammi initially took up reading, and when she had exhausted the Urdu stock in Balham and Tooting libraries, Aamer Bhai bought her a new television. Deprived of her lifelong partner, her devoted silent listener, she turned to television and with remote in hand, confined to her bedroom, for the first time she found the freedom to watch what she liked when she liked. She unleashed Pakistani politics, love, sex and endless Indian and English soaps, the plots of which she narrated to everyone, whether they were interested or not.

Once the initial fascination with all the channels had passed, she stuck with Islam Channel, Asian channels Geo and ARY, submerged in a world of religion and Pakistani politics; talking out-loud to the presenters. She effortlessly mocked the interlocutors: 'what rubbish' 'stupid fool,' 'ought to be shot', commenting as if she had an audience. Once she had acquired her free unlimited prepaid phone, she became a regular caller on the daytime talk shows and often got through. The TV presenters came to know her by name and were happy to have a well-informed caller with strong opinions and excellent Urdu to fill their airtime.

'Oh hello, Mrs. Ahmed. How are you today?'

'Never mind my health *baita*. No one want's to hear an old lady moaning. Who is this on your show today? At least call someone who knows what they are talking about. Now what would these politicians know about schools in Pakistan? All their children are studying *here* in England!'

She talked to her sisters Wazir Khala and Shama and Baby Khala, also widowed and now living in the States with their sons, exchanging news of the family. She called Baji and me to inform us about who passed away in the neighbourhood, repeating the same perennial questions. Occasionally, she would ask Ather or one of us to drop her to one of her friend's houses, or they would come over, usually in a group. She looked forward to going to the weekly lunch club, when she has the chance to dress up and catch up with the weekly gossip with other Asian ladies.

Ammi stayed with me and shared my bed when Asif was abroad. We talked intimately and affectionately in a manner we had never done before, giggling like teenagers at a sleepover. One night she teased me about my 'not so secret affair' with Khalid.

'You think I didn't know?' she asked, looking at me mischievously, a roguish smile on her lips.

I bit my lip, unable even now, to admit my fascination.

I loved her more than ever at that midnight hour. Her eyes danced and the corners of her lips twitched as she alternately laughed at herself or became solemn. We talked late, into the early hours of the morning, about Abbu, about Zia Mamo, about old times, reminiscing about my idyllic childhood.

'Go to sleep now; you have plenty to do in the morning,' she'd finally say. 'I'm used to staying awake; you need your sleep.' Then, a few minutes later, I'd hear, 'Are you asleep? Remember when your Abbu…' (I never heard her refer to Abbu by name), as she evoked yet another memory from my past. 'Who would have thought I would outlive him? It would have been better if I went first.'

'Ammi, Abbu wouldn't have survived a day without you!' I said.

'I suppose not. He always prayed that he would go before me. But a woman is nothing without her husband. They say life goes on... indeed it does, but without him, I feel I am a burden. I never felt like that when he was alive.'

I hugged and consoled her, reassuring her that she was not a burden on anyone. Something new now evolved in our relationship, like the companionship of equals. How snug, how warm, how comfortable I felt is impossible to put into words.

After Ammi went home she called me to tell me she was missing me. That was the first time she had expressed her love in words. I was touched. She has become more fragile, her memory of present events is less clear, though her memory of the distant past remains as sharp as ever. She remains a loved and respected elder in the family, surrounded by her six children, nineteen grandchildren, and two great-grandchildren, all of whom adore her. Ammi is a blessed and content lady. May she remain so – always.

A few years after Abbu's demise, after several heart attacks, Zia Mamo too, joined Abbu, leaving another void in my life. Abbu and Zia Mamo remain the two people I miss every single day at every point in my life, happy or sad.

Abbu left a hole in my life that can never be filled. Initially, it was unbearably strange to live without him. Each night I prayed hard for his salvation. It was a long time before he wasn't the first and the last person I thought of every day. To this day I miss and pray for him every night. Abbu's memory is as comforting as the warmth of the sun on a winter's day. It ushers me through life – with certain *ghazals*, with the tasting of the first mango of the season, with Turkish delight, with fish curry and rice, with bold colours and bric-a-brac in market stalls... I guess people remain immortal as long as they remain on the lips of the living. It is curious how the memory of his death lingers. Though it is not as painful as it used to be, it is forever present, like a fruit that's always in season.

Even today people remember him as one of a kind. They praise him with kind words and affection as they bless his soul. What more can one ask for? We take comfort in thinking he had a good life and a good send-off. Unlike most that are lost to oblivion within a few years, he will be remembered for his poetry. I hear it is being taught at Harvard University in a course on Post-Partition Contemporary Poets of Asia. I guess that's enough accolade for anyone.

Closing my eyes I can see Abbu with his crooked grin and kind face shining like the moon against the dark sky, sitting in his favourite seat, rocking

Kashif in his lap; watching TV with his long thin legs outstretched on the velvet sofa; reciting poetry in full flow, his head tilted to one side, bowing slightly and touching his forehead with his hand in his *Lucknawi* style, acknowledging accolade. I take solace in quietly reading a prayer to bless his soul. We gather annually to honour his memory; to pray and to recite his poetry on 4th November.

53
REFLECTIONS

I think Abbu would be happy to look over his shoulder. I'm sure he can stand tall and proud before his Maker and say, '*I came through*'. His greatest wish, for which he had made that epic journey to England, and all his life struggles, were for the betterment of his future generations. It paid off. His dream was to give his children a good education and a better standing in life. He succeeded.

Baji is a sought after interpreter. Shano has her own successful interior design business. After working as a librarian for many years, Nunni runs her own beauty salon. Ather has his replacement window business, and Muz is a brilliant carpenter specializing in loft conversions. Although he threw a wobbly after his divorce, he dusted himself down and picked himself up again. What would make Abbu even prouder is that nearly all of his grandchildren are professional, cultured, moral individuals, making their mark in British society.

Abbu and Ammi firmly believed in providence. They always said that one's *kismet* is written by God at birth. But I sometimes feel guilty, having had so much better luck than many of my friends and siblings. Having had an untroubled childhood, nearly all my memories of growing up are of feeling loved and happy. As a child I wanted to be a doctor but was satisfied with my career as a biochemist. Later, I drifted into teaching and writing. I have benefitted from my education and upbringing, which taught me to think for myself and make the most of life. I am blessed that the green tentacles of envy have never embraced me. By the grace of God and my parent's blessings, my *kismet* has served me well. For years my passion swept me along, propelling me to achieve beyond my physical capabilities. Now that has melted into thin air, like early morning dew in the sun. I am happy and content with my lot.

I know that the development of humanity is affected by more than just genes. It is influenced by genealogy, community, culture, education, geography, language and even the star one is born under, or as Abbu put it: *kismet*. I am blessed with a loving, caring husband who has supported me and helped me achieve my dreams. Without him and my children I would be like a destitute woman, robbed of her worldly belongings. I hope I have passed on some of Abbu and Ammi's genes, culture and finesse to my children. I pray that the Almighty blesses them with good *kismet* in their lives. I find myself praying out loud for their wellbeing and realize the anguish my parents must have gone through when we were growing up.

I have always been proud of my heritage and my roots. My past, sweet and sticky like molasses, has brought up many conflicts and struggles within me, but I think I have come through well. Despite having lived in Britain for most of my life, and appreciating Western culture and all that is good in it, especially freedom of thought and liberation for women, I remain very much a Pakistani. Only now do I realize the strength of my roots and the colourful threads with which my life has been woven and made me who I am. They have enriched my life into a vibrant canvas as bright and as luxurious as the silk I am so fond of. Not only do I want all the hues in the rainbow to colour my life and those of my children, but I want it all embellished in silver and gold.

Abbu always said: 'Reach for the stars and you'll touch the sky. This is your life. Live it to the full. *Carpe diem*. This is your world; make it better for yourself and others. You know what is right. Do it.'

تندی باد مخالف سے نہ گھبرا اے عقاب
یہ تو چلتی ہے تجھے اونچا اڑانے کے لیے

Tundi-e baad-e-mukhalif se na ghabra ay uqaab
(Don't fear the intensity of opposing-wind, O'falcon)

Ye tou chalti hai tujhai ooncha urranai ke liye
(It blows to help you reach greater heights.)
~ Sayed Sadiq Hussain Shah

The pinnacle of my life, so I thought, was when my book, *Comprehensive Practical Biology for A' Levels,* was listed as a recommended text in the Cambridge syllabus. I thought Abbu would have been proud of me. But in hindsight, I think the most important and incredible achievement in my life is that Asif and I have raised four wonderful children – each a distinguished and unique individual, with qualities that surprise and surpass us.

I pass on the same message to my children, though when I look at them I wonder what Abbu would have made of the younger generations' condescension, especially when my highly educated and articulate offspring brandish words like 'atheist' and 'agnostic' as carelessly as 'hello' and 'good morning'; words I couldn't even comprehend at their age. I find myself wondering, with a crushing sense of devastation, if it is a failure in their upbringing, or merely a sign of progress. What have we lost to gain this augmented awareness? Was it all worth it? I guess if there are winners there have to be losers.

I recall Abbu reading Rabindranath Tagore:

He whom I enclose with my name is weeping in this dungeon. I am ever building this wall all around, and as this wall goes up into the sky day by day I lose sight of my true being in its dark shadow.

I take pride in this great wall, and I plaster it with dust and sand lest a least hole should be left in this name, and for all the care I take I lose sight of my true being.

With these thoughts I look at the multifaceted kaleidoscopic images of my life; I realize I am like the passing water in a stream, always being replaced, as insignificant as a single drop but significant in mass. I know my presence will vanish like the ripples I have caused within it, but standing still has never been an option. With a deep sigh I tidy my unruly hair, rub the cross-stitch rose imprint from the pillow on my cheek and look at the wrinkles around my eyes, wishing I could iron them out as I do my clothes. I observe the dark patches under my eyes and press the chipmunk pouch on either side of my full lips, and smile. I note that my smile has gradually inverted into a frown. Seeing my thinning hair that I had only dyed a week ago already showing grey roots, I remember John Major's comments about his education in his first address to the House: 'Never had so much been said about so little'. I smile and whisper, 'Never has so little needed so much attention,' and move away from the mirror, promising to take better care of myself. Squeezing my eyes shut, I enjoy the red hew filtering through my eyelids, and focus on the last observed image. I allow my mind to drift into nothingness.

> *Farewell dear flowers, sweetly your time ye spent,*
> *Fit while ye lived, for smell or for ornament,*
> *And after death for cures.*
> *I follow straight without complaints or grief,*
> *Since if my scent be good. I care not if*
> *It be short as yours.*
> ~George Herbert

> *I am like the remnants of a cloud uselessly roaming the sky, O my sun ever-glorious! Thy touch has not yet melted my vapour, making me one with thy light, and thus I count months and years separated from thee.*
>
> *If this be thy wish and if this thy play then take this fleeting emptiness of mine, paint it with thy colours, gild it with gold, float it on the wanton wind and spread it in varied wonders.*
>
> *And again when it shall be thy wish to end this play at night, I shall melt and vanish away in the dark, or it may be in a smile of the white morning, in a coolness of purity transparent.*
>
> ~ Gitanjali, Rabindranath Tagore

HISTORICAL BACKGROUND
TO THE PARTITION OF INDIA

The documented history of the Indian sub-continent dates back over 4,000 years to the Indus Valley Civilization at Harappa and Mohenjo-Daro. By 1850 AD, India had a population of over 200 million. Britain, on the other hand, had no indigenous written language till almost 3,000 years after India. Its population was about 16.6 million at the time. How then did Britain manage to take over and rule India from 1757 to 1947, is beyond comprehension. The keys seem to have been cunning, superior weaponry, a strong profit motive and above all, Eurocentric confidence.

The Mughal Empire was established in India in the early 1500s, and was immensely powerful. One of the most influential Mughal Emperors was Shah Jahan, who expanded the empire and accumulated enormous riches. He made Islam the official religion of India. He also built the Taj Mahal as a tomb for his favourite wife, Mumtaz.

The Mughals took great pride in being patrons of the arts. Painting, literature, architecture and lavish gardens flourished under their rule. Through them, Indo-Persian culture reached a pinnacle of refinement and beauty. This influence can be seen in the arts, cuisine, gardens and even in the Urdu language. At their peak, the Mughals ruled almost all of India – including all the territory that is now Pakistan, most of Afghanistan, and even parts of Iran.

For centuries the Viennese controlled the trade in silk, spices, fine china and precious metals. But as soon as the Portuguese rounded the Cape of Good Hope in 1488, the sea lanes to the Far East opened and the European powers competed to acquire Asian trading posts of their own. The Viennese monopoly ended. Initially, the Europeans in Asia were solely interested in trade, but over time the driving force became the acquisition of territory.

After several unsuccessful attempts to trade in India, King James I of England sent a personal envoy, Sir Thomas Roe, to the Mughal court. He succeeded in persuading Emperor Jahangir to trade with India and the East India Company was established in 1612. It gradually strengthened its hold, developing its own army, composed of British troops as well as native Hindu and Muslim soldiers called *sepoys*. This army was far superior and more disciplined than the armies of the Indian kings.

By the 1720s, increasing peasant revolts and sectarian violence threatened the stability of the Mughal throne, and as various nobles and warlords sought to control the weak emperors, the Indian empire began a long and slow process of decline. Powerful new kingdoms emerged and began to chip away at Mughal land holdings. Meanwhile, other European powers, competing for control in India, sought alliances with the shaky states that inherited Mughal territories. The British benefitted from these internal squabbles and signed treaties with the insecure local kings, allowing them a little local autonomy in exchange for protection and representation in international affairs by the English.

Before the arrival of the British in India, Muslims, Sikhs and Hindus lived in harmony, side by side; their lives intertwined like the strands of hair in a plait. The British followed a divide-and-rule policy in India, cunningly sowing the seeds of segregation and causing inequality. They acquired vast territories by playing one Indian ruler against another and making the Indians believe that it was only their presence in India that prevented a bloodbath. Even in the census they categorized people according to religion, treating them as separate communities. They inducted vast numbers of Sikhs and Hindu *sepoys* into the army. The Muslims mistrusted the British and by and large refused to learn English or associate with them. This became a severe drawback as they found Hindus were preferred for positions of power.

Gradually, accumulating a vast amount of wealth from the people and the kings, the British gained more power and captured nearly two-thirds of India. British merchants made a fortune in India and returned home with tales of a grand life. Laden with rugs, jewels ornaments and paintings, the likes of which Britons at home had never seen, they were often derided by those in British high society as 'nabobs', the title for an official under the Mughals.

British colonization fundamentally impacted the religion, economy and social environment of the native Indian people. While they exploited India, the British also brought long term benefits. They established factories, schools and universities, to introduce Western ideas and to incorporate the concept of democracy. They established law courts, civil services and transport. Vast railway and communication networks were built that helped to knit the previously independent regions of India into a whole, enabling progress.

The real turning point came after the Battle of Plassey (*Palashi*) in 1757, which saw 3,000 British soldiers of the East India Company pitted against the 5,000-strong army of the Nawab of Bengal – Siraj-ud-Daulah, and his French East India Company allies. However, torrential rain spoilt the Nawab's cannon powder while the British managed to protect theirs, leading to the Nawab's defeat. After this victory, the British East India Company took political control of almost two-thirds of the sub-continent, marking the start of the British Raj in India. The later Mughal rulers held onto the throne but were simply puppets of the British.

The economic policies of the East India Company were resented by the Indians. Gold, jewels, silver and silk had been shipped off to Britain, stripping India of its once abounding wealth in precious stones. The land was reorganized under the harsh *Zamindari* system, to facilitate the collection of taxes. Farmers were forced to switch from sustenance farming to commercial crops such as jute, indigo, jute, tea and coffee, which resulted in hardship for farmers and caused food prices to soar.

During this period, the Industrial Revolution was beginning in Britain. Large cotton textile mills had been established in England and these mills needed raw cotton. This raw material was bought in India at very low prices and sent to England to feed the Manchester mills. In return, a vast quantity of British-made cloth was sold in India. In time, everyone, even the weavers of fine cotton and silk, were compelled to sell their cloth solely to British traders, at prices decided by them. Anybody found selling to a merchant other than the British was severely punished. No duty was charged on British goods coming to India. Indian exports to Britain, however, were subjected to high import duties. The result was that the Indian handloom cottage industry suffered and the locals became unemployed as people were compelled to buy costlier British cloth. The British also introduced advanced technology with the intention of selling manufactured goods and machines at high profits since labour was cheap. This extraordinary source of wealth was crucial in expanding the public and private infrastructure in Britain, and in funding British expansion in Asia and Africa.

Resentment toward the British had been building for some time and the new policies which allowed the annexation of certain territories, heightened tensions. The Indians felt violated. The British had cunningly conquered India with the help of the Indian *sepoy*, yet the Indian soldier was not treated on par with his British counterpart. Indians were regarded as second-class citizens in their own country and denied higher positions despite their abilities. British families lived in cantonments, at a distance from Indian settlements. Private schools and clubs, where the British gathered for social interaction, became symbols of exclusivity and snobbery. Indians were traded as slaves to various British colonies. Indian farmers, weavers, traders, craftsmen, kings and nawabs, were all unhappy. British insensitivity to and distance from the peoples of India, created such disillusionment in their subjects that the end of British rule became inevitable. By early 1857, a breaking point had been reached, leading to mighty revolts.

The mutiny of 1857, was a turning point in the history of the British in India, when *sepoys* rose up against the British in Meerut and massacred the British from there to Delhi. The traditional story is that the Indian *sepoys* mutinied because the newly issued rifle cartridges were greased with pig and cow fat, thus making them unacceptable to both Hindu and Muslim soldiers alike. The Hindus worshipped the cow while the Muslims considered the pig a vile animal. While there may be some truth to this, the fact remains there were many and far more cogent causes for the rebellion.

The uprising spread throughout British India, after which only 8,000 of the1,40,000 *sepoys* remained loyal to the British. Following the revolt, lurid reports of massacres and atrocities circulated in newspapers and illustrated magazines in Britain. More British troops were dispatched to India and they eventually succeeded in putting down the mutiny, resorting to ruthless tactics to restore order. Many of the *sepoys* who surrendered were executed by the British. The city of Delhi was left in ruins. Religious and cultural centres were closed and the properties and estates of those participating in the uprising were confiscated. Reforms were instituted, which included tolerance of religion and the recruitment of Indians into the civil service; promising equal treatment under British law – something which remained only on paper. The British government abolished both the Mughal dynasty, which had ruled India for three hundred years, and the East India Company. The British Crown assumed full rule in India and came to be popularly known as the British Raj (British Rule). The representative of the Crown was the newly appointed Viceroy.

The British were fearful of a potential threat from the Muslims, former rulers of the sub-continent. To gain their favour, the British helped establish MAO College (Mohammedan Anglo-Oriental College) in 1875, in Aligarh – an institution from which leaders such as Mohammad Ali Jinnah and Liaquat Ali Khan of the Muslim League, and the ideology of Pakistan, emerged.

Meanwhile, World War I began and Britain declared war on Germany on India's behalf. Under British rule, India contributed significantly to the British war effort, providing men and resources. The princely states donated huge amounts of cash as well as manpower. By the end of the war, India had an incredible 2.5 million-man volunteer army. Indian troops fought in Italy, Burma, North Africa, and elsewhere, and 87,000 Indian soldiers died in combat.

But British rule was widely resented and the Indian independence movement gained currency. The campaign was led by the very class of Indians the British education system had helped to produce – Gandhi, Nehru, Jinnah, Dadabhai Naoroji, Vallabbhai Patel, etc., who were all educated in England. They read about the concepts of fair play, justice and democracy, but observed that the British seemed to leave these values and practice at home when they arrived in India.

Although British control of India continued, by and large peacefully, through the remainder of the 19th century, many orthodox Hindus and Muslims were alarmed by Western education and social reform and the festering bitterness among the disinherited and taxed farming class. The justice system was inherently unfair to Indians. The official Blue Books, entitled *East India (Torture) 1855–1857*, that were presented to the House of Commons in the 1856 and 1857 sessions, revealed that Company officers were allowed many appeals if convicted or accused of brutality or crimes against Indians. With the British rapidly expanding their control, many Indians wondered what the political future was for Indians in India.

In 1898, Lord Curzon became Viceroy of India and launched some unpopular policies, resulting in the 'Quit India' nationalist movement. The Muslim League had formed as an opposition to the Indian National Congress (INC). As soon as the Muslim League was formed, Muslims were placed on a separate electorate, introducing the idea of separatism of Muslims in India. British colonial government now tried to play off one against the other. But the two political parties came together for the common goal of getting the British to quit India.

In April 1919, over 5,000 unarmed protestors

gathered at a pro-independence rally at Jallianwala Bagh in Amritsar. General Dyer ordered his British troops to fire on the unarmed crowd, killing an estimated 1,500 unarmed men, women and children. Following this massacre, Gandhi called for complete self-government, saying: 'When a government takes up arms against its unarmed subjects then it has forfeited its right to govern. It has admitted that it cannot rule in peace and justice.' General Dyer was, however, not satisfied with the massacre, and continued to flog men publicly and used other methods of brutal repression. As word of the Amritsar massacre spread through India, hundreds of thousands of formerly apolitical people joined the INC and the Muslim League.

In the 1930s, Gandhi became the most prominent figure in the INC. Although he advocated a united India, with equal rights for all, other INC members were reluctant to join with Muslims against the British. Realizing the disadvantage of Muslims in a democratically Hindu-controlled India, Mohammed Ali Jinnah, leader of the Muslim League, began a public campaign in favour of a separate Muslim state, while Gandhi and Jawaharlal Nehru of the INC called for a unified India.

During World War II, the British once again expected India to provide much-needed manpower and financial help for the war effort. But the INC opposed sending Indians to fight and die in a distant foreign war. After the treachery following World War I, they saw no benefit for India in such a sacrifice. However, the Muslim League decided to support Britain's call for volunteers, hoping to gain British favour in support of a separate Muslim nation in post-independence India.

In the decade preceding World War II, India was ravaged by the impact of the severe worldwide Great Depression, resulting in mass unemployment. It created tremendous tensions, exacerbated during the war by inflation and food shortages. Rationing was introduced in Indian cities that had sent mass shipments of rice to feed the army, resulting in the great Bengal famine, during which over three million people died.

In 1942, Britain sent Sir Stafford Cripps, with constitutional proposals, to offer future dominion status in return for help in recruiting more soldiers. Gandhi and the INC did not trust Sir Cripps and demanded immediate independence. The INC began the 'Quit India' movement. In response, the British jailed the INC leadership. Mass demonstrations flared across the country but were crushed by the British army. Muslim League may have arrived at a secret agreement with Sir Cripps, in return for allowing Muslims to opt out of a future Indian state.

Before the war had even ended, public opinion in Britain had swung against expansion of the empire. Winston Churchill's Tory party was voted out of office and the Labour Party voted in during the 1945 elections, calling for immediate independence for India, and gradual freedom for other colonial holdings.

After the war, soldiers who had joined Germany and Japan to fight the British, stood trial in Delhi's Red Fort, in 1946. Forty-five prisoners were court martialled on charges of murder, treason and torture and convicted. However, widespread public protests forced the commutation of their sentences. During the trial, sympathetic mutinies broke out in the Indian Army and Navy. The final months of British rule were marked by a naval mutiny, wage strikes and demonstrations in all major cities. During these conflicts, the British colonial government remained aloof, as it concentrated on the business of negotiating a speedy transfer of power.

As independence neared, the country began to spiral towards a sectarian civil war. On 17th August 1946, violence broke out between Hindus and Muslims in Calcutta. The trouble quickly spread across India, and an orgy of sectarian violence resulted in hundreds of deaths on both sides in various cities across the country.

Finally, in February 1947, the British government announced that India would be granted independence by June 1948. The announcement came soon after the victory of the Labour Party in the British general election of July 1945, amid the realization that the British state, devastated by war, could not afford to hold onto its over-extended empire. The last Viceroy of India, Lord Louis Mountbatten, could not persuade the Hindu and Muslim leadership to agree to form a united country. With the country descending into chaos, Mountbatten accepted the formation of two separate states and moved up the date for independence to 15 August 1947.

Sectarian violence flared again as independence approached. In June 1947, representatives of the Hindus, Muslims and Sikhs agreed to divide India along sectarian lines. The Sikhs campaigned for a nation of their own, but their appeal was denied. Hindu and Sikh areas were to stay within India, while predominantly Muslim areas were to become the nation of Pakistan.

With the decision in favour of partition made, the parties faced an almost impossible task of fixing a border between the new states. The Muslims occupied two main regions in the west and east, on opposite sides of the country, separated by a Hindu-majority section. In the wealthy and fertile region of Punjab, the problem was extreme, with a nearly even mix of Hindus and Muslims. Neither side wanted to relinquish this valuable land. On the other side of the peninsula, the state of Bengal was in a similar state of chaos. Also, through most of northern India, the two religions were mixed, along with Sikhs, Christians, and other minority faiths.

A British lawyer, Cyril Radcliffe, who had little knowledge of India, was drafted to draw the border, using out dated maps and census material. He drew a line right down the middle of the province of Punjab, between Lahore and Amritsar. Communities, families and farms were cut in two. On both sides people scrambled to get to the 'right' side, or were driven from their homes by their one-time neighbours. Communities that had lived together for centuries turned on each other in one of the worst communal massacres of the 20[th]century. The once peaceful land imploded as people were forced out of the villages they had lived in for generations. Trains full of refugees were set upon by rioters from both sides and all the passengers massacred. Fifteen million people fled, depending on their faith, to get to the 'right' side of the border. Over half a million were killed in the melee. A similar situation occurred in Bengal.

The British quit India in August 1947, after ruling India for two hundred years. India and Pakistan won independence following a nationalist struggle lasting nearly three decades. Although Pakistan celebrated its Independence on 14 August and India on 15 August 1947, the border between the two new countries was not announced until 17 August 1947.

Many attributed the massacre to the chaotic manner in which the two independent nations came into being, caused by the hurried nature of British withdrawal. By delaying the announcement of borders, the British managed to avoid responsibility for the worst fighting and the mass migration that followed. Britain, the once great colonial power, looked on as India burned.

In the British Census of India in 1941, Kashmir registered a Muslim majority population of 77%, a Hindu population of 20% and Buddhists and Sikhs comprised the remaining 3%. Hence, it was anticipated that Kashmir would accede to Pakistan when the British departed. However, Hari Singh, the Hindu Maharaja, hesitated to do so. Pakistan launched a guerrilla onslaught to frighten him into submission. The Maharaja appealed to Mountbatten for assistance, and the Governor-General agreed on the condition that he accede to India. The United Nations was then invited to mediate in the quarrel. The UN mission insisted that the opinion of the Kashmiris be ascertained, but India insisted that no referendum could occur until the state had been cleared of irregulars. As the referendum was never conducted, relations between India and Pakistan soured, and eventually led to two wars over Kashmir, in 1965 and 1999. Today, India has control of about half the area of the former princely state of Jammu and Kashmir, while Pakistan controls the other third. The two nations remain at loggerheads and the dispute festers to this day.

Ethnic and religious differences within East and West Pakistan also stymied early attempts to agree on a constitution and formation of an efficiently functioning civil administration. This failure paved the way for a military takeover of the government in 1958, and later a civil war in 1971, which saw the division of Pakistan and the creation of the separate state of Bangladesh. Ever since then, military rule has been the order of the day for the most part in both countries.

The assassination of Mahatma Gandhi on 30 January 1948, by a Hindu fanatic, strengthened the hand of secularists within the Indian government. Politicians endorsed a constitution which led to the holding of the first democratic elections in India, in 1951, making it the world's largest democracy, while consolidating governmental authority in the Indian sub-continent.

Qutubuddin Aziz (journalist and diplomat), wrote in *Quaid-i-Azam:* Jinnah and the Battle for Pakistan: *In hindsight and on the basis of reliable historic documents which have now been bared and made public, one wonders whether Mountbatten's planning and execution of the design of the grab of Kashmir for Nehru's India was personal revenge on Jinnah for having refused him as the joint Governor General Of Pakistan and India in 1947.*

Maulana Abul Kalam Azad wrote in his book, *India Wins Freedom*: *It was not Jinnah who created Pakistan it was Nehru. I used to think of him as a friend of Muslims. He was questioned as to why so much land was given to Pakistan when Muslims only are of twenty-five per cent representation; he said that this agreement is not the last word. This caused a great stir amongst the Muslims. Even before Partition, the Hindus were talking about going back on the agreement. Gandhi apologised, touched Mohammad Ali's feet, but Jinnah realised there was no option but to have a separate nation for Muslims.*

But in the ebb and flow of historical events, it is ever the common people, innocent of political ambition and yearning only for a better life for themselves and their families, who are tugged under in the tow tide. So it was with my family of migrants. Some of us survived and became stronger; others perished forever, victims of the horrors of history.

GLOSSARY OF URDU WORDS

Aandhi: dust storm

Abba/Abbu: father

Allah-o-Akbar: Allah is Great

Allah shuker: thank God

Aloo chana chaat: potato and chickpea savoury snack

Amma/Ammi: mother

Annas: coins

Ashraf-ul Mukhlooqat: the best of God's creations

Aya: nanny

Ayatul-Kursi: protective prayer from the *Quran*

Azaan: call to prayer

Badshah: king

Baita: child/son

Baite: child/daughter

Baji: older sister

Besharam: shameless

Bhabi: sister-in-law (brother's wife)

Bhai: brother

Bhangra: type of dance

Billi: cat

Bismillah: I begin with the name of Allah

Buddhi: old woman

Budmaash: scoundrel

Chacha: uncle (father's younger brother)

Chambeli: fragrant Jasmine-like flowers

Chana: chickpea

Chillum: clay container for holding ambers in a *hookah*

Chocki: wooden platform

Chohi-moie: touch-me-not plant

Chowkidar: caretaker/security guard

Choolai: chickpeas

Choona: slaked lime

Chorni: thief

Dadi: paternal grandmother

Dahi-ballas: gram flour and yogurt savoury snack

Desi: local

Devrani: sister-in-law (husband's younger brother's wife)

Dholki: drum

Dhoti: loin cloth

Dulhan: bride

Dupatta: sheer scarf

Dusterkhan: tablecloth

Eid Mubarak: Happy Eid

Eiddi: monetry gift given at Eid

Eid-ul-Fitr: Muslim festival to celebrate end of Ramadan

Ekka: horse drawn carriage

Ghazel: rhyming poem

Gali: lane

Gandairi: small pieces of sugar cane

Ghee: clarified butter

Gol-guppay: savoury snack

Goras: the Whites

Gown: village

Gulab jamman: sweet balls in sugar syrup

Gul golai: sweet dumpling like snacks

Gurdwara: Sikh place of worship

Halal: kosher

Harami: bastard

Hazoor: term of respect

Hookah: hubble-bubble

Hulva: sweet made with semolina

Halwai: sweet maker

Huwa: Eve

Imambara: Shia place of worship

Imam zamin: amulet

Jalebis, ladoo, burfi, gulab jamman: Indian/Pakistani sweets

Janaza: burial casket

Jethani: sister-in-law (husband's elder brother's wife)

Jharoo: thin twigs tied together and used as a broom

Kalgha: celosia

Kalima: declaration of faith

Khala: maternal aunt

Khuda hafiz: words at departure, 'in the care of God'

Kirpaan: sword carried by Sikhs

Kismet: fate

Kowain kai mainduck: toads in a well

Kugou ghori: little animals/toys made of clay

Kurta: loose fitting top worn by both men and women

Kath putli: puppet

Kutha: bark of a tree, used in *paan* (beetle leaf)

Kutti: bitch

Larki: girl

Lucknowi: from Lucknow

Lussi: yogurt and milk drink

Muhajir: refugee

Maidaan: open ground

Mamo: maternal uncle

Mashallah: May Allah protect you

Mashki: water carrier

Masairi: comfortable bed

Matum: ritualistic self-flagellation

Mazaar: shrine

Meena bazaar: fair/fete

Mersias: Shiat songs of praise

Mithai: sweets

Misri: crystallised sugar

Moazin: person who calls out to prayers from a mosque

Maulvi: priest

Mooras: jute stools

Motia: fragrant white flowers

Malung: devotees at a shrine

Mundi: market

Munjun: charcoal/ herb powder used to clean teeth

Mushaira: soiree where poets recite their poems

Mashuk: goatskin used to transport water

Mashki: water carrier

Mutka: earthenware pot for storing water

Naan: flat bread

Namaz: prayer

Namaskar: Indian salutation

Namatkhana: a wooden cabinet with wire mesh panels

Naani: maternal grandmother

Nawab: elite during the Mughal period

Nazar lagna: cursed by the evil eye

Neem: broad leaf tree

Nika: wedding ceremony

Nunni: tiny

Nuqsheen: embellished

Nasal bigaar: black sheep of the family

Paan: betel leaf; often chewed with tobacco and areca nut

Paandan: container holding ingredients for making *paan*

Paincha: trouser edge

Paisa: coin

Pakoray: onion bhaji

Paindo: derogatory term for villager

Palung: a wooden frame bed, woven with twine

Para: mercury

Paranda: hair braid

Paratha: fried flat bread

Patahni: female from northern Pakistan

Pathan: male from northern Pakistan

Pepal: a variety of tree

Phookni: a metal tube used to blow and kindle a fire

Phopi: aunt (father's sister)

Pithoo garam: an outdoor ball game

Pulao: fried rice

Pugli: crazy/mad

Purri: fairy

Qameez: shirt

Qoom: nation

Qurbani: sacrifice

Raat ki Rani: flowers which are particularly fragrant at night

Raveri: sugar and sesame seed snack

Rotti: thin unleavened flatbread

Sadqay: term of endearment/darling

Salaam Alaykum: Muslim greeting 'Peace be with you'

Samosa: savoury filled pastry snack

Saresh: a kind of glue

Sarotta: cutter used to slice areca nuts

Shahenshah: Emperor

Shalwar: baggy trousers worn by both men and women

Sheer khurma: rice, vermicelli and milk dessert

Sherwani: long coat

Sooji ki barfi: sweet snacks made with semolina

Sukh chayn: a variety of shady tree in Asia

Sunyai: listen

Tandoor: clay oven in which *naan* is made

Tonga: horse drawn carriage

Tava: hotplate for cooking *chapattis*

Taweez: amulet

Taya: uncle (father's elder brother)

Tazias: constructions carried in religious processions, depicting the tomb of the martyred family of the Prophet [PBUH]

Thara: platform over open drain

Thukht: wooden platform used for sitting

Tikka: barbecued pieces of meat

Tukkal: name of a fancy kite

Tusbih: rosary, string of beads used for prayer

Tuva: hot plate

Waheguru ji ki fateh: Sikh chant of victory (wonderful Guru)

Walaikum Assalam: response to Muslim greeting (Peace be with you too)

Zalzala: earthquake

Zari-karchob: gold/silver embroidery

Zarda: sweet rice dish

Zindabad: long live

BIBLIOGRAPHY

Dominique Lapierre & Larry Collins, Freedom at Midnight

Patrick French, Liberty or Death

Qutubuddin Aziz, *Quaid-i-Azam* Jinnah The Battle for Pakistan

WEBSITES

http://history1800s.about.com/odthebritishempire/tp/indiatimeline01.htm

http://asianhistory.about.com/od/colonialisminasia/p/profbritraj.htm

http://archive.org/stream/cu31924021963586/cu31924021963586_djvu.txt

https://prezi.com/oexx2_hz21_d/untitled-prezi/

https://www.ukessays.com/essays/history/history-of-the-british-raj-history-essay.php

https://www.ukessays.com/essays/history/history-of-the-british-raj-history-essay.php

http://www.newworldencyclopedia.org/p/index.php?title=British_Raj

https://au.answers.yahoo.com/question/index?qid=20130225175934AA6FHsN

http://history1800s.about.com/od/thebritishempire/tp/indiatimeline01.htm

http://www.bbc.co.uk/history/british/modern/partition1947_01.shtml

http://www.murrieta.k12.ca.us/cms/lib5/CA01000508/Centricity/Domain/1814/The%20Partition%20of%20India.pdf

https://prezi.com/pl7qz5wt2pcz/partitioning-of-india/

https://www.coursehero.com/file/6553498/Exercise-9/

https://en.wikipedia.org/wiki/Federacy

http://www.bbc.co.uk/history/british/modern/partition1947_01.shtml

ACKNOWLEDGEMENTS

My heartfelt thanks to:

Najma Shamsi: Baji, you have always been more than just a sister; you are my best friend; always will be. Thank you for stoking the embers. It was wondrous reliving our delightful childhood together. As so aptly put by Jane Austin in *Emma*, 'Where shall we see a better daughter or a kinder sister or a truer friend?'

Ammi: For your amusing anecdotes and blessings.

Nadir Chacha, Nasir, Mamo Saba, Shama Khala and Wazir Khala: For raking up your past, especially painful memories.

My husband *Asif*, and children *Kashif, Nimra, Samirah* and *Saif*: For your support and encouragement.

My early readers: Thank you for not saying it was rubbish, and for your support, encouragement and invaluable advice.

David Grant: For not only reading my book and giving constructive feedback but cooking for and feeding me.

Attia, Sidra, Rehana, Rimmel, Imman, Zeeshan, Soufyan, Asghar and Jenny Oxman, and my friends at City Lit.

Jonathan Barns, Caroline Netzler, Conor Montague: My teachers at City Lit.

WISH TO PUBLISH WITH US?

We are always keen to look at interesting content across genres. Please email your submission to: **submissions@leadstartcorp.com**

The submission should include the following:

1. SYNOPSIS
A summary of the book in 500 – 1000 words. Please mention the word count of the manuscript.

2. SAMPLE CHAPTERS / POETRY
A couple of chapters from the book; these need not be in order, just send the best two chapters of the book. Or a few poems if the same is a collection of poetry.

3. A NOTE ABOUT THE AUTHOR
An interesting note about yourself (about 200 words).

4. ADDITIONAL INFORMATION
- Target audience
- Unique selling proposition
- List of illustrative content (if any)
- Other comparative titles
- Your thoughts on marketing the book

26741875R10345

Printed in Poland
by Amazon Fulfillment
Poland Sp. z o.o., Wrocław